"I HAVE MISSED YOU, TESORO."

Arturo's dark eyes gleamed, his voice rich with seduction.

Quinn snorted. "You're really going to do this, now? Try to get me back into your bed?"

With a quick grin and a shake of his head, Arturo leaned back in his chair, eyeing her wryly. "Why do you think I am not sincere?"

"Not sincere that you've missed me or that you want me back in your bed?"

"You were the one who brought up the bed, *cara*, not I." His expression, faintly mocking, turned serious. "I have missed you."

By Pamela Palmer

Vamp City Novels

A KISS OF BLOOD
A BLOOD SEDUCTION

Feral Warriors Novels

A LOVE UNTAMED
ECSTASY UNTAMED
HUNGER UNTAMED
RAPTURE UNTAMED
PASSION UNTAMED
OBSESSION UNTAMED
DESIRE UNTAMED

PAMELA PALMER

A KISS OF BLOOD

A VAMP CITY NOVEL

AVON

An Imprint of HarperCollinsPublishers

AVON BOOKS
An Imprint of HarperCollins*Publishers*
10 East 53rd Street
New York, New York 10022-5299

Copyright © 2013 by Pamela Palmer
Excerpt from *A Blood Seduction* copyright © 2012 by Pamela Palmer
ISBN 978-0-06-210753-4
www.avonromance.com

First Avon Books mass market printing: July 2013

Avon Trademark Reg. U.S. Pat. Off. and in Other Countries, Marca Registrada, Hecho en U.S.A.
HarperCollins® is a registered trademark of HarperCollins Publishers.

Printed in the U.S.A.

10 9 8 7 6 5 4 3 2 1

This one's for my mother, Pat Palmer, who taught me to believe in myself, to embrace life's changes as grand adventures, and to understand that home isn't a place but a loving family. You've always been my role model, Mom.

ACKNOWLEDGMENTS

Thanks, as always, to Laurin Wittig and Anne Shaw Moran—friends, critique partners, and sisters of my heart—for always being there for me. Life would be so much less fun without you.

Thanks, too, to Kelly Poulsen, Kyle Poulsen, and Shannon Silkensen. And to Jeaniene Frost for your fresh eyes and wise counsel. Also to the real Amanda Morris, who won my contest to name a character and lent me her name.

A very heartfelt thanks to the wonderful team at Avon Books—Pamela Spengler-Jaffee, Jessie Edwards, Chelsey Emmelhainz, Art Director Tom Egner, and everyone else who had a hand in getting my books to readers. Most of all, thanks to my editor, May Chen, for friendship and unwavering support over and above our wonderful working relationship.

Finally, thanks to Keith for too many things to name. And to my readers. Without you, my stories would just be daydreams. You're the ones who truly bring my worlds to life. Thank you.

A Kiss of Blood

CHAPTER ONE

Four more days until Quinn Lennox's life, as she knew it, was over.

Quinn paced the lamplit living room of her apartment on the George Washington University—GW—campus, pulling the gun from the small of her back, dry-cocking, aiming, releasing. The magazine, filled with alternating wooden and real bullets, sat snuggly in her back pocket, ready to be slammed home at a moment's notice.

In truth, her normal life, if her life had ever been normal, had ended a month ago, when she and her brother Zack stumbled through a crack in the world and found themselves fighting for their lives in the dark vampire otherworld that, impossibly, shared physical space with much of Washington, D.C., and had for 140 years.

Washington, V.C., the vampires called it. Vamp City.

God help her, how was it possible there were vampires and werewolves and sorcerers?

She picked up her water glass, downed it, then continued to pace, continued to practice drawing the gun she'd bought last week. Because two things were going to happen on the equinox in four days, if not before.

One: The immortal son of the sorcerer who'd created Vamp City would renew the crumbling magic, releasing Zack from the grip of the magical illness that had him nearly bedridden. She hoped.

And two: The vampires now trapped by the magic's failure would once more be free to travel between worlds as they pleased, and the vampire master, and sadistic monster, Cristoff, would almost certainly send his goons after her. She'd escaped him twice now. She'd never escape him a third time, not if he caught her again.

Which meant he couldn't catch her.

Unfortunately, hopping on the next flight for the other side of the world wasn't on her list of options. Not yet. Arturo had warned her that she and Zack might have become infected by Vamp City's failing magic and might fall ill if they left the area before it was renewed. For once, that vampire had told her the truth.

Against her wishes, Zack had allowed his parents—Quinn's dad and stepmom—to sweep him home to Pennsylvania. After a couple of days, Quinn had managed to convince him to return to D.C., but by then it had been too late. He'd already started to sicken in a wholly unnatural way. Magically sicken. There was nothing she could do but hope that Vamp City's renewal would heal him. And if it didn't?

Her stomach cramped, her jaw clenched as her grip tightened on her gun. She'd have no choice but to breach the gates into that world again and to try to enlist the aid, once more, of the vampire who haunted both her dreams and her nightmares. Arturo Mazza.

Hopefully, it wouldn't come to that. The last

thing . . . the *last* thing she wanted to do was return to that vampire hell.

To the vampires, of course, Vamp City was utopia—a city where the sun never shone, where they could enslave and hunt humans without fear of retribution. A place where the vampires, werewolves, and other immortal creatures could live their lives in the open. In freedom.

But even utopias have a dark side, and Phineas Blackstone, the powerful wizard the vampires had paid to create their dark city, had engineered a brilliant one—a death trap finally sprung two years ago. The moment the magic began to fail, all vampires within the city's boundaries had become instantly caught, unable to escape. Soon, the sunbeams from the real world had begun to break through—slowly, at first, then more and more frequently until it became clear that their world was dying. And with it, every soul trapped within—vampire, werewolf, and immortal human alike.

Only by renewing Vamp City's magic would they be saved. And the only one who could renew it was another sorcerer, a strong one. Both of Phineas Blackstone's immortal sons had tried and failed.

Two years later, a month ago, as the situation neared critical, Quinn stumbled into that world. And they believed she was the one they'd been waiting for.

The sound of a car horn blared on the street outside her apartment, making Quinn's hand jerk as she aimed at Zack's computer monitor and pretended to fire. She'd always known she was different, but never in a million years had she dreamed she was an honest-to-goodness *sorceress*. It still didn't seem real. Yes, weird things happened around her sometimes, but she didn't have any real power. A little, maybe. Power she couldn't call when she needed it and that she couldn't control when it did decide to appear. Which was worse than not having any at all.

Cristoff had forced her to try to renew the magic, and she'd failed. But later, Arturo had seen her eyes glow—the sign of serious power, he said. He told her she had the power to save them, yet he'd helped her escape his master, Cristoff, and set her free, claiming that Phineas Blackstone's immortal sons would ultimately find a way to renew the magic.

None of that made a lot of sense. And if there was one thing she knew, it was that Arturo played fast and loose with the truth. He was a first-class manipulator. But he'd also become her protector and, in a strange sort of way, her friend. And her lover. He'd developed feelings for her, she was sure of it, as she had for him, as much as she hated to admit it. Despite his faults, and they were legion, she'd seen goodness inside that male.

In the end, he'd saved Zack from certain death, then stolen her from his master's dungeon and set them both free. An unlikely heroic, altruistic sacrifice for a vampire who'd betrayed her twice.

From the moment he set her free, part of her had been waiting for the other shoe to drop. Hence the gun, the wooden stakes she'd taken to carving, and the switchblade she's taken to carrying. She and Zack were free and safe, and she intended to keep them that way. They weren't going back there. If Vamp City imploded, taking its sadistic vampires with it, all the better.

But even as she thought that, she knew she didn't really want Arturo dead.

Shoving her gun into her waistband, Quinn crossed to the window and pushed open the lower half of the double-hung, enjoying the brush of cool September air over her skin. Across the narrow street stood one of the GW dorms, half the windows lit like the spots on a domino, the other half dark, the students still out and about campus despite the fact that the sun had set more than an hour ago.

Zack and his best friend Lily, both GW seniors, should have been out there with them, though more than likely they'd have been right here, side by side in front of their computers either playing some high-action fantasy shoot-'em-up or designing one. But Lily had disappeared, as so many people around D.C. had in recent months. Quinn suspected she'd fallen through the same door into Vamp City that she and Zack had as they'd searched for her; but they'd never found her.

Lily was most likely dead. Humans didn't last long among the vampires. And Zack . . . poor Zack was suffering not only from the magic sickness but from grief and depression as well. Her sweet, easygoing brother had not emerged from Hell unscathed.

Quinn straightened, hoping her neighbor, Mike, would come over as he did most evenings and give her something to think about other than vampires and lost friends, and something to listen to other than the ticking clock. In his company, she could pretend, if only for an hour or two, that she lived a normal life in a normal world. Even if nothing could be further from the truth.

But as she turned from the window, a familiar chill skated over her skin—a feeling she knew presaged the bleeding together of the two worlds. Those in Vamp

City would feel the bleed-through as an earthquake. During the day, the quake would be quickly followed by sunbeams bursting overhead like light through a dark piece of hole-riddled construction paper. The vampires would flee the sunlight, or die if they were unlucky enough to be standing in the wrong place when the sunbeams appeared.

But in the real world, Quinn alone felt the change, thanks to her sorcerer's blood. She alone could see through the shadowy breaks like windows into the other world. And since one of those breaks stood in front of her apartment, just outside her window, she turned back and bent low, unable to resist another glimpse of that world.

Created in 1870, a doppelganger of Washington, D.C., at that time, it was a world without streetlights or paved roads or electricity except in those few homes that had been hooked up to generators. She stared at the deserted, moonlit street and the line of crumbling row houses in a section of Vamp City that she knew to be largely uninhabited.

The street in that otherworld appeared deserted tonight. She heard no sounds but those of the real world, which continued to carry to her ears—a car driving down the street, the tick of the clock, the banter of college kids walking along the sidewalk below her window, discussing their fantasy-football picks.

Out of nowhere, a young man in shorts and a T-shirt stumbled into the dark Vamp City street, falling to his hands and knees in the dirt. Quinn gasped. One of the fantasy-football kids must have slipped between the worlds as he'd passed through the break. Every day, thousands passed through unaware and unaffected, but every now and again, one slipped through. As Lily probably had. As she and Zack definitely had.

While the kid struggled to his feet, Quinn heard his friends' voices below, shouting for him from the real world. Shouts the kid would never hear. Only she could hear both worlds at once when they bled into one another like this.

She watched as the young man leaped to his feet, staring around him in stunned silence, his body language projecting disbelief, shock, and slowly dawning terror. Her heart ached for him because she'd been in his shoes just a few weeks ago. And she knew what he'd soon learn—that he had every right to be afraid.

His friends would tell the cops that he'd been right there, then just wasn't—the same story reported over and over again on the news from others who'd been with one of the missing. But the cops wouldn't find him. They didn't have a clue what was going on. And they couldn't do anything about it even if they knew.

Her breath caught. She might be able to save him if she hurried, if she raced into that world and snatched him back out before the break closed.

Before she could question the wisdom, she was racing for her front door. Thanks to her sorcerer's blood, she alone could travel both ways through a sunbeam. She'd escaped that way once before. And she'd helped others do the same.

As she dashed down the hall and into the stairwell, her logical mind began to question the wisdom of this action. The breaks were unpredictable, some lasting close to an hour, others only a minute or two. If she ran into that world to save the kid, and the break closed before she got out again, she'd be stuck, unable to return to Zack until and unless she could make her way out through another break. And Zack needed her.

But she couldn't just leave the kid there. Not if she could help him.

She ran through the lobby. By the time she reached the doors to the street, her heart was pounding, sweat beading on her brow. She pushed open the glass door, just feet from where the break began and the magic would suck her in. In that dark column, she saw the Vamp City world and watched with dismay as two horses and their riders circled the kid. She gasped as one of the riders threw a lasso, roping the young man like a steer.

Fury ignited inside her. But caution and experience held her back because she recognized the overlarge heads and ears of the riders and knew them to be inhuman Traders with inhuman strength.

Yes, she was armed and dangerous, but with only a week's worth of target practice under her belt, she was probably more dangerous to the kid and the horses than to the Traders. Her chances of taking on two Traders and winning were slim to none. Even as the thought settled, two more Traders rode up to join the first pair. If it were Zack, she'd go anyway, no question, even if it meant getting caught herself and delivered to Cristoff. But Zack was upstairs. And he needed her.

As she watched helplessly, the Trader with the rope hauled the kid onto the back of his horse. The kid's cry for help ceased abruptly as the break between the worlds closed as suddenly as it had opened, leaving Quinn staring once more at the modern D.C. street and the small crowd that had begun to gather around the friends of the missing boy.

Quinn backed away from the door, pressing a shaking hand against her now-pounding forehead. She felt sick that she hadn't been able to help him, that she'd had no chance of getting him out of there for all her supposed sorcerer's power. Turning toward the elevator, she made her way back to her apartment, her skin ice-cold, because she knew what awaited him. She'd been in that world twice and wouldn't have survived either trip if not for Arturo's intervention.

Once more in her apartment, she sank onto her sofa, dropping her head back, feeling the frustration and defeat press down on her. Vamp City needed to die. Unfortunately, the Traders weren't tied to Vamp City and would probably survive the destruction. And there was no telling how many vampires lived in the real world. V.C.'s demise wouldn't eradicate all the vampires in the world, not by a long shot.

And she wasn't sure she wanted it to. Arturo . . . She shook her head, her feelings for the male so conflicted. From the moment she'd stumbled into that world, he'd been, in turns, her captor and protector, her lover and betrayer. And in the end, her savior. He'd gotten past her defenses as no one else ever had, partly because she'd had no way to avoid him. And partly because he'd understood her as no one else did. He was the only one in her life who'd known exactly who and what she was, right from the beginning, and accepted her anyway. She missed that. Despite everything, she missed *him*.

A low rap sounded on her apartment door, a quick-tap knock she recognized as Mike's. With relief, she headed for the door, glad for the promise of company and the illusion, however fleeting, of normalcy.

As she peered out the peephole into Mike's smiling face, a sense of calm settled over her, a calm she hadn't felt all day. The tense misery of the past minutes eased out of her shoulders as she unhooked the chain and twisted the dead bolt to let him in. Mike had moved into the apartment across the hall a few weeks ago, while she was caught in Vamp City. She'd met him the first evening she got back and he'd pushed right past her usual reserve to become a welcome, undemanding friend. A writer, he lived alone, working from home. He'd taken to bringing over a bottle of wine about this time every night. She, in turn, always had dessert ready and waiting.

She opened the door and smiled, stepping back to let him in. He was a good-looking guy despite his untrimmed hair, his unshaven jaw, and the three-inch scar that ran down one cheek, a remnant from a fight with his brother as teenagers, when they'd shattered a sliding glass door. Dressed in a plain black T-shirt tucked into well-worn jeans, his gray eyes sparkling with life and laughter, he was a welcome ray of light in the dark mire that had become her life.

Mike's smile faded, his brows lowering as he studied her. "You look like you've seen a ghost."

The man was far too perceptive. "I'm fine. It's been a long day." The understatement of the year. She'd felt every single one of the day's 86,400 seconds tick by. "What did you bring tonight?" she asked, eyeing the bottle of wine in his hand.

He held it up with a flourish. "Chateau la Peyre Saint-Estephe Bordeaux." The French rolled off his tongue as if he'd been born to it.

"Will it go with banana cream pie?"

Gray eyes crinkled with laughter. "Everything goes with banana cream pie."

They fell into their nightly routine, Mike uncorking the bottle and pouring it into the two wineglasses that Quinn had waiting while she served up whatever dessert she'd made that day. Dessert was the one thing she could still get Zack to eat.

But her own appetite had fled beneath the sick feeling of helplessness as she'd watched that boy being captured. While Mike seated himself on her sofa, wineglass in one hand and a dessert plate in the other, she followed with her own glass and took a seat on the reading chair across from him.

"No pie?" he asked.

"I'm not hungry."

Fortunately, there was no attraction between them. If there had been, she'd have stopped these nightly visits as soon as they began. After all, she was leaving town the moment Zack was well. Hopefully, in four days. There was no sense getting involved with a guy she'd never see again.

She'd done that all too recently with one far-too-handsome Italian vampire.

"How's the book coming?" she asked, needing to steer her thoughts away from Vamp City and vampires, and the tragedy she'd just witnessed.

He gave her a pained smile. "Three steps forward, five steps back."

"Ouch."

"No one ever said writing was easy. I spent half the day wandering in front of the window trying to understand why my protagonist left the scene of the crime three chapters back, only to realize he wouldn't have."

As Mike launched into the details of his latest thriller novel, Quinn took a sip of wine, sinking back into her chair, enjoying the calm, mellow tones of Mike's voice. And wishing, despite herself, that she were with another—one arrogant, controlling, and manipulative vampire within whom she'd found shades of both the hero and the villain. A male she'd trusted with her life. And a vampire whose word she'd never been able to trust at all.

Mike paused to take another bite of pie as he eyed her with what she'd come to think of as his writerly scrutiny, as if she were one of his characters, and he was trying to figure her out. He'd never succeed, of course. Humans didn't believe in sorceresses, or vampires, or immortal otherworlds. And she wasn't about to clue this one in.

"How are you really, Quinn?" His tone was compassionate, as if he could see her falling apart at the seams. Every night he asked the same question, in the same way, then never pressed when she gave him her stock, trite answer, for which she was grateful. It wasn't like she could ever tell him the truth.

"I'm fine. Tired and worried about Zack, but things will be better once we get home."

She'd told him that Zack's best friend was one of the many missing persons in D.C. and that Zack was suffering from depression as a result. That they were moving back to Pennsylvania to get him away from the memories. She wasn't sure Mike believed her. If only she could tell him the truth. If only she had someone to confide in other than Zack, who was still too traumatized by all that had happened.

Mike rose, smiling at her with understanding. He really was a nice man. Watching her with that studious look, he opened his mouth, then closed it slowly as if he'd decided against saying whatever was on his mind.

"Get some sleep, Quinn. Everything looks brighter in daylight."

Quinn snorted and smiled. "Profound."

Mike grinned at her. "That's the smile I like to see."

She said good-bye and let him out, locking up behind him, then went to check on Zack, to see if she could coax him into eating a little pie.

As she eased open Zack's door, the light from a streetlamp lit his face, a face that had aged during his brief captivity in Vamp City, making him look older than his twenty-two years. His was still an engaging face, if harder than before, framed by overlong curly red hair. If her own hair had looked like his, instead of being blond and straight, they'd have looked rather startlingly similar, despite being only half siblings. They'd both inherited their dad's lanky height, green eyes, wide mouth, and straight nose.

"Zack?" she asked, flipping on the light. "How about a slice of banana cream pie?"

His eyes opened slowly. The circles beneath were dark as bruises, the whites an unnatural shimmery gray.

She swallowed, aching at the sight of him.

"No thanks," he murmured, then rolled away from her.

Quinn turned off the light and closed the door behind her, then sank back against the wall. He'd be fine after the equinox, after the magic was renewed. She had to believe that. But the equinox was still four days away.

And deep inside, she was terrified that Zack might not live that long.

The sun was low in the sky the next afternoon as Quinn strode down Twenty-first Street, her gun wedged snugly at the small of her back beneath the leather jacket that was a little too warm for the September day, two wooden stakes in her inside breast pocket, and a switchblade in the front pocket of her jeans. A breeze played with her hair as she kept a sharp eye out for anyone . . . or any *thing* . . . suspicious.

She'd spent a couple of hours at the firing range, as she did every day, now. A week wasn't a long time to become proficient, but she could handle a gun, and her aim wasn't half-bad. A month ago, her self-defense capability had extended no further than the Tae Kwon Do moves she'd learned as a kid. She was still no warrior, but she was armed, now. And wary. And prepared to do whatever it took to keep her brother and herself alive.

As she neared the street where she lived, she passed a couple of college kids walking down the sidewalk, their backpacks slung over one shoulder, lattes in one hand and cell phones in the other. Just a month ago, Zack had been one of them, making plans with Lily to move to California next summer. when they both graduated. Last week, before she'd taken a temporary leave of absence from her job as a lab tech at the National Institutes of Health in Bethesda, Quinn had run some surreptitious blood tests on her brother, hoping to find something physically wrong that human medicine might be able to cure. Some reason for his failing health and his shimmery gray eyes. Something other than magic. She'd found nothing.

God help them both if the equinox came and went, and he got no better.

Her thoughts in turmoil, she turned onto her street, stepping off the curb to pass a small pack of chattering coeds. But as she stepped back onto the sidewalk, she caught sight of a pair of males not ten yards ahead with ears a little too large on heads slightly too big for their bodies.

Traders.

Her heart stopped, then took off like a flock of doves as her feet suddenly rooted to the sidewalk. The girls she'd just passed grunted and complained, now forced to walk around her. Ahead, one of the Traders turned to his companion, revealing his profile, making her breath catch in her throat. Because she recognized him. These weren't just any Traders but the same two who'd caught her the second time she entered Vamp City, the pair who'd sold her to the slave auction. If they saw her, they'd recognize her in return, no doubt about it.

She reached into her pocket for her switchblade, then, pivoting on her heel, turned and slipped back around the corner, her gaze flying out in every direction, her heart thundering in her ears.

What were they doing a block from her apartment? Coincidence? Or had they somehow tracked her? Were they even now heading for her home?

And Zack was there alone.

Even if the Traders were looking for her, they might try to take him instead. Or hurt him if he got in their way.

She yanked out her cell phone and called Zack's

number. He could go to Mike's. He'd be safe there; though what excuse they'd give Mike for such a cloak-and-dagger move, she had no idea. Maybe Zack would come up with something reasonably plausible and not too alarming.

But Zack's phone rang and rang, flipping to voice mail. Dammit. If only she could call Mike, but the slip of paper with his number on it was still sitting on her kitchen counter. She'd never put his number in her phone.

Gripping her switchblade, Quinn began to run. Circling the block from the other direction, she entered her building from the back door instead of the front and hurried up the stairs, avoiding the elevator. When she reached her floor, she pulled her gun, then peered cautiously into the hallway. Empty.

Her pulse thundering in her ears, she eased her way down the hall, relieved to find her apartment door closed and, apparently, untouched. A good sign, unless Zack had opened the door and let them in.

Quickly unlocking the door, she slipped inside to find Zack snoring softly on the sofa. Locking the door behind her, she did a swift search of the apartment. Everything appeared normal if she didn't count the way the beam of sunlight illuminated the gray cast of her brother's skin.

Shoving her gun into her waistband, she shook Zack's shoulder.

"Zack, wake up. We need to leave." He made a sound that might have been a question, but his eyes failed to open. "Zack!" Still, he didn't respond.

Panic bubbled up, shattering her desperate calm. He was too big for her to carry. And the Traders were too damned close.

Running to the kitchen, she snatched up the slip of paper with Mike's phone number. "It's Quinn, Mike," she said when he answered.

"Quinn. What's the matter?"

She took a deep breath, forcing herself to slow down. "Nothing. I just . . . Zack's sick. I need to take him to a doctor, but I'm having trouble getting him awake. Can you help me get him down to the car?"

She'd expected a swift, "Of course." Instead, her question was met with silence. She'd probably interrupted his writing, probably screwed up everything he was doing. Still . . .

"It'll only take a couple of minutes, Mike."

He sighed, his tone regretful. "Quinn, I can't right now. Maybe in a couple of hours? I'm—"

Whatever else he said was drowned out by the crash of her front door. Whirling, she stared as the two Traders pushed their way into her apartment.

"Quinn?" Mike's sharp voice rang in her ear.

"Don't come, Mike." She pulled her gun and backed toward the sofa and Zack. "I'm fine. Don't come!" Mike might be a well-built male, but unless he possessed X-men-like talents, he wasn't likely to be able to protect himself from supernatural creatures, let alone be of any help to her. He'd wind up in the slave auction at the mercy of bloodsucking vampires. Or dead. And that was the last thing she wanted.

If she was lucky, her power might decide to make an appearance. If not, she had other weapons, now. Tossing her phone onto the nearest chair, she aimed her gun at the closest Trader's face.

He just grinned at her, sending chills down her spine despite the sunlight warming her back. "You don't really think that toy is going to stop me, do you, girlie? You've got quite a reward on your head."

As she'd both hoped and feared, her latent sorcerer's power started to tingle in her blood, the weird, unnatural heat crawling beneath her skin. For all she knew, her eyes were glowing. One of these days, she'd like to be standing in front of a mirror when it happened so that she could see for herself.

The reality of firing her weapon at an assailant swept over her, at once exhilarating and terrifying. What if her bullet went wide, slamming through a wall and into another apartment? What if it didn't, and she tore a hole through a living creature's brain?

As the pair started slowly toward her, she pried her left hand away from the gun, holding it up, palm out and pointing toward her would-be captors. Taking a deep breath, she willed her power to come to her call, to push them back. But nothing happened, as usual, when she needed it.

"Come any closer, and I'll shoot," she warned.

A third person appeared in the doorway behind them. *Mike*.

"This isn't your concern, Mike. Please leave."

"Push them toward me, Quinn. Use your power and push them toward me. There's too much sun."

She froze at his words, her scalp going cold. Had Zack told him about her powers? No one knew. No one! Except Arturo. And the rest of the vampires.

Mike's words slowly sank into her brain. *There's too much sun*.

Too much sun.

Quinn swayed, the blood draining from her face as understanding crashed over her. Mike was a bloody freaking vampire. No, not *Mike*.

"Micah," she breathed. Arturo had told her he had a friend . . . a *vampire* friend . . . named Micah who lived outside Vamp City. "You're Micah."

"Yes."

Her mouth hung open, her eyes going hard as flint as the implications bombarded her. Arturo had sent his buddy to watch her. He'd known right where she was the entire time. He'd never set her free at all!

And suddenly she understood why Mike . . . *Micah* . . . had hesitated when she'd asked him to help her get Zack to the car. Her car was on the street, in full sunshine.

Without warning, the two Traders lunged for her.

"Use your power, Quinn. Now!"

There was only one power she trusted. She aimed and fired at the lead Trader, once, twice, but aiming at a moving target was a lot harder than at a stationary paper silhouette, and she had no idea if she'd hit him. He wasn't slowing!

With her third shot, he flew back. Micah disappeared, and, a second later, so did the Trader who'd hit the floor. Both materialized moments later in the dark foyer, Micah's skin smoking from that short dousing of simple daylight. Not even direct sunlight.

But she had no chance to celebrate. Before she could swing her aim to his companion, the second Trader was upon her, ripping the gun from her hand. Though she fought him with everything she had, he pinned her easily, wrenching her arms behind her back. In her peripheral vision, she saw him make a fist, as he'd done the last time he caught her. He'd knock her out, and she'd awaken in Cristoff's dungeon. Or within the clutch of Cristoff's torture-loving hands.

Raw terror slid through her veins, making the power inside her crackle and spark. But when she tried to use that power to throw him off, it failed her. Naturally.

A blur caught her eye, then the Trader at her back was gone, joining his buddy a heartbeat later in the shadowed foyer, slammed up against the wall by a second male, this one scorched and charred beyond recognition.

As the acrid smell of burning flesh raked her nose, the male healed, slowly at first, then more and more quickly, revealing a handsome, dark-haired vampire she knew all too well.

Arturo.

CHAPTER TWO

Quinn stared at the vampire who'd assured her he would be trapped in Vamp City until the magic was renewed. A myriad of emotions hit her at once—disbelief, despair, terror. Fury.

Did his freedom from V.C. mean the magic had been renewed? If so, it hadn't helped Zack, not at all. Or had the vampires being trapped been just one more of a long string of Arturo's lies?

He turned to her, his dark gaze colliding with her stunned one, his eyes filled with hard determination as he turned back to the Trader in his grasp.

"How did you find the sorceress?"

As the Traders struggled ineffectively against the far stronger vampires, Quinn searched for her gun, spying it against the wall behind her reading chair. She reached for it, picking it up as Arturo's voice dropped to that hypnotic tone of his that appeared to work as a low-level mind control. What she always thought of as his Obi-Wan voice.

"Tell me how you found her."

The Trader fought to free himself to no avail. "We saw her a couple of days ago but lost sight of her near here. We've been looking ever since. Today, we saw her again and followed."

Arturo glanced at Quinn. "Is he telling the truth?"

His gaze pinned her, his eyes at once hard with violence and soft as he waited for her reply.

Her heart pounded, her mind racing as she tried to make sense of his being here, as she tried to untangle all of his lies. "I don't know. All I know is that they're the ones who caught me and sold me to the slave auction a couple of weeks ago."

With a brief nod, Arturo reached into the Trader's chest and pulled out his heart, killing him instantly. Mike did the same to his companion.

Quinn swayed from the shock of the violence as the bodies fell to the floor. She wasn't sorry to see the Traders dead, but . . . good grief. Death meant nothing to the vampires. *Nothing.* But, of course, she knew that.

Even as she reeled, the bodies turned to smoke, evaporating. Definitely not human.

As the vampires turned toward her, keeping to the shadows of the hallway, Arturo pulled a handkerchief out of his back pocket and wiped the blood off his hands.

Vampires. In her world, her apartment.

"Has the magic been renewed?" she demanded.

"No." A hint of guilt flashed through Arturo's expression. "You are the only one who can renew it."

But she'd known that. On some level, she'd known he hadn't really let her go. "You lied."

"You were safer here. Cristoff could not reach you."

"But you could. You have." She frowned. "You're not trapped by the magic. Are none of you trapped? Was that just another of your multitude of lies?"

Arturo spread his hands. "I did not lie, except about myself. I am one of few who were not within the city when the magic began to fail. I was not caught by it, and am still able to come and go as I please. As can Micah. Most within Vamp City are trapped there."

"You wanted me to feel safe here, didn't you? And to not try to escape."

He shrugged, then propped one shoulder against the wall just inside the shadows. As usual, he was dressed, head to toe, in black—a silk shirt tucked into dress pants—the fit of the clothes setting off his lean, muscular build to masculine perfection. Dark hair, cut short, framed high cheekbones, a well-defined jaw, and a beautifully sculpted mouth. Even his skin had the kiss of a warm Mediterranean sun, though he hadn't been near sunlight in centuries. Damn him for a handsome, lying bastard.

"You are no longer safe here, *cara*. The Traders might have stumbled upon you by accident, as they claim, or they might have been sent to capture you, as I suspect. Others will follow."

She lifted her gun and aimed it at his chest. "You're not taking me back there."

His gaze flicked to her gun with a hint of amusement.

Her brow rose. "Wooden bullets."

His amusement fled. "I will keep you safe, *cara*."

"You'll hand me over to Cristoff again."

"*No.*" He stepped forward, then pulled up on a curse as the daylight once more began to sear his skin. "I will not give you back to him."

"I don't believe you," she snapped. She ought to just shoot him, shoot them both, and be done with it. Though with their vampire superspeed, they'd probably just step out of the way of the bullets.

And Mike . . . dammit, she'd thought he was her friend.

"Quinn," Mike . . . *Micah* . . . said, drawing her gaze. "Arturo's promised he'll not hand you over to Cristoff this time, and I can assure you he won't. He screwed himself good by taking you from Cristoff in the first place."

"Cristoff knows it was him?"

"No. Cristoff is on a rampage to find the traitor who freed you. He can never know it was Arturo and Kassius, or their lives are forfeit. Mine, too, now. Since your memories can't be erased, if Cristoff gets his hands on you, he'll learn the truth. Our only recourse now is to hide you and find a way for you to renew the magic without Cristoff's ever finding out we were involved."

Which meant that after it was done, they'd have to ensure she was silenced. She had no illusions about what that meant though it didn't mean they'd succeed. Still, if what Micah said was true—and having met Cristoff, she suspected it was—Arturo couldn't let her get anywhere near his sadistic master.

She still wasn't going with the lying bastard.

Shoving her gun in her waistband, she moved to Zack and shook his shoulder. How he'd slept through gunshots, she didn't know. "Zack, get up."

To her relief, he rolled over to face the room, blinking sleepily, his hair a mass of tangles, and a pillow mark on one cheek. His skin looked more gray than before, the dark circles beneath his eyes more pronounced. And his eyes . . . The whites had turned nearly silver.

"*Dio,*" Arturo muttered, then turned an accusing gaze at Micah. "You didn't tell me."

At the sound of Arturo's voice, Zack glanced up. "What's *he* doing here?"

Micah stared at Zack with a frown. "I didn't know. I haven't seen him in days."

"Arturo lied about not being able to leave Vamp City," she told her brother, acid on her tongue. "And Mike is his vampire bitch. Liars, all," she added with disgust. "We're getting out of here."

Jumping from a second-story window onto a concrete sidewalk probably wasn't the best idea, but their options were limited, with vampires blocking the only door. Then again, maybe they wouldn't have to jump. There was a construction crew working halfway down the block. If she leaned her head out the window, and yelled, "Fire!" ten bucks said they'd bring her a ladder.

"Quinn," Arturo said, his voice hard with warning, as if he'd read her mind. "Zack is suffering from magic sickness. He'll die if you don't reverse it."

She glared at him. "Right. And of course that means returning to Vamp City with you. No thanks."

Arturo opened his mouth as if to argue, then closed it again, his frown deepening. "How long has he been ill?"

As much as she wanted to ignore him, his worried tone had her answering. "More than a week. You told me he'd sicken if he left the area. He left." Enough of this. She turned and lifted the sash on the window, flicking away a dead fly to reach the rusted screen latch.

Micah spoke to Arturo behind her. "You said Kassius sensed something when he bit her. That Zack has somehow gotten tangled in her magic."

Arturo grunted. "But he has no idea what that means. Nor do I."

"His eyes . . ." Micah's voice rose slightly as he addressed her. "Quinn, I've seen magic poisoning before. If we don't figure out what's causing Zack's, Ax is right. He's going to die."

She straightened slowly and turned to face them with a you've-got-to-be-kidding look. "So his leaving town didn't cause it? That was just another lie?"

Arturo shrugged, a hint of a smile lifting one corner of his mouth. A smile that didn't reach his eyes. "I prefer to call it a lucky guess."

She just stared at him, the fury seething, burning. "What in the hell did you do to him?"

His expression turned serious, perhaps even puzzled. "Nothing. I do not know why he's sick. Perhaps it was leaving the area. Perhaps it was leaving Vamp City. Perhaps it was something else."

Damn him to hell. Lies, lies, lies. If there was any truth buried anywhere within that, how was she supposed to know? Whirling toward the window, she began prying one of the screen hooks loose.

"You would jump, *cara*?" Arturo asked quietly. "You will injure yourself. In Zack's weakened state, he might not survive at all."

She ignored him and pried the second screen hook loose, then glanced back to find the two vampires watching her.

Arturo's gaze caught hers and held fast, frustration and determination swirling in those dark eyes. "Even if you escape, you cannot hide from me, Quinn. After your last escape, I put a magical tracer on you. I may not be able to follow you during daylight, but come nighttime, there is nowhere you can go that I cannot follow. How do you think Micah found you so quickly?"

Unfortunately, *this* she believed because Micah had introduced himself to her just hours after Arturo freed them. As soon as the sun had gone down.

Her blood steamed. Maybe she'd shoot him after all. Shoot them both.

"I want to go back, Quinn," Zack said, sitting up slowly. "I want to go back to Vamp City."

Zack's quiet words stopped her cold. She met her brother's tired gaze. "They made you say that."

"No." He swallowed and looked away. "I want to see Lily again before I die."

"You're not going to die."

He turned back to her, his eyes older than she'd ever seen them. "Yeah, I am. Something's happening to me. I can feel it. And I'm not going to survive it."

Her breath caught. He sounded so sure, but he was wrong. He had to be wrong. "You'll be okay once the magic is renewed." Her own words, repeated so many times, came out automatically. But the moment she heard them, she froze. Her gaze flew to Arturo as the truth crashed over her with a shattering understanding. She was the only one who could renew the magic. Phineas Blackstone's sons couldn't do it. There was no escape. Not for her.

She sank down onto the sofa beside Zack, stunned. "I have to go back to renew it."

Her brother took her hand. "No. Blackstone's sons . . ."

"Can't. That was just another of Arturo's lies."

Zack said nothing for a moment, but his grip tightened. "Don't go back, Quinn. Let them die."

"Renewing the magic might be the only way to save you."

"Don't worry about me. Stay here," Zack urged.

"No, *leave* here. Leave now and drive as far and as fast as you can. You can get away."

"I'm not leaving you." Certainly not *to die*. Just a month ago, she'd been bracing for the day he left *her*. When he graduated. When he moved to California with Lily. *Lily*. He said he wanted to see her again. *Again*.

Quinn turned to stare at her brother. "Did you find Lily when you were there?"

Zack released her and looked away. Slowly, he leaned his long frame back against the sofa and closed his eyes. "She was at Castle Smithson." Where he'd been a slave. "She was a maid or something."

Quinn felt the words like a blow. He'd known all along where the girl was, yet he'd said nothing. *He'd left her behind.* "Why didn't you tell me?"

His jaw hardened, tightening in that way it used to when he was small, just before the tears started. "What difference did it make? It's not like I could save her. I couldn't even save myself. I was fucking useless."

Oh, Zack.

Her gaze swung to Arturo on a surge of hope that he could help save Lily as he'd saved Zack. But as she stared at that handsome, charming visage, as the vampire's mouth began to open, she turned away, chastising herself for forgetting, even for a moment, that she couldn't trust a word he said. He would promise her anything to get her out of the sunlight and back within his reach. Then he'd take her back there, use her to renew the magic, then try to kill her so she could never be captured by Cristoff and reveal what she knew about her escape from his vile master.

She turned to Zack. "You can't go back there.

Your chances of seeing Lily are next to zero, you know that." If the girl was even still alive. "You'll just be enslaved again."

"I will find her for him," Arturo said quietly. "And I will keep all three of you safe."

Zack's eyes snapped open, hope flaring within those sickly depths.

Quinn threw the vampire a look of disgust. "He's a liar, Zack."

"He freed us, didn't he?"

"Did he? And yet, here he is."

In the distance, she heard the wail of sirens.

Zack took her hand again. "Leave, Quinn, I mean it. Let that godforsaken place die."

"And let you die with it? I'd give my life for you," she whispered, emotion clogging her throat. "You know that."

He dropped her hand, pulling in on himself as he scowled. "Why? I'm nothing. You're the one with the X-man-like power. Figure out how to work it, then come back and kill the vampires that survive Vamp City's destruction. You'll be a hero, Quinn. Why waste all that on *me*?"

"Because I love you."

"I love you, too," her brother said matter-of-factly. "So do what *I* want this time. Let me go."

Let him go.

Swallowing hard, Quinn shot to her feet and turned away, staring, unseeing, out the window as her emotions knotted together until she didn't know what she was feeling, let alone what to do. The last thing, the *last thing*, she wanted was return to Vamp City. Nothing good awaited her there, only the threat of torture and the risk of death. But how could she walk away, *run* away, knowing Zack was going back there? Because whether or not going back there cured him, Zack's chance of survival in that place was miniscule unless she went too.

Her magic wasn't much, but it had saved him once. And maybe he really did need her to renew Vamp City for him to be okay. Assuming she could figure out how.

The sirens were growing louder. Glancing down at the sidewalk, she saw people hurrying away from the building as if they'd heard a fire alarm.

Or gunshots. Crap.

She whirled back. "The police are coming."

Arturo nodded toward the door. "Come, *cara*. We cannot leave the building in daylight, but you'll be safe in Micah's apartment."

She just stared at him. "From the cops, maybe." The wail of the sirens tore at her eardrums, and her nerves. Dammit, dammit, dammit. "Can you use your mind control to make them believe nothing happened?"

"Slowly, yes. But not if they grab you. Then I may have no choice but to fight them off."

And then cops could get hurt. Or worse.

"Come, *cara*. Quickly."

The moment she got within his reach, she'd be going back to Vamp City. But maybe Zack wouldn't have to. And the alternative was an almost certain trip to the local police station. And maybe jail.

She huffed with resignation. "All right. Let's move this discussion to Micah's." Fortunately, his apartment was just across the hall.

Quinn strode back to her bedroom, grabbed the small duffels she'd packed days ago in case they had to run at a moment's notice, then returned to the foyer. Arturo watched her as she approached him, his eyes dark and enigmatic.

Her heart began to beat crazily as she closed the distance between them. She told herself it was from the adrenaline and the sirens. It had nothing to do with the chemistry that had flared between them from the start, or the whiff of his scent, familiar and heady, that triggered memories of pleasure, of friendship, of betrayal.

"The coast is clear," Micah said, peering out the door. They crossed the hallway into an apartment lit only by lamplight. Room-darkening curtains had been nailed across the windows, canceling out every hint of daylight.

Micah closed and locked the door, then turned to her, his eyes serious, yet gentle with the concern she'd seen in them so often. "You're safe here, Quinn. Please believe that if you believe nothing else."

For a moment, he was her writer friend again, and she found herself asking him the question she most needed an answer to.

"Will Zack get better if I renew the magic?"

Micah hesitated, as if weighing his words. "I don't know. It's likely. It's also possible that he'll get better just by returning to V.C. Regardless, there are people there who might be able to figure out what's wrong with him." His mouth tightened with regret. "I'm sorry, Quinn, but he needs to go back."

Her instincts told her he spoke the truth, yet all he'd really told her was that Zack might die either way.

She turned to her brother, who'd sunk down onto the sofa. "Stay here. Stay in D.C."

"No."

"I'll call Dad and ask him to drive down, then I'll renew the magic, find Lily, and come back to you."

"No, Quinn." Her brother straightened, staring at her with the pride of a grown man. "*I'll* find her."

"You're too sick."

"I'll be better once I return to V.C."

"You don't know that."

Zack's gaze unfocused as if turning inward. A moment later, he nodded. "Yes, I do. I'm going back." In his eyes, she saw a strength that hadn't been there a month ago. A conviction. And she realized she wasn't going to talk him out of this.

She wasn't sure she should.

Quinn turned away, digging her hands into her hair, hands that were beginning to shake. Because all of her carefully erected plans were shattering at once. She had no choice but to go back, now—she knew that—to renew the magic and to try to see Zack and Lily safely out of there again, even if it was the last thing she accomplished of her own free will. Zack had always been the most important person in her life, and she wasn't about to turn her back on him now, when his life was at stake.

Outside, the sirens died, car doors slamming shut as the cops swarmed the building.

"It will be dark enough to leave within the hour," Arturo said quietly. "Will you come willingly, *cara*?"

She was surprised that he bothered to ask, now that she was back in his clutches. Then again, she was armed. And even without wooden bullets, an unwilling sorceress could be a dangerous companion, as she'd proved on more than one occasion even if she hadn't been in full control.

He needed her.

The balance of power between them had shifted subtly but profoundly.

"I have promised to find Lily and to keep all of you safe, Quinn. All I ask is that you save my friends and my world in return."

She met his gaze. "I'm not sure Vamp City needs saving."

Dark eyes studied her. "Even if it's the only way to keep your brother alive?"

And that was the real heart of the matter because there was nothing she wouldn't do to save Zack. And Arturo knew it. She'd made it abundantly clear on her previous visits. Zack was her Achilles' heel.

But Arturo had his own problems now. He'd almost certainly screwed the pooch when he'd taken her from Cristoff, which meant his own survival likely depended on his protecting her. She might not be as powerful as the vampires, but she had leverage this time that she'd lacked before, and she understood far better the game they played. Not only would she never again automatically trust a word they said, but she was the only one with a snowflake's chance in Hell of saving their friends and their world. They needed her alive, and they needed her cooperation.

She met Arturo's gaze, that knowledge in her eyes. "I'll go back, and I'll renew the magic. But there are going to be conditions. And if you betray me again, Vampire, I'll let your world die."

His brow lifted, and she knew he recognized the hollowness of her threat. As long as Zack needed the magic renewed, she'd renew it. But he didn't call her on it. Instead, his expression turned serious, his gaze gripping hers. Slowly, he nodded, a single downward dip of his head. "I will not betray you again, Quinn. Never again, *cara*. Someday, you will believe that."

She doubted that. But it was a moot point. She was going back to save her brother. And the only one she intended to trust was herself.

CHAPTER THREE

Through Micah's closed apartment door, Quinn could hear the cops storming her own apartment, then spilling back into the hallway.

At the pounding on Micah's door, Quinn tensed, but when she started to rise, to hide, Arturo shook his head. "You're in no danger."

Quinn eyed him skeptically. "And the cops?"

"They are in no danger, either."

Though she couldn't see the door from the leather sofa where she sat in Micah's living room, she heard Micah explaining that he'd heard a car backfiring on the street. The front door closed, but Micah didn't return.

Quinn glanced at Arturo. "Did he leave?"

"Yes. He'll move among the cops, using mind control to convince the majority that there were no gunshots. Once they leave, we can go. It's almost full dark."

"Where do you plan to take us that Cristoff won't find us?"

"To a friend of ours. You will both be safe there, I assure you."

She snorted.

"You do not trust me, *cara mia*." The words were soft, almost sad. But his gaze unsettled her pulse in a way that was all too pleasant. All too annoying. "I am sorry for the necessity of my lies."

"Necessity? And are you sorry, too, for the lies you're telling me now? That you'll tell me in the future?"

His mouth tightened, but he didn't answer.

"Where does your friend live?"

"I cannot tell you more. Doing so would endanger him should you fall into the wrong hands."

"Which you've promised won't happen," she countered.

He dipped his head. "I have. But some things are out of even my control."

She gave him a look of disgust. "Of course they are." Unable to remain still for another second, she rose and began pacing, wishing she could look out the window. But the only way to do that was to pull out her knife and slice away the heavy fabric. It wasn't worth it.

Within the hour, she'd be leaving everything she owned behind. Again. But she felt no slam of grief. Barely even a twinge of regret. She liked her job well enough, but it had never been her life. Her friends she'd let slip away as the evidence of her "weirdness," her magic, had begun to mount. And none of those friends had ever been more than casual acquaintances. Zack was the only family she had. At least he was the only one who mattered. And he was going with her.

There were things she'd miss, of course. Sunlight. Starbucks. Her cell phone. But otherwise, she would leave little behind of consequence.

The front door opened and Micah slipped inside. "We're good," he said, as if it had been a foregone conclusion. And it probably had.

"Are you going with us?" she asked.

"I am."

That pleased her, probably because she was still inclined to think of him as her wine-and-dessert buddy rather than Arturo's vampire spy. Which was a mistake.

Micah glanced at Arturo, a question in his eyes that had her spidey sense flaring to life. Especially when Arturo nodded.

"What?" she demanded.

Arturo was the one who explained. "Micah has an ability to glamour others for short periods of time. A day or two at most."

Micah grunted. "Only a few hours today, I'm afraid. I haven't fed for a while."

Quinn frowned, ignoring the feeding comment. "What do you mean 'glamour'?"

Micah's expression gentled. "I'll essentially place a mask over you, giving you the face of another woman except for your eyes, which cannot be changed. It won't hurt. You'll barely feel it, in fact. But no one will recognize you until the glamour wears off."

"So if we're stopped, no one will know me even if they've seen me before."

"Precisely."

Arturo grunted. "Unless you lose control of your magic."

Zack leaned forward on the sofa. "This I've got to see."

Quinn glanced at her brother, then crossed her arms over her chest. The glamour would be an excellent defense if they came upon Cristoff's men, which they could easily do. But she just didn't know how much she could trust Micah despite her admittedly biased instincts that, vampire or not, he really was her friend. She hated not knowing. And hated the fact that if she was going to work with them to get the magic renewed without Cristoff's knowing, she was going to have to trust them, at least to some extent.

Micah stood before her, studying her. "Your blond hair is too striking, I think. Your features too even, too attractive."

Arturo made a sound like that of a jealous male. As if he had any right. But Micah ignored him. Instead, he lifted his hands, touching her cheeks with cool fingertips. She wondered if his vampire coolness was the reason he'd never touched her or made a single move on her when she thought he was Mike. Would she have realized what he was if she'd felt how cool his skin was? She'd like to think so, but she just didn't know.

As he stroked her cheeks with the pads of his thumbs, he watched her with kind eyes. Mike's eyes.

Her gaze fell to his cheek. "That scar didn't come from a sliding glass door, did it?"

"No. It was a gift from the Gauls who slaughtered my family and enslaved me when I was twelve."

The Gauls. She stared at him, feeling bludgeoned all over again by the reality of who he was. He might have Mike's eyes, but this male was a centuries-old vampire. And she'd do well to remember that.

Slowly, his eyes closed. Cool hands splayed across her cheeks, barely touching her, and suddenly her flesh began to tingle. The feeling spread into her scalp and down her neck, into her body, a sensation that felt odd but not particularly unpleasant.

"Fuck," Zack breathed.

Micah pulled his hands back, the tingling dying away as he opened his eyes and began to smile.

Quinn turned to where Zack stared at her wide-eyed.

"You don't look like you. You look . . . weird, sis."

"Thanks a lot."

Arturo, watching her intently as he did so often, gave a satisfied nod.

The suspense was killing her, so she found Micah's bathroom, flipped on the light, and stared at the brown-haired stranger in the mirror. She was no beauty, though she hardly considered herself a beauty in her true form. The woman staring back at her looked, as Zack had said, a little weird. Her features were off. Too small, too close together. The only things that hadn't changed were her eyes.

She felt Arturo's presence a moment before he stepped behind her. "Micah made your features just unbalanced enough to make the eye draw away, which is precisely what we want."

"This is all a game to you, isn't it?"

His gaze met hers in the mirror. "It has never been a game with you, *tesoro*. You confound me. You have, in a matter of weeks, upended my well-ordered life."

Quinn snorted. "I've upended *your* life?"

Humor leaped into his eyes, a smile lifting the corners of his mouth. "Touché."

His scent, one that had always reminded her of almond liqueur, wafted over her again, reminding her of heat and passion, of strong arms and desire beyond bearing. But that was another time. And she was another woman. One who, *please God*, was no longer fully dependent upon him for survival. In either world.

"Explain something to me," she said, meeting his gaze in the mirror. "Why did you free me when doing so put you in such a dangerous position with Cristoff?"

His mouth tightened, then twisted. "I could not bear to see you in pain. I did not think past that." His hands rose to cup her shoulders, his long fingers cool against the skin bared by her tank top. But as he started to pull her back against him, she pulled away, shrugging him off.

"*Cara* . . ."

She whirled on him. "Don't, Vampire. Just . . . don't. Don't *cara* me. Don't try to pretend you have feelings for me. Over and over you've warned me not to trust you, and I've finally listened. I'll work with you to renew Vamp City and to save my brother, but that's all. We're not friends anymore. And we're not going to be lovers again."

She turned away, and he stopped her with a hand on her arm.

"You are wise to doubt me, *tesoro*. I have given you little reason to do otherwise. But I will win your trust. I will do whatever I must to keep you safe. You will see."

She met that intense gaze, then turned and left the bathroom without replying. What was there to say?

Arturo followed her back to the living room, where Zack sat, looking far too sick.

Micah stood. "It's time to go. I'll get the Jeep."

Arturo tossed Micah the keys, and her onetime neighbor left the apartment, vampire-fast. Zack rose slowly and Quinn joined him as they started for the door, Arturo close behind. Quinn stepped into the hallway, eyeing her closed apartment door, and wondered if she'd ever come back here.

It would take a miracle to get them all out of Vamp City alive.

But she'd never been one to give up. And she wasn't about to start now.

CHAPTER FOUR

Quinn sat rigid in her seat in the back of the Jeep Wrangler as she prepared for yet another return to Hell. Zack sat beside her, asleep against the window. Arturo drove with the top up to hide his passengers as much as possible while Micah rode shotgun as the vehicle sped through the D.C. streets toward the Kennedy Center and the Boundary Circle that separated the real D.C. from Vamp City.

The scientist in her began to frown as she tried to understand how the two cities occupied the same physical space. Magic, she knew. But still . . .

She glanced at Arturo. "If you're outside the Boundary Circle, say crossing into the District from Virginia, how do you choose whether to drive into Vamp City or remain in D.C.? Clearly, the magic doesn't automatically pull you into V.C., or you couldn't have reached my apartment." Or anyplace within the space occupied by both.

Micah was the one who answered. "At the moment that we hit the Boundary Circle, the magic tries to embrace us. We can either push it away and remain in D.C. or allow it to pull us into Vamp City. There are some vamps who can't push it away, they haven't the ability, and are therefore always pulled in. They can only travel the parts of D.C. where the two worlds don't overlap. Humans and weres can't embrace the magic, so can never enter V.C. without an escort, except for those handful of humans who've been slipping in by accident through the sunbeams, and we have no idea why that's happening. Traders can come and go as vampires can. Or as vampires could before the magic began to fail. They alone are not trapped by the failing magic."

Quinn's mind still struggled to wrap itself around the concept. "So how does that work for a car?"

Micah smiled. "You ask difficult questions, Quinn."

"I'm a scientist."

"Perhaps you need to think more like a sorceress. Magic is a far more potent force in Vamp City than science."

As they reached the Kennedy Center, Quinn could see the Shimmers like a faint wall of water vapor sparkling in the moonlight across the grounds. She'd seen them all her life, nearly invisible walls in various parts of D.C. that were always in the same spots, never moving, never wavering. It wasn't until recently that she'd realized what they were—the boundary of Vamp City. A boundary no other human, to her knowledge, could see.

The sight of it now made her pulse kick, sending a shiver of cold skating over her skin even as a flush of heat dampened the back of her neck. Because they were going in.

Arturo pulled into the Kennedy Center drive as if he were heading for the parking garage, a drive cut straight across by the Shimmer. As they neared it, she tensed. As they passed through it, the hair rose on her arms, the air prickling her skin in a cool, ticklish dance. But they were still in the real world, the Kennedy Center looming large beside her.

"What happened?" she asked.

Beside her, Zack moaned as he had every time he'd passed through a Shimmer since their escape a week and a half ago, which was another reason she suspected the magic of Vamp City was at least partially at fault for his illness.

"Nothing," Arturo said, making a tight U-turn in the middle of the drive, and suddenly she understood. Her apartment was within the V.C. boundary. To enter Vamp City, they first had to leave it. Which they'd just done.

Now, they were going in.

Turning off his headlights, Arturo accelerated as he drove back toward the waiting Shimmer. As they hit it, the hair rose on Quinn's arms a second time, and darkness swallowed her, the true dark of a night world without electricity. A shiver went through her that had a little to do with the air flowing in from the open front windows, air that turned instantly cooler by a good ten degrees, and far more to do with the primal fear of being back in Vamp City.

This time, Zack's moan sounded less like pain and more like one of relief, as if the magic had finally quit strangling him. She prayed it was true.

The Jeep began to pitch and bounce over uneven ground, leaving the paved streets for an open, rutted field in the vampires' 1870 version of her world. Thank goodness vampires had excellent night vision. Without headlights, she could see nothing but the dim glow of the vehicle's instrument panel and its reflected light on Arturo's profile. His jaw was set, tension radiating down his arms and shoulders. A tension her own body echoed though she hoped his meant he was worried about what would happen if they were caught and not that he was bracing for her reaction when she learned what he really had in mind.

She'd kill him if he betrayed her again, especially with Zack at risk, now, too. "Who does Cristoff think took me?" she asked, needing the sound of voices to drown out the pulsing silence.

"Ivan and his men," Arturo replied.

"The ones who tried to stop us from leaving?"

"Yes."

As they'd ridden for the Boundary Circle the day Arturo and Kassius set them free, one of Cristoff's more vicious guards and his troop had ridden upon them, recognized her, and realized Arturo was trying to free the sorceress. A battle had ensued. Ivan and his troop were dead.

"Cristoff believes Ivan took you and escaped Vamp City."

"And the rest of his troop?"

"He thinks that they either defected or, like Ivan, were not actually trapped by the magic. It has long been suspected that some who claim to be trapped here are not."

As her eyes adjusted to the dark, the ghostly, twisted shapes of dead trees began to appear, silhouetted against the moonlit night sky. Even as a thrill of dread crawled along her scalp, she admitted to herself a dark fascination with this night world. She'd always loved the dark. As a child it had been the only place she'd ever truly been able to hide from the stepmother who'd hated her.

"So how many vampires aren't trapped? How many of you are there in the real world?"

Micah glanced back. "Before the magic began to fail, there were over three dozen of us that I knew of in D.C. alone, about half tied to the kovenas within V.C. Nearly a dozen of them got caught on the wrong side of the Boundary Circle when the magic began to fail, trapping them inside. They'd come in for the Kovena Cup, our annual vampire soccer match. Halfway through the semifinal game, the first sunbeam broke through just outside the coliseum. Several vampires died, and no one who was in Vamp City at that moment has been able to leave since. The magic's failing was like a switch being flipped. The same switch Phineas Blackstone flipped in the 1870s when he attempted to make Vamp City a death trap."

She'd heard what had happened next back then, that Cristoff had cut off two of Phineas's young son's fingers before persuading the sorcerer to renew the magic and disable his death trap. And once he had, Cristoff killed the sorcerer. Vamp City had remained intact ever since. Until two years ago. Who or what had flipped the switch this time, no one knew. At least, that's what she'd been told.

"What were you two doing that night?" she asked the vampires, since they obviously hadn't been at the Kovena Cup.

"Destroying a Ripper nest in Adams Morgan."

Ahead, she could make out the silhouettes of decrepit houses and row houses. Not until they passed the crumbling corpse of the White House would they start to see signs of habitation. With a lurch, the Jeep flew over a low embankment and onto the packed dirt that passed for roads in this place, as they had in the real D.C. of 1870.

"Are there a lot of Rippers in the area?"

"More now than there used to be," Micah told her. "With so many Emoras trapped within V.C., there are fewer to hunt them."

"Is it your job to hunt them?"

"It is, and I take it seriously. Rippers are vicious, without conscience."

The Rippers, she'd learned, were a different race of vampire, one who fed exclusively on blood, whereas the Emoras, the more prominent race, fed on both blood and emotion. They claimed the Emoras were the more humane of the two races.

Quinn scoffed. "You just described most of the Emoras I've met. If the Rippers are worse, God help us all."

Micah glanced at Arturo, then looked back at her. "You're right, Quinn. Many of the Emoras of Vamp City have become every bit as bad as the Rippers, but they didn't used to be. Most of the nearly five hundred vampires that first moved into Vamp City continued to hunt in the human world as they always had—fear feeders scaring their victims as they fed on them, then wiping their minds and sending them on their way. The pain feeders haunting the hospitals, the old folks' homes, and the neighborhoods, feeding simply by standing outside the bedroom window of a human in childbirth or in pain from disease or injury. And the pleasure feeders . . ." He smiled. "Throughout the ages, the brothels have been our favorite places to feed and hunt."

So Micah was a pleasure feeder. She'd wondered. "So why did they change?"

"We're not sure, not entirely. And as with most things, the answer is complicated. We'd always had to remain under the human radar, and suddenly didn't. A number of the vampires brought in their human companions. And when those humans began to turn immortal, recruiting more humans to serve us became a simple matter of offering immortality. They came willingly and happily. For a time."

They passed the White House, its abandoned, crumbling appearance the symbol of everything wrong in this place, but Quinn only glanced at it this time, far more interested in Micah's story.

"Most vampires continued to leave Vamp City at night to feed in the old ways. The coliseum was originally built for vampire sports, not gladiator battle. We held rugby and football matches, among other things. And, if you can believe it, we enjoyed the arts. One night an entire theater company was enthralled and brought in to perform a play, then returned to their beds without any of them the wiser."

Quinn shook her head, knowing her face was a mask of disbelief. "What happened?"

"Some would tell you we got bored and slowly reverted to our natural inclinations, free of human retribution." Micah glanced at Arturo. "Those of us who've remained outside, who live in the real world, disagree. We've watched the changes in those we've known for centuries. The magic of Vamp City has had a corrupting effect on many of those who live within its borders, disintegrating souls and consciences."

"My conscience is just fine," Arturo muttered.

Quinn snorted. Right.

"You still have one, Ax. Which, considering what's happened to most in Vamp City, is saying something. Your conscience was always strong. Even so, you've not been unaffected. Not by a long shot."

Arturo lapsed into a brooding silence.

Quinn turned to watch out the window as a horse and wagon passed them on the wide dirt road, driven by a male dressed in Civil War garb. A vampire, no doubt. In the back of the wagon sat three people dressed in modern clothing. New captives? It was hard to tell in the dark, but their hair appeared to lack the phosphorescent glow of Slavas—humans who'd turned immortal, as all humans apparently did in this place if they survived their first couple of years.

Her stomach cramped as she wondered who they'd left behind—wives, children, parents? And with sorrow at what she feared they'd suffer in this place.

"So there weren't always slaves here?" Quinn asked, skeptical. "Or torturing and killing just for the sport of it?"

"There have always been human servants—humans who willingly, or not so willingly, serve their vampire masters. But the influx of humans solely for sport and food didn't start in earnest until a few decades ago. Even that didn't become widespread until a couple of years ago, when the magic began to fail. The depravity since has spiraled out of control, Quinn." Micah glanced at Arturo. "And even those with honor in their hearts have turned a blind eye."

Arturo's jaw tightened, but, again, he said nothing.

Quinn watched the passing landscape, the well-lit houses in the inhabited areas, streets that in modern D.C. were now lined with high-rise office buildings.

"*Cara*," Arturo said, drawing her gaze to his in the rearview mirror. "If we are stopped and anyone asks, you and Zack are Micah's slaves. He is leaving you at my house while he helps me search for the missing sorceress."

"All right." There was much to be said for getting their stories straight.

They turned onto Fourteenth Street, and she knew they were close to Arturo's house. She'd been there before and knew it to be on F Street, only about a block from the Treasury. In 1870, F Street had been primarily residential, unlike its twenty-first-century twin.

Several minutes later, Arturo pulled into the alley that ran behind his house and parked the Jeep. Too fast, he was out of the vehicle and slinging a still-sleeping Zack over his shoulder as if her brother wasn't close to Arturo's size, as if he weighed nothing.

Micah emerged from the vehicle at normal speed and opened her door for her. As she climbed out, she heard a man's scream on the wind some distance away. The sound clawed through her, raking open every memory of the terrors she'd known in this place, setting them free like nightmares flying through her mind. No one should ever be made to scream like that.

"Quinn?"

Mike's voice penetrated the darkness, jarringly wrong in this place. But it focused her, grounded her. Screams were a common sound in Vamp City.

God, she hated this place.

With a shiver, she moved quickly toward the house, preceding Micah through the back door and into a kitchen that was, if not modern, at least a far cry from its 1870s roots. This was the one room within Arturo's home that was fully electrical, with 1970s appliances and modern, recessed lighting.

The kitchen was empty, the faint smell of freshly baked bread lingering, reminding her she hadn't eaten anything since breakfast. The tension in her back and shoulders eased now that they'd reached Arturo's home. Oddly, she felt safe here. Arturo might have scared her mindless the first time he brought her here, feeding from her fear, believing he could take her memory of it later. But he'd never attacked her. She'd never been physically harmed in this house. And she never would be as long as Cristoff and his goons didn't find her here. For all of Arturo's faults, she believed that. He wouldn't hurt her. Not physically.

As they started down the hallway, Ernesta, one of Arturo's servants, bustled out of the living room, motioning with her hand for them to follow. Quinn knew that the matronly, Latino-looking woman wasn't human, though exactly what she was, Quinn had yet to learn.

Quinn entered the living room to find Arturo setting a disgruntled Zack on the sofa.

"I could have walked," Zack grumbled.

"You were sound asleep," Quinn countered. It might be wishful thinking, but she thought he looked a little better, his skin tone less gray, the circles under his eyes a little less pronounced, though the "whites" of his eyes had turned fully silver. "How do you feel?"

Zack ran a hand through his shaggy curls and met her gaze with a spark of life that had been missing for the past ten days. "Hungry."

"Have Susie prepare a meal for two," Arturo told Ernesta, then sent Micah a questioning glance. When the other vampire shook his head, presumably not interested in human food, Arturo added, "And send Horace in."

Micah settled his big vampire body on one of the chairs. As Quinn joined Zack on the sofa, Horace, Arturo's sole male servant, appeared in the doorway. He was a balding, stocky male with a graying beard that glowed with a Slava's phosphorescence.

"Master." He said the word as a soldier might say "Captain" to a respected and revered commanding officer.

"What news, Horace?" Arturo asked, crossing one ankle over his knee.

The older man stroked his bushy beard. "Well now, a new sunbeam broke through right outside the slave auction yesterday, just as it was ending. A wide one, wider than anyone had ever seen. More'n fifteen vamps were caught in it, including that bitch Francesca."

Quinn started with surprise, and no small amount of relief. She'd briefly been one of Francesca's slaves and was delighted that no one else would suffer that monster's torment.

"Any word on the sorceress?"

Quinn frowned, wondering why he was asking Horace about her when she was sitting right there.

"Nah. Some say she's a shifter and turned herself into a bug and escaped Cristoff that way. Others say she's far more powerful than Cristoff knew and transported herself out of his prison. But no one's seen her."

"Thank you, Horace. I need you to send word to Mukdalla. Tell her I have a couple of gifts for her, and I'm in immediate need of transport to pick them up."

With a deferential nod, Horace turned and left.

Eyes narrowed, Quinn turned to Arturo. "What was that all about? He doesn't know who I am?"

"You're glamoured, *cara*."

She grimaced. "Right." She'd forgotten about that.

"But it wouldn't matter either way. He doesn't remember having met you. None of my servants do. Nor do they remember seeing Zack."

"You took their memories?"

"I did. And I'll take them again when we leave. For their protection as well as yours."

Quinn leaned forward, her arms on her knees. "What's the plan, Vampire? Don't leave me in the dark. I assume Zack and I are the gifts in need of transport?"

"You are." He leaned forward, mirroring her, until their faces were but a couple of feet apart. As he watched her, his eyes softened, deepening, his gaze probing as if he meant to coax her to lower her defenses. Instead, she leaned back, putting distance between them.

His brows flickered down in disappointment, his expression clearing, turning military cool once more. "Later tonight, we'll transfer you to a place of safety."

She frowned. "You're not going."

"You go nowhere without me. Micah and I will follow at a distance, keeping watch over you. We will rendezvous with you there."

"Wherever 'there' is."

With a gleam in his eyes, he gave a nod, then glanced at Micah. "Show Zack to the dining room, *amico mio*. I should like a moment alone with Quinn."

She wasn't sure she wanted a moment alone with him. But she said nothing as Micah gave his friend an assessing look, then rose. "Let's find you some food, Zack."

Zack jumped up more quickly than he'd moved for days, easing the clamp around her heart. When they were alone, she turned back to the vampire, curious and wary.

Arturo watched her, searching her face . . . No, not *her* face. "I have missed you, *tesoro*," he said quietly, his dark eyes gleaming, his voice rich with seduction.

She snorted. "You're really going to do this, now? Try to get me back into your bed?"

With a quick grin and a shake of his head, he leaned back in his chair, eyeing her wryly. "Why do you think I am not sincere?"

"Not sincere that you've missed me or that you want me back in your bed?"

"You were the one that brought up the bed, *cara*, not I." His expression, faintly mocking, turned serious. "I have missed you."

She cocked her head. "How did you happen to be at Mike's . . . Micah's . . . this afternoon? Have you been spying on me, too?"

"I prefer to call it watching over you. Protecting you. I have spent as much time with Micah as I could though not as much as I would have liked. I caught a glimpse of you only rarely though your emotions were my constant companion. Your worry nearly drove me to distraction. I thought your fear was that vampires would find you. But your fear was for Zack, not for yourself. I did not realize Zack was sick." He leaned forward again, eyeing her intently. "I do not like it when you suffer."

She just stared at him, feeling like he'd kicked her in the chest. "You have a funny way of showing it." Twice he'd turned her over to his sadistic master.

The vampire looked down at his hands, his breath

leaving his body on a sigh. Slowly, he lifted his head, meeting her gaze with eyes so dark, so deep, she knew if she wasn't careful, she could fall into them and never find her way out again.

"I am sorry, *cara mia,* for what you suffered at Cristoff's hands. I knew he would be angry, but I did not think he would . . ." His hands curled into fists, his jaw turning rigid. "I could not stop him, Quinn. A vampire never questions his master's words or actions unless he intends to challenge him for his position."

"Which means?"

"To have objected to Cristoff's punishment of you would have been tantamount to calling him out, to declaring my intention of killing him and taking his place. Which, of course, would have meant he'd have immediately ordered my death in return. Kassius would have sided with me, as would Bram, who was in the stronghold at the time, and perhaps others. In all likelihood, we'd all have died. And then you'd have had no one to look out for you."

Sincerity rang in his tone, regret throbbed in his eyes, and instinct told her he spoke the truth. She'd seen enough of Cristoff to believe that he'd allow no questioning of his actions. Still, she wasn't about to let him off the hook that easily. She said nothing.

"He was not always this way, Quinn. He was honorable once. Despite being a pain-feeder, he was never cruel except to his enemies." He looked down at his clasped hands. "Micah is right. Many of us have changed, particularly since the magic began to fail. Cristoff most of all."

He looked up, dark eyes pulling at her once more. "I have hope, Quinn, that when the magic is renewed, he will once more become the man—the vampire—he once was. Ruthless to his enemies, yes. And as I fear he will always see you as such, you can never go near him. But not sadistic, as he has become. Do you know he used to refuse to cause pain? We used to walk the battlefields, just walk them, gorging on the fear and the agony the humans inflicted upon one another. He has lost his soul, cara. I have hope he may, with the magic's renewal, find it and become that male again."

"Do you really believe that's possible?" Cristoff was as soulless, as evil, as any creature could possibly be.

"I must."

For the first time, she realized how honestly devoted Arturo must have been to Cristoff at one time. And how hard it must be to watch a man you've admired, and perhaps even loved, turn into a monster. If, that is, you hadn't done the same.

She'd never known Arturo to be a monster, but just how fully functioning his conscience was now, or had been in the past, she had reason to question. She'd be a fool to trust him any more than she had to.

"I hope you're right. For all of our sakes." A benevolent Cristoff might be far easier to escape. She rose.

Arturo followed. "I will never let him hurt you again, *cara mia.*" His fingers curled around her upper arm, and he stepped closer. "*No one* will hurt you again. I vow it."

"You can't make that promise. And I don't need you to. I can take care of myself."

He dipped his head, his nose brushing her hair. "Nevertheless." His head dipped farther, his lips tasting the side of her neck, sending shivers dancing through her blood. Her mind urged her to put distance between them, but her body remembered all too well the delight she'd known at his hands and resisted. His scent of almonds and moonlight invaded her senses and her body came alive at his touch. Her pulse raced. It would be all too easy to give in, to let him lead her upstairs and drown her worries in passion and pleasure.

Instead, she pulled away.

"Don't, Vampire. We're not going to be lovers again. We're not going to be anything."

"Now it is you who lie, *tesoro*. If only to yourself." He watched her with disappointment. "You respond to my touch as few ever have. And I to yours. Your merest kiss turns my skin warm. You cannot deny this."

"It doesn't matter. If you want me to save your world, then that's how it's going to be."

His mouth tightened, but the only emotion she saw in his eyes was regret. "So be it. Join your brother and eat, *cara*. I have things to discuss with Micah."

As she led the way to the dining room, she was all too aware of him at her back, too physically aware of him on every level. There was something about him that drew her like a moth to flame. It would be all too easy to give in to the pleasure she knew he could give her, indescribable pleasure that had haunted her dreams since the last time she was in his arms.

But the closer she let him get, the more likely she was to trust him again. And that was something she refused to do.

CHAPTER FIVE

Quinn found Zack at the dining-room table devouring homemade rolls as fast as he could butter them up and shove them into his mouth. The room was lovely in an old-fashioned fussy kind of way, the walls papered dark red, a gold-and-crystal chandelier hanging above an antique, ornately carved table. Gilt-framed paintings lined the walls, some exact duplicates of originals that would go for millions at auction in the real world . . . if the originals didn't already hang in museums.

"Your brother looks better," Arturo commented behind her.

Quinn nodded. "It's amazing. He really did need to come back here."

"I have told you the truth, have I not?" Arturo's cool fingers stroked the side of her neck.

She stepped away from him. "Lucky guess."

"Educated guess."

"Regardless, thank God it worked."

As Quinn reached for the chair at a right angle to her brother's, Arturo pulled it out for her. She met his even gaze. Whatever else he was, she'd always known him to be a gentleman and a charmer.

With a nod, she took the seat he offered as Micah strode in from the kitchen, a bottle of Corona in his hand. "You need limes, Ax."

"I'll have Ernesta run up to the Safeway," he replied dryly. "A word?"

As the two vampires left the dining room, Quinn reached for one of the rolls from the heaping basket. "You're hungry."

Zack nodded, waiting to reply until his mouth wasn't entirely full. "Starved." His gaze met hers. "I really felt like I was dying, Quinn."

"And you don't now?"

"No. Dying from lack of food, maybe."

Ernesta bustled into the room with two plates piled high with large slabs of piping-hot lasagna, returning moments later with heaping bowls of salad. It was far more food than Quinn needed. Fortunately, if Zack didn't slow down, he'd wind up finishing off his portion and hers, too. For a moment, she just watched him, feeling her eyes burn with relief. She'd told herself all along that he'd be fine, that the magic would be renewed in time to save him. But she'd been lying. She'd been gut-ripping terrified that her beloved brother was going to die. And while Vamp City was probably the most dangerous place in existence for a human, there was no denying it was where he needed to be right now.

As Quinn dug her fingers into a warm, soft roll and spread a dollop of what appeared to be freshly churned butter on one side, she eyed her brother thoughtfully.

"What is it?" Zack asked, catching her gaze.

She hesitated to bring up the questions that had been weighing on her since his revelation earlier, but decided if he could eat like a four-hundred-pound weight lifter, he could answer some questions, even tough ones.

"Tell me about Lily, Zack. Was she . . . okay?" In many ways, she didn't want to know the answer to that. It was hard enough watching the torture of strangers, but hearing about the suffering of a young woman she'd already begun to think of as her future sister-in-law was going to hurt.

But Zack just gave her his customary shrug. "She looked tired."

Tired. "That's all?"

"And sad."

Okay. "But not bruised? Or hurt?"

His brows lowered, then lifted as understanding widened his eyes. "God, no."

Quinn released the breath she hadn't even known she was holding. "Good. That's good."

She took a bite of lasagna, but Zack's gaze fell to his own plate, his hand turning a soft roll into a hard ball of bread.

Slowly, he looked up again, staring at nothing. "The first time I saw her, she was standing in the upstairs window with a load of towels or sheets or something. The second time, she was in the kitchen carrying a bucket and a mop."

"So they were using her as a housemaid." Quinn didn't voice out loud her fear that the girl had been used for far more. For far worse. Many vampires were depraved in the extreme. The way Zack was mangling that roll told her he was thinking the same.

"Zack, why didn't you tell me you saw her?"

For several moments, he didn't respond, didn't act as if he'd heard her. "I don't know."

When he failed to expound, she suspected that was the only answer she was going to get. In his defense, he probably didn't know why. She remembered how down on himself he'd been after they were reunited. How Arturo had told her he blamed himself for not being able to save the women he cared about.

And what if he *had* told her he'd seen Lily right after they'd escaped Vamp City? Would she have tried to go back in after the girl? The thought of it weighed on her like a pile of bricks. Selfishly, she was glad she hadn't been forced to make that decision.

Until today, she'd suspected Lily was somewhere in Vamp City, but she hadn't known for sure. Now she did. If Arturo could spring Zack from the gladiator camp, he could find a way to get Lily out of Castle Smithson. And he would. Because they were partners now, God help her.

The next time she escaped Vamp City, it would be with Zack *and* Lily.

She just hoped there was a next time.

Lily Wang slid her hand across the gold satin sheet, smoothing it across the modern mattress, satisfied that there were no bloodstains. She moved quickly, efficiently, silently, as she changed the sheets in the upstairs bedrooms . . . bed*chambers* . . . of Castle Smithson, as she had every day since her capture. Changing the sheets, working in the bedrooms at all, was a tricky proposition. She'd yet to be caught, yet to be raped. At least that she knew of. With the vampires' ability to enthrall and steal memories, it was always possible she'd experienced things she didn't remember.

But she was nothing if not prosaic. If she didn't remember, and had been left with no injuries, then nothing had happened. Period.

The trouble was, if she stayed here long enough, something would happen. It was just a matter of time, she knew that. She'd already been bitten several times. That was unavoidable in a coven . . . *kovena* . . . of vampires. More than once, she'd been grabbed from behind as she walked through the halls, doing her chores. It never took long and didn't hurt. As much as she hated to admit it, the sensation of vampire sucking was actually kind of pleasant . . . except when the vampire pulled out messily, dripping blood onto clean towels, and she had to send them back to the laundry.

For the most part, though, she was a shadow, moving through the halls silently, drawing little or no attention. And she intended to keep it that way. When the time was right, she'd move silently right out of this castle, out of this hellhole, and find her way home.

Her parents were frantic at her disappearance, she knew that. And she'd missed all of her classes for weeks. She'd have to reenroll next semester, which meant graduating a semester late. And if she did that, Galaxy Gaming might rescind the offer of employment they'd made to her. And to Zack.

Zack.

Pain slammed into her at the thought of him, making her gasp. The tears she'd so far managed to keep at bay burned her eyes. She tried so hard not to think of him, but he was with her always, his presence steadying her, giving her strength. Even though she knew he was probably dead.

Poor Zack.

The first time she saw him in the yard behind Castle Smithson hauling a wheelbarrow full of bricks, she'd felt such a tangle of emotions—joy, shock, regret, despair. Somehow, he'd become one of the missing, too. Eventually, days after he'd arrived, he'd caught sight of her and called to her. And the hurt in his voice when she'd hurried away, ignoring him, still cut her to the quick. But she knew what happened when vampires thought two slaves cared about one another. The pair became the sadistic vampires' new favorite playthings.

Zack had only ever thought of her as his best friend, but he was as loyal as they came and would have suffered if they'd hurt her in front of him. Her feelings for him went far beyond friendship and had since the first day he'd smiled at her. She loved the redheaded loon. And she'd been terrified that the vampires would see it.

So she'd ignored him. And the next day, they'd sent him to the gladiator camp to be prepared for the Games. In a computer battle, Zack could beat anyone. But in real life, with real swords?

The thought of him in that arena, facing a deadly opponent, was almost too much to bear.

She pulled the satin coverlet over the bed, then replaced the colorful pillows. Top sheets and blankets were never required on vampire beds since the bloodsuckers didn't sleep. Beds were for two things only—sex and feeding. Often at the same time, from what she'd seen. And heard.

Picking up her dwindling pile of clean sheets, she slipped out of the room, heading for the next. She was halfway down the hall, when a man appeared at the top of the stairs. A vampire with hunger in his now-white-centered eyes. And he was staring right at her.

She froze, her heart beating a fast, frantic rhythm. Maybe he'd only feed from her and not take her to one of the beds.

He smiled, tipping his head back in pleasure, clearly a fear-feeder enjoying her anxiousness. Slowly, he lowered his head and peered at her curiously. "Why the fear, little human? Still taken aback by the eyes?" He smiled, revealing sharp twin incisors. "And the fangs? Have you ever felt them pierce the tender flesh between your legs?"

Her heart rate spiked, and he felt it, his smile broadening.

"I have," a brash, tart, and wonderfully dear voice said behind her. "And what I like even more is some vampire mouth sucking on my huge-ass tits. Forget that scrawny-ass Asian. She's flat as a board and as cold as you are. What you need is some warm, soft Jazlyn."

The heavyset, dark-skinned Jazlyn brushed past Lily, heading straight for the vampire.

The vampire's expression turned amused. "She fears me, Warm Soft Jazlyn. You don't."

"No. But once you show her the real joys of vampire-loving, she'll lose that fear. Which would be a shame, wouldn't it? 'Sides, I'm in the mood for some vampire cock-loving. Ain't never sixty-nined with a vampire."

Jazlyn was too wise, and far too experienced, for her eighteen years. Lily only had a vague idea of what a sixty-nine meant, but the vampire's eyes lit with interest.

"Come, then."

Jazlyn threw Lily a wink over her shoulder, then walked right up to the vampire and slid her hand between his legs. With a grin, he took that hand and led her into the nearest room and closed the door.

Lily darted into the next bedroom, pulling the air in through her nose, fighting to settle her racing heart before she had every fear-feeder in the castle hunting her down.

That was too close.

She exhaled deeply, at once relieved and sad for her friend, although Jazlyn had assured her she really did love sex with the vampires. Despite Lily's being three years older, Jazlyn had usurped the role of protective older sister the first night Lily arrived. She'd taken one look at Lily, and said, "Damn, girl! You still a *virgin?*" Lily hadn't replied, but it hadn't mattered. Jazlyn had gone on to tell her she hadn't been a virgin since her cousin raped her when she was eleven. The girl was often prickly and tough, at least with others. But she was always there for Lily. They exchanged confidences on their pallets at night, and whatever extra food one or the other had managed to stash away. Most nights, they fell asleep pressed back to back, sharing body heat in the cold storeroom where the female slaves slept. And more than once, Lily had felt Jazlyn's hand slip into hers, the girl-woman seeking a child's reassurance that she wasn't alone. That everything was going to be all right, when both of them knew nothing would ever be right again.

Lily knew it was ridiculous to care about her virginity in a place like this when most were struggling just to hold on to their lives. But Jazlyn was fiercely determined she should protect it, especially after Lily had told her about Zack. Jazlyn refused to accept that he was gone, preferring to think of him as some romantic hero, a David who'd undoubtedly slain Goliath.

But Zack was just a young man, and an inexperienced one at that. Lily had known he was the one for her the first time she met him. She'd recognized him on some gut-deep level, as if she'd always known him and had simply been waiting for him to show up in her life.

He hadn't recognized her in return, unfortunately. Not in the same way. As friends, yes. Totally. But he'd been dating a girl at the time and had continued to for a while longer. Even after he broke up with that girlfriend, he'd dated others, though never seriously. And less and less. In the past year and a half he'd dated no one, spending all of his time with her. But never once had he made a move to indicate she was anything but his best friend.

She'd believed that eventually, when he was through with school and settled in his career, he'd begin to think about finding a wife. And when that happened, when he was finally open to the idea of love and marriage, he'd realize what Lily had always known. That they belonged together.

Now that would never happen. Because Zack was lost to her. Even if he hadn't died in the Games, she didn't have any idea how to find him. All she could do now was survive and find a way to escape this place. She would do it for her parents, who she knew were heartbroken at her disappearance. And she'd do it for Quinn, who had to be frantic at her brother's vanishing.

Mostly, she'd do it for Zack. Because as long as her love for him lived inside of her, Zack lived.

CHAPTER SIX

Quinn took her seat beside Zack in the back of what appeared to be an old hay wagon, then turned so that Arturo could wrap a rope around her wrist to make it look like she was tied. The wagon was partially covered by a canopy stretched across the top of curved bows, falling to within eighteen inches of the wooden sidewalls on each side, allowing her a view if she ducked her head just a little bit.

"Don't fidget," Arturo warned. "Or the ropes will fall off. They're barely hanging on to your wrists." When he was through, he moved to the other side of the wagon. As he reached through and "tied" Zack's wrists, his gaze found her. "If anyone approaches, keep your eyes closed, *cara*. It would not do for anyone to see your eyes glow if your power sparks."

"I know, Vampire," she said testily. "You've reminded me three times."

"You're acting like a helicopter parent, Ax," Micah chided, coming to stand at the foot of the wagon. "Hover, hover, hover. Quinn's a smart girl."

Arturo grunted. "You haven't seen her in the full throes of her power." Truthfully, he had reason to be concerned. She was nearly sick with worry that they wouldn't make it out of Gonzaga kovena lands . . . Cristoff's lands . . . without being stopped. If anyone figured out who she was, and that Zack was her brother . . . The thought caught in her throat until she could barely breathe around it.

Arturo rounded the wagon and reached for her, his hand curling around her knee. "*Cara mia*," he said softly, "I'll not let anything happen to you."

She swallowed, annoyed that he could feel her emotions. "Neither will I."

His mouth tightened just a fraction. With a nod, he straightened and turned to the two Traders who would drive the team of horses. "Off with you."

One of the Traders flicked the reins, and, a moment later, the wagon lurched forward. As they braced themselves against the sudden movement, Quinn and Zack exchanged wary, worried looks. So many things could go wrong, even if the two vampires really were wholly on their side this time.

Quinn had been shocked by Arturo's inviting the two Traders into his living room earlier. Her only experiences with them had been bad ones. But she supposed all Traders were no more coldhearted mercenaries than all humans were Mother Teresas. Arturo had introduced them as friends and told her they could be trusted. And so, for now, she'd reserve judgment. Allies might well make the difference between life and death in this place. Twice she'd struck out on her own in Vamp City, and twice she'd been caught. And that was before she had a price on her head. With Cristoff's entire guard contingent searching for her, her situation was far more precarious.

Plus, where would she go? If there was a safe haven anywhere in Vamp City, she didn't know about it. She took a deep breath and let it out slowly. She'd trust the vampires until they gave her a reason to doubt their motives. In the meantime, it wouldn't hurt to keep an eye open for alternatives.

The wagon rattled along the dirt road, the wheels hitting pits and rocks, knocking Quinn into the rails closest to the Traders often enough and hard enough that she was going to have bruises. At least she and Zack sat deep in the shadows, where they'd be the least likely to draw attention if anyone saw them.

They'd left the city behind quickly and without incident—urban structures hadn't extended much past downtown in 1870—and now traveled through the woods. The dead woods. The only trees that grew in V.C.—and they grew in abundance—were dead ones. Which twisted her scientific mind into knots. But there was only so much that science could explain in a world created from magic.

Quinn ducked her head, peering out, wishing she could see some sign of Arturo and Micah in the dark. She'd feel better if she knew they were close by. Arturo had promised they'd follow at a distance, keeping watch without making it obvious they were associated with the Traders and their human cargo. And as the wagon had pulled out of Arturo's yard, she'd seen him and Micah mounting horses, so she had to believe the trip was going as planned. A plan that, hopefully, she wasn't going to have to kill Arturo over.

On the bright side, she and Arturo had developed some kind of link when he first sucked her blood—an unusual link that allowed him to sense her emotions and allowed him to speak to her telepathically. She wasn't sure why it had formed. Maybe because of her magic. To her knowledge, he never heard her thoughts in return, so if they got into trouble, she wouldn't be able to call for help. But the moment her terror spiked, he'd know.

She shivered at the thought that he'd been right across the hall, in Mike's apartment, on and off the past couple of weeks. Had he felt her dreaming about him? And she had, on too many occasions, dreamed he was back in her arms and in her bed. Heat began to rise into her cheeks. Of course he had. No wonder he'd been so quick to want a few minutes alone with her.

A faint light caught her eye in the distance, and she peered out again, recognizing the windows of a house. She wondered who lived there. Vampires? Werewolves? That probably depended on where they were.

From what she'd learned on her previous visits, Vamp City was in the shape of a disc, its borders a circle extending approximately three miles in every direction from the spot they called the Focus, where Phineas Blackstone had originally summoned the magic to create it. Vamp masters had laid claim to land around the outer circle for their kovenas, the vamp equivalent of mob families. The unclaimed lands between them were called the Nod. The wild and dangerous inner lands were called the Crux, home to the werewolves and the Rippers.

"Do you know where we're going?" Zack asked quietly.

"No clue. How are you feeling?"

"Hungry."

Quinn rolled her eyes, then smiled to herself. He'd eaten enough for four men less than two hours ago. Zack was definitely feeling better.

"There'll be food where we're going," one of the

Traders commented, his voice low and scratchy. Apparently, Traders not only had good night vision but good hearing. They ought to, considering the size of those ears.

A moment later, the same Trader spoke again. "We've got company coming."

Unfriendly company, if his tone was anything to go by. Beneath the sound of the wagon and their own horses, she heard another rhythmic pounding. Horse hooves.

"Rippers or werewolves?" she asked quietly.

"Neither. Quiet, now."

Neither meant they were vampires. Emoras. Possibly Cristoff's men.

Her pulse began to pound though not yet tear out of her chest. A healthy dose of fear wasn't a bad thing if any of these vamps were fear-feeders. There would be no hiding from them, and a human tied in the back of a Trader's wagon *should* be afraid. Very, very afraid.

Her mind spun with options. She still had her weapons. But reaching for one meant untangling her hands from the ropes and giving away the fact that she wasn't really a captive. Nor could she afford for her power to start glowing in her eyes. If she started the fight, she and her allies might be able to end it, but maybe not before one of these vampires got away to spread the tale that Arturo and Micah were in league with the sorceress.

No, her best defense was to play the role she'd been given—captive—and trust Arturo to do what he did best: lie.

The sound of the horses' hooves grew steadily louder until it sounded like there must be a dozen of them. But when the dark forms finally coalesced, circling the wagon, she could make out only four. In the faint moonlight, three appeared to be males, or were at least dressed like males. The one in the long split skirt and fancy white blouse was clearly a female.

The Trader called, "Whoa," bringing the team, wagon, and Quinn to a lurching stop.

One of the vamps climbed off his horse and leaped into the wagon, vampire-fast, sending Quinn's heart squeezing into her throat and her hand itching to grab for her gun.

Arturo, this would be a good time to make an appearance.

The vamp reached forward and grabbed Zack's hair, wrenching her brother's head back, as if baring his neck for the strike.

Quinn, furious, clenched her hands into fists to keep from staking him. A tingling heat flared in her palms and began to crawl up her arms, beneath her skin.

Shit. Her eyes. She squeezed them closed, praying she'd done it in time. If she hadn't, she'd surely have heard the vampire's exclamation. Unfortunately, keeping her eyes closed did nothing to calm the growing need to protect her brother. Which only made the power beneath her skin burn hotter.

Beside her, she could hear Zack struggling against the vampire's hold. Zack sounded mad. At the first sound of his pain, she was pulling her gun, her secrets be damned.

The vampire called to his friends. "This one's got some height to him, but little muscle mass. Still, he could be of use."

"Take him," one of his companions replied.

"These two are already sold," the deep-voiced Trader said calmly. "I'm just delivering them."

The female vamp laughed. "Looks like you're going to have to pay back the money then. Finders, keepers," she added in a singsong voice.

Quinn fought to calm herself, to douse the power now burning in her veins. Beside her, Zack grunted, and she felt him moving, or being pulled, away from her. The soft thud of Zack's ropes hitting the wooden floor of the wagon sent a bolt of cold fear shooting up her spine. The creepy tingling beneath her skin grew worse.

The closest vamp began to chuckle. "You were about to lose this one anyway."

He thought Zack had worked himself free. Of course he would.

Without warning, she felt the hard press of cold hands on her jaw and gasped, her heart leaping until it thundered in her ears. Only by sheer force of will did she manage to keep her eyes closed and her hands behind her back.

"This one's plain as mud, but serviceable. Open your eyes, chippy." He squeezed her jaw hard, until her eyes began to water. "I said, open!"

But there was no way in hell she could do that, not unless she wanted to give up the game. Because she knew her eyes must be glowing by now. She could feel the energy surging through her veins, wild and uncontrolled, and a new thought had her head pounding. If her power flew free, the vampires might be tossed away from her. But Zack could get caught in it, too, and hurt.

Her hands began to shake with the force of her struggle to hold a lid on the power. The best thing she could do was calm down, but that wasn't happening, not with a vampire threatening to break her jaw.

Her whole body began to shake like a volcano ready to blow. Beneath her, even the wagon started to vibrate.

"What the hell are you doing, chippy?" the vampire growled.

The vampires circling the wagon shouted. "Sunbeams!"

"It's nighttime, you moron. There's no sun in either world at night."

The hair on Quinn's arms lifted, and she knew the worlds had opened nearby. Suddenly, she could hear the dull roar of traffic and that constant buzz of electricity that most were never aware of until it was absent. A car alarm bleated in the distance.

It was all she could do not to open her eyes, to see the world she'd left behind. The power crawled through her veins, cutting even as it burned, seeking a way out. If something didn't give soon . . .

We are coming, cara mia. Arturo's voice rang in her head. *Remain calm.*

Right. Calm. She had a vampire ready to claw her eyes open, and she was shaking so badly from trying to hold back the power that, for a minute, she'd thought she'd caused the earthquake that had opened the break between the worlds.

"Ho, there!" Arturo called, the sound of hoofbeats carrying to her beneath the sounds of her world. "By order of Cristoff Gonzaga, I demand to know who and what you take from his lands."

The Trader with the deep voice replied. "Slaves, Arturo Mazza. Just slaves who came in through a sunbeam."

"Mazza?" The vamp holding her released her suddenly. "Bollocks."

"A sunbeam on Gonzaga lands," Arturo continued smoothly, "which makes them Cristoff's property. You know what happens to those who steal from Cristoff, Trader."

"Just searching for one of my escaped freshies," the vamp who'd been accosting her said, moving away. "This one isn't her."

Ha. No shit, Sherlock.

And just like that it was over. A moment later, over the loud rumble of a truck, she heard what sounded like horses galloping off into the night. Was it Arturo who'd scared them off, or the threat of what Cristoff would do to them?

She didn't know and, at the moment, didn't much care.

"They are gone, *cara*," Arturo said, his voice drawing near. "But keep your eyes closed. The glow will be seen far in the distance." She felt his hand cup her knee "You are shaking like a leaf."

"I'm not in control." She pulled her hands from the ropes, stretching them in front of her. "Get Zack away from me. Get everyone away from me."

"I have a better idea."

She felt Arturo's arms slide beneath her knees and behind her back. "What are you doing?"

"Moving you away. If your power flies, it may spook the horses."

She couldn't argue his logic. He lifted her into his arms, and she curved her arm around his neck and held on tight as he began to run. Being in his arms felt so natural, so right, so . . . safe. It was a mistake to feel that way, she knew it. And yet on some gut-deep level, she trusted him. She always had, which was why his betrayals had cut so deep.

The wind raked at her face and hair, but strong arms held her tight. And as quickly as the ride began, it ended.

"Where did you take me?" Quinn asked breathlessly, struggling not to open her eyes.

"A quarter of a mile from the others, no more." He set her on her feet. "Release your power, *bella*. It is safe here."

"That's easier said than done." If she knew how to release it, she'd have fired her energy at the Traders in her apartment instead of her gun.

"Lift your hands and blast me, Quinn."

She tried, willing the power to fly, but nothing happened. And she was still shaking.

He gripped her jaw as the other vampire had, though not enough to hurt her. "Think of all the times I lied to you," he said harshly. "Remember how I delivered you to my master knowing he would hurt you. I stood there and watched him hurt you, Quinn, and did nothing to help."

His voice ached with regret, but the memory was too fresh, too raw, and he was right. She wanted to hurt him for it, dammit. She needed to make him pay for what he'd done.

The fury rose slowly, melding with the power fighting to escape. She slammed her hands against Arturo's chest, pouring her anger into him. And suddenly, he was gone, the power tearing through her fingertips. And then she was flying back, too, slamming into the hard ground, burning alive on a backdraft that tore through her body, making her cry out from the agony.

"Quinn!"

As she lay in the dirt, gasping for air, cool, gentle fingers stroked her head. "You're hurt."

The wind knocked out of her, she gasped for air, but the power was already draining away. "Are my eyes . . . ?" She blinked them open and closed again.

"The glow is gone."

She opened her eyes to find him bent over her, his face tight with concern.

"I'm fine, Vampire." She sat up, stifling a groan, and reached behind her. "My gun." It must have flown free when she landed. As she pushed to her feet, Arturo picked up something off the ground, her gun, and handed it to her.

Shoving it in her waistband, she looked at him with surprise. "You really trust me with this?"

"I ask you to trust me, *cara*. The least I can do is trust you in return."

"*I've* made no promises not to hurt you."

"You have not." His expression was serious, but gentle. "You have honor in abundance, and I do not believe you'll try to kill me unless I deserve it."

She considered that. "There are times already when I've thought you deserved it."

"I know. I am sorry, *tesoro*."

And she believed he meant it. "How far did I send you flying just now?"

"A good twenty feet. That was quite a blast."

She snorted. "Too bad I didn't get to see you land."

His mouth kicked up, his eyes crinkling at the corners. "You'd have enjoyed that, would you?"

"I would."

His expression sobered. "The power caught you, too. You could have been hurt."

"My power doesn't like me." As they started back toward the others, she glanced at him. "Vampire, do you think it's possible that I caused the worlds to open this time?"

Silence. "Why do you ask?"

"I started shaking from the force of the power. The next thing I knew, the wagon started shaking, then the ground. It wasn't until then that the hair rose on my arms, and I started to hear my world. Usually, the shaking comes last, not first."

Her looked at her with fathomless eyes and shrugged.

Quinn lifted her brows. "It would seem that not only might I have the power to save your world. I might also be able to hasten its destruction."

They returned to the wagon, and she and Zack resumed their captive pose. As the wagon bounced over the rutted terrain, questions bombarded her mind. *Had* she caused that last break in the worlds? It made a certain kind of logical sense that a sorceress's power could affect the magic of a sorcerer-created world.

That kind of power could act as a potent threat to hang over the vampires' heads should they ever consider betraying her again. Unfortunately, in truth it was just another factor of her magic that she couldn't control. Every time the sunbeams broke through, Vamp City came a little closer to dying.

And now, it seemed, so did Zack.

CHAPTER SEVEN

Quinn lost track of time as the wagon continued on toward its unknown destination, Arturo and Micah once more disappearing into the darkness. The ride made her teeth clack until she finally locked her jaw against the jostling. With her power dissipated, she felt fine again, at least.

As they started down a dead-tree-lined path, she turned and peered between the seated Traders, able to make out some kind of dark structure against the moonlit sky. Was this their destination? It appeared quite small and unassuming though unassuming wasn't a bad quality for a hideout.

As they drew near, she realized the house wasn't as small as she'd first thought. It was, in fact, a small mansion. Lights shone faintly from around the edges of almost all the windows, behind curtains or shades of some kind. She had some time to absorb the true size of the place as the wagon slowly circled the house. In the back jutted a small, covered carport. What would they have called it in 1870? Portico, maybe. It would provide protection against the rain and some measure of privacy to those coming and going.

The Traders drove the wagon under the portico roof and far enough through that Quinn and Zack would alight from the back in that covered, protected space. As the wagon came to a lurching stop, the back door of the house opened, illuminating the space in a swath of low, warm light. A man stood silhouetted in the doorway, a tall man with broad shoulders and what appeared to be long jet-black hair tied at the nape of his neck. His features remained in shadow.

"Did you meet with any trouble?" the man asked, his accent faintly Middle Eastern.

"Vamps from York's kovena tried to abscond with our slaves," the smaller of the Traders said as the pair alighted from the wagon. "Until Arturo threatened Cristoff's wrath."

The man grunted. "Serves them right."

Quinn pulled her hands from the loose ropes and followed Zack as he scooted from the back of the wagon. As they approached the door, the man stood back, inviting them in with a smile and a flourish. "Welcome."

When Zack started forward, Quinn grabbed his arm. "We'll wait for Arturo and Micah."

The man lifted a brow, his smile fading to a look of understanding. "They'll be arriving momentarily, but not through this door. Guests come to the front. It would seem odd to anyone watching if they were to enter this way."

The larger of the Traders started for the door. "Only Traders and slaves use the back."

"Those we wish to appear to be slaves," the man said quietly. "Come inside, sorceress. You will be safe here, I promise. And safer inside than out."

Quinn took a deep breath and let it out slowly, then started forward. Zack followed. As she stepped into the house, the man turned to the side to allow them entrance, revealing an intriguing face. His bone structure was strong and attractive, his eyes tilted slightly, with a shape that spoke of a hint of Asian ancestry, except that they were as blue as a clear summer sky. In those eyes, she saw no cunning, no cruelty, just a wealth of curiosity and intelligence.

"I'm Neo," he said, his voice as deep and rich as his skin tone, his mouth tilting up into a hint of a smile.

"Quinn. But you knew that."

His smile widened, reaching his eyes in a way that had surely slain more than a few feminine hearts. "I did." He ushered them into a back room that appeared to be at once storage room and office, a desk on one wall piled with paper and ledgers and books. She wondered what kind of paperwork could possibly be needed in Vamp City, where everyone appeared to simply take what they wanted. "We shall wait here for your friends."

"Are you a vampire?" Zack asked Neo, a hint of challenge in his tone that surprised Quinn.

Neo met his gaze, then gave a small nod. "I am. But perhaps not the kind you're used to meeting here."

"*I'm* intrigued," Quinn murmured. "Exactly what kind are you?"

Humor lit his eyes. "The good kind. I was brought to V.C. as a slave in 1973 and turned into a vampire eight years later. But I have never lost my conscience. Nor have I ever accepted what I am." He shrugged. "I did not choose to be turned and have not forgotten what it's like to be a slave. Nor have I ever forgiven the Traders and vampires who stole my life from me at the age of twenty-two."

His vehemence surprised her and rang convincingly true. Was it possible for a vampire to continue to identify with his human origins even after he was turned?

"Yet you work with Traders."

"They are not the ones who stole me off the streets of D.C. And you will learn, Quinn Lennox, not all Traders are the same. Just as all vampires are not. Nor humans, for that matter."

"How do you feed?" she asked him.

"Blood and fear."

"You don't act like a fear-feeder."

His mouth twitched in the semblance of a smile. "I feed quite adequately on those who already fear. I've no need to cause it."

"Then you're an anomaly around here from what I've seen." She cocked her head as she studied him. "If what you say is true."

He watched her steadily, then shrugged. "I have no need to lie to you. I am who I am, sorceress. You will have to accept help from some in this world if you are to survive. But accepting help is not trusting, not entirely. Trust is something that must be earned."

She couldn't have said it better.

Voices in the hallway had her glancing at the open door as Arturo appeared, Micah close behind him. Relief snaked its way through her, easing her mind, if only a little. She might still have walked into a trap, but her instincts told her that wasn't the case, that she and Zack really were safe here. As safe as they could be anywhere in Vamp City.

"Come," Neo said, and started toward the door. "I wish for the others to meet our guests."

Arturo motioned for her to precede him, and she did, Zack behind her. Neo led them down a narrow hallway, through a comfortable-looking living room, and into a library lined with bookshelves. One set of shelves had been opened like a door, revealing a long, wide staircase leading down into a well-lit basement. She wondered what the trick was to opening the hidden door, then decided Neo had intentionally not revealed it to them.

Arturo started down the stairs first this time, Quinn and Zack behind him. They were less than halfway down the long stair when she heard something heavy and creaking behind her and looked back to find Neo closing the bookcase. She supposed that was a good thing. If anyone got inside the house who didn't belong, they'd have trouble finding the way down here.

The question was, if she needed to, would she be able to find the way out?

The room that came into view was large and open, and surprisingly inviting, dotted with leather sofas and chairs of various sizes. In the center sat a large oval table upon which a small feast had been laid out—platters of small sandwiches, cheese and crackers, raw vegetables and dip, and a host of what appeared to be tiny cheesecakes.

Behind her, Zack made a sound of appreciation.

Two women stood beside the large table, one of whom appeared to be of the Trader race, her shoulders as broad as a linebacker's, her face wide, her eyes glowing bright orange.

The other woman was petite and pretty, with long, wavy dark hair that glowed with the phosphorescence that marked her as an immortal human, or Slava.

To Quinn's surprise, both women smiled and

moved forward to greet Arturo warmly, each getting a kiss on the cheek from the vampire in return. Arturo turned, gripping Quinn's shoulder lightly.

"This is Quinn Lennox, though you'll have to wait until Micah's glamour wears off before you're able to see her true likeness."

"This is Mukdalla," he said, motioning toward the Trader female.

The Trader smiled and reached for Quinn's hand. "It is my pleasure, sorceress. You are most welcome here." Quinn had thought the woman homely at first glance, but the wisdom radiating from her eyes and the warmth of her smile had Quinn reassessing.

"It's nice to meet you, Mukdalla."

Mukdalla's glance slid from Zack to Quinn, and back again. "Siblings? You have the same eyes."

Quinn sighed. She was glamoured, for heaven's sake, and still the woman saw the resemblance. She'd learned the hard way that it was not in Zack's best interest to be revealed as her brother. Loved ones could be used against you too easily in this place. But it seemed that he'd been revealed anyway.

"My brother, Zack."

"Hello, Zack," Mukdalla said kindly.

Arturo nodded to the other woman. "This is Dr. Amanda Morris."

"Just Amanda, please." The woman extended her hand, shaking Quinn's, then Zack's. "In my old life, I was a family practitioner."

"You still have a practice," Neo said behind them. "It's just changed a bit."

Amanda snorted. "You might say that." Her gaze returned to Zack, peering at him a little too long and in a doctorlike way that had Quinn tensing. "I was captured several years ago, escaped my master about a year later, then was captured and bought by Cristoff."

Quinn winced. "I'm sorry."

Amanda's gaze met hers. "I'm not. Kassius kept me away from the house and, upon learning that I was a doctor, had me brought here." She looked back at Zack. "I'd like to do a brief examination of you, Zack, if you'll allow it."

Zack eyed her warily. "What kind of exam?"

Amanda's voice warmed. "I just want to check your temperature and take a quick look at your eyes."

Quinn's gaze sharpened. "Why are his eyes silver like that? He's not . . . ?" The thought made her stomach clench. "He's not turning Slava already, is he?"

"Not Slava, no. Only the hair glows once we turn Slava." She held up her hand, her expression kind. "Let me grab my things. I'd like to do my examination before I offer a prognosis."

As the doctor hurried off, Neo ushered them forward. "Have a seat and help yourselves to the food. We have much to discuss."

"What is this place?" Quinn asked.

Arturo pulled out a chair for her. "Sit, *cara*."

She did, and the others took their seats around the table, Arturo on one side of her, Zack on the other.

"I do not easily give up my secrets, sorceress." Neo shrugged. "But perhaps if we trust you with our secrets, you will find it easier to trust our motives in return." He glanced at Mukdalla.

The Trader female nodded and turned to Quinn, clasping her hands on the table in front of her. "Most vampires and Traders capture humans and bring them into Vamp City. Neo and I have made it our life's work to funnel as many of them back out again as we can."

Quinn stared at her, then at Neo. In their eyes, she saw a passion, a crusader's zeal for a cause they believed in. She turned to Arturo. "Weren't you the one who told me a vampire might play with his food but he never sets it free?"

His brows flicked upward and down again. "I told you many things that I did not necessarily believe."

"So you set people free?"

"I help where I can. As you can imagine, there are many who would destroy Neo's operation were they to learn of it. We must be very careful not to draw attention to the work done here."

She stared at him, feeling as if she were seeing him for the first time. So many untruths and half-truths hiding facets of the male. Facets that her instincts had recognized. She'd trusted him too many times because of that, because despite his glibness, she'd sensed honor in him. And maybe she hadn't been entirely wrong after all.

"At one time," Neo told her, "our work was far less than it is now. Before the magic began to fail, many of the humans brought into Vamp City against their will were the miscreants—the murderers and rapists and wife-beaters. The drug addicts and gangbangers. Those we will never free back into D.C. society. The humans would not thank us if we did. But now, with the magic failing, those who trolled for the human dregs are trapped here and can no longer hunt for them. As the city crumbles, the demand for blood grows, and the consciences of the vampires who need it disintegrate. The Traders grab whomever they can, and many of the vampires who once cared do no longer."

"Neo and I run an underground railroad to free as many of the innocents as we can," Mukdalla continued. "Amanda treats the injuries many of the fresh slaves arrive with. We feed them, heal them both physically and mentally, stealing their memories of this place, then smuggle them out in Traders' carts."

"Those who've not yet turned Slava. Those who can still escape," Quinn clarified.

"Yes."

Quinn glanced at Arturo, and she found him watching her, his eyes dark and deep.

Amanda returned, claiming her attention as Zack swiveled in his chair to face her. The doctor pulled a thermometer out of her doctor's bag and slid the nodule into his ear. When it beeped, she removed it, then grabbed her penlight and flicked it into first one eye, then the other.

"How are you feeling, Zack?" she asked, putting the light back in her bag.

"Fine."

"Only for the last few hours," Quinn qualified. "He had no energy or appetite until we brought him back to V.C."

"How long have you been ill?"

"I don't know. A week."

"He was fine when we left Vamp City ten days ago. At least I think he was. But he spent several days in Pennsylvania and started feeling dead tired almost immediately."

Amanda listened, nodding. "His temperature is over 101."

Quinn frowned. "I thought he was better."

"He's feeling better, from what you describe. Which is not unusual with magic poisoning."

Her stomach sank. He wasn't well. Not yet.

"I feel fine," Zack repeated.

The doctor nodded. "And you'll probably continue to. Once the magic of V.C. is renewed, I'm sure you'll be fine." She moved around the table, taking a seat beside Mukdalla. But her gaze flicked to Zack, the small creases between her eyebrows telling Quinn there was more she wasn't saying. And it wasn't good.

Her stomach tightened.

"Let's get started," Neo said. "We have much to discuss."

Clenching her jaw against the need to question the doctor further, Quinn forced her attention on Arturo as he began to fill the others in on the situation—that she was the only sorcerer the vampires had found who might be able to renew the magic. That he believed she had power but that she could not access most of it and could not control what she could. He told them what he'd told her, that his plan was for her to renew the magic without Cristoff's being the wiser. That her life and theirs depended upon it.

"The Blackstone brothers will have to be involved," Arturo told them. "They were there when their father renewed the magic the first time after attempting to spring the trap and destroy us all. Sheridan is the only one who remembers the ritual."

"Can they be trusted?" Neo asked, his expression making it clear he doubted it.

"I do not know," Arturo admitted. "They have no love for Cristoff, but the hold he has over them is prodigious. It is impossible to know whether they will help Quinn without being forced." He lifted a brow. "But I am happy to force."

"It may be a moot point if we can't free the sorceress's magic," Neo countered. "And we have little time. The equinox is only a few days away, and it's unlikely Vamp City's magic will last until the winter solstice. The next strong power day," he added for Quinn's benefit. He glanced at her. "I would read your magic for myself, sorceress."

"What do you mean 'read'?"

Arturo's hand covered her arm, squeezing lightly. "Where I taste magic, Neo feels it through touch."

"I'll barely touch you, Quinn," Neo assured her. "And only your face."

God, she was tired of having to trust vampires. But when Neo reached her chair and motioned her to stand, she complied, turning to face him. He was a tall man, a couple of inches taller than Arturo, and smelled pleasantly of Mediterranean spices and warm climates. As he reached for her face, she instinctively tensed, then forced herself to relax. The last thing she wanted to do was call up her power in this place filled with humans. Zack wasn't the only one she might injure.

Taking a deep breath, she eyed Neo. "Tell me what you're going to do."

His blue eyes were kind. "I will touch your face, Quinn. Just that. Through my fingertips, I'll be able to read your magic. Yes?"

She'd never been comfortable with strangers touching her. Or friends, for that matter. It wasn't in her nature. And there was no telling what a powerful vampire could do with a touch. Micah had changed her entire appearance. But she needed to understand her magic.

"Yes. Do it."

Neo watched her a moment longer, as if he were as cautious about touching a sorceress as she was about being touched. Finally, he lifted his hands again and pressed his fingers lightly against her cheekbones, his thumbs resting on her chin. Dark lashes dropped, hiding those incongruously blue eyes. After a moment, his lashes rose again.

Releasing her, he stepped back, his brows drawing together. "You have power, sorceress. And yet . . . I don't know. There's something odd about it. As if it's been caged."

"Kassius said the same," Arturo told him.

"I know of someone who may be able to tell you more," Mukdalla said. "A fae by the name of Tarellia. Do you know her?" she asked Arturo.

"We've met, but I've not seen her in decades. Tell me where she lives, and I'll fetch her."

Mukdalla shook her head. "She'll not leave her house—you'll have to take the sorceress to her—but she lives in the Nod, not far from here. It's a safe enough journey."

"There are no safe journeys, my friend. You know that. Quinn will remain here. I'll bring the fae to her."

"You will go to the fae, Arturo," Neo said, his tone brooking no argument.

Arturo smiled a smile that didn't reach his eyes as his voice turned Obi-Wan. "It will be fine, Neo."

But Neo only shook his head. "You'll not sway me, Arturo. You bring too many to my home. You'll compromise all our safety. No more. You must go to the fae. There is too much at stake."

Arturo's jaw hardened, but to Quinn's surprise, he didn't argue further or attempt any more mind control. "We'll go tomorrow. I do not wish to run across York's vampires again. Not with Quinn."

Neo nodded. "We are in agreement, then." He motioned to the platters of food. "Eat. Enjoy. Now that the sorceress is here, we have a chance. This is cause for celebration. If you'll excuse me, I have work to do upstairs."

Once Neo left, Micah and Arturo moved off to one side of the room to talk in private. While Zack refilled his plate, Quinn placed a couple of finger sandwiches on one of her own, then joined the vampires. She was through being left out of discussions.

"I'm going to have to report to Cristoff in the morning, first thing," Arturo said, as she approached. He met her gaze, apology in his eyes. "It's been several days, and he'll have someone out looking for me if I don't."

The thought of him with Cristoff curled her stomach.

He either felt her uneasiness or saw it in her face, for he said, "It will help us not at all for Cristoff to know I'm his traitor. He'll send his troops after me to get to you. And he might well succeed."

"I know." And she did, logically. It didn't mean she had to like it. "When will we visit the fae, then?"

"Afterward. My visit with Cristoff will be short."

"I'm staying here," Micah added. He cocked his head at her, a smile lifting his mouth, a kind Mike smile. "You look . . . lighter, Quinn. Like the weight of the world is no longer weighing you down. I'm glad. It's Zack, isn't it?"

It amazed her that, despite all the revelations—that he was a vampire, that he'd been spying on her—he was still Mike. He was still her friend. Either he was a heck of an actor or he'd never acted with her at all. She was inclined to believe the latter.

She found a smile for him. "I was worried about him. I still am, but far less now that he's threatening to eat Neo out of house and home."

Micah grinned, then gave her shoulder a friendly squeeze and turned to walk away.

Quinn glanced at Arturo as she picked up one of the finger sandwiches. "I need a word with you." She took a bite, the sandwich melting in her mouth.

A gleam entered his eyes. "You can have whatever you want of me, *cara,* you know that."

She snorted. "You say that so glibly."

His mouth quirked up. "It was, perhaps, meant to be suggestive rather than glib."

She chose to ignore that. "I want to take Zack with us to see the fae tomorrow."

"It is too dangerous."

Her spine stiffened. "Your only interest might be in my magic, but my primary concern is his health. I need to know why my magic's hurting him and if there's some other way to help him."

He reached for her, lifting a lock of her hair, studying it as if the glamoured color fascinated him. His gaze slowly lifted to hers. "We will put the question to Tarellia. Perhaps she will sense the connection as Kassius did. If we are fortunate, she'll understand what she senses as Kassius did not. If she wants to see Zack, then we will take him to her. But it will be far safer for both of you if we don't have to do that. Your brother will be fine here."

She didn't like the idea of leaving Zack behind. But the last thing she wanted was for Cristoff to figure out he was her brother. Cristoff already knew she had one and had threatened to hurt Zack in order to force her hand.

Quinn set down her plate on a nearby table. "All right. He'll stay here." She turned to him. "What about Lily?"

He frowned. "Freeing her will not be easy, *cara*."

"Vampire . . ."

"I did not say I cannot free her, *cara*. I simply said it will not be easy. The master of Castle Smithson, Lazzarus Nica, is no friend of Cristoff's. We have no diplomatic ties with that kovena whatsoever. I cannot step foot on his land. Nor can any member of Cristoff's kovena or those in alliance with him, which eliminates Neo, before you ask. I have already sent word to Kassius. He will enlist the aid of an ally in another kovena."

"He won't know what she looks like."

"Her name is Lily. She is young. She will know of you and Zack. If she is there, and he can get in, he will find her."

"How long will it take?" She'd come to realize things took time in this place without cell phones or public transportation, where most travel of any kind was fraught with danger.

"I hope no more than a few days." His gaze deepened. "I will find her, *cara*. I promise you." He lifted his hand, stroking her cheek briefly with his knuckles. "And then, perhaps, you will begin to trust me."

CHAPTER EIGHT

The sound of fighting and a chorus of cheers carried from deeper in the basement of Neo's safe house. Quinn glanced at Arturo warily, but he seemed unconcerned as he motioned her to follow.

"What's going on?" he asked, as they approached the table where Mukdalla and Amanda sat sipping coffee and chatting. Across from them, Zack continued to eat though more slowly than before.

To Quinn's surprise, Amanda smiled. "Training. Mukdalla's husband and a few of the others are working with the escapees, teaching them to defend themselves in case we can't get them out cleanly. There's little they can do against vampires, but with proper training, they can learn to fend off Traders."

Quinn glanced at her brother. "Zack, why don't you go have a look?"

He gave her a baleful look. "I'm tired."

"Zack . . ."

"I said I'm tired," her brother snapped, then pushed himself to his feet, shoved his hands in his pockets, and turned away.

Quinn stared at him in hurt surprise. Her once easygoing brother had changed during his captivity in Vamp City. And while she understood, his occasional harsh words toward her—so alien—still took her aback.

Amanda gave Quinn a sympathetic look as she rose. "I'll show you to your rooms." She walked toward one of half a dozen hallways that led off of the main room like spokes of a wheel.

Quinn waited for Zack, then followed as Arturo brought up the rear.

"Either the house is bigger than it looks, Dr. Morris, or you've built tunnels down here," Quinn commented.

"Amanda, please. And yes, there are tunnels. An entire barracks, for that matter, with kitchens and living quarters. Most of the house is hidden underground."

"This is where the escapees hide?"

"Yes. We accept only the freshly caught. Those who've turned Slava can never return to the real world and are therefore turned away."

"Except you."

She glanced back with a soft smile. "I'd not yet turned Slava when I arrived here."

"So you could have escaped. Neo would have helped you."

"He tried to, yes." Her expression turned inward. "I decided I was needed here more than I was at home. Not everything can be cured with a vampire bite."

"You fail to mention the main reason you stayed," Arturo said, his voice almost teasing.

Amanda laughed. "Oh, him."

Quinn smiled. "A man?"

"He's my husband, now."

"A vampire?"

"A Slava. He was already involved in helping Neo. Now we do it together."

Quinn wondered at the depth of emotion that would make a woman give up life in her own world to remain in this place of perpetual dark. Especially when the object of that emotion could so easily die, leaving her trapped for eternity.

She couldn't imagine ever feeling that strongly for anyone. Except Zack. What if renewing the magic didn't work, and he had to stay here? Could she leave V.C., leave him behind in a perpetual battle for his life, while she flew to another part of the world, never to see him again?

No. And she prayed it never came to that.

The hallway Amanda led them down emptied into a living area where half a dozen people sat reading or playing chess by the light of several oil lamps. None were Traders or had the phosphorescent hair peculiar to Slavas, but whether they were humans or vampires, she couldn't tell.

All six turned when they walked in, eyeing her and Zack curiously. One man eyed them warily, tensing as if he were preparing to run . . . or fight, if he had to. The word *traumatized* came to mind. A couple of them smiled, but none said anything, nor did Amanda speak to them as she led Zack and her through the room and down yet another hallway, this one lined with doors on either side. Some of the doors were open and Quinn saw one or two twin beds in each, a bedside table, and little more. Spartan, but clean, and since the occupants were free to come and go as they wished, and free from attack by vampires, a luxury hotel couldn't be any more welcome to most who arrived here.

Several doors down, Amanda stopped, motioning to an open doorway on either side of the hall. "These are your rooms." The doctor entered one, using a Bic to light an oil lamp on the bedside table. "The bathroom is at the far end of the hall. It's a community bath, but there are several shower stalls, and the water is warm enough, if not as hot as you might like."

Quinn glanced back the way they'd come. "Those people . . . Are they all escapees?"

"Yes. They'll be out of V.C. by week's end, if all goes as planned, with no memory of where they've been."

Zack walked into the room and sat on the bed with a sigh. "I wish I had a computer."

"You're not tired," Quinn murmured. That, at least, was a good sign. "Why don't we go watch the training for a little bit?"

The self-loathing in Zack's expression slew her. "Why? So I can add to the catalog of all the things I can't do?"

To Quinn's surprise, Arturo took a seat on the bed beside him. Zack glanced at him with suspicion, then turned to study his hands, where he'd clasped them between his knees.

"When I was sixteen," Arturo said quietly, "I watched a vampire kill my mother." He turned to study his own hands. "I didn't even try to stop him. I did nothing, just stood there in shock as the blackguard drained her dry, then dumped her body onto the dirt floor of the shack where we lived."

Quinn's heart clenched with misery for him, for the teen he'd once been. She glanced at Amanda, who stood beside her, empathy and sorrow warm in the doctor's eyes.

Zack looked at him, his brows drawn. "You were just a kid. There's nothing you could have done."

"I was the man of the house and nearly full-grown. And I have never forgiven myself for not trying to save her even though I know, now, that there was nothing I could have done. Not then. Not with the knowledge I'd lacked at that point in my life. Vampires can be killed by human hands, Zack. Learning how to battle them takes time, and skill. Even then, you must take your opponent by surprise if you are to have any chance of success. But the skills can be learned by anyone with the drive and the persistence to learn them."

Zack glanced at him, a moment's hope flaring in his eyes, then dying away. "I'm not a fighter. I've never been any kind of an athlete. I'm too skinny."

"The best fighters have both strength and cleverness. Cleverness is a gift one is born with, but strength can be acquired. I suspect you are quite clever, Zack. If you wish, you can become a good fighter. But you'll have to work hard. It will not happen overnight. Your Lily would be impressed, would she not?"

Zack's gaze returned to his hands. "Are you going to rescue her?" His tone was stiff, but a thread of life wove through the words.

"Yes. It will not be easy, but the most important things in life rarely are."

For long seconds, Zack said nothing. But finally he looked up and met Arturo's gaze, a light in his green eyes that hadn't been there moments before. "What do I have to do? To fight vampires?" The question was filled with more wariness than determination, but the words were the right ones.

"I will speak to Neo. He's trained many a human, and some of those humans have remained with him. They'll work with you if you wish."

Zack licked his lips, his shoulders hunching as if preparing to be humiliated all over again. But he nodded. "Okay."

Quinn felt a quick clash of emotions—pleasure at that admittedly small spark of life in Zack's eyes but terror at the thought of him fighting at all, let alone bloodsuckers. This was right, though, and she knew it. This was what her brother needed, a reason to live, and the confidence that would come from being able to defend himself, at least against other humans.

"Arturo's right, Zack. You've got the smarts to find your opponent's weaknesses and exploit them." She shrugged. "You can learn the rest."

"Okay. But not tonight."

"Not tonight," Quinn agreed. "Get some sleep."

Arturo rose and followed Quinn and Amanda out, pulling Zack's door closed. When he looked up, Quinn met his gaze with a small smile.

"Thank you for that," she said quietly. He'd given Zack an incredible gift—permission to be weak and a way to get stronger.

Arturo's dark eyes turned as soft as a summer night. "You're welcome."

Amanda entered the other room to light the lamp, and Quinn followed her. "Tell me what's really going on with Zack, Amanda."

The doctor glanced at her. "I've told you the truth. I don't know what'll happen."

"I saw the way you were frowning earlier. You know more than you're saying."

The doctor sighed and straightened, the lamp-light flickering behind her. "I've only seen eyes like his once before, and I never figured out what caused them."

"What happened to the other victim?"

Her mouth compressed, and she looked away.

"Amanda?"

Slowly she met Quinn's gaze. "She died."

"How long after you first saw the signs?"

"Three weeks. I'm sorry."

Three weeks. Quinn swayed. Arturo gripped her shoulders from behind, steadying her.

Amanda reached for Quinn's hand. "It's very possible that renewing the magic will save him. There's no reason to panic. Not yet. But I don't think it will benefit him to know this. The brain can be a powerful force in healing."

Quinn took a deep breath, gathering her control, and pulled away from both of them. "I agree. Is there anything he should or shouldn't do? Does he need to rest? To eat more food? Less food?"

The doctor shook her head. "Honestly, I don't know. Nothing my other patient did or didn't do appeared to matter. I'd recommend he do whatever he feels like. Magic doesn't attack the body in the same way a virus does. There's no need to conserve energy to fight it. The equinox is just a few days away, Quinn. Let's trust that renewing the magic will cure him, hmm?"

If she *could* renew the magic. A knot formed beneath her breastbone. He'd been acting so normal . . .

"I'll leave you to get some rest," Amanda said, her eyes full of apology.

"Zack will be fine once the magic is renewed, *cara.*"

Quinn swung around to face him, then grabbed the door and closed it, barely managing to keep from slamming it because . . . *dammit* . . .

She turned on him. "You all keep forgetting that *I don't know how.* I've *tried* renewing it with the ritual, with both Blackstone brothers right there. And I failed, Arturo. I *failed.* Why in the hell are you so convinced I'm going to succeed the next time?"

He stood by the wall, watching her with quiet eyes in such counterpoint to her turmoil. "Because we shall figure out what is hampering your magic."

"And what if we can't fix it . . . *in four days?* The equinox is almost here. What if it passes, and I don't have the magic and never have enough power to renew the magic on a null day?" Her eyes began to burn, her chest caving. "He's going to die, and I can't stop it."

She saw him move through the blur of her tears, felt gentle hands grip her shoulders.

"We shall not let him die."

"I know he's not well. His eyes are still silver. But he's been acting so normal, I started to believe . . ." The tears began to fall in earnest, and she was helpless to stop them. *Three weeks.*

Cool fingers stroked her hair. "I will not let him die."

She blinked against the tears, searching his face. "Don't pretend he matters to you."

His hand gripped her jaw, his eyes almost harsh. "He matters to you. He is everything to you. And you matter to me."

"The salvation of your city and your friends."

"If that is all you were, my life would be so much simpler, *tesoro.* So much colder. And I would have remained blind to what has happened to my city and to my people." His hands cupped her face, his thumbs wiping the tears from her cheeks. "I will not let him die, *cara mia.* I will not."

He pulled her into his arms, and she let him, burying her face against his shoulder as the grief and the fear swept through her on the torrent of tears. He held her, stroking her back, her hair. All her life, she'd cried alone except for those times when Zack had snuck into her room and lain down beside her. He'd always known when she was hurting, he'd always come, even if just to curl up on the rug beside her bed and play his Gameboy.

She'd never wanted to need anyone. Perhaps because she'd never had anyone. Except for Zack. But Arturo's strong arms and willing shoulder felt so damn good. So . . . right.

As her tears subsided, his lips brushed the curve of her ear, then pressed softly against her temple. For all of his faults, he could be the most gentle of males when he chose to be.

Slowly, she pulled back until she could see his face. Blinking back the last of the tears, she met his soft gaze and found herself pulling one hand from around his neck to stroke his cool cheek.

"Thank you."

He kissed her forehead, then continued to watch her with eyes as dark and deep as the night sky and as warm as down. Her heart began to stir, to fill. Her pulse lifted. She'd never been able to remain unaffected by this male, no matter how hard she'd tried.

And right now, right here, she no longer cared to try.

Her gaze dipped to his mouth. Her breath caught. The hands at her back jerked slightly, then splayed, pulling her closer as his head dipped to find her lips.

She met him halfway.

Their lips brushed, cool to warm. Excitement shivered inside her as her body awoke, as it always had, to his touch. His scent wrapped around her, almonds and moonlight, drowning her in sensation. He kissed her, tasted her. As she parted her mouth, his tongue swept inside to stroke hers in a tangling, dueling caress.

Her arms snaked around his neck, her fingers burrowing into his soft hair as he pulled her tight against him, making a sound deep in his throat, a sound of pleasure and satisfaction. But not of wild need, though the need was there, beneath it all. The kiss remained tender and sweet, a gift of comfort, of pleasure. A silent plea to trust. A promise to take no advantage.

His lips left her mouth, trailing slowly over her cheek to lay sweet kisses along her cheekbone and the corner of her eye, her earlobe and the curve of her jaw. Each savored, each caressed, each pulled at that place inside her that had lain empty and untouched for so very long.

His hands roamed her back, one moving into her hair as he claimed her mouth again, deepening the kiss, making her heart race with pleasure and excitement. His body was growing tense, his erection growing thick between them. And in his mouth, she felt his fangs elongating.

A chill skated down her spine, then evaporated in the memory of the last time they'd made love and the ecstasy she'd known from his bite. Passion hazed her thoughts, her mind drugged by his taste, his kiss.

Slowly, he pulled back, kissing her lips, then tipping his forehead to hers, his flesh now as warm, his breath as ragged, as her own. But though his hands continued to curl against her back and in her hair, he made no move to resume the kiss or to take it further. Instead, he released her, cupped her face with his hands to settle one more soft kiss upon her mouth, then moved to the door.

When he turned back to face her, she saw that his pupils were white with hunger. But those eyes watched her only with softness.

"Sleep, *bella*. Come morning, we will ride for Tarellia's."

Quinn pulled in a ragged breath. "Ride?" Until a couple of weeks ago, she'd never been on a horse in her life, and she still wasn't sure she liked them.

Slowly, his pupils slid back to black. "The Jeep draws too much attention. It yells, 'Arturo Mazza,' when I would prefer to slip through the shadows unseen."

"Then I guess we ride."

He gave her a small smile. "Good night, Quinn."

Then he turned and left, leaving her staring at the empty doorway, bemused. He'd swept the rug out from under her, then made no attempt whatsoever to get her into bed. And she wasn't sure that he wouldn't have succeeded. Was this a new game he'd decided to play? She didn't think so. But she was too tired, and too worried about Zack, to think straight.

Wiping the last of the tears off her cheeks, she sank down on her bed, feeling the weight of the world on her shoulders once more. Zack was so much more than just her little brother. He was all she had, all she'd ever had. And she would risk everything and anything to keep him safe.

What scared her so badly was that everything she had might not, in the end, be enough.

CHAPTER NINE

Arturo strode up the front walk of Cristoff's castle just before sunrise, or what would be sunrise in the real world. The veil between the worlds was thin today, the crisp, cool Vamp City breeze interspersed with slightly warmer air vaguely scented with diesel, sunshine, and the occasional whiff of greenery and coffeehouse.

He climbed the wide brick steps, tension radiating down his spine as he prepared, once again, to lie through his teeth. He was adept at lying, had in fact made a career out of it thanks to his gift of *persuasion*, the ability to exert low levels of mind control on others, even other vampires.

But he'd rarely lied to his master, and it had never set well with him. At one time, Cristoff had been almost as close a friend as Kassius or Micah or Bram. Many a time, the two of them had played chess, or hunted together, or discussed human and vampire politics for hours on end. They'd hit it off from the beginning, soon after he, Kassius, and Bram arrived at the Gonzaga kovena looking for a new start, a new family after their previous master's death. That other Gonzaga Castle, of three centuries ago, was where they'd met Micah, one of Cristoff's progeny.

It was Arturo who'd quickly become Cristoff's favorite; Arturo whom Cristoff had treated as the son he'd never had; Arturo who'd found in Cristoff the father he'd longed for growing up a bastard.

But Micah was right. The Cristoff of old was gone, changed over the years, most markedly in the past two. And all he could offer the Cristoff of today were lies.

The front doors of Gonzaga Castle opened. "Arturo," the guards said in unison, nodding to him with deference as they stood back to admit him. "Cristoff is in the pool."

Arturo acknowledged them and strode into the mansion's ivory marble foyer. As usual, vampires lounged, played, and fucked on every available chaise and surface, if slightly less boisterously than the last time he was here. Were they finally beginning to realize their immortal lives were in danger? Despite the magic's failing, few vampires truly believed they'd die. No immortal believed in his own death until it came for him.

As he strode through the gaming room, dodging the poker and billiards tables, regret washed through him for all that had changed and all that had been lost. Most of all, he regretted that his once-beloved friend and master had become the enemy, though Cristoff could never know.

Above all, Quinn must be protected. She was the sorceress who must save their world and with it the lives of some of his very best friends. But his need to protect her went deeper. Far deeper. From the moment he'd first come upon her, she'd confounded him. He'd been drawn to her from the start, ensnared by her beauty and her courage even as he'd tried to tell himself she was simply a means to an end and meant nothing to him. For a time, he'd believed that. Ultimately, her safety was all that had mattered. She was sunshine and light, strength and vulnerability. And she'd begun to awaken his dormant honor, igniting within him emotions he hadn't even realized had died, and a craving for a softness that had long eluded him—her smile, the touch of her hand, the sweet music of her quiet and all-too-rare laughter.

He thought constantly of taking her into his arms, of laying her down and sinking into her lovely body. But he refused to cajole or seduce this time. She'd changed since he saw her last. She'd become more sure of herself, more wise to the ways of his world. And too wise to his own ways to trust him easily again. If ever.

But she'd changed him, too. He no longer felt like the male he'd been before. Perhaps, as Micah believed, she'd merely reawakened his conscience.

Arturo stepped through the open doors onto the deck, stopping beside the pool, where Cristoff swam laps. On his next turn, Cristoff spied him. Two laps later, his master pulled himself from the water and took the towel a female Slava rushed into his hands. Cristoff's shoulder-length bleached hair was slicked back from a strong-boned face, the small black beard that fell from his chin, like a duck's tail, dripped with water.

Pale blue eyes pinned Arturo. "Have you found her, my snake?"

"No, Master." The lies ran easily from his tongue. "But I am following a lead. Ivan has escaped with her into the real world and hidden her well, but I will find her. I vow it."

"The equinox nears." Cristoff turned and snapped,

"Monroe! Morgenstern! Attend me now." A moment later, two guards came running, one from inside the house, the other from the yard beyond the pool. Both, Arturo knew, had been loyal to the deceased Ivan. "Kneel before me," Cristoff growled, wrapping the towel around his waist.

The two guards fell to their knees, their faces betraying their confusion.

"Where is Ivan?" The question was quietly spoken, but Cristoff's tone and eyes were hard.

"I do not know, Master," Monroe stated. Morgenstern echoed his compatriot. And Arturo knew they told the truth.

Cristoff's mouth compressed into an ugly line and he reached for them both, pressing his palms to their foreheads.

As one, the two guards gasped, then began to scream.

Arturo stared, stunned. Cristoff was using his mind blast, one of the most powerful weapons known to vampires, one gifted to very few—the ability to slowly pulverize his opponent's brain with a simple touch of his hand.

"I don't know, Master!" Morgenstern cried. Blood began to leak from his ears.

"I haven't seen or heard a word from him since the sorceress disappeared," Monroe swore.

His face a mask of fury, Cristoff pulled away from them and the pair slumped, gasping for air.

"Go," Cristoff snapped. "Get out of my sight. If I discover you've lied to me, I will kill you."

The two guards struggled to their feet and hurried away as the other vampires around the pool stared in stunned silence. In all the centuries Arturo had known him, Cristoff had never used his mind blast against one of his own. The old Cristoff never would have, not unless the vampire had directly challenged him.

But the attack had not quelled Cristoff's fury. He grabbed the Slava who'd handed him the towel, threw her down onto the hard pool deck, lifted his foot, and brought it down hard.

"Where is that bitch? Someone find me the sorceress!"

The crack of ribs accompanied the woman's agonized screams.

"*Where is she?*"

Slavas would heal most injuries quickly enough. The words Arturo had told himself a hundred times flowed through his head, but this time found no purchase. There was no excusing such barbarity, such cruelty against not only an innocent, but one of his own.

Arturo clenched his fist against the need to do *something*, and struggled to keep his face a mask of indifference. How had he remained complacent in the face of Cristoff's brutality for so long?

His pulse thundered in his ears. It was Quinn whom Cristoff attacked in absentia, Quinn who would suffer his rage if he ever got his hands on her again.

"Find her," Cristoff said, turning to Arturo, his voice more plea than demand. "If anyone can, it will be you, my snake. You'll find her, and you'll return her to me. You've never failed me, my loyal one. Never."

For a moment, Arturo saw the echo of the friend Cristoff used to be behind the mask of the monster he'd become. Could he be saved? Was the old Cristoff still in there?

He prayed, for all their sakes, it was so.

"I will not fail you, Master." And he wouldn't. Quinn would renew the magic of Vamp City, saving them all. Then she'd disappear back into the real world before Cristoff discovered that his snake was also his traitor.

"Go." Cristoff waved him off with a casual motion, and Arturo strode from the pool deck and the castle.

As Arturo passed through the great wrought-iron gates, he felt sick at his stomach at what he'd witnessed and stunned that such a display would not have fazed him even a couple of weeks ago. He'd felt nothing before. Nothing.

Micah was right. His conscience really had been in hibernation. But it was no more. Quinn had changed him, he was certain of it, with her kiss and the sunshine that seeped inside him, warming his flesh, every time. *That* was magic, the same magic that would renew Vamp City.

Assuming he found a way to free it for her.

He must.

And Cristoff must never find out.

Quinn woke after a restless night. Or maybe it was just a few hours. It was impossible to know without the morning sun shining in a window. Or a bedside clock. She fumbled for the lighter, flicking it, then glanced at her watch in the light of the small flame. Eight thirty. In the morning, she assumed.

Climbing out of bed, she padded across the hall and

quietly opened Zack's door to find him sound asleep, hanging off the small bed in three different directions as he snored softly. Closing his door again, she stood still and listened, hearing voices in the distant rooms, and a short burst of laughter. Taking a deep breath, she let it out slowly, easing the tension from her shoulders. Safety and welcome pervaded this place.

Grabbing her jeans, a cotton sweater, and clean underwear, she took a quick shower, then dressed. When she'd donned her boots and armed herself, she followed the smell of coffee and food back into the room with the conference table, where they'd gathered last night.

Neo, Mukdalla, and a male Quinn hadn't seen before sat at one end, empty plates in front of them, steaming coffee mugs in hand. Neo looked up at her with surprise, and no recognition, shooting to his feet in a move that was distinctly threatening. In a vampire flash, he was across the room, his hand around her neck.

"Who are you?"

"Quinn," she choked, reaching for her stake.

His eyes narrowed, then lit with sudden understanding. He released her and stepped back as she pulled the stake clear of her jacket pocket, ready to wield it.

"My apologies, sorceress. Your glamour's worn off."

Quinn's heart was about to leap out of her chest as she stared at him, shaken from the sudden attack and the reminder that weapons only worked against vampires who weren't expecting them.

"Are you okay, Quinn?" Mukdalla asked worriedly.

"I'm fine." Neo hadn't hurt her, he'd just startled her half to death. "On the plus side, I'm now fully awake."

Neo smiled, but his expression remained apologetic. "I saw a stranger in our midst and thought we'd suffered a breach. I forgot you'd been glamoured." He motioned to the table. "Come. Fill a plate and join us as we adjust ourselves to the real you."

As her pulse slowly calmed, Quinn served herself from warming dishes filled with scrambled eggs, sausage, and hash browns. Behind her, the others returned to their discussion, tossing about names, arguing whether their first concern should be the mom with the three kids or the young man whose ailing mother was dependent upon him for support. Quinn assumed they were deciding whom to include in their next escape attempt and was glad the decision wasn't up to her.

As she approached the table, Neo rose and pulled out the chair to his right for her. She sat, wondering if the gentlemanly manners were the norm with vampires or with males in general who'd been born before a certain time.

"How did you sleep?" Mukdalla asked cheerily, claiming the seat across from her, her eyes bright with warmth as if Quinn, whom she barely knew, was her favorite person in the world. And maybe she was. After all, it was Quinn who they believed would save their world.

It was odd to have so much weighing on her shoulders. The hopes of a world she still wasn't convinced should be saved.

"I slept well," she told the other woman. "Zack's still asleep."

Mukdalla placed her hand on the arm of the male beside her. "This is my husband, Rinaldo."

The male nodded. "It's a pleasure to meet you, Quinn."

"You, too."

Rinaldo wasn't a handsome man, not by any stretch of the imagination—his face was too long, his mouth too small. But he was no Trader, which was interesting. And his eyes, when he glanced at his wife, shone with love.

"He's a vampire," Mukdalla said, answering Quinn's unspoken question. "We've been married for over four hundred years.

Quinn's eyebrows shot up. "Congratulations?"

Neo chuckled. "Immortality takes some getting used to. It's rare to find a mate one wishes to share eternity with."

Mukdalla's expression turned serious. "Rinaldo and Neo are both trapped by the failing magic. I don't have to tell you how thrilled I am that you're here, that you're going to renew the magic."

"I'll do whatever I can." Quinn hated to keep reminding them she had no idea if she'd be able to call the power she'd need to do it. And she couldn't give voice to the nagging question of whether she even should. The more vampires she met, the more confused that question became because she was beginning to suspect there really was such a thing as a good vampire. Fortunately, that wasn't a decision she had to make. As long as Zack's life was entwined with V.C.'s magic, she would do everything she could to renew it.

At least two vampires would survive either way.

"Where's Arturo?" she asked, cutting a bite of sausage. "And Micah."

Neo answered her. "Micah is upstairs, keeping watch. Precaution only. We take turns. Arturo had to run an errand."

An errand. "Cristoff." Her appetite fled at the thought.

"Yes."

"Cristoff doesn't know about this place, does he?"

"Absolutely not." Neo looked horrified at the thought. "Only those you've met know about us, and a handful of others, both vampires and Traders."

She glanced at Mukdalla who was sipping her coffee. "I'm curious about something."

Mukdalla smiled. "You can ask anything."

"What are Traders?"

"Ah." Mukdalla set her mug down. "We've been called by many names. The most common being *demon*."

Quinn's eyes widened, her jaw dropping before she snapped it closed.

Mukdalla's smile widened. "Precisely why we prefer the term Traders."

Rinaldo covered Mukdalla's hand. "True demons are nothing like your popular culture, or your religious texts, portray. They are no more inherently evil than humans; nor do they reside in any subterranean sauna. Like vampires, they are immortal though not indestructible. Unlike us, they are born, not made."

"There are actually many races of demon," Mukdalla added. "The Traders are just one, but the most common in Vamp City. The fae are another."

"Fae," Quinn murmured. "Fairies and demons. I suppose I shouldn't feel shocked."

"Humans always do when they first learn of the

supernatural," the other woman said kindly. "The best thing you can do is remember that we are all individuals with our own hopes, our own needs, and our own senses of right and wrong."

"Don't judge the book by the cover, you mean."

"Yes. Exactly. But a healthy dose of wariness with those you don't yet know—especially those more powerful than you—is a very good thing."

Quinn turned back to her breakfast, and the conversation she'd interrupted with her arrival resumed, flowing around her. When she was finished eating, she rose. "Where should I take my plate?"

"Leave it." Neo stood. "Come, Quinn. I have someone I want you to meet, then I want to show you something. As a scientist, I think you'll find this of interest. As the sorceress, I want your reaction."

He had her attention. Glancing down the hallway that led to their bedrooms, she saw no sign of Zack. Turning back, she followed Neo down a different hallway to a fully outfitted gym lit by oil lamps. The equipment, of course, was all of the nonelectrical variety—stationary bikes, NordicTrack skiers, weight benches. Half a dozen people were working out, four men and two women, all in shorts and T-shirts, a couple in bare feet.

"Jason," Neo said, and one of the men lifting weights reset his weight bar and stood to quick attention, his bearing distinctly military.

Neo turned to Quinn. "This is Jason Grimes. Arturo asked me to find a trainer for Zack before he left this morning, and Jason has agreed to do it. Quinn Lennox," he told Jason.

The man wiped his hand on his shorts and extended it to her. "Nice to meet you."

Quinn sized up the man, liking the kindness she saw in his eyes. "Zack . . ."

Jason nodded. "Arturo talked to me about him before he left, that he's untrained and very down on himself for not being able to protect the women he loves." Something hard and pained moved through his eyes. "My wife and I were captured together over a year ago. I didn't stand a chance against those fuckers . . . pardon me, ma'am . . . and we were separated." Emotion tightened his features, and he looked away for a moment, gathering himself. When he turned back, fire burned in his eyes, but also compassion. "I'm an ex-Marine, ma'am. I understand the Marine way of training raw recruits. Your brother does not qualify for such a method. He's already been to Hell and back. What he needs now is a return of his dignity and the tools to take control the next time. As much as any human is able against the immortals. I'm happy to help him with that."

"Thank you, Jason."

As Neo turned away, Quinn followed him back through the main room and down yet another spoke of the wheel of the sprawling safe-house underground. "Was Jason's wife killed?"

"He doesn't know. He's been all over this city, slave to three different vampires, but he's never found any sign of her. I keep offering to get him out of V.C., but he refuses to go without her even though he must know she's probably dead. We're looking for her, too, now. At the moment, he's being forced to keep a low profile." Neo snorted. "He took out nearly a dozen vamps in his escape from his last master."

"How long does he have before he turns Slava and is stuck here for good?"

"Six months at best. Honestly, I doubt he'll leave even then. Not without her."

She ached for the man. "Love can be a terrible burden sometimes, can't it?"

"It can. You've risked much to save your brother." Neo turned, studying her as they walked, a smile breaching his face. "You're not what I expected, sorceress."

Quinn peered at him. "Why? Were you expecting me to show up in flowing black robes with a wand in my hand?" She meant for the comment to be light, and failed. She'd never been comfortable with what she was, and she didn't like that everyone here knew.

"I meant no disrespect, Quinn," Neo said softly, the smile dying from his eyes.

Quinn sighed. "I know. I didn't mean it the way it came out. I just . . . I don't think of myself as a sorceress."

He nodded, understanding in his eyes. "It's hard to change your self-image overnight. Been there, done that."

She peered at him. "Is that what happened to you when you became a vampire?"

"It is. As I told you, I was a slave here for years. I *hated* the vampires."

"Yet you became one."

"Not by will, I assure you. The one who turned me did so just to infuriate me . . . or kill me. Most who are turned don't survive. But I did. And the first thing I did was kill him for it."

"Have you killed . . . others? Humans?"

"No, though it was a near thing a couple of times."

"You have more self-control than most."

"Either that, or I simply have more passion for my self-professed calling."

"Saving people."

"Giving them the freedom to return to their world, to the sunshine, as I so desperately fought . . . and failed . . . to do myself. It feels like a losing proposition, sometimes. For every human I free, other vamps and Traders bring in two more. But I feel like I thwart the grand scheme with every person I get out of here. And I never tire of watching the joy and tears in the eyes of those I help send home."

Quinn nodded. "I get that. I freed half a dozen slaves through a sunbeam a few weeks ago." She thought of Marcus and the others she'd handed out of Vamp City that day. Soon after escaping with Zack, she'd looked up Marcus and spoken with his wife on the phone, who'd burst into tears of gratitude when she'd told her who she was. Marcus had wanted her to come meet his wife and daughter, and she'd promised to. Sometime. Now she wondered if she ever would. His wife had told her they'd all made it out safely. Celeste, who'd been a newly turned Slava, had had a heart attack as she'd traveled through, but Marcus was trained in CPR and had been able to get her heart beating again. She was fine. Her hair had even turned back to normal.

Apparently, Slavas reverted to their true age upon leaving VC. That sudden aging, even if they weren't too old to live, tended to kill them. Celeste had only been immortal for a year, and, still, without Marcus's intervention, she'd have died.

Neo watched her with interest. "You clearly have power, to be able to free slaves through a sunbeam, Quinn."

Her mouth twisted. "Someday I'm going to be a force to be reckoned with."

"It will happen," he said kindly. "You've not yet come to terms with it. You've not yet embraced it."

"I've spent too many years hating it. Have you come to terms with being a vampire?"

"I have."

She looked at him with surprise and was met with a quick grin. "I've learned to appreciate the benefits of incredible strength and speed, of never suffering pain or injury for more than minutes at a time. And to appreciate the fact that I never age. Immortality is a gift, Quinn. One I never asked for, but one I have come to enjoy. Once you learn to control it, your power will be a gift to you."

He was an interesting man, Neo. She felt comfortable with him. "Don't you miss the sun?"

"I do, though I've found ways around it. Until the magic began to fail and I became trapped, I used to frequent the movie theater in Georgetown on a regular basis. In the dark safety of that theater, with the films rolling, I could immerse myself in your world and pretend I lived once more in the sun. It might have been a false, Hollywood sun, but I thoroughly enjoyed it. And I miss it."

She followed him into a large storage room at the end of one of the tunnels. A deserted room far from anyone else. Neo seemed nice enough, but he was still a vampire. And she suddenly wondered if anyone would hear if she shouted for help.

"You're in no danger, Quinn," Neo chided softly. "I wish only to show you something that you'll find interesting."

"I'm not afraid."

"Perhaps not. But your tension has risen."

"You can feel it."

"A little. I'm very sensitive in that way, able to feed off of almost any wariness. That's why I have so little need to cause true fear. Everyone who comes here is at least wary. Most are thoroughly terrified." He looked at her evenly. "If you'd rather wait for Arturo or Micah, I'm fine with that. But there's something I need you to hear. I believe there's a permanent break in the worlds down here."

She met his gaze and saw no subterfuge. And at the high peel of childish laughter deep within the storeroom, her eyes widened and she motioned Neo to lead the way through the stacks and stacks of boxes that appeared to fill the room. As they walked, the music carried to them, followed by voices.

But when they turned the final corner, there was no one there.

Neo smiled with bemusement and drew his finger to his lips.

As she listened, she realized the music was a children's tune on television. Overlaying it were the voices of children. And a woman.

"Are you finished with your cereal? Aidan, where's your vitamin? Did you eat your vitamin?"

A little girl piped up. "He fed it to the roses."

"Aidan . . . did you put your vitamin in Mommy's rose vase again? *Son* . . ."

Quinn smiled, meeting Neo's gaze, a hundred questions on her tongue. Neo escorted her back through the path of boxes until they could talk quietly without being overheard.

"I hear them regularly when I'm in here. We all do. Since you can travel out through sunbeams, I was wondering if you can find a way through there. If you can, it would save us untold efforts in getting slaves out through the Boundary Circle though I imagine Aidan's mother would have a heart attack."

"Let me see if I can find anything." Quinn retraced her steps, following the sound of the television show, but though she searched, she could see no sign of the break and no way to breach it. And she should be able to, even inside.

"No go," she whispered, shaking her head.

Neo shrugged. "It was worth a try." He smiled. "That kid entertains me. You should hear the places Aidan's stashed his green beans."

They started back, but had gone only a few yards when the floor began to shake suddenly and violently. The boxes stacked high on either side of them began to wobble and rock. And they began to fall.

Neo grabbed her, curving around her as cans of food rained down on top of them. One can clipped her on the elbow, another on the foot, smarting. Finally, after more than a dozen seconds, the quaking stopped.

Neo pulled back, looking down at her without letting her go. "Are you all right?"

She nodded. "A sunbeam."

"Yes."

And Arturo was out there, somewhere.

"Mommy?" The voice of the little girl—Aidan's sister? She didn't sound scared, but annoyed. "Mommy! Aidan dumped rice in the fish bowl."

Neo's eyes lit with laughter. "That kid's got a food fetish."

Quinn laughed quietly, meeting Neo's warm gaze. She liked this vampire.

He tensed suddenly, releasing her slowly. She straightened and turned to find the source of Neo's tension. Arturo stood in the path, his eyes hard as flint.

He was jealous and he had no right to be. And no reason.

"Vampire," she said coolly, and started toward him. "Neo just saved me from being crushed by cans of food. How's Cristoff?"

As she started to brush past him, he took her arm lightly, but possessivley, his eyes shifting toward Neo, a warning in their depths. "We'll discuss it later. It is time we left for Tarellia's."

Men and their pissing contests.

"Release me, Vampire," she said quietly as they headed back to the hallway.

Instead, his grip on her arm turned to a light caress. "I heard the crash, *tesoro mio*. I feared you would be injured."

He'd come to save the day and found another male had done so already.

Her pique with him dissipated and she turned to him with a sigh. "Thank you for coming to my rescue, Vampire, even if it wasn't needed."

His eyes warmed. His cool hand slid down her arm, his fingers sliding between hers.

Oh, Vampire, what am I going to do with you?

She gripped his hand in return.

CHAPTER TEN

As they reached the main room, Arturo turned Quinn to face him. "Your glamour has worn off." He released her hand to touch her hair, his fingers lifting a lock and letting it slide through his fingers. "Micah will have to repair your glamour before we leave. I shall let him know." He looked unhappy, but she sensed his mood had little to do with her glamour. Or finding her with Neo, for that matter. And everything to do with Cristoff.

"You haven't told me how your visit went this morning."

He closed his eyes, and when he opened them again, they were filled with shadows and she knew her instincts were right. "He is not the man I knew."

"What does he think happened to me?"

"He believes what I have told him—that Ivan took you into D.C. and that I am looking for you and will return you to him as I did before." He lifted a lock of her hair again, then dropped it, pinning her with a gaze that glowed with fervor. "He will never get near you again."

Neo caught up with them, and Arturo glanced up, his jaw hardening. "We will leave in an hour, *cara mia*. Get some breakfast if you have not already done so."

Moments later, she rapped softly on Zack's door. When he didn't answer, she opened the door to find him still sound asleep. "Zack."

Her brother blinked, his eyes opening slowly. "What's the matter? What time is it?"

"We're in Vamp City. Time doesn't matter, but breakfast is going to be gone if you don't get out there soon."

To her amused relief, he swung his legs over the side of the bed and shoved himself to his feet without hesitation. "Where?"

"The same place as last night." But when he would have brushed past her to escape the room, she blocked his way. "Hold on a minute."

She pressed her hand to his forehead, beneath his mop of red curls. He felt hot to the touch. Definitely feverish. Fear curled in her stomach. "How do you feel?"

"Hungry."

With a roll of her eyes, Quinn stepped back. "Go eat." But as Zack hurried out of the room, Quinn watched him with worried eyes, then followed more slowly. In the main room, she grabbed a cup of coffee as he filled a plate to overflowing, then joined him at the now-empty table.

Briefly, she told Zack about the trip to the fae's. She'd expected him to take her explanation with his usual equanimity, but he turned to her with stubborn eyes.

"I'm going with you."

"I suggested that to Arturo. But he feels that the more of us who go, the more attention we'll draw. Two of us can get in and out of there safer than three."

Zack's mouth tightened, a flash of self-loathing crossing his face as his shoulders slumped. Without another word, he went back to eating.

Quinn's heart clenched. He'd be of no help protecting any of them, including himself, and they both knew it.

Her brother was on his second helping of everything when Jason walked in. The ex-Marine poured himself a tall glass of water and joined them.

"Is this Zack?" he asked.

Quinn introduced them. "Jason's offered to . . ." She wasn't sure how to put it. *Train you? Whip you into shape?*

"Your sister tells me you'd like some fighting tips. A few basic moves anyone can use."

Zack glanced up, his eyes sharp and angry, before returning to his meal. He must see this as one more blow to his already battered pride.

"Nothing crazy," Jason assured him. "I can show you the workout equipment they have here. It's a pretty impressive assortment, considering where we are. And I can give you some basic exercises to get you started. But first we'll warm up together and work on a few basic defensive moves. Not right away. You need a chance to digest your breakfast first. Maybe in an hour?"

Zack nodded without looking up.

Quinn met Jason's gaze with apology in her eyes, but he waved it away.

"We'll go at whatever speed you're comfortable with, Zack," Jason said as he rose again. "I'll see you in an hour."

"Thanks, Jason," Quinn said. When he'd left, she watched her brother. "You're stronger than you think."

Zack made no indication he'd heard her. Or believed her.

A short while later, Neo, Arturo, and Micah walked in.

Quinn looked up. "Time to go?"

"Not yet. You need your glamour renewed."

Micah gave a huff. "Everyone wants a say this time. Apparently, they weren't impressed with my last effort."

He sounded so put out she had to bite back a smile. She rose and squeezed Zack's shoulder. "I'll see you when I get back."

But as she started to turn away, she felt her arm snagged by a gentle, overwarm hand and turned to meet her brother's soft gaze.

"Be careful, sis."

She covered his hand with her free one, love welling up thick inside of her. "I will. Don't forget Jason."

"I won't."

He let her go, and she crossed the room to join the three males. The three vampires.

As they headed down a different hallway from where she'd slept last night, Arturo slid his hand under her hair to cup the back of her neck in a decidedly possessive move. Staking his territory. She met his gaze, warning him silently to cut the he-man theatrics. She expected to see a flash of the charmer, the vampire who cajoled and seduced. But no light entered those dark eyes. His grip on her neck tightened fractionally, as if resisting her demand, before letting go.

They entered a small sitting room, one as spartan as the bedrooms, though instead of a bed and nightstand, this one sported two dark gray sofas at right angles and a smattering of end and coffee tables.

Micah lit the oil lamp on one of the end tables, then closed the door. "We don't need an audience for this."

Quinn glanced first at Arturo, then at Neo. "Looks like we've got one anyway."

"Make her a redhead," Neo said. "I've always been partial to redheads."

Arturo sent him a scathing look. "I want her skin and hair dark. Perhaps she'll not stand out like a diamond in the twilight."

Micah threw his friend a ribbing look. "That was poetic, Ax. I'm impressed." He turned to her, humor still lighting his eyes. "Do you have a preference, Quinn? A favorite actress, though I won't copy her exactly. You'd only draw more attention that way, not less."

She started to shake her head, then glanced at Neo, considering. "Can you make me look like Neo's sister?"

Neo looked surprised but pleased.

Arturo scowled.

Micah grinned. "That I can do." Like before, he closed his eyes, lifted his hands, and touched her cheeks with his fingertips, stroking them with the pads of his thumbs and the barest of touches. Her flesh began to tingle, the sensation spreading along her scalp and neck, then down into her body, as before. Finally, he opened his eyes, the grin spreading across his face slowly.

"Damn, Neo," Micah said. "You make a stunning woman."

Neo snorted. Arturo's scowl only deepened.

"I need a mirror," Quinn said.

"Mukdalla has one." Neo led her from the room and down two more, Micah close behind, Arturo following more slowly. When Neo's quick rap went unanswered, he opened the door, lit a candle in a holder by the bed and lifted a hand mirror on the bedside table, handing it to Quinn.

She took it gingerly, then stared at a woman who was, as Micah said, rather stunning. A woman who in no way resembled her, except for the green eyes.

Quinn set the mirror back on the bedside table, then turned fully to Arturo, who watched her from the doorway. "What do you think?"

He frowned. "It is not a look I would have chosen."

"You have to admit," Neo murmured with a chuckle, winking at her, "I do make a fine-looking woman. Though it's your own beautiful eyes, Quinn, that steal the breath."

Was Neo intentionally poking the tiger? Served Arturo right. But the temperature in the room dropped a good ten degrees as Arturo's eyes turned glacial. If they got into a fight over this, she was going to be pissed as hell.

"It's time to go," Arturo snapped, then turned and walked away.

Quinn rolled her eyes with exasperation and followed him out. She needed to say good-bye to her brother, first, but when she reached the main room, she saw no sign of him. As she started toward the gym, Arturo suddenly appeared out of nowhere, blocking her way.

"You will come, sorceress. Now."

She just stared at him, her anger sparking. "I'll join you in three minutes after I've told Zack I'm leaving." What was the matter with him? If this was about her new look . . . Heaven help them both. He'd better get used to it, or she was going to end up staking him before the day was out.

Turning her back on him, she strode down the hall to the gym, glad to find Jason showing Zack how to block a punch. Zack appeared interested and engaged, and that's all she could ask for. Jason glanced at her standing in the doorway, and Zack did the same, both without a hint of recognition. Of course they wouldn't know who she was beneath the glamour. She kept forgetting what she looked like.

Instead of introducing herself, she turned away and went to rejoin the vampire, who'd begun to act more like a lion with a thorn in his paw. She found him waiting impatiently by the stairs just as Micah joined him.

She turned to Micah. "Will you let Zack know we left, please?"

"Sure, Quinn." He accompanied them upstairs and opened the back door for them. "Be good, kids," he quipped. "No fighting, and be home in time for dinner. Call if you're going to be late."

Quinn snorted. Arturo ignored his friend as he ushered her out the door and into the dusky twilight of a Vamp City day.

"Where are the horses?" Quinn asked as they started walking away from the house.

"The barn." His voice was sharp and cold, which just made her angry.

"What's gotten into you?"

His mouth turned harder if such a thing were possible. "Neo oversteps. I do not want his hands on you."

"They haven't been!" They strode quickly toward the barn door, their strides fueled by their mutual anger. "He's never made the slightest move on me, and if he did, it would be none of your business."

Suddenly, her back was up against the wall, her body pinned by that of a furious vampire.

"It is my business. *You* are my business." Arturo's enunciation was slow and cold and dangerously precise. "You are mine, Quinn Lennox. *Mine.*"

She gaped at him, speechless. "I'm not your *slave*. I've never been your slave, and I'm never going to be!"

"Not my slave." At her words, at her vehemence, his anger seemed to ease. He gripped her jaw with long, cool fingers. She tried to jerk away, but he held her fast. His voice lowered, softened. "You are mine, *cara*. The sunshine that warms my flesh. My sunlight." His hold on her jaw tightened, though not unduly so. His expression grew tormented. "Do you have any idea how much I want you? Yet I do not push you. You have lost your faith in me. You are angry with me for handing you over to Cristoff and, *dio* Quinn, *you have a right to be.*"

He released her suddenly, turning away, running a hand through his hair. "The things I saw today . . ." His voice was low with anguish. "I have watched his atrocities for months, *years,* and felt too little. Felt *nothing.*"

Quinn stared at him, her own anger slipping away as she realized how shaken he really was. This wasn't about Neo. This was about Cristoff.

"What happened at Gonzaga Castle this morning, Arturo?" she asked quietly. Not that she really wanted to know. She didn't.

When he didn't answer, she reached for him, sliding her hand down his back. She felt him tense and shudder. Slowly, he turned back to face her, his expression revealing little, but his eyes burned.

He took her face in his hands. "He will never touch you again. I vow it." His shoulders sank, his forehead tipping against hers. "*Mio dio*. You've changed me, *cara*. I cannot decide if I should thank you or hate you for it."

"Micah's glad."

"Yes. As am I." One of his hands began to stroke her hair.

"Does my hair feel different? Like Neo's hair?"

He pulled back and smiled, though the smile only briefly reached his eyes. "No. The glamour is nothing but illusion. It is your silky hair I feel." His knuckles brushed her cheek. "Your soft skin. Your scent that I smell." He leaned in to briefly press his lips to forehead. "You that I taste."

Slowly, he pulled away. "Come." He held out his hand to her. "I will endeavor to be less of an ass."

She grinned at him and slipped her hand in his. "That's all I ever ask."

The smile he gave her was soft but still filled with shadows.

"I'm sorry, Vampire. Sorry for what you've lost. It's incomprehensible to me that Cristoff could have ever been a good man, but I've only ever known the monster. It must be very hard to watch a friend lose his soul."

He lifted their joined hands and brushed a kiss over her knuckles. "I believe I now understand the frustration and sorrow I've witnessed in the eyes of my own friends too often these past couple of years.

While my soul was not fully compromised, neither was I unaffected. I was not the man they knew."

"And now you are again."

"I hope so."

And how could he know for certain when he hadn't realized he'd changed in the first place? she wondered. But unless he was playing them all, he had absolutely changed. For the better.

"I like the real you, Arturo."

She glanced at him and caught the smile light his eyes. "I like you, too, Quinn." He squeezed her hand. "Let us get this errand over and done with so that we might return to Neo's before lunchtime."

"I'm all for that."

He pulled something out of his pocket with his free hand and proffered a roll of SweetTarts. His weakness, she remembered. With a smile, she took one and popped the tart candy into her mouth.

If she wasn't very, very careful, she could be in danger of liking this vampire entirely too much.

CHAPTER ELEVEN

Quinn rode beside Arturo, enjoying the wind in her hair and the feel of the horse beneath her. She was starting to understand the appeal of the animals, she decided. Especially one as calm and easy to control as the one she was on now.

"Choose a name," Arturo said, when they'd ridden a short distance.

"Pardon me?"

"A name for me to call you as my Neo-look-alike slave. One you will remember to answer to."

"Neo-look-alike," she muttered, and he smiled, pulling a smile from her, reminding her how much she'd enjoyed his company once. His mood had lightened as they'd ridden, and she was glad. "Jillian," she said without thinking. "It was my mother's name."

"Jillian it is, then." He cut her a chiding look, even as the humor lingered in his eyes. "Endeavor to act at least a little like a servant if we come across others, yes? You needn't act obsequious."

"Obsequious isn't in my dictionary. Or my nature."

"I've noticed."

As they rode, Arturo gave her a few riding tips, and she felt like she was really starting to get the hang of it by the time they entered a small cluster of

log houses that looked like they'd been built somewhere on the prairie a couple of hundred years ago.

Quinn glanced at Arturo. "What exactly is a fae,
anyway? I'm assuming they don't fly."

He smirked. "They do not have wings, no. They
are humanlike and gifted in the ways of clairvoy-
ance. Think Tolkien's elves, though perhaps not quite
so attractive."

"Not so attractive" turned out to be an understatement. Minutes later, Arturo dismounted, turning to
her, then standing back to allow her to dismount on
her own.

He nodded with approval. "You're getting the
hang of it."

Arturo rapped on the split-wood door of one of
the houses, and a face appeared in the front window.
Male or female, Quinn couldn't tell, but the mouth
was comically wide, the eyes slanted downward,
giving the person . . . the fae . . . a look of sadness despite the wariness in those pale orbs. The face disappeared as quickly as it had appeared, and, a moment
later, the door opened. The sad-eyed creature, apparently a female, if the simple, old-fashioned dress was
anything to go by, eyed Arturo with antagonism.

"You are not welcome here."

Quinn looked between them in surprise. Then
again, he'd admitted he'd had few dealings with the
fae.

But the great diplomat . . . the great manipulator
. . . wasn't about to be put off. His voice low and
hypnotic, he said, "You have nothing to fear from us.
We ask only to speak with Tarellia."

The woman watched him carefully, the rigid line
of her shoulders easing just a little.

"Who are you?"

"I am Arturo Mazza."

"Mazza," she muttered, then frowned. "Cristoff's snake." She spat onto the dirt beside the porch, disgust in her words.

Arturo said nothing for a moment. When he spoke, his words were even more hypnotic than before. "I mean you no harm. I am here on a diplomatic mission and only want a word with Tarellia, then I will take my leave." He leaned forward slightly, and said in a conspiratorial whisper, "I bring gifts, woman. I carry with me the latest seasons of *CSI* and *So You Think You Can Dance.*"

The last was the clincher. The fae's eyes lit up like Christmas-tree bulbs. "Dance! And AA batteries for the DVD player?"

"And batteries."

Quinn stifled a disbelieving smile. Every time she thought she had this place figured out . . .

The fae eyed her with distaste. "The human stays outside."

He shook his head as if he knew he had the upper hand now. "My slave goes where I go."

The fae frowned, then waved them inside. "Come, both of you."

They followed the now-excited woman through a tiny, if quaint, sitting room and into another, slightly larger room with a fire in the hearth. In a rocking chair in front of the fire, in a dress of bright red velvet, sat a female similar in appearance to the first, her eyes not quite as sad-looking.

She looked up when they entered, her gaze wary.

"What is this?" she asked the first woman sharply.

"He wishes to talk to you, Tarellia. He brought

the latest season of *Dance*!" Her face glowed with happiness.

The fae in the red dress, her yellow hair piled high atop her head in a classic beehive, rolled her eyes and waved them in. "You discovered her weakness."

Arturo gave a charming smile. "I've found it to be the weakness of half of the population of Vamp City."

"What brings you here, Arturo Mazza? I've not seen you in an age." Tarellia motioned to the straight-backed wooden chair beside the hearth. "Sit."

Arturo glanced at Quinn with apology and did, leaving her standing as he would any servant. He clasped his hands and settled them on his lap, bending slightly forward. But though on the surface he might look friendly, something about him reminded Quinn of a tiger ready to strike.

Apparently Tarellia thought the same, for her gaze turned sharp, wary.

"I came upon some information of interest some-time back . . . Martine."

The fae's rocking stopped abruptly, her hands slowly clasping the arms of her rocker. "No."

Quinn had no idea what was going on, but clearly the fae had once gone by another name. Martine. And wasn't happy to be found out.

Arturo leaned back, propping one ankle on the other knee, his body language saying "game, set, match." "I am very good at keeping secrets, Tarellia. And I have secrets to share."

The fae, whose face had drained of color, watched him sharply. "What kind of secrets?"

Arturo said nothing for several moments, letting the silence stretch.

The fae leaned back in her rocker, her grip on the arms easing. "I am very good at keeping secrets, too, Vampire."

With a slow nod, Arturo smiled though the smile didn't reach his eyes. He held out his hand to Quinn, motioning her forward.

"I want you to read my slave, Tarellia. Tell me what you sense."

The fae's eyes narrowed, turning to Quinn with interest. Slowly, she rose to her feet, barely reaching Quinn's shoulder. Taking Quinn's hand between both of hers, she closed her eyes. For minute after minute, she didn't move until Quinn began to wonder if she'd fallen asleep.

Tarellia's eyes snapped open suddenly, and she dropped Quinn's hand as if it had burned her. Whirling toward the fire with quick, jerky movements, the woman pulled down vials and jars from the rough-hewn mantel, then began mixing herbs and what appeared to be oil in a small ceramic bowl on the table beside her rocker, crooning all the while in a soft, singsong voice. *This is what a witch should look like,* Quinn thought. But Tarellia was the fairy. The real witch in the room could do nothing more than stand there in her leather jacket and watch.

The concoction smelled foul, and Quinn hoped to high Heaven the fairy didn't push her to drink it. To Quinn's relief, Tarellia threw the oil concoction onto the fire in a spitting hiss of flames, then turned back to her, grabbing Quinn's hand once more, her grip surprisingly tight.

Closing her eyes, Tarellia threw her head back and began to croon.

Quinn glanced at Arturo over her shoulder, seeing

the small frown between his eyebrows. Clearly, he wasn't sure what was going on, either . . . or didn't like it. Which calmed her own nerves not at all. They stood like that again, frozen, for what felt like twenty minutes though it was probably only four or five. But as Quinn's muscles began to jerk in protest, Tarellia's eyes flew open. Releasing Quinn, she blinked, brushed her hands on her dress, then turned back to her rocking chair with slow, calm movements, and took her seat as if nothing had happened.

Quinn backed away, then turned and tried to pace the tiny room, her restless muscles in desperate need of movement.

Slowly, Tarellia turned to Arturo with eyes that held a hint of wonder. "You've found a sorceress."

Arturo nodded. "None can know."

Tarellia frowned. "She must save Vamp City."

"She will. But Cristoff cannot be trusted not to hurt her. And I'll not have her hurt."

The fae cocked her head with interest. "You defy your master. And one such as Cristoff." A smile bloomed bright and delighted across her face. "Secrets indeed."

Arturo gave a nod, his expression rueful. "Indeed." He glanced at Quinn, meeting her gaze. "She has no control over her power, Tarellia. Most cannot sense that she has magic at all. Why is that?"

The fae's visage had turned calm, serene. "The sorceress is cursed."

Quinn frowned, meeting Arturo's surprised gaze. Cursed? Seriously?

"By whom?" he demanded.

Tarellia gave a small wave. "Are you not familiar with the Levenach Curse?"

Now it was Arturo's turn to frown. "I suspected her of Blackstone blood, not Levenach."

"She has both. It's impossible to say how far back the bloodlines converged. Her Levenach magic is dormant, of course, thanks to the curse. But it would appear that the curse is also strangling her Blackstone magic." She shook her head. "I've never seen a sorcerer with both Levenach and Blackstone blood, so I cannot be sure."

Quinn watched them, her mind awhirl. Magic and curses and sorcerers. Her heritage. Her *life*. She wanted to shake her head, to deny any of it could possibly be real. And yet, she knew better, now. The whole thing made her stomach ache.

If she was cursed . . .

Her blood pressure began to rise. "Does this mean that there's no hope for my magic? That there's no way for me to renew the magic of Vamp City?" Heaven help her, Zack would die. She slammed Arturo with her gaze. "Why is this affecting Zack?"

He looked at Tarellia. "What effect, if any, might the crumbling of Vamp City be having on her power?"

A thoughtful looked entered the fae's eyes. "Vamp City was created with Blackstone magic, which her Blackstone blood no doubt responds to. But . . ." She turned and peered at Quinn hard. "Two or three years ago . . . what did you do?"

Quinn frowned. "What do you mean?"

"You may have been the trigger. Did you come into your magic then? Attempt a spell?"

"A *spell*?" Quinn shook her head. "Three years ago . . ." She blinked. "I moved to D.C." She'd lived in Bethesda, Maryland, until Zack started college at GW.

"Within the Boundary Circle?" Tarellia demanded.

"Yes."

The fae nodded. "That's it. The trigger. *She* is the reason the magic began to crumble after all these years."

Quinn gaped at her. The trapped vampires, the sunbeams breaking through, the humans disappearing right and left—Lily. *Zack.*

"I did this?" Her gaze swung to Arturo, and she found him watching her with surprised, troubled eyes.

"Not you, per se," Tarellia said. "But your battling magics. Blackstone blood called to Blackstone magic, but the curse somehow infected Vamp City's magic and slowly began to trigger the demise."

"If I leave—move away from D.C.—will the magic stop crumbling?"

"Nothing will stop or reverse the disintegration but the Renewal ceremony, which you will complete using your Blackstone magic."

"But I can't reach it. The curse . . ."

Tarellia held up a hand. "Free the magics, one from the other, and you will have access to your Blackstone power."

"Can you help her with that?" Arturo demanded.

A sad look crossed the fae's face. "No. I haven't the gift, and the only fae this side of the Atlantic who does is aging."

"Tell me, woman," Arturo demanded.

"Vintry. He's been Fabian Neptune's sage for nearly two hundred years."

"How much time does he have?" Arturo asked.

"Days. Perhaps only hours, now. I will know when

he dies, and I've not felt his death, but I know it's near."

Quinn looked pointedly at Arturo. "Zack?"

The vampire nodded at her unspoken question. "Is it possible the sorceress could have somehow entangled another in the magic? Someone who accompanied her into Vamp City on a sunbeam."

The fae cocked her head, her mouth pursing. "When it comes to battling magics, anything is possible. Renewing the magic should solve all problems."

Arturo rose. He turned to the fae, his expression grim. "Secrets, Martine. If anyone asks, I sought only your aid in locating the missing sorceress, which you were unable to give me."

The fae nodded, her expression once more tight. "Of course."

"Thank you, Tarellia," Quinn said.

As Arturo ushered Quinn out of the room and house, the sad-eyed fae followed them to their horses, grinning happily. While Quinn mounted, Arturo pulled the two DVD sets and a pack of AA batteries out of one of his saddlebags, along with a large package of Oreo cookies.

The woman's joy knew no bounds. "Oh, this is a fine day, a fine day." As she bounded back into the tiny log cabin, Arturo mounted.

"Are we going to find Vintry?" Quinn asked when they were out of earshot of the small settlement. She was still reeling from the revelation that she was suffering from some kind of curse.

"We? No. I will take Micah. The Gonzaga kovena has diplomatic relations with Fabian's, but the two are not friends. Cristoff has been . . . aggressive . . .

in recent years. The other vamp masters do not appreciate it."

"I can imagine." Cristoff's brutality knew no bounds. "If there's not much time, I should go with you."

"No."

"Vampire . . ."

His expression turned obstinate. "Do not demand this of me, *cara*. I cannot keep you safe there."

"Is he another pain-feeder?"

"He is a pleasure-feeder. And you are not going near him."

His determination to keep her out of harm's way was admirable. And appreciated. But from what Tarellia said, Vintry was nearly out of time. Which meant Zack was, too.

Micah would see her side, she was almost certain. She'd save her arguments for Neo's. Besides, other questions crowded her mind.

"Tell me about the curse."

Arturo frowned, his eyes scanning the horizon in every direction before he finally began to speak. "Legend has it, the Levenach Curse is centuries old, perhaps millennia, placed by the Black Wizard, from whom all Blackstones are descended, on his arch enemy, the wizard Levenach."

"They obviously hated one another."

"Levenach had stabbed the Black Wizard with a blade empowered to kill him. With the Black Wizard's dying breath, he swore that none of Levenach's heirs would ever again have access to their magic."

"How is a curse like that lifted?"

"It isn't. Only the one who performed the curse can lift it."

"And the Black Wizard died moments after uttering it."

"Yes."

She could almost imagine that she felt the curse twisting around her organs, choking them. A curse that she was stuck with for life, for it could never be lifted. But perhaps it didn't matter. Not as long as she was able to access her Blackstone magic.

"So if we can reach Vintry in time and get him to disentangle my two magics, I should be able to renew Vamp City and, hopefully, free Zack from its effects. Will it be enough to keep my battling magics from triggering the crumbling again?"

"I do not know. Once you have renewed the magic, you must leave D.C. regardless. You'll never be safe from Cristoff. Never."

As they rode, the cool breeze caressed her cheeks and lifted strands of her hair. But her mind was in turmoil, questions darting every which way. Unfortunately, most were questions Arturo had no better answers to than she did. Who had her Levenach ancestor been? How powerful might she be if not for the curse?

If only there were someone to ask, some relative still living from that side of her family. But her mom had been an only child and had lost her parents at nineteen. Then she'd died herself when Quinn was only two. If any of them had possessed magic, Quinn had no way to know.

"What did Tarellia mean when she said Vintry is aging?" she asked aloud, one question Arturo should be able to answer.

"The fae are not entirely immortal. They live two to three millennia before they begin to grow old.

But once the aging begins, it happens very quickly. Within weeks of its onslaught, the fae will wither and die."

That was sad, in a way, and yet perfect, too. Who wouldn't love to live for lifetimes, retaining their youthful appearance and strength right up until their last days?

Arturo coaxed his horse into a canter, urging her to give it a try. For a short while, the increased speed kept her mind engaged on the riding and off the questions.

Suddenly, Arturo pulled up, muttering something low and short in Italian. Then, "*Cara.*"

She managed to bring her horse to a stop, though she suspected her mount of reacting more to Arturo's than her own inexperienced attempts at control.

"What's the matter?" Quinn asked quietly. But she knew the moment she saw the dark forms beginning to slink out from behind the trees a short distance ahead, more than a dozen of them. Huge, pelted, four-legged forms. Wolves.

Werewolves.

Arturo eyed the wolves with dismay, his muscles tensing for the fight that was almost certain to come. The werewolves snarled, circling them, sliding out from behind the trees.

Mio dio, this was not good. The wolves were hungry, and while they might attack him, it was sweet human flesh they craved. Quinn's flesh.

His muscles tensed. They would not get it. He would not let them harm her.

His horse nickered with fear. Quinn's mount

began to shy, and he urged his own closer, grabbing her reins to keep hers from throwing her.

Options ran through his mind, lightning fast. Diplomacy? His power of *persuasion* almost never worked on werewolf minds, not when they were in their animal forms. His only real option was to grab Quinn and run.

Trust me, cara.

Snatching her off of her mount and into his arms would be easy. But the wolves, while not as fast as he was, had an uncanny ability to track a vampire's movements. Breaking through the line that now surrounded them would not be easy at all.

"No," she said quietly, her voice tight with strain. "Don't touch me." The telltale glow of power leaped into her eyes even as she pulled and cocked her gun. "Where should I aim?"

"The head. It will slow them down the fastest."

"But not kill them?" She was shaking from her struggle to keep hold of the power.

"Not necessarily."

Tension knotted his muscles as the need to snatch her away warred with the certainty that he must do everything possible to aid her in maintaining control. He prepared, as she did, for the only other option.

Fight.

The ground began to quake. A crack of thunder rolled across the skies. Sunbeams burst through in the distance, at least three that he could see.

Quinn's gaze flew to his, her eyes widening. Wild. She was losing control. "I did that," she gasped, clutching the reins with one hand while the gun in her other vibrated badly. She'd never be able to hit anything like that.

Hold on to the power, cara. *We stand a better chance if you remain mounted and in control.*

"I'm trying."

As the wolves slowly closed in, saliva dripping between jagged teeth, Arturo drew his knives. Somehow, he had to keep them from her. All of them.

If his heart could still race, it would be racing now. If the sweat could still roll from his brow, it would be rolling.

Then lose control hard, Quinn. Send them flying and make your escape.

"What about you?"

I shall follow. Because she'd never get away from this hungry pack, not without help.

The blast happened suddenly, hitting him like an eighteen-wheeler. He went flying off his horse even as his mount stumbled and pranced, barely missing him. As his mount shied from the encroaching wolves, Arturo leaped to his feet and flew toward Quinn.

But so did the wolves.

Quinn lifted her gun and fired, but the sound spooked her already skittish horse, and it reared. Somehow, Quinn managed to hold on, but her control of the animal was negligible at best.

As Arturo started for her, a second power blast sent him tumbling back into the wolves. And this time when he rose, he was cut off. Twelve beasts stood between him and Quinn, half snarling at him, the other half circling her as if ready to pounce.

Quinn fired another shot. And another.

His head began to pound, his muscles tensing as he drew his sword and attacked the closest wolf. "She is the only one who can save Vamp City. Do not harm her!"

But the wolves reacted with only more relish, and his stomach twisted with the certainty that they'd heard . . . and likely believed . . . the old wives' tale that consuming the flesh of a sorcerer would convey the power to the one who ate him. A wolf with a sorcerer's power would have no reason to fear the demise of Vamp City. He would, presumably, walk away unscathed.

It was a foolish belief. And one that could get Quinn killed.

Hacking at the wolf in front of him, killing him, he pushed his way toward her, but two more leaped at him in wolf form. He fought them, too, crazed with fear that the beasts would begin to tear at Quinn's flesh before he could reach her.

More shots rang out. He had no idea how full her magazine was when she started, but sooner or later, she would empty it.

Her emotions blasted him—fear, anger, determination. So far none of them included pain.

A second wolf's blood spilled beneath his blade, and a third. But there were too many of them!

Once more, Quinn fired, but when her mount reared this time she lost her precarious hold.

Arturo went berserk as she fell, as he watched the wolves leap at her. He roared with fury, but as he attempted to fly to her, wolves tackled him from all sides, dragging him to the ground. As he fought them, one tore a chunk out of his leg, making him howl with pain and frustration. He swung his sword, finding flesh and fur before sharp teeth tore through the wrist of his sword hand. He moved to shift his sword to his left hand, but another huge furry body plowed into him, knocking him flat.

Before he could fight his way free, a chain slipped over his head, tightening around his neck.

Silver. The one thing that could render a vampire all but powerless. *Mio dio.* It didn't burn him, didn't physically hurt him. But already he could feel the strength flowing out of him and feel his senses dulling.

Quinn! he shouted telepathically. *Fight them off. Find your power and save yourself. Run. You must run!*

Instead, she fired another shot.

"We come in peace," he said out loud, his voice low and hypnotic.

"Gag him," a rough voice said nearby. "Silence his *persuasion.*"

A gag was forced into his mouth by a were now in human form, snagging on his fangs. Arturo tried to fight free, but with the silver around his neck, he was now powerless against the far greater strength of his captors. Several more of his attackers shifted into human form and began trussing him up like a lamb for slaughter.

Pain exploded in his head . . . *Quinn's pain* . . . driving him mad in his need to reach her. A moment later, her emotion flickered out as she fell unconscious. He went feral, struggling against his bonds, to no avail.

Out of the corner of his eye, Arturo saw one of the now-human weres rise, flinging Quinn's limp form over his shoulder. To his desperate eyes, she appeared whole. Unharmed.

His vampire heart began to beat again.

Several of the weres shifted human. "Let us eat her here!" one cried. "If we take her back, there won't be enough to go around."

"The alpha alone will decide her fate." The one carrying her, the largest of the group, glanced at Arturo. "If you need a bite, take it from that one. Just don't kill him. Yet."

Arturo, too, was lifted and slung over a shoulder. His breath had returned with the evidence of Quinn's survival, but his mind remained awash with disbelief. Never in six hundred years had he let himself be captured by werewolves.

But he'd been more concerned with Quinn's safety than his own.

He still was.

CHAPTER TWELVE

"There you are."

At the sound of Jazlyn's voice, Lily looked up from scrubbing the floor in one of the castle's many bathrooms.

"Come on, girl. The vamps want all the freshies in the master's hall right now. You don't want to be the last human wandering around up here."

No, she didn't. Lily dropped the scrub brush in the bucket of soapy water and set the bucket under the sink, where no one would trip over it.

"Thanks, Jaz. What do they want?"

Jazlyn bit her lower lip. "I don't know, but it can't be good. Group gatherings aren't ever a good thing."

The two girls hurried downstairs, slipping into the gathering in the master's hall along with half a dozen other stragglers.

The master's hall looked much as the real Smithsonian Castle's west wing did in the real world, with its high, vaulted ceiling and intricate woodwork. But the red sandstone walls were now brown with smoke, the once-lovely windows boarded over against errant sunbeams. Chaises covered in stained floral silks and worn brocades lined the walls upon which sat more than two dozen hungry vampires.

Lily's pulse raced, as she knew the other female slaves' did. She could almost smell the fear, and knew the vampires, at least those who were fear-feeders, could taste it. And most of the vampires at Castle Smithson, along with their master, Lazzarus Nica, were fear-feeders. From what she'd heard, fear-feeders were the most common of the emotion-feeding vampires. Lazzarus, thank Heaven, apparently disliked the taste of pain. And while he enjoyed pleasure immensely, he was a male who preferred other males. From what she'd been told, new male slaves were sent either to the yards to work, or to the hall, to be prepared to pleasure the master.

The females were put to work as house slaves and blood donors though the hetero male vamps were free to use them at will.

"Many of you are new to Vamp City," a feminine voice rang out, and Lily had to peer around Jazlyn's shoulder to get a glimpse of the woman speaking, a vampire by the name of Marguerite.

On the dais at the end of the hall, the vampire master, Lazzarus, lounged on a chaise, surrounded by the three well-built, half-naked males who seemed to accompany him everywhere. Other males, fully naked, sat or lay upon pillows around his feet, most with the phosphorescent hair of Slavas.

"Some of you came to us through the slave auction, many of you did not. For those who are not familiar with the auction, let me explain. Because within the next couple of days, half of you will be transported back there."

Gasps and small cries sounded throughout the gathering, one girl breaking into sobs. Most of the slaves, Lily included, merely looked at each other with wariness and trepidation. It was clear who'd come through the auction and who hadn't.

Marguerite continued. "Within Castle Smithson, you have known relative safety. In the slave auction, you will not. You will be enthralled or knocked unconscious, then shackled to the other slaves at the ankle. In recent months, it's become customary to kill a slave or two in front of the others to feed the gathering vampires."

Behind her, one of the girls whispered in a broken voice, "It's really like that. It's just like that."

Lily's head began to pound at the description of the violence. She knew Vamp City was bad, but she'd never seen anything so barbaric in Castle Smithson.

"When the vampires' hunger has been satiated, the shackled slaves are led to the auction dais where, one by one, their finest attributes are displayed for the bidding horde, whether that means breasts or buttocks, courage or screams. You'll be sold to the highest bidder to be used for food, labor, sex, or simply to be tortured and killed for your master's feeding pleasure."

Lily's stomach began to quiver badly enough that she thought she might be sick. Why were they telling them this? But a quick glance around the room told her. The vampires all appeared to be in the throes of incredible pleasure.

Lazzarus and his vamps fed on fear. And the hall was now wild with it.

Was it possible this gathering was just a setup to create the fear? Or were many of them really doomed to experience the slave auction firsthand?

"Over the next few days, we will be deciding which of you to sell and which to keep. Work hard, cooperate with your masters to the fullest, and you'll remain a Smithson slave. Do not, and I guarantee you will find yourself wishing you had. Now, go!" She clapped her hands. "Return to your duties."

The women rushed from the hall, scattering in all directions as they ran to prove themselves worthy of remaining. Lily mimicked them—the worst thing to do in such a case was to stand out, especially as one who didn't believe what they'd been told. But the fact was, she didn't. Oh, she believed they'd sell slaves to the auctions. That part was true. But not those who weren't working hard enough. Hard work wasn't something the vampires particularly prized, from her estimation.

No, what Lazzarus and his vampires prized most was fear.

Hurrying back up to the bathroom where she'd been working, she pulled out her bucket and resumed her scrubbing.

Most of the female slaves in that hall today had come into the kovena within days of Lily. A new wave of terrified captives. The only two that Lily knew had been here for a while were perpetually terrified creatures. But over the past few weeks, most of the new wave had settled in. And settled down. Many had become enamored of their vampire hosts, eager for their attention. Over the past weeks, most of them had all but lost their fear. Until today. The threat of the slave auction had stirred their anxiety, but that would only last so long. Soon, they would all be sold. Lily was sure of it.

She didn't intend to be here when that happened. Which meant she had to plan her escape. And fast.

She'd heard rumors. Not all of the girls had been

new to Vamp City when they were brought here. Some had escaped other masters and been caught again. They'd shared stories of slaves escaping through the sunbeams, and stories of a man called the Guardian who protected slaves and helped them escape Vamp City altogether.

Lily figured she could decide whether or not to seek the Guardian once she was on her own. And she could get out of there, she was almost positive. The trouble was Jazlyn. The girl wasn't small, quick, or quiet. Trying to get them both away without the vampires' noticing might well reduce her chance of success from one in ten to one in ten thousand.

Lily took a deep breath, dipping her brush back into the soapy water as she exhaled slowly, with a heavy sigh.

She and Jazlyn were in this together, now, whether that meant escaping in unison or suffering the slave auction hand in hand.

Lily couldn't . . . *wouldn't* . . . leave her friend behind.

Quinn woke with a groan, her arms at once numb and in pain, as if they'd been pulled out of their sockets. Her mouth ached where a cloth gag bit into the corners. She felt herself hanging, her wrists caught tight in . . . *manacles*. But her feet were dragging the floor.

Stumbling, she righted herself, pushing herself to her feet, easing the pressure on her wrists, which were, apparently, chained to the stone wall behind her. If only she could as easily relieve the pounding in her head.

The last thing she remembered was . . . *wolves*.

Her heart began to race as it all came back, how the wolves had surrounded them, attacked them. How, for once, she'd managed to use her power for defense, but she'd been unable to keep Arturo from getting caught in it, too. How impossible it had been to hit the wolves with her bullets even at close range. Or, if she had hit them and didn't know it, how impossible they'd been to kill. Only one had gone down, and he hadn't stayed there for long.

Ultimately, none of it had been enough. One of them had shifted into a man and slammed his fist into her jaw. Lights out.

Had Arturo gotten away?

Blinking, she found herself deep in the shadows, ribbons of light teasing the dirt floor beneath her feet as a torch flickered outside the bars of her prison cell, just out of sight.

Why would they chain her up inside a prison cell? Talk about redundant. Then again, they knew she was a sorceress. Maybe they thought this would keep her power in check. Wouldn't they be in for a surprise? She doubted chaining her would stop anything. Anything but her ability to escape.

Rolling her shoulders eased the ache in her arms as she listened to the faint rumble of voices in the distance. Above her, the ceiling appeared to be nothing but rock, as if she were deep beneath the ground.

A prisoner of werewolves.

Hell.

Tipping her throbbing head carefully against the rock, she sighed, her heart rate slowly returning to normal, which under the circumstances, it probably shouldn't. If they had an ounce of sense, they'd real-

ize she was the only one who might be able to save
Vamp City. They'd be fools to hurt her.

"Vampire?" she called softly, but no reply met her
ears. Her heart clutched as it occurred to her that he
might not have survived.

The thought stunned her. He *had* to have survived.
Arturo Mazza could not be gone. Not after six hundred years. Not like this.

No, he wasn't dead. She refused to believe it. But if
he were free, she wouldn't still be in this cell. He was
probably chained up, too, somewhere.

Well, one of them was going to have to get them
out of here. It might as well be her.

The manacles were tight around her wrists—too
tight to pull her hands through—so she tried yanking the chains free from the wall behind her. That
didn't work. Not the human way, at least. Closing
her eyes, she concentrated, imagining the manacles
popping open, imagining the chains flying free and
not . . . thank you very much . . . knocking her out in
the process. Still nothing.

Arturo?

No reply, of course. He'd never been able to hear
her thoughts. And all she heard in return was her
stomach growling with hunger.

Tipping her head back, she railed at her sorcerer's
power to be of some use, dammit.

Suddenly, she heard something. The creak of
hinges nearby.

She went still, her pulse accelerating. At the sound
of footsteps, her mind sighed with relief even as her
muscles tensed, and her heart began to race.

A shadow appeared on the ground outside her
cage, and grew, followed closely by the appearance

of a man—a big, heavily muscled, and thoroughly naked man with broad shoulders, a bushy mop of light brown hair, and a beard to match. Though incredibly well built, he was not a particularly good-looking male, his mouth too narrow, his eyes the color of cement and just as hard.

He wasn't alone. Two other naked males followed behind him, neither quite as big, or hairy, but both as well built. Werewolves, no doubt. One, a young man with peach fuzz across his upper lip, came to stand beside the bearded were, but the other, a bald male, hung back.

"Find the key," the bearded one said. He eyed her with excitement and a hunger that made her flesh want to crawl right off her bones. And suddenly Quinn thought she understood the reason for the redundancy in her imprisonment. Her chains were to keep her and her magic in. The cage was to keep the werewolves out.

Quinn felt the power buzz beneath her flesh. *Finally.*

Peach Fuzz began searching.

"Gunroth . . ." the bald man said disapprovingly. "You'll be banished for this."

"Who cares? We'll be stronger than all of them put together. And when the city's magic fails, we alone will be safe. We'll be free."

"It's not here," Peach Fuzz grumbled.

Gunroth's mouth turned as hard as his eyes. "The alpha must have it. We'll just have to find another way in." He pushed out of the doorway, rooting around in what sounded like a metal box or locker, then returned with what looked like . . . *lock picks.*

Hell. Come on, power.

The bald one threw a look of disgust ceilingward and walked away.

"Are we going to fuck her before we eat her?" Peach Fuzz asked far too eagerly.

Eat her?

Quinn's magic began to spark and spit beneath her skin. There had to be a way to turn this energy into something more useful than power blasts although a power blast might be welcome in a few minutes if they got that door open. The energy began to quake inside her.

"We won't have time," Gunroth said as he began digging at the lock. He glanced back, realizing his second companion was gone. "Fuck." He stepped up his efforts, his movements growing increasingly frantic.

Quinn heard the telltale click of the lock. Terror flared. Her heart pounded. They were going to shift into their animals, rip into her with their fangs, and *eat her.*

Like hell.

Gunroth swung the door of her cage wide open, grinning even as he shifted into wolf form, his teeth sharp and gleaming.

As she stared at the vicious animal, Quinn willed the power to fly, to throw him back. Beneath her, the ground began to shake.

As Gunroth stalked her, Peach Fuzz shifted into a smaller wolf behind him and followed him into her cell. Two vicious animals intent on killing her.

She embraced the terror rising inside of her, focused it, drawing it in to feed her power. *They're going to kill me, they're going to kill me, they're going to kill me.*

Finally, the energy burst free, sending both wolves flying—Peach Fuzz out through the door of her cage, Gunroth into the inner bars. But two seconds later, they were on their feet, coming back for more. And with the energy dissipated, she didn't have any more to give.

Shit, shit, shit.

In the hallway just outside, she heard the low, vicious growl of yet another wolf, and her heart sank. She was so dead.

But to her astonishment, the smaller wolf, Peach Fuzz, sank to the floor, whimpering in supplication. The larger, Gunroth, tensed as if suddenly torn. But he made his decision quickly enough. He leaped at her, mouth open wide as if ready to take the biggest chunk out of her he could get.

Her pounding heart stopped suddenly as a third wolf raced into her cage, taking Gunroth down. Sharp fangs snapped closed inches from Quinn's thigh, then Gunroth was on the floor, his wolf's neck caught tight between the other wolf's jaws. He gave a whine of submission, and the larger wolf released him, backing off him to shift into a man in a process that was neither fast nor slow and appeared to cause little pain.

Quinn stared, her heart thundering as the male eyed her with a hard gaze. He was taller than Gunroth, his shoulders massive, his dark hair falling in waves to his shoulders, his eyes black as a Vamp City night.

"Leave us," he snapped.

Peach Fuzz and Gunroth ran in wolf form, Peach Fuzz whining as he went.

Quinn stared at the male, wondering if he'd saved

her from death or simply meant to keep her all for himself.

Stepping forward, he gripped her jaw, forcing her to meet his gaze. "I will remove your gag, sorceress. But if you utter the first word of magic, I'll snap your neck and eat your remains. Is that understood?"

Quinn nodded. An easy promise since she didn't know any magic.

The shifter did as promised, untying the gag and pulling it from her lips, tossing it on the floor.

Moving her lips, stretching her sore jaw, Quinn watched him.

"Are you the one Cristoff searches for?" Black eyes bore into her, and she hesitated, knowing Arturo didn't want the wolves knowing any more than they had to. At the moment, she could pass for someone else, thanks to her glamour. But if they didn't get out of here soon, the glamour would fail, and they'd know the truth, and know they'd been lied to. And she was pretty sure this male would not appreciate being lied to.

"I am. As far as I know, I'm the only one who can save Vamp City."

"Then why did you run?"

Apparently, all of Vamp City knew she'd gone missing.

She swallowed, wondering how much to tell him. Arturo was so much better at this than she was. "I didn't run. Cristoff was torturing me. One of the vampires didn't like it and got me out of there."

"The one who was with you just now?"

"No. Another." That, at least, was the truth. Technically, Kassius had been the one to spring her though at Arturo's request. "How did you know Cristoff lost the sorceress?"

"All of Vamp City knows. The fact that a sorceress had been found spread like wildfire. The news that she'd subsequently been lost spread just as fast."

"The vampire I was captured with . . ." Her breath caught. "Where is he?"

"In the trough." He sniffed her, his nose in her hair, dipping to her neck.

The magic that had never died sparked again beneath her skin.

"What's the trough?"

The alpha straightened. "You do not smell of magic. Yet your eyes are glowing."

"It's what happens when I'm threatened."

He watched her with interest. "Then I do not threaten you. Not now." His eyes narrowed even as he sighed. "In truth, I'm not sure what I'm going to do with you."

She'd like to ask him what the options were, but was afraid she wouldn't like any of them. "What's the trough?" she persisted.

"The feeding tray where my wolves will feast off of him. Food is scarce. And while vampire flesh is tough and stringy, it renews constantly as long as we don't accidentally kill him."

My God. They were eating him alive.

She had to swallow back the bile. *Oh, Vampire.*

"It distresses you that the vampire suffers," the wolf leader murmured, surprised. "He may not have freed you, but you care for him just the same."

She had to learn to hide her reactions better. "He's not like some of the others." She remembered another woman, a Slava, saying the same about another vampire, one Quinn had watched die at the hands of furious humans. Delilah. "You're not the alpha of the Herewood pack, are you? I know Narina's sister, Delilah."

"I am not." He looked at her with interest. "How do you know the alpha's mate's sister?"

"I met her a few weeks ago. I'd like to see her again."

"We are enemies of the Herewood pack."

Of course they were. That would have been too simple. "My arms are killing me. How about we have this discussion with me no longer chained?"

"What am I to do with you? I'd rather leave you here, but I'm afraid another of my wolves will try to break in just as Gunroth did." With a grunt, he strode to the side of the room, where she now saw a small safe tucked into the wall. Turning the dial one way, then the other, he finally opened the door and removed a small set of keys.

Returning to her, he unlocked the cuffs at her wrists.

Quinn lowered her stiff arms, swallowing a groan as the blood began to circulate through her limbs again.

"Turn around."

Quinn looked at him warily. "Why?"

"You will be bound one way or another, sorceress, or you'll not leave this cage."

She stared at him. With a scowl, she turned, not fighting, barely wincing, as he pulled her wrists and cuffed them together.

"Come," he said.

She followed him out of the cage. "Free the vampire."

The alpha glanced back at her with amusement. "My wolves need sustenance. Would you take his place?"

"You know I won't." Arturo would survive it. Probably. She certainly wouldn't. But it had been worth a shot.

He led her through a maze of hallways and up a long stair into what was apparently the main part of a house that had seen far better days. Wallpaper, long faded, covered only strips of walls, the rest having fallen or worn off. The ceiling sagged, the wood floors creaked with every step. And the few furnishings looked like they'd come from the city dump.

Though the house appeared relatively large, if nowhere near the size of Cristoff's castle, it looked like it had been lived in continuously since the 1870s and never updated or adequately maintained. If ever a house looked like it should be haunted, this was it.

The place reeked of dog . . . or wolf, which wasn't too surprising, considering. Though a few people—well-muscled and naked people—walked about or lounged on the furniture, they had to vie for room with more than two dozen wolves. The animals were everywhere.

At her appearance, they lifted their snouts, as if sniffing the air, and turned to watch her with interest. Several leaped to their feet, one licking his lips as he tracked her with hungry eyes.

Quinn's skin crawled, and she found herself edging closer to the alpha.

Did wolves do nothing but lie around, threatening their food? If this were her pack, she'd order them to find some tools and get to work fixing up the house. But maybe wolves just didn't care about the looks of their living space.

They'd probably care if the roof fell on their heads.

As if hearing her thoughts, the alpha said, "It's

solid, despite what it looks like. Most of my wolves spend the majority of their time outside. They're far more wolf than human." He eyed her with a warning in his eyes. "You'd do well to remember that."

Quinn swallowed, her gaze fastened on one who watched her as if she were a fat little rabbit. "It's rather hard to forget."

A man's yell of pain carried from outside, jacking her pulse through the roof. She knew that voice. *Arturo.*

She had to get him out of there. But how? An energy blast was too temporary to do her much good. She'd watched how quickly the wolves had righted themselves after being thrown back. And her gun was gone.

No, she needed another idea.

"Why do you eat vampires and humans?" she demanded. "Why not deer. Or chickens?"

The alpha glanced at her, his expression bored. "I'm sure the deer and chickens prefer we eat you." He shrugged one massive shoulder. "We actually prefer beef or pork. And while we've never been successful raising our own in this place, we're happy enough with cuts straight from the market."

She looked at him askance. "All you need is a *grocery-store* run?"

He scowled. "Do you *see* a grocery store around here?"

"There have to be markets."

"Run by Traders, yes. We are at war with the vampires, at war with the Traders."

"Maybe you wouldn't be if you quit eating them."

The gaze he turned on her was filled with annoyance. "We did not turn on them in that way until we had no other choice. When the magic first began to fail, the vast majority of the Traders fled, unwilling to risk their hides since no one knows for certain what will happen when Vamp City disintegrates. As the shipments declined, the wolves began to go hungry. Unfortunately"—his mouth tightened—"a couple of rogue wolves from the Herewood pack ate the last Traders who were providing us meat."

"So now the Traders won't come near you."

"No."

"And you're trapped in Vamp City, too?"

"We have been trapped since Vamp City's earliest years. Like the human Slavas, the weres here turned immortal and now can never leave."

This place just got more and more complicated.

"What if I could get you a shipment?" To free Arturo, she was certain that Micah would find a way to smuggle the contents of a butcher store into Vamp City.

For the first time, the werewolf looked at her with something approaching interest. "I have forty wolves, sorceress. That is a lot of mouths to feed. How would *you* procure such a feast?"

"I actually have better connections than you might think." It was odd to realize that was true.

"But that would mean releasing you. And trusting you. And that would be foolish."

"You have a reason for me to return."

The werewolf scoffed. "He is a vampire. Not reason enough." His hand sliced the air. "No more. I am through discussing this."

She wasn't through, not by a long shot. But she'd bide her time. And hope the vampire still had time.

As hungry eyes bored into her back, the alpha

led her into a room, a study that looked like it belonged in a different house. A large desk dominated
the room, and bookshelves lined the walls. A woman
sat on one of the chairs, wearing what appeared to
be a sleek green satin nightgown, but at least she had
something on, unlike the two muscular, naked males
standing on either side of the hearth, each with a
glass of amber liquid in his hands.

The tableau had a genteel quality about it. Or it
might have had if not for the dangling penises.

The three looked at her with interest and the same
hunger she'd seen in the other wolves' eyes. She remembered too well how Gunroth had leaped at her
as he'd sought to eat her.

Her jaw turned rigid, sweat gathering at the back
of her neck as the suspicion that she'd been led to
a private slaughter raised its ugly head. Once more,
sparks began to dance and burn beneath her skin.

"The sorceress?" the woman asked.

"Yes." The alpha began searching through the
books on his shelves. "The rumor that sorcerer flesh
empowers the eater refuses to die."

One of the males scoffed and took a sip of the
liquid. Probably whiskey. "It's a stupid myth. There's
not an ounce of logic to it."

"And yet the pack continues to believe it," the
woman murmured.

"We need her alive," the alpha said. "The magic of
Vamp City must be renewed."

"We could feed them her legs," the second gentleman drawled. "She'd survive that. At least long
enough to renew the magic."

"You take my legs, and I won't be renewing any
magic." But the thought of it sent chills along her

spine just as Cristoff's threat to cut off her feet had. "Nor will I procure that shipment of meat for you that I offered your alpha."

She'd expected . . . hoped . . . to see some spark of interest in their expressions. Instead, they just eyed her with amusement.

"Why did you let her out?" the woman asked, her tone deferential but curious. Straight, shoulder-length hair framed an attractive, middle-aged face.

"Gunroth picked the lock on her cage. I'm not going to be able to let her out of my sight." The alpha made a sound of satisfaction and pulled down one of the books. "Here we go. I've done a lot of research on the old ways, recently, seeking a strategy for surviving the magic's failing. Long ago, when the world was full of sorcerers, the wolves often aligned themselves with a magic wielder for protection." He glanced at Quinn. "And power."

"The sorcerers shared their power willingly?" one of the men asked.

"At times," the alpha said cryptically. "The protection went both ways."

"How?" the woman asked.

"The moon ritual." The alpha flipped through the book. "Ah, this is it. Waiting until a full moon would be best, but it's not necessary."

"What exactly is the moon ritual?" Quinn asked. Inside, she was terrified—that Arturo was going to die before she could get him out of that trough, that the wolves were going to kill her before she could renew the magic and save Zack. But if werewolves were anything like real wolves, the last thing she could afford to do was show that, or any, weakness.

"It speaks again," one of the males drawled.

Quinn glared at him. "*It* thinks you might look better as a toad."

The male stared at her, his eyes widening a fraction. "You wouldn't."

If only she could. She snorted. "Try me."

"Enough," the alpha said without heat. "You'll survive the ritual, sorceress, but the moment the ritual is over, word will be sent to Cristoff that we have you."

"*What?* Do you really think he'll bring you meat? He'll kill you, werewolf. He'll slaughter your pack or capture them for torture. He's the last person you want to call."

The alpha glanced up at her as if she were a difficult student interrupting his class. "Cristoff will pay handsomely to get you back."

She wanted to scream her frustration. What could she possibly say, or do, that would make a difference to them?

The alpha continued to peruse the book. "We'll perform the ritual tonight at midnight." He glanced at Quinn. "Make yourself comfortable, sorceress. You're not leaving this room until then. And neither am I."

Midnight. And it apparently wasn't even night yet. That was hours from now, hours more that Arturo would be eaten alive. Hours in which Vintry might die. And she still didn't know what the moon ritual was or what it would cost her.

The only bright spot in any of this was that Arturo had talked her out of bringing Zack with them. At least her brother was safe.

But she and Arturo were in a world of hurt.

CHAPTER THIRTEEN

Sweat ran down the sides of Quinn's face, sliding through her hair and between her bare breasts. If she'd been dressed, her clothes would be drenched with perspiration, but the wolves had declared that she had to be as naked as they were for their moon ritual. Standing in the center of a circle ringed by five bonfires, she wasn't sure she minded the lack of clothes. She certainly didn't stand out. And, technically, it wasn't even her body on display. Micah's glamour had yet to wear off.

No, of far more concern was the fact that she was tied to a stake in the middle of the open ground, unable to run if any of the three dozen wolves racing around her decided to turn and take a bite out of her instead. Her only protection were the four human werewolves—the alpha and his friends, who stood with their backs to her, presumably to keep the other wolves from getting too close.

Though it was called a moon ritual, Quinn could see no sign of the moon peeking through the thick layer of clouds above. The breeze blew lightly. She wondered at the wisdom of building open fires in a land filled with dead trees.

The alpha began to chant in a deep, rhythmic voice, words that hardly sounded human. As she watched, the racing wolves slowly stopped, then began to change into human form, taking up the chant. One of them ran outside the hot, hot circle, returning moments later with a large white bucket filled with something.

Paintballs.

Quinn watched in bemusement as the wolves picked out one at a time, squeezing the paint on their naked skin in streaks and swirls of yellow, blue, and red. Paintballs. Quinn shook her head. The were-wolves' ancestors were either rolling in their graves or cackling with glee. Even life as a primitive could be enhanced by modern invention, she supposed.

As the chanting grew louder, the wolves slowly abandoned the paintball bucket, dividing into five separate groups, each one encircling one of the bon-fires, dancing around it.

Quinn's skin began to itch. The magic beneath her flesh had died down after she'd slammed Gunroth and Peach Fuzz back when they'd tried to attack her in her prison cell, and she had yet to be able to build it up again. During the interminable wait for mid-night, she'd tried a dozen ways to convince the alpha to let her and the vampire go, but with her hands tied and her magic unresponsive, she'd had little leverage and made no headway.

Her magic was back, finally, but in a way she'd never felt before. Instead of crawling beneath her skin, the power danced across the surface, a sensa-tion growing more uncomfortable by the minute as it turned to a feeling of pinpricks, then pinches.

Quinn gasped as the pinches turned increasingly painful.

"What's happening?" she demanded.

"You will share your power with us." The alpha reached into the bucket and pulled out several paintballs. He tossed one each to his companions, who began to paint their bodies as the rest of the pack had already done.

"What do you mean by *share*?" She was beginning to feel as if invisible hands were attempting to pry the skin from her body.

The alpha met her gaze, his eyes hard. "Ancient sorcerers shared their power with the wolves on a regular basis. You will do the same."

But the ancient sorcerers' power hadn't been chained by a curse.

"They did so willingly!" She presumed so, anyway. "Free me and my companion, and I'll give you what you want. Hurting me, perhaps even killing me, will buy you nothing."

But the alpha ignored her as he and his four compatriots began to circle her, chanting words different from the others'. Discomfort turned to true pain until tears pooled in her eyes, and she was struggling to breathe.

"Stop this!" she cried.

Suddenly, the alpha was in her face, his visage ferocious as he pressed sweaty palms against her sweatier temples. "You hold back on us, sorceress," he growled. "Give it up!"

"I'll give you nothing if you're going to hurt me!"

His hands turned to fire, burning through her skull, and she screamed from the pain. She fought to throw him back with her mind, struggled to pull away from his fiery hands . . .

And suddenly the light went out. The night went silent.

The alpha jerked back, his hands lifting from her sweat-soaked skin. "What did you do?"

"What happened?" She couldn't see him, couldn't see anything but the flames from the bonfire that felt permanently etched onto the backs of her eyelids. Good grief, if he weren't standing here with her, she'd suspect she'd died.

But, no, she was still tied to the stake, her skin still burning, though the pain was becoming less and less with every passing second. Despite the lack of light, the heat and scent of the bonfires lingered as if they'd been here and were now gone. As if something or someone had sent them all away, wolves, fires, everything.

"What did you do?" the alpha growled again.

"I didn't do anything!" Not intentionally, anyway. *Could* she have done this? And what was *this*?

She heard the alpha move away, heard him stumble back, swearing. "There are walls all around us. You've caught us in some kind of trap. Some kind of bubble."

Quinn's eyes went wide, a chill sliding down her spine. A bubble. Wasn't that exactly what Vamp City was, only on a far grander scale? Was that what she'd done here, duplicated the small space around her? What if this was how Phineas Blackstone had discovered his own ability to create other worlds?

As her eyes adjusted to the dark, she began to see shimmers all around her, like black opals. The walls of the bubble, the walls of the magic. Good God Almighty, *she had power.*

Against that opalescent darkness, a shadow moved, and she felt a hand grip her jaw hard.

"Undo it!"

Not only did she have power, she had leverage. "Untie me."

He growled. "Perhaps I'll just kill you."

"Killing Blackstone didn't undo Vamp City. If killing me fails, you'll be stuck here forever."

Silence. The hand disappeared. "You've created an alternate world," he breathed.

"Apparently so."

"*How?*"

Ha. "Magic. Untie me."

"If you created this place, you can escape it."

"I can also take you with me. If I want to." Probably. She'd pulled humans through sunbeams; there was no reason to think she couldn't pull a werewolf out of a bubble she'd created assuming magic worked with any kind of logic whatsoever. "But first, we're going to come to an agreement."

She saw the dark shape of the male move against the black opal background and felt his breath on her cheek. His hard body suddenly pressed against hers, reminding her in a startlingly raw manner that they were both naked. His thick penis brushed her thigh. It was flaccid at the moment, but she suspected a determined male could change that.

A shiver of fear rippled through her, but she pushed it away. She'd waited too long to get the upper hand. She wasn't about to let him steal it now.

"You're in no position to negotiate," the wolf alpha growled.

Quinn snorted. "*Au contraire*. I'm in a damn good position to negotiate. Now that I've created one of these things, there's a good chance I can make more. The next one might just catch your entire pack."

He pressed against her hard, his menace barely controlled. "You will release me *now,* sorceress."

"Well, here's the thing, dude. The only way you're getting out of here is if I take your hand and lead you out. Which means *you're* going to release *me.* Now. My arms are tired."

He growled low, but a moment later, he was gone and she felt his fingers pulling the ropes from her wrists. The moment she was free, he grabbed her and jerked her toward the nearest wall.

Quinn felt the magic pulling to suck her through, but she pushed against it and felt the male at her side stumble back even as he kept tight hold on her.

"We're not leaving until I say we are," she told him smoothly, stifling a smile. She rather enjoyed having the werewolf under her control. For the moment.

The alpha's fingers dug into her arms, and he jerked her around, pulling her hard against him, letting her feel the erection that now protruded from his body.

"I will hurt you, sorceress." But he was holding the losing hand, now, and they both knew it.

"See, that's where your threat goes awry, wolf man. I know what your ultimate plan is, to hand me over to Cristoff. And there is nothing you can threaten me with . . . *nothing* . . . that is worse than what he'll do to me if he gets his hands on me again. Besides, we both know you can't kill me, or even hurt me badly enough to risk it. Because if I don't renew the magic, if Vamp City fails, you and your pack are toast."

She felt the rhythm of his breathing change, the menace easing down, the frustration skyrocketing. But the hard grip on her arms didn't change.

If he were another male, she might try a more diplomatic approach, a bit of stroking his male ego, perhaps, or injecting a bit of friendliness into the exchange. But real wolves responded to authority and power above all, and she suspected werewolves did, too. Any show of niceness would only be construed as weakness, and that was a thing she couldn't afford.

"We both want the same thing, wolf—to get Vamp City's magic renewed. You've seen what I can do. And I can assure you, my power is growing by the day. I've barely tapped into it. I could become a powerful ally. Or I *will* become a dangerous enemy. Your choice."

His grip on her tightened, fractionally, revealing his frustration. "What do you mean you've barely tapped into your power?"

She briefly considered how much to tell him, then decided she didn't have a lot to lose by holding back. She had far more to gain by making an ally of this male.

"Apparently, I've got more power than I know what to do with, but it's being hampered by a curse. I need to free my magic before I can save Vamp City, but the only two who can help me are the vampire in your feeding trough and an aging fae who is dying as we speak. I'm running out of time, wolf. And we're all going to suffer if I fail. You could help me. And I'll help you and your pack in return."

"Cristoff is the only one who can renew the magic."

"Cristoff has Phineas Blackstone's sons under his control. I'll probably need their help, but they can't renew the magic, or they'd have done it already. Cristoff wants me because he likes power, but I don't need him. I can absolutely renew the magic without him." God help her if she couldn't.

Silence fell as the werewolf released her. He looked up as if admiring her handiwork, as if contemplating her offer. "You have power, sorceress, there's no doubt of that."

"I can also get you food, wolf. I can arrange a shipment of meat from one of the local grocery stores."

He was quiet for several more minutes before he apparently came to a decision. "Free me from this bubble, and I will free you and your vampire companion. You will send the food at once. And when you come into your power, you will return and share it with us."

"And *not* tied to your stake."

"As an honored guest. I give you my word."

"I hope your word means more than a vampire's."

"My word is granite. Solid and unbreakable." His voice told her she'd offended him by questioning that. But he added in a less harsh voice. "I'm beginning to think you will make a better ally than dinner."

Quinn made a sound of amusement. "I appreciate that. Are you ready to get out of here?"

"Most ready."

"Me, too."

She reached for his hand and felt his fingers curl tightly around hers as if he feared she'd try to escape and leave him behind. Leading him, she started for the black opal wall. But when, by all rights, the magic should have embraced her, it threw her back, taking the wolf with her.

"Sorceress," he snarled, grabbing her again.

"I didn't do that on purpose! I'm still figuring out how all this works."

He plowed into her suddenly, knocking her to the ground and landing heavily on top of her.

"Wolf," she gasped.

He was off her a moment later, then slamming into her again, knocking her down when she tried to get up.

"*What are you doing?*" she cried.

He curved his arm around her shoulder, pressing close. "The walls of your bubble . . . they're shrinking."

Oh, shit. Quinn reached out her hand, feeling the rubbery surface against her fingertips. Reaching in the other direction, she found it again. Too quickly. Like the wolf said, the walls were shrinking. And her hand wasn't going through.

Her heart began to pound. She'd made this world. She had to be able to get out.

The rubbery feel crowded them from every direction, knocking them one way, then the other until they had nowhere left to move. Slowly it pressed them together, Quinn's back to the alpha's chest, growing tighter and tighter.

As the bubble compressed, as Quinn felt it brushing her face, she threw her hands up, trying to make space for her mouth and nose. With a bolt of pure terror she realized that soon she wouldn't even be able to breathe. It was as if they were being wrapped in cellophane, the air being slowly sucked away.

"Sorceress!"

Her own freaking magic was going to kill her, and no one would ever know. Zack would never know.

I won't die here.

The power began to dance beneath her skin, sparking, tripping, burning her flesh as badly as the lack of air was beginning to burn her lungs. Recognizing that this was her chance, she embraced the terror, embraced the fear that her death would mean Zack's death, too.

And suddenly her magic tore loose.

Heat, light, and sound blasted her, sweet sweaty air tore into her lungs as the bubble burst, as she and the wolf collapsed, together, onto the ground, light-headed and gasping.

Wolves circled her, snarling, snapping inches from her face. But as she threw up her hands to ward them off, the alpha leaped to his feet, shouting.

"Halt! Down. Now!" The wolves backed off, and the alpha helped her to her feet. "Just as Blackstone created Vamp City, the sorceress created a small bubble of a world, a place for us to talk, and negotiate, in private." That was one way to spin it. "Once the sorceress has renewed the magic of Vamp City, she will return and share her power with us. Bring the vampire in the trough to me. He's her protector and henceforth will not be harmed."

Releasing Quinn, he lifted both hands. "Douse the flames."

As the wolves began scooping up dirt to put out the fires, the alphas' three friends gathered close around them.

"You trust her, then, Savin?" the woman asked.

"She holds no love for Cristoff. He's tortured her."

The woman nodded as if that answered her question. The enemy of my enemy and all that?

A couple of minutes later, Arturo was led forward, naked and stumbling. Quinn gasped at the sight of him, her stomach roiling until she thought she might be sick. His bloody legs were more bone than flesh. His skin was paler than she'd ever seen it, his eyes gleamed white-centered with hunger, though he kept his fangs behind his lips.

Quinn's heart twisted to see the powerful vampire brought so low. "Have you fed him?" she demanded.

The werewolf who held him shook his head.

Quinn gave the alpha a look of disgust.

He lifted his hands. "I thought he was dinner."

Quinn strode forward, pushing the werewolf male away, taking Arturo's ice-cold arm. "You need to feed. Drink from me."

Arturo shook his head, his eyes glassy, but focused on her. "No. Not you. You are unharmed?" His voice was hoarse from screaming. Lines of strain bracketed his mouth.

"I'm fine. You need to feed."

"No, *tesoro mio*. Your blood is too sweet." He sounded exhausted. "I will not be able to stop."

How many hours had he suffered? She went lightheaded at the thought of the pain he must have endured.

The alpha stepped forward. "The sorceress has negotiated your release, vampire. Both of yours. I hope you will honor the terms of that release."

Quinn eyed him with a question. "What terms? The food shipment?"

"That, and the vampire shall never attempt retribution for what was done to him here."

Those terms. "The second is up to him, though I suspect that allowing him to feed on one of you might alleviate his need for retribution."

Arturo nodded slowly. "It might." He turned to her, his eyes going hard even as they flickered with pain. "I felt your terror soon after you awoke. Were you harmed?"

"No. One of the wolves tried to reach me, but the alpha here stopped him."

"Let me seek vengeance on the wolf who tried to hurt her," Arturo said to the alpha. "Then I will give my word to this treaty."

"You cannot kill him."

"Agreed."

Savin yelled, "Gunroth!"

A moment later, a large gray wolf slunk slowly toward them.

"Shed your fur."

The wolf's eyes gleamed, hard and belligerent. But a deep growl from the human throat of his alpha had the wolf hanging his head in submission. And a moment later, Gunroth the man was standing before them, his mouth hard, his eyes shining with fear.

"This is the wolf who tried to reach your sorceress. He disobeyed my direct order and picked the lock of her cage intending to eat her, Vampire. You will not kill him or the treaty is forfeit. Short of that, you may feed from him thoroughly and with my blessing. Seek your vengeance on him for what was done to you and for what he intended to do to your companion." Savin's gaze turned to the wolf. "And he will submit, fully, or be banished from this pack."

The bearded werewolf began to visibly shake, the whites of his eyes gleaming with light from the dying fire, but he nodded.

Savin stepped forward and removed the silver chain from around Arturo's neck. Arturo turned to Quinn. "I do not wish for you to see this, *cara*. Turn away. Please."

With a deep sigh, she did as he asked, not only turning away, but walking away.

She heard the snarl, the rip of flesh, the scream of pain, and felt no pity. Gunroth would have torn into her with the same level of viciousness, knowing she'd never heal, knowing he was killing her. And while it might not have been personal, she'd have been dead all the same.

The female friend of Savin's stepped beside her. "I'll fetch your clothes and the vampire's."

Quinn looked at her. "And my weapons."

The woman glanced at Savin, who nodded. By the time the woman returned, the noise had died down to mere groans. Then, finally, to nothing.

Quinn quickly dressed and armed herself. Arturo joined her, looking almost normal again if still a bit pale. As he dressed, she watched him. "Feel better?"

He gave her a brusque nod. If he had more to say, he wasn't saying it within wolf hearing.

To her surprise, another of the werewolves led their horses to them. "I figured they'd eaten them," she muttered to Arturo.

"No one kills a horse," he said. "They are far too valuable."

"Unlike humans," she added darkly.

Savin joined them, and Arturo met the alpha's gaze, a powerful vampire once more. "I will abide by the terms of the sorceress's treaty; however, I would add one more condition."

Savin lifted a brow.

"Cristoff searches for her. He would hurt her, and I would not have it."

"I have no use for Cristoff. No one will know you were here."

Arturo gave a nod, then turned to Quinn. But before he could usher her to the horses, she turned to the wolf. "Good-bye, Savin."

"I look forward to the shipment, sorceress. And to your return. In the meantime, I will provide you a wolf escort—" The alpha jerked back, staring at her. Gasps peppered the air around them.

Quinn cocked her head warily, but Arturo cleared up the mystery. "Your glamour has worn off."

Quinn glanced at her hand, now gleaming pale in the firelight. She met Savin's shocked gaze with a rueful shrug. "Now you know what I really look like."

The alpha stared at her a moment more, then began to laugh. "Working with a sorceress will take some getting used to." To her surprise, he took her hand in a move that was distinctly friendly. "Anytime you are in the Crux, shout my name, and if my wolves are within hearing distance, they will provide you safe escort."

"I will. Thank you."

Arturo helped her onto her horse, then mounted his own. As promised, several wolves escorted them for quite a way before falling back. Arturo lifted a hand in thanks as the two of them continued on, alone.

"I'm sorry you went through that, Arturo," she said quietly. He looked a thousand times better than he had when they'd first pulled him from the trough, but he still didn't look well. "Will you heal completely?"

"I'm fine."

"Vampire . . ." She ached for him, for what he'd endured. His yells would echo in her ears for a long, long time.

"I'm fine, Quinn. Leave it at that." But his tone said otherwise. And she hurt for both of them.

He needed time to heal, physically, mentally, and emotionally. But there was no time. If they wanted any chance of saving Vamp City, and Zack, they had to reach Vintry as quickly as possible. There was no way in hell she was letting Arturo seek out the dying fae in this condition, without her. They would head for Fabian's castle together.

Even if Arturo fought her every step of the way.

CHAPTER FOURTEEN

As Quinn and Arturo rode back to Neo's, Arturo was silent. Brooding. The landscape was dark as pitch, and Quinn couldn't see a thing, but her horse seemed to be able to follow Arturo's, so she gave the horse his head and concentrated on not falling asleep in the saddle. She was exhausted. But with Vintry's life going quickly down the drain, sleep was a luxury she couldn't afford.

The rumble of the earth startled her into full wakefulness. Moments later, flashes of light appeared here and there across the landscape. Not sunbeams—it was the middle of the night. But streetlights, car headlights, the nighttime glow of the city. She could see them, sprinkled through the dead trees and it gave her chills.

"It's getting worse," she murmured. The bleedthroughs were everywhere.

"Did you tell them my name?" Arturo's words took her by surprise, yanking her thoughts back to the wolves. He still sounded so . . . spent.

"No. I was careful about that. They didn't seem to recognize you."

"Wolves . . . are Kas's job."

Kassius, she knew, was a vampire and a wolf. A werevamp. "I imagine it is. Does he get along with the other wolves?"

Silhouetted against a distant bleed-through of a streetlamp, she saw Arturo glance at her though she couldn't read his expression. If she had to guess, she suspected he wasn't sure he liked that she knew that Kassius was a wolf. She wouldn't have known if Kassius hadn't bitten her to get the truth out of her at Cristoff's insistence. And if she hadn't stolen a few truths from him in return.

"No," was all he said. And even that word seemed to cost him.

They fell once more into silence. She had things to tell him—the bubble, for one. But now wasn't the time, so she held her tongue and kept an eye out for more trouble.

Movement caught her eye in the distance. A couple of figures on horseback silhouetted against an office building's nighttime lights.

"We've got company," she murmured, preparing to reach for her gun. Or maybe her knife since she wasn't sure how many bullets she had left.

"It is Micah and Neo."

It always surprised her that he could see so well in the dark. From what she'd been able to gather, vampire senses were not superhuman, exactly. They weren't that much better than her own. Except for their night vision, which was a huge advantage.

Arturo turned toward the other two vampires, and they met in the middle a few minutes later.

"Where the hell have you been?" Micah demanded. "We've been looking everywhere for you." He frowned, peering at Arturo closely. "You look like hell. When was the last time you fed, Ax?"

Arturo ignored the questions. "Fabian's. ASAP."

Quinn's jaw dropped. "After what you've been

through? You need time to recover." But even as she said the words, she heard the fallacy in them.

"No time," he said, voicing her thought. He turned to Neo. "Take Quinn."

"No way. I'm going with you."

"You're staying," he snarled.

"No," she replied calmly. "I'm not."

Micah looked from one of them to the other. "Ax, you look terrible. What happened?"

When Arturo made no move to reply, Quinn did it for him. "Wolves. He's been in their feeding trough almost since we left here."

Micah whistled low, turning to his friend. "And you haven't fed."

"He has," Quinn replied, when Arturo remained mute. "He just did."

The bleed-throughs disappeared suddenly, the worlds closing once more. And once more she couldn't see her hand in front of her face.

"Are you okay, Quinn?" Neo asked, his voice warm with concern.

"They didn't hurt me. The alpha and I came to an agreement . . . after I almost killed him. I promised them a shipment of beef and pork, by the way. I hope you can help me honor that. I suspect they could be valuable allies."

The silence that met her request had a heaviness that told her she'd made a mistake. Or overstepped.

"Is that a problem?" she asked.

"Mukdalla's son was killed trying to deliver store-bought meat to the wolves six months ago. The wolves killed him."

Quinn's heart clenched. "Poor Mukdalla. But Savin said the wolves that killed the Traders were from the Herewood pack, not his. I made a promise, Neo. We'll have more trouble with the wolves, not less, if I fail to honor it."

"Discuss this later," Arturo snapped, startling her. "We need to go."

Suddenly, there was a flurry of movement between the vamps and she heard Micah's low curse. She hated not being able to see!

"Back to Neo's, Ax. You're in no condition to go anywhere like this. There's too much at stake to risk screwing this up."

"What happened?" she demanded, as the horses started forward again.

"He nearly fell off his horse," Micah told her. "I thought you said he fed."

"He did. I thought he did. It certainly sounded like it."

"I fed," Arturo grumbled, but he sounded completely exhausted.

"What's at Fabian's?" Neo asked.

When Arturo didn't answer, Quinn did, suspecting he was using all his concentration to stay on the horse.

"Tarellia said that Fabian's sage, Vintry, is the only one who might be able to help me free my magic, but he's aging. There's not much time. And that was yesterday morning."

They continued in silence until, finally, the faint lights of Neo's house appeared between the trees. They rode into Neo's courtyard, and Quinn dismounted easily, handing her reins to one of Neo's men—vampire or human, she wasn't sure. Neo led the way in through the back door, and Quinn followed, Arturo and Micah close behind.

"Your eyes have turned white, Ax," Micah murmured as they closed the door behind them. "He needs blood, Neo. And fear. A lot of it."

Neo frowned. "I'll send someone, but you must ensure he doesn't accidentally hurt her."

"I'll stay with them."

Neo called to one of his people. "Bring Marissa to 3A. At once." To them he said, "She just arrived last night and is still utterly terrified."

"I'll clear her mind when he's through," Micah assured Neo. "She won't be harmed."

Though Quinn followed them downstairs, she remained in the hallway as Micah led Arturo into one of the bedrooms, and a young woman was escorted there soon after. The door shut behind her, and a moment later, her bloodcurdling scream tore through the underground.

Quinn went rigid.

Neo squeezed her shoulder. "He's not hurting her, you know that. He's scaring her because he has to. Because he has to feed."

"I know." She looked at him. "I swear he just fed from a wolf."

"Who probably had little fear in him."

She wasn't so sure about that, considering what Arturo almost certainly did to him. With a shake of her head, she moved away. "Do you know where Zack is? I can't listen to this." The poor girl was *terrified*.

"It's the middle of the night. He's probably in bed."

"Right." It was so hard to remember night and day in a land without a rising and setting sun.

But when she checked his bedroom, she found it

empty. As she headed back into the main room, she caught sight of Mukdalla's vampire husband.

"Rinaldo."

He turned to her with a smile. "Sorceress."

"Do you know where my brother is?"

"With Jason, I believe. Last I saw them, they were in the study." He pointed down yet another hallway. "Third doorway on your left."

Quinn thanked him, the muscles of her neck and shoulders easing as the screaming finally quieted. She found Zack sitting at a long table in a room lined with bookshelves. He was shoulder to shoulder with Jason as they peered at something in Zack's hand. A Gameboy.

"Damn, you're good," Jason muttered. "It's my turn."

Zack grinned. "Give me a computer or game player, and I can kick anyone's ass."

Jason grunted, accepting the Gameboy. "You'll be kicking vampire ass by the time I'm through with you. One more game, then we get some sleep."

"I'm not tired."

"I am."

Quinn watched them, glad that Zack and Jason seemed to be getting along. Happier still that Jason had, wisely and amazingly, found a way to remind Zack of the things he *was* good at.

She walked fully into the room, joining them at the table. "Hey."

Zack looked up, relief in his eyes. "You were gone a long time. Everything go okay?"

"Yes and no. We found the fae, but she can't help me. There's someone else we have to find. We may be gone a couple of days."

"*Days?*"

"It's hard to tell. Nothing happens quickly in this place."

"And you're still not going to let me go?"

She shook her head apologetically. "We'll be going in undercover." At his frown, she added, "I'll be fine, Zack. Arturo and Micah are going with me."

"Any word on Lily?"

Quinn shook her head, hating the disappointment that tightened her brother's jaw. "Arturo's sent someone to find her. As soon as Arturo hears anything, I'm certain he'll let you know."

She slid her hand against the side of Zack's neck and grimaced. He was hotter than before.

"If Arturo's not going after her, I am."

Jason set the Gameboy down, meeting Zack's gaze calmly. "Then come morning, let's get back to work. If you attempt a rescue untrained, you could hurt her more than you help her. Training is key."

Zack stared at him morosely, then released a hard huff. "I know."

The thought of Zack's attempting a rescue attempt on his own terrified her. But Jason was a good, calm influence. And Zack did need to learn how to fight, if only to protect himself.

Zack glanced at her again. "How soon are you leaving?"

"I'm not sure. Arturo's getting a bite to eat . . ."

Jason snorted.

Zack eyed her with concern. "Be careful, sis."

She gave into the urge and kissed him on the cheek. "I will. You, too." Then she headed back to the room where Arturo fed, needing to know the vampire was going to be okay.

She only had to cool her heels in the hallway for a few minutes before the door opened, and Micah stepped out, the girl at his side, smiling, the two fang wounds on her neck barely visible and already healing.

"What kind of dance?" Micah asked kindly, meeting Quinn's gaze with a knowing look before turning back to the girl.

"Jazz mostly, but I take one ballet class a week, and I've been thinking about trying hip-hop."

As the two disappeared down the hall, Quinn stepped into the doorway. Arturo sat on the bed, his head in his hands.

"Better?" she asked quietly.

"Come in, *cara mia.*" He lowered his hands and looked up at her wearily. His eyes were back to normal, but he still looked tired and beaten. Maybe it would just take time for him to recover.

She sat beside him and took his cold hand in hers, then gave in to the urge and leaned against him, resting her head on his shoulder. "I'm sorry."

She felt his mouth buss her hair.

"That feeding didn't help you, either, did it? You're so cold. I've never felt you so cold."

"It is not blood that I still require. Nor fear."

Her brows drawing together, she straightened and looked at him. His eyes were normal, his fangs not elongated. "What do you need?"

He stared at her, his own brows lowered as he reached up to caress her cheek. "It makes no sense, *bella,* but there is one thing and one thing alone that I crave. That I must have."

"What?"

"You. Your sunshine. Your warmth." The thumb

that slid softly across her bottom lip trembled subtly.
"Your kiss." The depth of need in his voice, in his
eyes, caught at something deep inside of her.

With shaking hands, he framed her face, his need
not quite hunger. Nor quite passion. But there was
no denying it existed. Her breath turned shallow as
he stared at her, as he stroked that unsteady thumb
across her lips.

"I must kiss you, *cara*. Do not deny me this."

"I won't." She reached for him.

He dipped his head, slowly this time, his mouth
covering hers, his cold, closed lips pressing against
hers, just that. But with that simple touch, she felt
the tension go out of him as if his body sighed. His
hands on her face gentled even more, a featherlight
caress. And she shuddered, a longing deep inside her
stirring, making her eyes sting. She'd been so worried
the wolves would kill him.

Lifting her arms, she slid her hands to the back
of his neck, then he was pulling her tight against
him, one hand in her hair, the other around her
waist as he swept his tongue into her mouth, claiming her, drinking of her as if she were the only thing
he needed to survive. Her body softened, heating,
as affection for this difficult, dangerous male surged
within her.

And still he drank of her kiss. His lips began to
warm. Beneath her hands, his flesh warmed, too.
And still he kissed her, making no move to do more.
The door was still open, but somehow she doubted
that would stop him if he wanted to coax her beneath
him.

Instead, he pulled away, his lips pressing a kiss to
her cheekbone, her eyebrow, her temple. Breathing

hard, he pulled her against him, pressing her head to his shoulder as he held her close. Just that.

"I failed you," he said softly, his tone devastated. "Again."

"No."

"I did not protect you."

Quinn pulled back, lifting her hand to his face, to his warm flesh. "You were battling a pack of wolves and a sorceress's magic at the same time. You may be fast, and strong, but you're not Superman." She stroked his cheek. "The only way you've ever failed me was in betraying my trust and handing me over to Cristoff. You didn't betray me this time, Arturo. I know you tried to reach me." Stroking his cheek again, she smiled. "You're warm. And you look better."

He didn't return her smile. Instead, as his hands caressed her hips, he watched her with a bemused expression. "I needed your sunshine."

She frowned. "You really did, didn't you? How can that be?"

"I do not know. You feed me in a way I do not understand. The girl's fear left me cold."

"Literally."

"Yes." He stroked her cheek. "You are becoming important to me in ways I would not have thought possible. I do not want to take you with me, *tesoro*."

I do not want to. Not *I won't.* They were making progress. "We're out of time, you know that."

"It is a terrible risk, *cara*."

"Isn't everything in this world? Vintry can't die before he helps me, you know that. We can't let that happen."

"Because of Zack."

"Yes. Of course."

He watched her for several thick moments. "If Zack were not tied to the magic . . . would you renew it?"

Would she? She looked away, uncertain what to tell him. There were good people here, she was convinced of that, now. But there was so much evil, too. Arturo believed the evil would lessen once the magic was renewed, but what if he was wrong?

"I don't know," she said honestly, meeting his gaze.

He looked at her in disappointment, then released her and rose. "Come, then. Micah will renew your glamour. And we shall go."

CHAPTER FIFTEEN

Quinn found herself drifting off to the rhythmic movement of her horse a short while later. Arturo and Micah accompanied her as they rode toward Fabian's stronghold, and Vintry. Before they'd left, Micah had renewed her glamour. She once more looked like Neo's sister, though this time with a Slava's opalescent glow in her black hair. The vampires agreed that it might help protect her since, apparently, *freshies*—mortal humans—were the coin of the realm at the moment. The best an enterprising Trader could do with a captured Slava was hope for a reward. But freshies were fair game and could be bought and sold at will.

Of course, by pretending to be a Slava, she ran a greater risk of being injured. The immortal Slavas were sometimes treated far more roughly—in Cristoff's house, brutally. Hopefully, since she supposedly belonged to Arturo, they'd leave her alone.

Micah had warned her that her glamour wouldn't last as long this time. Creating the glamour took a lot of energy, energy he needed time to renew. And before they reached the stronghold, he was going to have to glamour himself since the plan was for him to enter in the guise of one of Fabian's guards. Any way they looked at it, they wouldn't have much time.

The clouds had broken up a bit since their first ride tonight, allowing the moonlight to filter through. Why the moon and stars were visible through the Vamp City bubble, but the sun and sunlight, not to mention the real world, weren't, she didn't know. It scrambled her scientific mind. Despite the moonlight, she couldn't see much—her companions were little more than dark shadows on either side of her—but at least she didn't feel like she'd fallen into a well.

"So, what else do I need to know before we get there?" she asked the two vampires. They'd convinced her to leave her gun and stakes behind since both could be construed as weapons of aggression against a rival vampire master. But they had no objections to her switchblade. Everyone in Vamp City, apparently, carried a knife.

"Bring your patience," Micah drawled. "Especially with Fabian."

Arturo clarified. "I shall claim to be searching for the sorceress, which will be expected. But there are protocols to be followed in vampire politics and one does not simply march in, demand access to another kovena's stronghold, and march out again. I will be invited to partake of the festivities, if there are any, *cara*. At the very least, I will be expected to dine with the vampire master. It will take time."

"Something we don't have."

"I am aware. I will speed things along as quickly as I can, but he cannot become suspicious."

"While you're dining with Fabian, I can try to find Vintry."

"Absolutely not. You will stay close to me at all times. If for some reason that is not feasible, I will find a safe place to lock you away."

"I'm not helpless, Vampire."

"Perhaps not, but you *are* human. Once we've located Vintry, we will approach him together."

Arturo pulled up. When she'd managed to stop her horse, he turned to her. "We have reached the Crux. Traveling through will save us time if we can trust Savin."

The last thing any of them needed, especially Arturo, was a repeat of their time in Wolf Land. But she believed Savin had been sincere.

"Let's try it and see what happens."

"You're both insane," Micah muttered. But he followed as Arturo and Quinn started forward.

They'd gone no more than a hundred yards when three wolves appeared on the hillside not far from where Quinn thought they'd said good-bye to their previous escort.

"Savin!" she yelled. A moment later, one of the wolves shifted into a man, though it was far too dark to recognize him. "We need an escort across. Can you provide one?"

"Stick to your path, human. We'll accompany you."

Quinn lifted her hand in thanks.

As they started forward, Micah grunted. "That was either brilliant, or incredibly stupid. Then again, you promised them food, didn't you?"

"I also promised to share my power with them when I come into it. The alpha has seen what I can do."

"When you almost killed him? What exactly did you do?" Micah asked.

"I made a bubble."

"A bubble?" Arturo sounded confused. "Explain."

"I created a miniworld. Like Vamp City."

The protracted silence that met her revelation had her wishing she could see their expressions.

"How?" Arturo asked, clearly stunned.

"I'm not sure. The wolves were performing some kind of ritual to steal, or borrow, my power. It hurt, and I tried to make them stop, but my usual power didn't rise. The Alpha got mad that I wasn't cooperating and started crowding me. All of a sudden the two of us were standing in the dark, alone. The light was gone. Everything was gone—light, sound, the rest of his pack. I didn't know what had happened at first."

"You have the power of Phineas Blackstone," Micah breathed.

"I have the ability to do one of his tricks, at least. The bubble was small, no more than six feet by six feet, and it collapsed on us pretty quickly. But Savin was trapped, which gave me the leverage I needed to secure his promise to free Arturo and me. I told him that once I had my full power, I'd return and share it with them."

"What do you mean by the bubble collapsed?" Arturo asked slowly.

"It shrank in on us, then exploded." She decided to keep a few of the details to herself, for now. Like the fact that she'd nearly suffocated. And the fact that only when she was facing death was she able to find the power to save them.

The two vampires fell silent. At first, she wondered what they were thinking, but soon the silence, the soft breeze, and the rhythmic gait of the horse began to lull her to sleep. When her head fell, jerking her awake, she decided that silence wasn't her friend.

She'd better do something to stay awake, or she was going to wind up in the dirt.

"You called Fabian a rival. Where does rival fall, exactly, on the spectrum between ally and enemy?"

"Smack-dab in the middle," Micah told her.

Arturo, appearing to understand her need for conversation, gave a more detailed explanation. "Cristoff and Sakamoto are the strongest of the V.C. vampire masters and are mortal enemies. Since one is as powerful as the other, if in different ways, they maintain a balance. Two others—Fabian Neptune and Jean-Luc Oubre—are strong both in numbers and in power, if not as strong as the first two. The remaining five vampire masters and their kovenas have aligned themselves with one or another of the strongest four."

"So, since Fabian is aligned with neither Cristoff nor Sakamoto, does he maintain diplomatic ties to both in case one or the other attacks and tries to take his territory?"

"Precisely. Gonzaga maintains ties to all the kovenas except for Sakamoto's and the two smaller kovenas aligned with him, one of which, unfortunately, is Castle Smithson."

As they traveled through the empty lands of the Crux, Quinn saw the occasional home, lit by candlelight. It should be a welcoming sign, she mused. But vampires didn't sleep, and a lit house in the small hours of the morning probably meant Rippers.

They rode in silence, passing it without incident, and soon she recognized the bright swirling lights of the Focus in the distance, the dead center of Vamp City. It was the very spot where Phineas Blackstone had stood when he created this place. And it would be the spot where she would stand to save it.

The reminder of the potential threat of Rippers kept her awake better than any discussion, and the miles passed quickly. Finally, several wolves appeared on the opposite rise. Their escort howled, and the wolves took off the other way.

"We're leaving the Crux," Arturo told her before she could ask the question.

"I'm officially impressed," Micah said. "I'll be leaving you kids soon, but I *might* need a little assistance before I go."

His tone had her questioning the request, especially when Arturo replied with silence.

"What kind of assistance?" she asked finally.

Arturo grunted. "Micah needs to feed to ensure he has the energy to create his own glamour."

"He needs blood?"

"Sorry, Quinn," Micah said sincerely. "I'd rather not ask this of you. And . . . I need more than just blood," he added quickly.

"You're a pleasure-feeder." Surely he wasn't asking for sex.

"He will drink your blood," Arturo said. "I alone will be sharing your pleasure."

Which wasn't a huge improvement. "And just how do you plan to do that? I'm not into threesomes."

"Nor am I. Not with you."

She thought her mind might explode from the pictures his qualifier sent flinging through her skull. With a thorough shake of her head, she pulled her thoughts back to the problem at hand.

"No sex." She grimaced as she looked at the shadow she knew to be Arturo.

"Agreed." And by the sharp tone of his voice, she had no doubt he did. The jealous one had no more desire to touch her in that way in front of another male than she had to be touched.

Micah pulled up in a small copse of dead trees, dismounting. Arturo and Quinn followed, and the vampire took her reins, securing their mounts.

"Remove your jacket and give him your wrist, *cara*."

"I'd prefer her neck," Micah said, his tone telling her he was poking the tiger just as Neo had.

"You'd prefer to have her all to yourself for a few minutes," Arturo countered. "Or an hour. But you're not getting that, either."

Quinn slid her jacket off and felt it taken from her.

"You never did share well, Ax."

"With Quinn, I never will."

Micah took her hand, sliding her sweater up to her forearm. As he lifted her inner wrist to his mouth, the moon came out fully, and she saw the light gleam on the white pupils of his eyes and his growing fangs. He'd never looked less like her neighbor the writer. He was all vampire, now.

Arturo cupped her cheek, turning her to face him, pulling her gaze away from Micah as she felt the pinch of fangs in her arm. Arturo's eyes began to change, too, his pupils turning white.

"I am going to drink from you, *cara*. A very little. But enough."

Enough to make her orgasm.

"You're going to embarrass me in front of Micah," she countered, already feeling the heat of it in her cheeks.

"Your orgasm will feed him quicker and faster than anything else. And time is of the essence, do you not agree?"

Taking a deep breath, she let it out slowly, shedding her inhibitions along with the air. At least it was dark out here. "Go ahead."

Arturo stroked her face with his thumb, but his words were for Micah when he spoke. "Pull me off of her if I get lost."

A deep sound of agreement met her ears.

Arturo brushed her hair off her shoulder, baring her neck, and she tipped her head to the side, giving him full access. Two vampires, both wanting to feed from her, and she was letting them do so freely.

Trust came in many forms.

She felt Arturo's lips brush the sensitive skin at the curve of her neck a second before his fangs slid in. Her breath caught with anticipation, and she was not disappointed. He pulled gently, a small intake of blood, but the pleasure that ripped through her was anything but small.

Quinn gasped, her breath trembling into her lungs.

Arturo took a second, harder pull, and she cried out from the blast of exquisite pleasure that left her shaking with need, her body trembling, her legs weak, her body pulsing hot and low. With his third pull of blood, she came, hard and fast, her legs buckling beneath her. As the pleasure ripped through her over and over, she felt Arturo's arms around her, holding her close, his mouth moving from her neck to her jaw, to her cheek, to her mouth. And then they were kissing, touching, his hands in her hair, her free hand sliding over his muscular shoulder.

She barely noticed the pull on her wrist, didn't even realize it had stopped until Arturo pulled away, kissing her forehead, and she realized she had both arms wrapped around his neck.

In a flush of embarrassment, she pulled away, hazarding a glance at Micah who was watching them with the same look on his face she'd often seen on Arturo's when they first met—that rapturous look of feeding pleasure.

"I'm going to hang around you kids more often," Micah said, his tone all too serious. "If it was half as good for you, Quinn, as it was for me . . ."

Quinn's face flamed hotter. "I'd rather not discuss my orgasm with you, Micah, if it's all the same to you."

He grinned. "No discussion necessary. I was there." He shook his head, his expression turning once more serious. "Don't let Fabian get a taste of that, or he may lock you two up and never let you leave."

Micah strode to where he'd tied his horse and quickly mounted. "On the plus side, I'm refueled to the top. On the downside, I've got a woody like you wouldn't believe."

"Micah . . ." Arturo growled.

With a laugh, Micah turned his mount with a wave. "I'll find you." Then he disappeared into the dark.

Arturo retrieved their mounts, then hovered over her as she reached for the reins. "He did not take too much?"

"I don't think so. I feel fine." To prove her point, she swung up into the saddle without any trouble. "That was . . . rather embarrassing." And more intriguing than she wanted to admit.

"We are vampires, Quinn. We are Emoras. Blood, pleasure, fear . . . we must feed."

"I know." She sighed. "I know."

They continued on until a large stone wall came into view on the hill in the distance. "Is that it?"

"It is. Do not forget your role, *tesoro*."

"I won't screw this up, Vampire. Not in that way, at least."

"I usually feel when the magic begins to claim you, but tell me early, yes? And I will try to help you keep it in check."

She glanced at him. "How?"

A smile claimed his mouth, leaping into his dark eyes, stealing her breath. "Distraction."

Quinn laughed. "I'm sure."

His smile softened. "How I like the sound of your laughter." Slowly, that smile of his died, his expression turning serious. "If you are in danger, do whatever you must to protect yourself. If you have to use your magic, do so. It is better for you to be revealed than harmed."

Quinn nodded. "All right. But I'm not leaving until Vintry frees my magic."

Arturo eyed her thoughtfully, then nodded. As they neared the gates, he glanced at her. "Are you ready?"

Quinn swallowed. "Sure. What can go wrong?"

Their gazes met, the knowledge leaping between them with chilling resonance.

Anything. *Everything*.

CHAPTER SIXTEEN

As Quinn and Arturo rode closer to the stone wall, to the stronghold of yet another vampire master, Quinn's tension mounted, and the shiver that went through her had little to do with the cool temperature of the air. Fabian Neptune was a pleasure-feeder, not a pain-feeder like Cristoff, though she wasn't sure that was much comfort. Especially given the fact that Arturo hadn't wanted her anywhere near this place.

She glanced at Arturo. "Do none of you feed on happiness? On love or joy?"

"Some do, but it makes them no kinder, *cara*. I knew a vampire once who required the joy of children. She hid in the shadows feeding from their giggling laughter, then snatched them up and sucked the blood from their bodies."

"All of it?" Quinn asked, horrified.

"Too much for them to survive."

"That's terrible."

"Yes. She was a vampire with no heart and little conscience. A monster, no matter how she fed. Feeding on joy did not make her good any more than Bram's need for pain makes him a monster."

She'd met Bram on her first visit to Gonzaga Castle. A good friend of Arturo's, he'd spent most of his time in the real D.C. as an emergency-room surgeon, healing humans even as he fed from their agony. He'd been visiting V.C. the night Blackstone's trap sprung and was now trapped, unable to return to his job or to the life he desired. He'd been a man in torment when she'd met him, forced to feed on the torture his master, Cristoff, preferred.

"This place is in the middle of nowhere," she murmured. "Northeast D.C.?"

"Yes."

They grew silent as they rode up the dirt track to the huge wall where two guards stood, dressed in black, armed with what appeared to be semiautomatic assault weapons. For the werewolves or other vampires?

"Arturo Mazza requests an audience with Fabian Neptune," Arturo said formally, pulling up two dozen feet away from the armed men.

Quinn pulled up behind him like the good little Slava she was pretending to be. The walls of this place had to be thirty feet high. Maybe forty. Atop stood two more armed vamps.

"State your business," one of the guards called down.

"Diplomatic in nature," Arturo replied. "I have news of the sorceress."

No one replied, but a quick look up revealed that the one who'd asked the question was no longer there. For several minutes, nothing happened. And there was no peering in. The two wide gates within the rock walls appeared to be solid steel.

One of those gates began to swing open. The guard from the wall stood in the opening and motioned them in. "Fabian wishes to see you."

As they knew he would.

Arturo's horse moved forward without any visible signal on Arturo's part. Quinn's horse followed. As they cleared the gates, she stared at the structure rising before her. As big as Gonzaga Castle, it looked like a freaking wedding cake. The curved walls were white stucco, the levels in three distinct tiers, smaller as they rose. Each of the upper floors was ringed in intricate and swirling banisters lit by the torches standing in regular intervals around the whole.

The windows, instead of glass, appeared to be cut crystal. Even the front door appeared made with crystal panels. It must weigh a ton. Then again, a vampire could probably lift a ton.

"Wow," Quinn breathed.

"Fabian enjoys the finer things," Arturo replied quietly.

That was one way to put it.

At the base of the steps, Arturo dismounted, and Quinn followed. A Slava ran toward them to take their horses, and the guard led them up what appeared to be cut-crystal steps and into a foyer that was a fairyland of sparkling light. The foyer's massive chandelier supported no fewer than five dozen lit candles.

The floor, mosaic tiles in whites and golds, depicted . . . Quinn's eyes widened . . . a thoroughly pornographic scene. She cocked her head, trying to see it from a better angle. Was that position even possible? Tearing her gaze away, she admired the walls covered in gold-leafed flowering vines.

A wide stair rose from the foyer, fanning out as it went up, the steps crystal, the railings pure gold draped in filmy white ribbons. On either side sat beautiful fountains tinkling with water. Though the

room certainly didn't run to her personal tastes, she
could not deny it was a feast for the eyes.

The guard led them through the archway to the
right and into a room of color and beauty. Yards and
yards of white silk draped the windows and walls,
which, considering the likelihood of spilled blood,
didn't seem like the wisest decorating choice for a
nest of vampires. But she didn't see any stains. The
fixtures here, as in the foyer, were all crystal and
gold. Flickering candles sat in hurricane glasses lining
a shelf that ran around the entire room, some eight
feet high. Large silk chaises in bright pastel prints
lined every wall though most remained empty. There
were flowers everywhere, filling vases, scattered on
the chaises and the floors, their fragrance perfuming
the air.

A bright blue mat covered the floor in the large pit
in the center of the room, reminding her of the kind
of springy mat she used to spar on in her Tae Kwon
Do dojo. Behind the mat, the room rose several steps
to a chaise that appeared to be made of pure gold,
covered in black velvet. And on that chaise, lounged
a man.

"Fabian," Arturo said by way of greeting.

The vampire master appeared to be in his early
forties though she knew he must be far, far older.
He had a pinched face and a bald pate around which
hung, like a fringe, thin salt-and-pepper hair. But his
eyes were sharp and assessing, gleaming with intelligence and power, and Quinn had little doubt he
was a very dangerous male despite the uninspiring
appearance.

Wearing only a pair of bright blue pajama pants,
Fabian held a tumbler of amber liquid in one hand

as he fondled the bare breast of one of the six Slava females who surrounded him. The women wore long, skimpy dresses of sheer, bright color that revealed far more than they hid. And every one of them had her hands on Fabian somewhere. While one ran her fingers through his hair, two massaged his bare feet, two caressed his arms and bare chest from either side. And one had her hand down the front of his pants almost certainly playing with, or stroking, his jewels.

Clearly, the pleasure-feeder enjoyed his own pleasure.

"Come in, come in," Fabian said. "Join me, Arturo Mazza."

Arturo stepped forward without giving Quinn any signal or apparent thought, but they'd discussed this on the ride, how she must act. Arturo had warned her to always follow him, to stand behind him when he sat, to remain silent, and to keep her eyes downcast at all times. Apparently, looking a vampire in the eye was a good way to catch his attention. Something few Slavas did willingly. And while she supposedly belonged to Arturo, the last thing they wanted was for Arturo to have to wage a battle over her.

Quinn followed Arturo up the steps. When he took a seat on the yellow chaise at Fabian's right, she moved to stand behind him, her hands folded in front of her, her eyes downcast.

"Your drink of choice?" Fabian asked Arturo. "I have a fine whiskey. An excellent Macallan."

"A man after my own heart," Arturo said warmly, his voice and attitude embracing his diplomatic role. "You have always had the best whiskey, Fabian."

Two Slavas darted from Fabian's side, one pouring

a splash of whiskey into a tumbler while a voluptuous blonde with breasts spilling out of her gown made a beeline directly for Arturo. She knelt on the chaise beside him and began to run her fingers through his hair, and over his face and neck, as the other handed him the tumbler.

Quinn clenched her teeth with annoyance.

Fabian's eyelids lowered to half-staff, a small smile lifting his mouth, then dying as his eyes opened with disappointment. "No pleasure, Mazza? And why is this? Have you taken a liking to men?" He lifted his hand as if to call one.

"No, Fabian. I simply have more pressing concerns."

"Nonsense. I've felt your pleasure before, my friend, and fed well from it. I would do so again."

Quinn felt the vamp master's curious gaze turn on her.

"Your Slava is quite attractive, Mazza. Perhaps it is her touch you enjoy?" When Arturo said nothing, Fabian pressed. "What is your name, lovely?"

"She is Jillian," Arturo answered for her.

"Touch him, Jillian. I would know if it's your touch he seeks these days."

Keep your touch light, cara, Arturo's voice whispered in her head. *As impersonal as possible. And think of unpleasant things. Your fear would be welcome, now, if you can keep it from triggering your magic. Your fear sours my stomach.*

Quinn swallowed hard, remembering Micah's warning. The passion that rose between her and Arturo was strong and heady. One Fabian should not experience. That shouldn't be too much of a problem. She doubted she could forget her surroundings or her audience long enough to feel true desire here, no matter who she touched.

Sliding her hands across Arturo's shoulders, the black silk of his shirt molded to his muscular form. He felt good, *smelled* good. But while she enjoyed the feel of him, nothing crazy stirred inside of her. Not with everyone watching. She could do this.

"Come now!" Fabian chastised. "Remove your shirt, Mazza. What is this false modesty? Do you intentionally try me?"

"Of course not, Fabian," Arturo said smoothly, unbuttoning his shirt and shrugging it off, revealing his beautiful male back and a fine set of shoulders dusted in Mediterranean sunshine.

Quinn slid her hands over that cool, gorgeous skin, struggling to cling to her indifference, but as Arturo settled back, as her cheek brushed against the soft springiness of his hair, as his intoxicating scent filled her lungs, her blood began to heat. He affected her too strongly and always had, and it was clear her body didn't care that they had an audience.

"That's better. Still . . ." Fabian waved his hand at his Slavas. "Fetch the elixir! They will both drink."

Arturo's shoulders stiffened. Quinn stilled as she watched two of Fabian's Slavas rise and snatch a pitcher of bright green liquid and two glasses from a table against the wall.

"Elixir?" Quinn whispered.

It will not harm you, cara. *And we have no choice.*

"Now, tell me this news of the sorceress, Mazza. Word reaches us that one was found, then lost. Some claim that she has no power. Others say she is powerful indeed."

"The rumors are true, Fabian. She is powerful,

able to hide her magic. And she is missing. I know her smell and would search your stronghold to find her. That is why I have come."

The Slavas stopped in front of Arturo, one woman pouring the green liquid into the glasses the other held. Then both were offered to Arturo.

"You think I have her?" The vampire master's voice rose with indignation and something stronger. A trace of alarm. "If that witch darkened my doors, I would send for Cristoff immediately. You know that."

"Of course, my friend," Arturo said, his voice soothing. "Cristoff knows well that you take no sides. But it is possible the sorceress has breached your walls without your knowing."

The vampire master scoffed. "Impossible."

Arturo handed Quinn one of the glasses of green liquid. "Drink," he said. Then tipped back his head and downed his own.

Quinn took the glass, eyeing the strange liquid warily. An elixir, the vampire called it. And what in the hell did that mean?

"If the sorceress were here, I would know," Fabian argued.

Quinn hesitated a moment longer before downing the glassful without taking a breath. A lemon-lime sweetness lingered on her tongue as she handed the glass back to Arturo, wondering just what she'd swallowed. And how badly they'd just been drugged.

"The woman has magic, Fabian. I have seen it with my own eyes. It is not beyond reason that she is here, and we need to find her, do you not agree?"

As if on cue, the ground began to shake, the crystal tinkling and rattling, one hurricane glass falling and shattering on the tiled portion of the floor. The couple on one of the few occupied chaises cried out, the glass just missing them. Through one of the dark windows, light erupted, though a distance away. Sunbeams breaking through from the real world.

Arturo glanced back at Quinn, but she hadn't been the cause of this one. Her eyes weren't glowing.

"Very well," Fabian conceded when the rattling had ceased. "You may explore my castle to your heart's content. After tonight's banquet."

"Time grows short, my friend." Arturo's tone remained affable. "Perhaps . . ."

Fabian's hand sliced through the air, a hard look crossing his face, one that reminded Quinn the male was probably a vampire master for a reason. One not to be crossed lightly. "You will remain until I say otherwise," he snapped. His expression eased, and he was once more the gracious host. "I wish you to enjoy the pleasures my golden palace has to offer. And I wish to enjoy your own pleasure." He made a quick move with his hand, motioning Quinn toward Arturo. "Come, come, Slava. Touch him, wrap yourself around him. Please us both."

Feel nothing, feel nothing, she told herself as she stepped forward and slid her palms, once more, over Arturo's strong shoulders. She forced her mind to another place, Cristoff's castle the day Arturo handed her back to her master, and Cristoff knocked her to the floor. But the feel of cool flesh beneath her fingertips combined with Arturo's warm, masculine fragrance sent pleasure rippling down into her body. Memories rose past her defenses, erotic memories of the last time she'd touched him like this, of the incredible heat, the blazing passion.

Cara. Even telepathic, his voice sounded breathless, as if he felt her body's reaction and shared it. Her pulse began to increase, her own breath growing shallow.

"Can't help it," she whispered. A strange warmth began to flow through Quinn's veins and down deep into her body, setting up a throbbing pulse between her legs.

The drink was a powerful aphrodisiac, cara. *Fight it as much as you are able, as will I.*

"You knew."

I feared, yes.

"Much better," Fabian said, a satisfied smile in his voice. "I wonder if I would rise to your Slava's touch as you do, Mazza. She is quite beautiful."

Arturo's body went rigid.

Fabian made a tsking sound, his voice sharp. "You would deny me a taste of your Slava, my friend?"

Arturo stilled, his posture visibly calming, though Quinn felt no softening of the tension in his muscles. Or her own.

"You would not enjoy her touch," her vampire said, his voice taking on the hypnotic quality of his *persuasion.* "She was broken early in her stay in Vamp City, and now accepts only me. The touch of another male, except for the most casual, often sickens her. Literally."

Fabian nodded slowly, as if everything Arturo said were undeniably true. "That would indeed be unpleasant. I've no desire to touch her, then." He shook his head as if trying to throw off the effects of the *persuasion.*

Fabian clapped his hands once. "Music! Come, my friends. Enjoy!"

People began to flow into the room from the various doors, most of them naked. Somewhere in the rafters above, a live band tuned up.

And still Quinn caressed Arturo's shoulders, her fingers moving of their own accord, finding their way into his hair. Heat flushed her skin, desire shortened her breath—a desire she always felt when she was near Arturo, heightened by Fabian's elixir.

In so many ways, they needed to get out of here. They had to find Vintry. But Arturo knew that as well as she did, and knew what risks he could and couldn't take with Fabian. Pleasure-feeder or not, their host was quick-tempered and, she suspected, unpredictable. There was no telling what he would do.

Under the thrall of Fabian's elixir, she had no idea what any of them would do.

Quinn was ready to crawl out of her skin.

Her breasts ached, her nipples were hard and sensitive, her blood pounded, her body pulsed with the need to feel Arturo's hands on her in return, on her breasts, her thighs, and stroking between her legs. The only time she'd ever felt anything like this fever of need had been when Arturo had made love to her after he'd saved Zack from the Games.

Her hands trembled as she stroked his bare chest, his shoulders, his neck and back. It took every ounce of control not to climb onto his lap and straddle him to try to find some small measure of release. And he was in no better shape. She could feel the tension in his shoulders and hear the harshness of his breath.

Of course, the *entertainment* Fabian provided did

nothing to ease her growing carnal need. For more than an hour, the music had pounded with a deep, erotic beat, designed to whip the dancers on the mat into a hedonistic frenzy. And it had done just that. While some had danced, most had grabbed and groped the nearest flesh, fondling, caressing.

As Quinn had stared, they'd begun to merge into groups of two and three, cocks sliding into hands, into mouths, into bodies, both male and female. Half a dozen males had formed what looked like a conga line, each grasping the hips of the male in front of him, until Quinn realized the only movement any of them were making was hip thrusting.

As she watched now, a female with white-centered eyes and elongated fangs rode one male while a second took her from behind. A third grabbed her face and shoved his cock down her throat as she grabbed his hips and pulled him closer.

A few weeks ago, such a tableau would have shocked Quinn. Now, she found the sight almost heartwarming. The only cries were of pleasure, even from the Slavas, though she wondered if any were actually here of their own free will. Without a doubt, all were under the thrall of Fabian's elixir.

In her current impassioned state, she found the sight of the foursome incredibly hot. She was so aroused, her own body so desperately in need of attention, that watching the others was almost more than she could bear. Especially with Arturo's flesh beneath her hands, his scent filling her lungs, his taste like the finest wine as she ran her tongue along the curve of his ear.

Her breath was completely ragged, her equilibrium destroyed. And hers wasn't the only one.

Without warning, Arturo pulled her onto his lap and began to kiss her as if he were drowning and she was the only one who could save him. His hands burrowed into her hair, his breath as rough as her own. He'd held on to control as long as he could, despite the smell of sex all around them, the sound of slapping flesh and passion underscored by the pounding, pulsing music. And the elixir flowing hot through their veins.

"Fuck her, Mazza," Fabian called. "Strip her down and fuck her."

Quinn tensed.

"Easy, *cara*," Arturo whispered against her ear. Then he dipped his head to her neck and bit her.

She screamed with pleasure as the first pull of blood shot her straight to orgasm. Her overheated body shattered, pulsing, the pleasure exquisite as he pulled on her neck again and again.

When he lifted his head, his eyes were white-centered and white-hot, his fangs long and streaked with blood. "*Mio dio.*"

"Mazza," Fabian growled over the swelling music. "You've taken me to the edge and left me there. Fuck her! *Now.*"

Arturo cupped her jaw, the heat in his eyes part real, part the product of the drug. But the concern and tenderness were completely genuine. "Not in front of the others. She'll not be able to tolerate it. Find us a screen for privacy."

We cannot avoid this, cara mia.

"I know." Heaven help her, she didn't care where they did it as long as he filled her and ended this pulsing, aching torture.

Minutes later, slaves erected dressing-room screens

all around them, though why they had such a thing in a place like this, she couldn't imagine.

"Fuck her, Mazza," Fabian called. "Or I'll do it myself, vomit and all."

Hidden at last, Arturo turned to her, his hands on her face, meeting her gaze. "I need you."

"Yes." But when she reached for her shirt, he grabbed her wrists, stilling them.

"I would have us not undress any more than we have to," he said against her cheek. "I don't trust him. Unfasten your jeans and get on your hands and knees."

With shaking fingers, she did as he asked, and, a moment later, he was pulling her jeans and panties down to her thighs, exposing her ass to the heated air. At once, she felt his hand on her, between her legs, his finger sliding deep inside of her.

She cried out from the pleasure.

"You are so wet, *cara*, so ready for this. For me."

She heard the zip of his pants, the quick rustle, then felt his hands grip her hips and his thick erection plunge deep inside of her.

She screamed, arching, pushing back to shove him deeper. "Harder, Vampire. Faster!" she urged, then gasped as his pounding took on a superhuman speed. She came again and again and again. Each time she shattered, she felt him with her in a way that wasn't quite physical, as if he embraced her, holding her as she came apart.

"*Cara*," he gasped, and she knew he was close. She rose again, and this time he joined her, slowing, jerking her hips tight against his as he roared, as the pleasure exploded. She felt his spirit wrap around hers, felt the sun on them both. In her mind's eye, she watched him tip his face up, smiling. The sun's warmth flowed down inside her, down into the deep, cold crevices of her being, of her heart. Their cries echoed around the room.

It was moments before she came back to herself, collapsing onto the chaise as Arturo pulled out of her and released her hips. She felt him stretch out beside her, and turned her to face him. For long moments they stared at one another, his fingers stroking her cheek.

"What you do to me," he breathed.

"That was . . . unbelievable."

He smiled, stealing what little breath she'd managed to reclaim.

"I saw the sun. I felt it on my face. And it didn't burn."

"I know." Which made absolutely no sense. "Was it real, or just the drug?"

He looked deep into her eyes, stroking her face. "It was you, *amore mio*. You give me the sun."

For long moments, they stared at one another, then Arturo blinked and began to frown.

"It is too quiet."

In a heartbeat, a human heartbeat, he was up, helping her to her feet and pulling her jeans up, helping her adjust her clothes, then quickly adjusting his own.

Arturo set aside the screen and, just like a bad dream, Quinn saw that all eyes were on them, most mouths hanging open. With a silent groan, she hazarded a glance at Fabian. He was watching them with a look of rapture, his eyelids heavy, his mouth open and panting.

A cunning smile broke slowly over his face. "My

friends, that was extraordinary. Never have I felt its like. If such a creature always creates such a response, no wonder she was used to the breaking point." He lifted a weary, sated hand. "She is all yours, Arturo, my friend. But you will stay here. With her. And pleasure us both."

Quinn felt Arturo tense. "Of course, Fabian. I shall be happy to be your guest for a while longer. Just as soon as I have found the sorceress and returned her to Cristoff, so that she might save our world."

Fabian's smile turned calculating. "While you search for the sorceress, Jillian will remain with me. Because then I know you will return, and quickly." His voice rose. "This Slava is not to leave the castle," he commanded. "Not unless she's with me."

Quinn's stomach clenched.

Arturo took her hand. "She will remain at the castle with you, Fabian, as you wish. But while I am here, I would have her remain by my side. It brings me pleasure."

Fabian's eyes narrowed as his gaze moved between them. His mouth tightened. But, finally, he nodded grudgingly. "While you are here, she is yours."

Her hand clung to Arturo's, her heart still pounding though the effects of the elixir appeared to have dissipated with their lovemaking.

"I must take my leave, for now, and search for the sorceress, Fabian," Arturo said calmly, his voice still husky with lingering passion.

"Later," the vampire master snapped. "Sit and fondle her. I am not through with you two."

Arturo's hand tensed around hers, but he did as commanded, pulling her onto his lap as the other inhabitants of the room resumed their inventive rutting. She curled her arm around Arturo's neck and stiffened only a little when his hand went to her breast, fondling her through her clothes. Despite the multiple orgasms, despite the elixir's effects having worn off, her body lit up again with that simple touch. And beneath her hip, she felt his erection once more begin to rise.

Fabian was never going to let them out of here. And, at this rate, Vintry was going to die before they ever got a chance to talk to him.

If he wasn't already dead.

CHAPTER SEVENTEEN

It was another hour, and three orgasms later, before Fabian finally acceded to Arturo's thinly veiled demand to find "Jillian" food and a bedchamber in which to sleep.

"See her fed, then return to me at once, Mazza," Fabian called, as they reached the door behind their guard escort. "Our feast awaits!"

They'd no sooner entered the back hallway when another guard stepped forward.

"I'll take them from here."

Quinn immediately recognized the voice if not the man. Micah.

The original guard nodded and left.

"I found Vintry," Micah said when they were out of earshot of the guard. He looked nothing like himself, his hair long and blond, his face broad as a bowling ball. His glamour was pretty amazing. Then again, so was her own. "He's in the dungeon, locked in a cell in the very back. Alone. They're afraid of his death wind. Access is through the second pantry, behind the wine casks, but I've yet to find the key to his cell."

Micah was speaking fast and low. "I asked him if he could help the sorceress, and he said yes, he could, but he would not. He hates vampires, wants us all to die, etc., etc. Then he started yelling bloody murder for me to leave. A bitter old cuss."

"I'd probably be bitter, too, if someone locked me in a dungeon to die," Arturo muttered. "We'll have to grab him out of there and run. Perhaps Tarellia can convince him to help us."

"You'll be implicated in his sudden disappearance. But you can spin it easily enough."

"I can. Find us an empty bedchamber close to the dungeon where we can set up base."

"Already done." He led them down a second hall with far too many doors, which meant the rooms were microscopic. Probably the Slavas' quarters. Pushing open one of the last doors, Micah stepped back for them to enter.

The room was just as she'd expected, a dingy little closet with a tiny bed that took up the majority of space. She took a seat on it since there was so little room to stand.

Arturo's hand rested on her shoulder, but he turned back to Micah. "I must return to Fabian for the feast, but once it is done, we'll move. Find the key."

"Roger that."

Arturo squeezed her shoulder. "Stay here, *cara*. I'll find you food. You should be safe here."

"I'll keep an eye on her," Micah promised.

Quinn wasn't entirely sure she wanted Micah keeping an eye on her. There was no way she was sitting here twiddling her thumbs while Arturo attended Fabian. Not when Vintry could be freeing her magic and might die at any moment.

As Arturo started for the door, the sound of a commotion erupted nearby, along with the unmistakable sound of a crying child.

Arturo froze.

"What's a kid doing here?" Micah muttered.

The two vampires strode forward as one. Quinn pushed off the bed and followed, horrified at the thought of a child's witnessing, let alone experiencing, anything that happened in Vamp City.

They didn't have to go far to find the source of the disturbance. A couple of doors down, the hall crossed with another. As they turned, Quinn caught sight of the two pantries Micah had mentioned, one with wine casks in the back.

A short distance farther, the hall opened into a huge kitchen. Standing in front of the door at the back, a trembling young woman cradled a towheaded boy. He couldn't be more than three or four, tears running down his cheeks as he hiccuped with sobs.

The pair were flanked by men Quinn assumed to be vampires, talking to a third dressed in guard's black.

One of the vamps smiled. "Found them outside, just wandering around. They must have escaped the Traders."

Arturo's eyes narrowed, tension stiffening his shoulders even as his face took on a casual, curious expression.

"Has the ban on children been lifted, then?" he asked with mild curiosity bordering on indifference. An indifference she sensed was wholly faked.

"Apparently so," the guard said, "since they were declared fodder for the next Games."

Fodder. Children . . . *toddlers* . . . sent into the arena to die?

Quinn swayed, grasping the nearest wall. Her gaze flew to Arturo as he and Micah exchanged looks, something passing silently between them. A question, a nod, a shrug.

"I've seen those two," Micah said, stepping forward. "They were running from Sakamoto's contingent several hours ago. I'd have grabbed them myself, but those who steal from Sakamoto have a bad habit of turning up dead."

The two vampires blanched. Sakamoto sounded a lot like Cristoff.

"They were alone," one of the two complained. "We didn't steal them."

"I'm heading out now to do a perimeter check. I'll see if the contingent is still out there and hand them back before Sakamoto declares war on Fabian's Palace."

The vampire pair stepped away from the woman and child like they'd suddenly become radioactive. "Sure, sure. Take them."

The woman stared around her, visibly shaken, pale as snow and clinging to her toddler for dear life. But to her credit, she wasn't crying or begging. Just trying to figure out how to keep her and her son alive.

"Come along," Micah said, gripping the woman's arm lightly. Quinn thought she saw him wink at the woman. "You don't belong here."

The woman didn't fight him, allowing him to steer her out the back door.

Arturo stepped forward. "My Slava is in need of food," he bellowed, drawing all attention. "Where can I get food?"

Most who'd gathered to witness the commotion dispersed. One woman hurried to him with a sandwich on a plate and a can of Coke. Arturo took them from her and walked away, brushing past Quinn without a glance.

Playing her role, Quinn followed him as meekly as she could manage back to her bedroom. But the moment she closed the door, she dropped the façade. "What's Micah going to do with them?"

Arturo handed her the plate, then opened the Coke for her, cocking his head in challenge. "What do you think a vampire will do with two fresh humans?"

Rolling her eyes, she took the Coke. "He's either going to set them free or take them somewhere safe."

"You're so certain?" The look in his eyes told her that her answer mattered. Very much.

"Yes, I'm certain. I saw the look on your face when you heard that kid, Arturo. You turned to stone."

"Children do not belong in Vamp City." His brows drew down in an expression of bafflement. "It is the *law*. It *was* the law. No children. Ever. When did it change? When did everything change?"

Now it was her turn to cock her head. "Your reaction was more than annoyance at unauthorized rule breaking. You were horrified."

"Yes." Arturo met her gaze for a long moment before answering her first question. "We are a quarter of a mile from the Boundary Circle. He'll find a way to set them free."

Thank God. But her curiosity was peaked. "You feel a certain protectiveness toward kids, don't you?"

"They deserve a chance to grow up."

She sensed there was more to his reaction. The situation had hit a nerve, but he clearly didn't feel like talking about it with her. Not here. Not now.

She picked up her sandwich. "Micah won't be able to get that key, now, will he?"

"Not yet, no. Unless he runs into trouble, he'll be back very soon."

As if trouble didn't stalk them at every turn.

Arturo eased past her. "I have to return to Fabian. Sleep, if you can. I'll fetch you when I am able. Lock the door as soon as I leave."

"Enjoy your dinner."

With a small smile, Arturo left, closing the door behind him.

Quinn got up and threw the dead bolt, one hundred percent certain it wouldn't actually keep out a vampire who wanted in. But it might dissuade one who didn't want to suffer Fabian's displeasure.

Returning to the bed, she wolfed down the sandwich and Coke. She was exhausted, desperately in need of sleep. But Vintry was still alive and might not stay that way much longer.

Her pulse began to escalate as she formulated a plan. Not only were there vampires out there, but most of them were males with no compunction about taking what they wanted from any human, female or otherwise. Especially a Slava.

She palmed her switchblade, opened the door, and peered cautiously down the hallway. When she saw no one, she stepped out, closing the door behind her, and strode the short distance to the second pantry, then ducked inside and slipped back to the wine casks visible in the light flickering in from one of the small wall torches in the hallway.

She found the door behind the casks just as Micah had described. Though wooden and old, it was well oiled and barely made a sound when she pulled it open. But whatever lay beyond was dark as a crypt. She was going to need a light.

Stealing across the hall, she pulled one of the torches out of its holder, hoping no one would miss

it before she returned. Once again, she made her way
to the cellar door and pulled it open. Her light illuminated a long, wooden stair and a dark void beyond.
A tingle of dread danced down her spine, though she
found it reassuring that Micah had just been down
there and lived to tell the tale.

Then again, Micah was a vampire.

Swallowing her trepidation, she closed the door
behind her and descended the stairs to the hard-
packed dirt floor. Lifting her torch, she saw that the
path led out from the stairs a good hundred feet,
lined on either side by rows and rows of prison cells.

Though she listened, she heard no noise. Another
chill skittered down her spine, and magic began to
buzz lightly beneath her skin as she strode down the
path, glancing into each cell. Empty, every one. Until
she reached the very last.

She found the old fae lying on a pallet on the
floor. He appeared small in stature, his hair almost
gone, his skin as wrinkled and leathery as any ancient male's, though this one was far more ancient
than any she'd come across in the real world. He was
wearing worn brown trousers and a flannel shirt that
looked as if it hadn't left his body in several decades.
His feet were bare, and he had one arm flung across
his eyes. What a lonely, sad way to die.

"Douse the damned light," he growled.

"Vintry?"

"What do you want?"

Spying a torch holder on the wall a few cells down,
she planted the torch and returned to Vintry's cell,
now cast into shadow.

"Tarellia said you might be able to help me."

"She lied."

Dying and bitter, just as Micah said. Not that she could blame him. "I know you'd just as soon Vamp City failed. But what will happen to the other fae if it does?" she asked softly.

"What do I care?"

Biting back her frustration, Quinn launched into the truth. "I'm a sorceress, Vintry. Apparently *the* sorceress. Maybe the only one left."

The old fae's arm moved, his head turning to peer at her through rheumy eyes. "You?" He couldn't have put any more derogatory disbelief into the word if he'd tried. The little prick.

"It's true. And my brother has somehow gotten tangled up in my magic. He's suffering from a magic sickness, and if Vamp City dies, he will, too. I'll do *anything* to keep that from happening."

He turned back, covering his eyes again. "I can't help you. Go away."

Not a chance. "Tarellia believes I have both Blackstone and Levenach blood. That my Blackstone magic is being obstructed by the Levenach curse. That as long as it is, I'll never have any real control of my magic. She believes you can help me break my Blackstone magic free of the curse."

Once again, Vintry lowered his arm and peered at her, but this time, the look on his face was different. Almost intrigued. "Blackstone *and* Levenach, eh? What's your name, girl?"

"Quinn Lennox."

His eyes narrowed, but he was no longer scowling at her. "Do you have the key to my cell?"

"No."

Her heart leaped as he pushed himself slowly and stiffly from the bed, his body bent and arthritic.

"Damned aging," he muttered as he crossed the floor and gripped the bars tight with one hand as if to stabilize himself. Then he held out his hand. "Put your hand through, girl. This might hurt."

She eyed him warily, but did as he asked. Wrinkled, gnarled, surprisingly warm fingers curled around hers as the old fae closed his eyes. Quinn stared at him, noting the profusion of age spots, the wisps of hair, the hook of a nose. His ears, she noted, had the slightest point at their tips, making her smile. He really was an elf. She was holding hands with an elf.

Suddenly, his eyes snapped open. He stared at her, his eyes, amazingly, filling with tears as he began to smile. "I thought I'd missed you."

"Excuse me?" She resisted the desire to pull her hand away.

"You are the one foretold, girl. The Healer." He patted her hand as she stared at him in stunned confusion. A gleam leaped into his eyes. "Is the snake with you?"

"Arturo? Yes. How . . . ?" Maybe Micah had mentioned him.

Suddenly, the old fae's eyes went wide, and he jerked away, stumbling back. But as he stared at her, his face softened with understanding, and he began to laugh. "Glamour."

She jerked her gaze down to her hand, her pale true hand. "Shit."

Vintry waved his hand. "Return with the snake, and him alone, and I will help you. He must be here, too." He turned away and began making his way back to the bed. "Now go!" he admonished, though his voice was warm this time. "Take the light with you. And don't delay, or I'll be dead." He began to cackle.

Quinn turned away, relieved, and more than a little dazed. The Healer? At least Vintry had agreed to help. The trouble was going to be getting Arturo away from Fabian in time. Oh, and the small fact that she'd lost her glamour. Again.

At least her room was close by. Quinn made her way swiftly up the stairs to the pantry, briefly debating whether to leave the torch in the prison instead of taking it with her, and decided against it. Vintry didn't want the light, and she'd need it to make her way through the pantry since she'd removed the light that had shone into the space in the first place.

Hearing nothing through the closed door, Quinn opened it slowly, wishing to hell she still looked like Neo's sister, then slipped into the pantry and closed the door behind her. The torch holder sat on the wall just across the hall, taunting her. Because as long as she held the torch, there was no hiding.

Squaring her shoulders, she stepped into the hallway and nearly ran into two passing vampire guards. Dammit.

"Who are you?" one of them demanded.

Quinn froze, heart pounding as she debated her options and came up with not a single decent one. Throw the torch at them and run? Right. Vampires were lightning fast. She could demand to be taken to Arturo, but admitting she'd been hiding behind a glamour, that he'd had the sorceress with him all along, would, best case, get them thrown out of the castle. Worst case . . . she didn't even want to think about it.

Going with instinct, she threw the torch at the nearest guard and pulled her switchblade. In the blink of an eye . . . a human eye . . . the torch was back in its holder, her blade was gone from her hand, and her wrist was caught tight in a vampire's hold. Too damn fast.

The vamp who held her began to smile. "She's a freshie, Bill. What's a freshie doing sneaking around our pantry?" He leered at her. "Trying to steal food from us, girlie?"

Quinn's heart began to pound. Magic started to tingle beneath her skin, but not quickly enough.

The guard turned to the hallway she'd first come down and pulled her along with him, striding fast and sure as if he knew exactly where to take her.

Her mind grasped for ideas even as she worried that Arturo would feel her emotions, her fear, and come for her, giving himself away. There was no fighting the vampires to get free. And she could think of nothing she could say that would help her. With dismay, she realized where the guard was leading her seconds before they entered the orgy dojo. The smell of sex hit her hard, along with the coppery scent of blood. Almost every vampire in the room had his fangs in someone, if not his cock.

Including Arturo.

She found him on the chaise where they'd metaphorically blown the roof off with their orgasms, a naked woman draped across his lap, his arm around her waist as he drank from her neck. He, at least, was fully clothed and appeared to be doing nothing but drinking.

Though he continued to feed, his eyes lifted as she entered the room, spearing her. She felt, rather than saw his surprise and his frustration with her. If she'd stayed in the room where he'd left her, losing her glamour wouldn't have mattered. No one would have seen her. But that was water under the proverbial bridge and she was in a boatload of trouble.

Though Arturo continued to watch her, he made no move even to acknowledge her. And he wouldn't, she realized. He *couldn't* without implicating himself.

The guard steered her around the edges of the room, toward the dais, where Fabian was being straddled by two women—one over his groin, riding him, the other over his mouth.

At the base of the dais, Quinn's captor stopped, silent and waiting for his master's attention. After less than a minute, the woman straddling Fabian's face began to sway, her skin looking alarmingly pale. With horror, Quinn realized Fabian had been eating her in the truest sense of the word, his fangs sunk deep between her legs.

Fabian gripped her tight, holding her against his mouth even as she collapsed, unconscious.

He was draining her dry! With his fangs sunk into her femoral artery, he would, within minutes, if he could drink that fast. It reminded her of the way some of the kids used to shotgun beers in college, opening a hole in the bottom of the can so that it poured quickly down their throats.

Fabian, she thought, stomach turning, was into shotgunning humans.

As she watched in horror, he tossed the woman onto the floor, like the empty vessel she now was. Blood running down his cheek, he grabbed the hips of the woman who fucked him, driving into her vampire-fast. But as he caught sight of Quinn, he slowed, then stopped.

Raising himself up on one elbow, he glanced at her guard.

"Who have we here?"

The magic beneath her skin began to sting.

"We found a freshie raiding the pantry. She must have snuck in from outside."

Fabian's smile bloomed slow and dangerous. "Steal from me, would you?" He waved his hand at the woman still attempting to ride him. "Go." Without hesitation, she pushed up and off him, moving away from the chaise.

Fabian sat up, his erection still thick and hard. "Bring her here."

Quinn's breath caught, the magic bubbling. If she didn't get control, her eyes were going to glow, and the gig was going to be up. The sorceress revealed.

His fingers tight around her arm, the guard pulled her up the stairs to stand in front of the pale, skinny Fabian. The vampire master rose to his feet as she approached, his hand reaching out to stroke her hair with surprising gentleness, even reverence.

"Beautiful. Like spun gold. Your skin like porcelain. Take off your clothes, lovely. I'll finish inside of you."

No way in hell. Her pulse tripped, escalating fast and hard as she considered her exceedingly limited options. This was the reason she should have held on to her stakes.

"Now, woman," Fabian snapped.

"Go to hell."

The hand in her hair tangled and jerked, and he pushed her head down toward his erection.

"I prefer pleasure to pain, but I will have obedience. Either you submit to me here, or I'll hand you over to my guards, to be taken away and used in any way they wish. Most of my guards are pain-feeders, in case you're wondering." He jerked her head up again, making her cry out from the ripping sensation along her scalp. "Submit."

She met his gaze, terror and fury twining inside of her, feeding the flame beneath her flesh. "*No.*"

Fabian jerked back, his face suddenly a mask of shock. Slowly he began to grin. "Well, well."

Ah, crud. Her eyes must be glowing.

Arturo, damn his vampire hide, finally decided to join her. He rose and moved to Fabian's side, smiling a hard, humorless smile. "Hello, sorceress."

CHAPTER EIGHTEEN

Arturo grabbed Quinn's arm roughly, turning on Fabian. "You've been harboring her."

Quinn's knees nearly buckled as Arturo took her out of Fabian's grasp. She'd inadvertently handed Arturo the upper hand and, to her vast relief, hadn't blown his cover at all. She just had another role to play now, as Arturo pretended to be discovering her here for the first time. Unfortunately, the relief was having no effect on her building power.

Fabian scowled, a hint of alarm in his expression. "I had no idea she was here. Cristoff must believe that. I've never seen her." His gaze slowly raked over her. "I would certainly remember if I had."

Arturo remained silent for several moments, acting thoroughly steamed. Finally, he released a frustrated sigh. Cristoff's snake was more than a first-class manipulator. He was a hell of an actor.

"Cristoff will be most pleased that you found her." His voice sounded conciliatory on the surface, but the underlying threat was unmistakable. "I am quite certain he'll send a gift of appreciation. But I must return her to Cristoff immediately. If he learns that I delayed in returning her to him once I found her, he will be furious, of course."

Fabian's expression shifted back and forth be-

tween consternation and frustration, clearly irritated
with the turn of events that now forced him to take
a defensive role.

His mouth twisted with annoyance. "Of course."

Quinn was trembling now as the magic burning
beneath her skin fought to get out. Slowly, the ground
beneath her began to shake, escalating quickly in violence. Crystal crashed to the tile floor, shattering,
snuffing candles. Vampires and Slavas alike cried out.

At any moment, her power would fly, pushing
them all back against the walls. And then what?
She'd never escape, not surrounded by vampires.
But Arturo might lose the upper hand, especially if
Fabian became enraged. She needed to find a way to
pull it back, tamp it down. She must!

The power turned on her suddenly. One moment
she was shaking as if she were about to blow. The next
she felt as if a dozen knives were slicing up her flesh.
With a cry, she doubled over from the ripping, ungodly
pain. It flayed her body, tearing at her mind until she
could feel nothing else and think of nothing at all.

The agony tripled as she was lifted and flung over
a hard shoulder.

"I will leave for Cristoff's when my Slava awak-
ens," Arturo told Fabian.

Quinn didn't hear Fabian's response if he made
one. She felt them moving, cried out in agony with
every one of his steps.

*I am sorry, tesoro. So very sorry. But he cannot
know how your pain slays me.*

A lifetime later, she felt herself lowered gently onto
a hard mattress. Cool fingers stroked her cheeks.
"*Cara mia.* Tell me what you need. Tell me how to
help you."

She reached for his hand, clinging to his strength. "I didn't want to throw you against the wall."

"So you swallowed the power."

"I suppose. It attacked me." Slowly, the pain began to die, and she released a pent-up breath as she realized she was no longer in danger of losing control.

A rap on the door had her opening her eyes and Arturo pulling away.

"Ax."

At the sound of Micah's voice, Arturo strode to the door to let him in.

"What happened?" Micah demanded.

Quinn struggled to sit up, the pain still darting across her skull.

Micah grimaced. "Your glamour didn't last, I see. At least you were hidden." He glanced from one of them to the other, frowning. "Someone saw, didn't they? What happened?"

Voice tight, Quinn told them everything.

"Fuck. Sorry about that." Micah sighed. "I can glamour you again, but it's not going to last long. I've about depleted my stores keeping my own glamour up. A little passion might help, but Quinn's clearly in too much pain to feed me any pleasure."

And that was the truth if there ever was one.

Arturo sat beside her and pulled her against him. His hand was cold where it brushed hers, and she took hold of it and lifted it to her aching forehead.

"That feels good," she murmured.

He kissed her hair, stroking her arm with his free hand until, slowly, the pain slid away. His gentleness tried to stir something soft deep inside of her, but she kept remembering the way he'd watched as Fabian threatened her, making no move whatsoever to come to her aid. She had to believe he wouldn't have let it go too far. He wouldn't have stood there and watched Fabian rape her. But she couldn't forget the way he'd watched Cristoff beat her senseless a couple of weeks ago and never raised so much as an objection.

She pulled away. "We have to go to Vintry. Immediately." She didn't dare leave this room as herself, not yet. Pulling up her sleeve, she strode to Micah and offered him her wrist. "Feed. I need you turn me back into Jillian."

Micah looked at her with surprise, his gaze swiveling to Arturo. But when Arturo started toward her, she held up her hand. "No. Just Micah. Just blood this time."

Arturo frowned. "*Cara*."

"Vampire . . ." She glanced at Micah, who was watching them curiously, though his fangs had already elongated. "Would you please eat? We don't have much time."

His expression bemused, Micah took her arm and lifted her wrist to his mouth, sinking his fangs painlessly into her flesh.

"You are angry with me," Arturo said quietly. "I would not have let him hurt you."

She met his gaze and saw the sincerity in his eyes. "That's good."

His mouth tightened. "You do not believe me."

For a long moment, she stared at him. "Honestly, I don't know, Vampire. You've changed. I know you've changed. And yet it was just two weeks ago when you watched Cristoff break my ribs and did absolutely nothing to stop him."

"I have explained . . ."

She sliced her hand through the air. "I know. I understand why you couldn't challenge him before and that your conscience was still half-buried. I even understand that racing to my aid today before it was absolutely necessary would have been the wrong thing to do. That with any luck the situation would turn to our advantage, which it did. None of that alters the way I feel right now."

Micah lifted his mouth from her wrist. "Kiss him, Quinn. Either kiss him or kiss me because without a complete feeding, I'm not sure I'll be able to call your glamour up."

Quinn stared at him hard, wondering if he was trying to take advantage of the situation, either for his own gain or his buddy's. She felt Arturo move up behind her, felt his hand slide lightly over her hair.

"I would not have let him hurt you, *cara mia*," he said quietly. "I will not let *anyone* hurt you. Never again."

Dammit. She didn't want this, this softening. And yet a part of her longed to believe him, longed to be back in his arms. She turned and met his gaze, her mouth tight. But she gave a brief nod, and that's all he needed.

His finger lifted her chin. His head dipped. Sliding his hand into her hair, he pressed his mouth to hers, a tender brush of lips, undemanding, and as gentle as dew on a rose petal.

Her response was slow in coming, but it was his gentleness that tore away her defenses. The breath she'd been holding trembled out of her on a sigh as her body melted against his. She lifted her arms and circled his neck, pressing her mouth more firmly to his.

His lips parted, stroking hers, then diving inside

when the last of her resistance gave way. And then thought fled, and she spiraled into sensation and passion and the certainty that this was where she belonged, where she'd always belonged.

Behind her, Micah cleared his throat. "That'll do it, kids. You did say time was of the essence?"

Quinn pulled away as Arturo lifted his face, his eyes as warm as his skin now. He cupped her cheek, then turned to Micah. "Did that help?"

"It did indeed."

Micah took her hand and pulled her in front of him to work his own personal magic. "Welcome back, Jillian," he said after several moments. "I'm afraid this isn't going to last long. Probably not much more than an hour."

Quinn nodded. "Then I'll have to be back in an hour."

As Micah reached for the doorknob, Quinn turned to go, and Arturo curled his hand around her shoulder from behind.

"Someday you will trust me implicitly, *bella*."

"I hope you're right, Vampire."

As it was, she trusted him far more than she'd ever thought possible given what he was. And what he'd done. But trust had never been something she gave easily. To anyone.

Quinn followed Arturo the short distance to the second pantry, slipping inside, while Arturo grabbed the torch, and Micah ran interference, distracting the only vampire close enough to see them.

The moment Arturo followed her into the pantry, Quinn opened the door to the dungeon and started down. Quietly, she led the way back to Vintry's cell.

This time, the old fae was sitting up, waiting for them, his eyes bright and excited. At the sight of them, he rose slowly, painfully, to his feet, a smile stretched across his face.

"The Healer and the Snake." But as he neared the bars, he frowned. "You've still not found the key?"

Quinn shook her head. "We haven't been able to look for it."

Vintry waved it away. "No matter." He reached a bony hand between the bars and grabbed Arturo's wrist. His eyes widened. "You're no vampire."

"I assure you, I am."

"You're warm."

Arturo nodded, a funny look sliding over his face as he glanced at her. "I've been kissing the sorceress."

Vintry made a comical and charming expression of surprise, then began to cackle. "Of course, of course." As his laughter died, he eyed Arturo seriously. "You were born to this world for a purpose. A purpose you must not forsake. The Healer needs you. And you her. Cleave one to the other, or all will be lost."

Quinn frowned at his words, but there was no time to ask questions. Not now.

Vintry reached for Quinn's hand, then set it on top of Arturo's when she gave it to him. "Hold her," he ordered Arturo.

After only a moment's hesitation, Arturo stepped behind Quinn, wrapping his arms around her and pressing his cheek to her hair. "How's this?"

Vintry nodded. "Fine. Better." He thrust both of his hands through the bars. "Take my hands, sorceress. Be quick. I've not much time."

Quinn did as he commanded, sliding her hands into his warm, bent ones.

The ancient fae closed his eyes. "Blackstone and Levenach, as you said," he murmured. "Honor. Good, good. Strong. Binding. Healing. You have great power within you, sorceress. Power that Cristoff will desire once he discovers you possess it." One eye opened, and he squinted at her. "You must not allow him to get it."

Arturo pulled her closer. "Cristoff will never touch her again."

Vintry turned that one eye on him, staring at him long and hard. "Untrue."

Quinn jerked.

Arturo's arm tightened. "I vow it," he snarled.

"Yes, yes, yes. It is you who needs her power, Snake. You who needs it." The old fae just closed his eyes again.

Quinn stared at him. Could he really see the future? Did he know that Cristoff would ultimately catch her? Dear God, was that really going to be her fate? She'd known it was likely from the moment she'd agreed to return to Vamp City. Still, she wouldn't change anything, not if it saved Zack.

"My brother," she began. "Is he somehow tied to my magic?"

"No. I sense nothing like that. Just the curse strangling your Blackstone magic."

"Then why is he suffering magic sickness?" she murmured.

"Don't know. I cannot tell you without seeing him for myself. Too late now."

Arturo's chin brushed her hair. "He'll be fine once you renew the magic of Vamp City."

For at least ten minutes they stood like that, Vintry silent, his eyes closed, holding her hands. Finally, he began to frown. "It is tangled, too tangled. I cannot free one from the other. Not entirely. The curse must be broken for that. Break the curse, and you will have the power you were born to, sorceress."

"But the curse can't be broken."

That eye opened again, squinting at her. "Aye, it can. Destroy Escalla. So long as Escalla exists, the curse lives."

Now it was Quinn's turn to frown. "Escalla? You mean Cristoff's sword?" She'd seen that jewel-hilted blade when Arturo first handed her over to that monster. Cristoff had taken her into his study, pulled the sword from a special case, and laid it in her hands. Then declared she had weak magic.

She turned to glance at Arturo, to question his previous statement that only the one who'd uttered the curse could break it. The Black Wizard who was long dead.

But he only shrugged as if he, too, were hearing this for the first time. And maybe he was. Besides, what difference did it make? If she could save Vamp City with her Blackstone magic, she and Zack were getting the hell out of here and never coming back. She had no need for magic in Australia. Or New Zealand.

All she'd ever wanted to be was normal.

Vintry opened his eyes. "I'll set free as much of your Blackstone magic as I can, girl, but it's not going to come easily. Or silently."

Quinn narrowed her eyes. "What do you mean?"

But he closed his eyes again and didn't answer for another several minutes. Finally, he opened both eyes and dropped her hands. "It is done. Hold on to your hat, girl, your magic is about to explode."

"*What?*"

"You have a few minutes. Maybe an hour. Now go!"

"What do you mean, *explode?*"

Arturo grabbed her arm. "We have to get out of here. Now."

As he started to pull her down the hall, Quinn called back, "Thank you, Vintry!"

"Cleave one to the other. Only together will you prevail!"

Quinn ran for the stairs, Arturo close behind with the torch. At the top, she eased open the door, then slipped into the pantry, the vampire close behind. Arturo strode into the hallway, replacing the torch, then grabbed her hand. And dropped it as if it had burned him.

"Come," he said in his best slave master's voice, remembering himself as he strode into the kitchen, presumably to steal away through the back door.

But they'd taken only a couple of steps when a voice sounded behind them.

"And just where do you think you're going?"

Quinn didn't have to turn around to know who'd spoken. She recognized the voice.

Fabian.

At the sound of Fabian's voice, Quinn dropped her gaze, fast, aware that if her eyes weren't glowing yet, they might start at any moment. She had no idea what Vintry meant by her magic's exploding, but whatever he meant, it couldn't be good. Not in a place like this.

She could feel the energy beginning to flow beneath her skin, not burning like usual but building, like steam looking for a way out.

Arturo spun around, his manner take charge and colonel-like. "The sorceress has vanished. We are looking for her."

"My men will search for her." Fabian's tone was sharp with annoyance and possessed more than a hint of cunning. The balance of power between the two of them had just shifted back into his hands, and he knew it.

Cold fingers curled around Quinn's arm. Fabian's fingers. "While they search, you two will join me. And feed me." He jerked Quinn off her feet, yanking her against him, palming her breast through her shirt. "This time, however, I will join you. I will have my cock inside of her."

Fabian gripped her face tight, forcing her to look at him. She tensed for his shock, terrified her eyes had begun to glow—that the Slava, Jillian's, eyes had begun to glow. But his expression revealed nothing but hard satisfaction.

"If my touch is going to make you sick, slave, then I'll tape your mouth closed. Which would be a shame. Your mouth is just one of the things I want to fuck."

She had to struggle not to spit in his face. All of a sudden, she began to shake as the energy built inside of her far more quickly and violently than it ever had before. A strange sensation began to bubble beneath her flesh, as if the skin were about to fly off her bones. As if she were about to *explode*.

The floor beneath her feet began to shake.

Shit, shit, shit.

The first blast sent them all flying a good fifteen

feet. Fabian pulled her with him as he flew, and she landed on top of him, knocking the breath out of herself. She slammed her eyes closed in case they were glowing and thanked whatever guardian angel looked out for sorceresses that Fabian had been holding on to her, or she might have been the only one left standing, which would have certainly given her away. As it was, all of them had been thrown to the ground—Arturo and Fabian's guards, as well as several Slavas.

Fabian surged to his feet vampire-fast.

"The fae," he muttered. "He's dead."

Quinn blinked. He thought the blast had been Vintry's doing? She remembered someone's saying something about a death wind.

Easing to her feet with her eyes all but closed, Quinn waited for Arturo to find her. But the pressure inside her was building all over again, much faster than before. The second blast erupted with no warning. Again, the vampires flew. This time, however, Quinn was prepared and dropped to her knees. Maybe she'd just stay there.

Strong arms gathered her close. Arturo's voice rang out close behind her. "That fae is going to bring the house crashing down!" She could hear the hypnotic *persuasion* weaving through his words. "Run!"

They did. When the third blast hit, Arturo slammed into the wall, keeping her tight against him, but protected. The plaster began to rain down from the ceiling. Pans and dishes crashed to the floor.

They were nearly to the door when the fourth hit. The windows broke. Rising, Arturo flung her over his shoulder, opened the back door, and ran.

"Keep your eyes closed, *tesoro*."

"I'm trying. What about Micah?"

"He should be waiting with the mounts."

"I'll kill the horses, if I knock them around like this."

"Maybe not. And we have no choice. They're our best chance of getting out of here."

Moments later, she was seated behind Arturo, her hands tight around his waist as her magic let loose yet again. The horses lurched, but righted themselves quickly, then took off, spooked by the sound of glass . . . or crystal . . . shattering all along the back curve of the wedding cake.

"They've already opened the gates," Arturo told her. "Everyone's fleeing." And a moment later, they were flying across the open ground. When no more blasts came for several minutes, Quinn lifted a hand to her face, opened one eye, and saw no glow against her palm.

"We made it," Micah said, as the two vampires brought their horses back to a walk. "Did you free your power, Quinn?"

Quinn grunted. "Something's gotten loose, that's for sure." She sighed. "I don't know. I'm not even sure how to tell."

She'd better figure it out soon. Tomorrow was the equinox.

"This isn't gonna work," Jazlyn hissed.

"If you believe it won't," Lily replied quietly, "then it won't. You must believe it will." They'd escaped the castle more than two hours ago and had been crouched behind the outdoor kiln ever since. So far, no one had ventured back there, but it was just a matter of time. It was dusk in the real world, Lily was fairly certain. She'd quickly picked up the nuances of light in this place—the black of night, which turned to twilight during the day. In the in-between times, dawn and dusk, the air took on a different quality, almost shimmering. And she was pretty sure the vampires' eyesight was just a little off at that time.

Conveniently, a Trader wagon arrived late afternoon most days, remaining at the castle for an hour or two while the Traders dropped off their goods and took orders for more, and often spent a little time in the kitchen eating and drinking and sometimes having sex with one of the slaves.

The Traders who'd come today had been inside, by Lily's calculation, for a little over an hour and a half. And the male slaves had just been called in for their evening meal. The yard was almost empty.

If they were going to sneak into the Traders' wagon, as was her plan, they'd never get a better chance.

"It's time, Jazlyn." Lily squeezed the girl's arm. "We can do this."

Jazlyn's pulse leaped beneath Lily's fingers. Lily had never seen the girl so nervous, which boded ill in a castle swarming with fear-feeding, and fear-sensing, vampires.

"You have to calm down."

"I can't! If they catch us . . ."

"They'll sell us to the auction, which they're going to do anyway. There's no downside to this escape attempt." Lily knew that wasn't true. The vampires could choose any number of horrible ways to make an example of them, but mentioning that to Jazlyn now would only make things worse. "Come on, Jaz. Let's go."

The wagon sat twenty feet from the back of the kiln and was still half-filled with goods destined for another house or castle. There were places to hide. They would never get a better opportunity.

"You go first, Lily. I'll follow."

"Jaz . . ."

The girl turned on her, her mouth hard. "I said, *go*."

"You're not coming." Lily could see it in her eyes.

Jazlyn's toughness melted, her eyes filling with tears. "This is your chance to get away, not mine. I can't climb into any wagon without spooking the horses, I can't fit into any hidey-hole inside. They'll see me the minute they look. And I *know* they'll catch me, Lily. I *know* it. And my pounding heart is going to give us both away. You go."

"Not without you."

The toughness hardened her face, then melted again. "Yes without me. You're a female ninja. You can disappear, and they'll never find you, and I need you to do that." The tears began to slip down her cheeks. "Don't you see, Lily? Don't you *see*? I can't watch you stripped and beaten. I can't watch you get killed like I did my sister. I *can't*." Her eyes flashed, her mouth turning mean even as tears glistened on her lashes. "I can take whatever those motherfuckers throw at me, but not that. You got to escape *for me*."

Tears burned in Lily's eyes, and she threw her arms around Jazlyn's neck, feeling strong arms circle her and squeeze her tight in return. She searched for words and found none. So she slipped out of Jazlyn's grip and stole, silently, into the wagon, curling up behind one of the crates beneath a beat-up old tarp.

Only minutes later, she heard the sound of voices.

The Traders', most likely, and one vampire whose voice she recognized from his constant bellowing in the yards. Her pulse began to race, and she struggled to bring it back down. Because she knew that that particular vampire was absolutely a fear-feeder.

As she felt the wagon lurch with the weight of the returning Traders, the vampire made a sound of surprise that boded ill and made her stomach cramp with dread.

"I taste your fear, human." The voice sounded so close, she knew he was peering into the wagon. "Show yourself at once, blood sack, or you're going to feel my lash."

Jazlyn's squeal cut through the pounding in Lily's ears. "I don't want to go to the slave auction!" Jazlyn cried, her voice growing louder, closer. She was running right up to the vampire! "Don't make me, please don't make me. I'll take your lash, or your fangs, or your cock. Just don't send me to that auction!"

The girl sounded hysterical. But Lily knew better. She was covering for Lily, making the vampire think it was her fear he'd tasted instead of Lily's.

"Go on!" the vampire called, and a moment later, the wagon began to move. Jazlyn cried out, this time in pain, this time for real.

Lily began to cry. As the distance between her and Castle Smithson grew, her tears fell in earnest, and she cried for Jazlyn, and for Zack, and for all the other girls she'd lived with these past weeks, many of whom were destined to suffer terribly. But not for herself. She refused to cry for herself. Because some way, somehow, she was going home.

When her tears were spent, she wiped her face and listened hard as the wagon rattled over rough ground.

With Jazlyn's help, she'd escaped Castle Smithson, but this was only the first of many challenges, she suspected. If this were an old-time computer game, she'd have completed only the first level.

If the Traders found her in the back of their wagon, or saw her when she tried to escape, she'd either be returned to Smithson or sold directly to the slave auction.

And whatever Jazlyn had suffered helping Lily escape would have been for nothing.

CHAPTER NINETEEN

Quinn clung to Arturo, pressing her cheek against his shoulder as she rode behind him on the horse. She was exhausted, worn-out by lack of sleep, by the bursts of power, and by the stress of keeping secrets and staying alive in an enemy stronghold. But she felt utterly exhilarated, too. Not only had they succeeded in finding Vintry and getting him to help as much as he could, but she was intrigued by his claim that she was the Healer, whatever that meant. And on a far more basic level, she was beginning to realize she enjoyed the rush of adrenaline. Escaping out from under the nose of a vampire master on a racing horse, with her goal accomplished and her secret intact, had been one of the most exciting things she'd ever done.

For the time being, the magic blasts seemed to have stopped. A couple of times, as they'd ridden, she'd pointed her palm or finger at a fallen branch and tried to make something happen—exactly what she wasn't sure. Maybe fly, maybe burst into flame. Just a bit of a quiver would have been nice. She'd thought that with her magic *exploding,* she'd have some ability to wield it. And maybe she would, once she figured out how.

"Are you still awake back there?" Arturo asked.

"Barely. What are we going to do now?"

"Good question. Until we know what you can do, and can be certain you're done blasting, we can't risk the humans at Neo's. Or the vampires, for that matter. The whole house could come down."

"Is there somewhere else I can go?"

"Neo has safe houses scattered all over V.C.," Micah said. "He'll know of somewhere safe."

"I have to see Zack."

"When we reach Neo's, I would suggest you remain outside, *cara*. I'll bring Zack out to you."

"How are you feeling, Quinn?" Micah asked. "Do you feel any different? More powerful?"

Even as tired as she felt, the power continued to flow beneath her skin like a creek beneath a thin layer of ice. "It's hard to say. Before, the power came and went, and when it started to rise, it hurt. It's never left me this time. But it doesn't hurt, and it doesn't feel like it's rising. More like it's part of me now, if that makes any sense."

Arturo reached back and squeezed her knee. "You need to test it, to learn what you can do. We'll work on that once you've gotten some sleep."

"She may get a chance to do that right now," Micah said quietly, his voice suddenly razor-sharp. "We've got company."

Quinn jerked upright, her gaze following Micah's. Indistinct shapes loomed on the hill ahead, in between the trees. Four of them. Men.

"Werewolves?" she asked.

"Rippers."

Adrenaline flooded her body all over again, washing away her exhaustion.

As they cleared the trees, she could see them more clearly. The four were on foot and looked like they'd just walked off the streets of D.C.—dressed in jeans, tees, and jackets.

"How do you know they're Rippers?" she asked.

"Look at their eyes," Arturo murmured.

She squinted, frowning. "They're red," she said with surprise. Red where the whites should be. "Does that mean they're hungry? Or are their eyes always like that?"

"The red presages violence. It means they intend to attack."

"Why? Can they tell I'm human?"

"No, we're too far. Their olfactory senses are sharper than an Emora's, but they are not that pronounced. No, they attack because they think they can. They outnumber us. And Rippers hate Emoras."

"We hunt them," Micah told her. "Hunting Rippers in D.C is one of my primary, and most satisfying, jobs for Gonzaga kovena. Not only are they monsters, but they're a danger to our race. They're careless with their human kills."

"Are these four trapped in Vamp City, now?"

"Probably. Any vampire—Emora or Ripper—who was here when the magic broke is trapped."

"Be prepared to grab the reins, Quinn," Arturo said quietly.

"You're leaving?"

"The moment the battle engages, take the horse and go. Call to your wolves for escort if you can."

She was glad he'd warned her because a moment later, the four Rippers disappeared in a blur. And then Arturo was gone and she was alone on the horse, sitting too far back.

The horse whinnied and sidestepped, and she grabbed the pommel. As the sound of snarls and the clank of steel erupted on either side of her, she struggled into the saddle, grabbed the reins, and inelegantly kicked the horse into gear.

But just as she thought she'd made her escape, movement ahead caught her eye. She saw the red first. And then the forms of more than half a dozen more Rippers as they stepped out from behind the trees. Holy hell. Several of them grinned, their fangs longer than Arturo's or Micah's, and sharper, their eyes as red as blood and cold with the promise of death.

The power beneath her flesh surged harder as her heart began to thud in her ears. If only she still had her stakes! Instead, she lifted her hand, attempting to channel that power. Aiming her palm at the middle Ripper, she willed him to fly backward.

To her amazed delight, he did, landing a good ten feet back with a shout of surprise.

She grinned, excitement sparking inside her. For the first time, she'd successfully called the power when she needed it. And without pain. This was going to be fun. But as she shifted her hand to aim at another, the Rippers blurred and were gone. Damn speedy vampires.

A heartbeat later, something slammed into her hard, knocking her off the horse and the knife out of her hand. She hit the ground back first in a blast of fiery pain. The breath left her body. Something landed on top of her.

Fangs sunk into her throat.

Shit, shit, shit.

Her mind went blank as instinct kicked in and she grabbed hold of the head latched onto her and . . . to her utter amazement . . . jerked it away. As if the vampire who'd attacked her was a seventy-pound weakling.

He stared at her, stunned. She slammed her palms against his shoulders and pushed him, hard, then stared wide-eyed when he flew back, landing on his butt by her feet.

Holy shit.

In a blur, he was standing over her, half-grinning, half-snarling. But not, she noticed, attacking. Not yet. Had she really just pushed him off her?

Quinn stared at him in shock, lifting one hand to the sticky wetness on her neck, aiming the other at him. He blurred to her right a good six feet. Quinn jumped to her own feet, rising far more easily than she'd expected to, and faced him.

He blurred, gripping her around the waist from behind, his fangs once more sinking into her shoulder. Lifting her knee, Quinn slammed her heel back into her opponent's and heard the incredibly satisfying sound of cracking bone.

The vampire released her with a roar. She spun, leading with her elbow, and knocked him flat. This was like some kind of dream.

She was freaking Buffy!

But just as she was beginning to think she might really be Superwoman, she was knocked to the ground again, this time by three vampires. And though she managed to temporarily dislodge one or the other, they just kept returning, two biting either side of her neck, one sinking his fangs into her upper thigh right through her jeans.

With fear tearing through her, and the knowledge that she only had moments to get them off before they drained her dry, the power beneath her flesh ran faster, harder. But though she pushed and bucked and *willed* her power to shove them away, nothing happened.

Her heart began to thunder in her ears. She wasn't helpless, dammit. She was *not* helpless. She had the power to save herself; she just had to find the way to call it.

Concentrate.

She imagined gathering that energy into a single, pulsing ball, then closed her eyes and focused all of her attention, feeling the power beneath her skin rush harder and swirl more violently.

One, two, *three*.

She imagined her energy ball exploding outward in a powerful blast.

The three vampires went flying.

For a second, relief made her boneless. She'd done it. But as she tried to rise, her body barely responded. As she struggled to sit up, the landscape spun around her. They'd taken too much of her blood. But she had to move. They'd be on her again any second, coming back to finish her off.

Battle exploded suddenly around her. She managed to stumble to her feet, but when she tried to take a step, her legs collapsed beneath her, and she went down hard. The next thing she knew, Arturo was holding her, talking to her, and the sounds of battle were gone.

"You are hurt, *cara mia*. They've torn your flesh." She opened her eyes as he lifted her onto his lap. "I'll take no blood, but I must bite you to initiate the healing." As her head fell against his shoulder, he dipped his head to her ravaged neck.

She felt cool fingers around her wrist and turned

to find Micah lifting her wrist to his mouth. He watched her, his white-centered eyes dark with concern. Mike. Her friend.

"Did you kill them?" she asked, but she already knew the answer.

Neither vampire replied for a moment. Then Arturo lifted his face to meet her gaze, lines of worry bracketing his eyes.

"They are no more. I tried to reach you sooner, but there were more of them than we realized. I am sorry, *tesoro*."

Already she was beginning to feel a little better, a little stronger. "I'm not. I needed the practice."

Arturo tipped his head against hers. "I would prefer you practice with those who are not trying to kill you."

Quinn gave a soft sound of amusement. "Me, too. Though there's no denying that the threat of death helps me focus."

Arturo swept her into his arms and stood, then handed her to Micah while he mounted. Micah handed her back and swung onto his own horse. Arturo tucked her tight against his chest, and they headed back to Neo's.

"**W**ake up, *carissima*."

The soft words, the kiss to her head, burrowed deep and sweet, far more deeply than Quinn had let herself feel in a long, long time, and for a moment the emotion stung, like warm water on hands that had grown too cold.

She straightened groggily, still on the horse, pulling away slightly from Arturo's chest. "Where are we?"

"Neo's. Micah has gone for Zack."

Blinking, trying to force her eyes to stay open, Quinn glanced at the familiar house looming close. "I really slept."

"You needed to."

A few minutes later, Neo and Micah came out through the portico, Zack following close behind.

Arturo swung down, then lifted her off the horse, setting her on her feet.

"Are you steady?" he asked, watching her carefully.

She still felt half-asleep, but no longer light-headed with blood loss. "I'm good."

He nodded and joined the vampires as Zack loped over to her.

Her heart swelled at the sight of her brother, her rock. "How are you feeling?" she asked, as he joined her. She reached for him, feeling his forehead. Hotter than before. So damned hot. A small kernel formed just beneath her breastbone, a terror that the fever would take him suddenly, stealing his life. And she wouldn't be there. She wouldn't know until too late.

"I'm beat," he admitted, but he sounded excited. "Jason's been working my ass off."

"That's good." She supposed. She stroked his hair lightly, aching from the love she'd always felt for him. Realizing what she was doing, she snatched her hand away, afraid she might accidentally hurt him with her power.

He peered at her curiously. "Did you free your magic?"

"To some extent. I could use a tutor."

Amusement crinkled his eyes. "Like Dumbledore?"

"Or Merlin."

Zack smiled, his grin swift and bright. "Too bad you can't enroll at Hogwarts. You need to practice."

"I do. Until I get it under control, I can't stay here. I'm still throwing energy, pushing people back. And there are too many who could get hurt around here. Too many humans."

"Where are you going, then?"

"I'm not sure. One of Neo's other safe houses. I shouldn't be far."

His mouth twisted with wry acceptance. "And I suppose I still can't go with you."

"Seeing as how you fall into the human category, no. I could break your bones . . . or your skull."

"Freaking Xena."

Quinn snorted. "I wish." Though she'd managed to channel Buffy for a while. Maybe, eventually, she'd be able to do that at will.

She hugged Zack hard, feeling his quick hug in return, then pulled back, letting him go. "Neo will come get me if you need me."

"I know."

"Love you, Zack."

"Love you, too, sis." He turned and loped back into the house, as if eager to get back to whatever he'd been pulled away from.

Quinn turned and joined the vampires, who were having a discussion of their own.

"We'll join you in twos or threes," Neo said. "I don't want anyone becoming suspicious."

Arturo nodded. "Agreed."

Neo smiled at her. "Hi, Quinn."

She returned the smile sleepily. "I'd like to talk to Amanda about Zack."

"She'll be joining you shortly," Neo told her. "We'll all be joining you. Immortals only, so there's no danger if your power breaks loose."

Another male strolled out of the house, and she recognized Arturo's friend, Kassius. Tall as a tree, with short, curly, dark hair, he was the one responsible for the Slavas in Cristoff's castle, and he watched over them like a mother hen.

He, too, gave her a quick, friendly smile. "Hello, Quinn."

"Hi, Kassius."

"What are you doing here?" Arturo asked, pleasure in his voice as he shook his friend's hand.

Kassius's expression turned grave. "They're bringing children into Vamp City."

"I know. Micah already smuggled one back out."

"Traders brought three in the last shipment. I bought them and brought them here." His mouth compressed, his jaw turning hard. "It's a damn good thing tomorrow's the equinox because this city has gone to hell."

"Can you stay for a couple of hours? We're about to discuss tomorrow. I'd like you there."

"I can stay for a little while."

Micah lifted a hand. "If Kas is going to accompany you, I'll stay here and feed. I'll meet you over there in time for the meeting."

As Micah and Neo turned back for the house, Rinaldo brought several fresh mounts around. Arturo gave Quinn a leg up on one, then he and Kassius mounted the other two. The three started off, Quinn between them.

A short while later, they pulled up in front of what appeared to be a deserted house—two stories with a crumbling porch, shutters hanging askew or missing altogether, and the glass of most of the windows shattered. An old-style haunted mansion, they'd call it in the real world. Here it was just one of hundreds of shells left to disintegrate by a population that needed far less housing than their doppelganger world provided.

Arturo swung down. "Wait here while I ensure it is safe." A moment later, he disappeared through the front door.

Quinn turned to Kassius. "Any luck finding Lily?"

He shook his head. "I sent a man to investigate. I'll let you know as soon as I learn something."

She nodded, praying they found Lily and got her out of there safely.

"You've found your power?" Kassius asked her quietly.

"I've found something. I'm still figuring out what I can do."

"It will come."

"I hope so. Kassius, I'm not sure if I ever thanked you properly for rescuing me from Cristoff's dungeon. But thank you."

He dipped his head in acknowledgment. "I was happy to do it. Happier still that Ax requested it. I had begun to fear we were losing him to the darkness, but you changed that."

"Your own conscience was never compromised, was it?"

"I don't believe so, no. I suspect my wolf blood is the reason."

"You're very loyal to Arturo."

"We all are. I would follow him to the ends of the earth, sorceress. I sometimes think I have."

CHAPTER TWENTY

"**A**ll clear," Arturo said, striding down the front steps of the crumbling house.

Before Quinn could dismount, Arturo was at her side, helping her down, sliding an arm around her waist.

"I'm okay," she told him.

"Good." But Arturo didn't remove his arm as he led her into the dusty house that smelled of age, rot, and mildew.

"I'm surprised these places are still standing after a 140-plus years," she murmured.

"Some are, some aren't. Lack of sun keeps them from rotting as quickly as they would have in your world. And perhaps, a touch of the magic."

Once they were in the house, Arturo released her and set about lighting candles and oil lamps, revealing walls and flooring as decrepit as she'd expected—chunks of plaster missing from the walls, the wooden floor lifted and broken in places. The furniture in the house was another matter. By rights, it should have looked as broken-down and ancient as the structure around it. Instead, a pair of worn, but by no means ancient leather recliners, flanked a new leather sofa. And against one wall stood half a dozen gray, folding metal chairs that looked like they'd been nabbed from the closest elementary-school auditorium.

There were no cobwebs, no signs of critter infestation. But she supposed there wouldn't be since there were no living things in Vamp City that the vampires hadn't intentionally brought in.

"How many people are we expecting for this powwow?" Quinn asked.

"There will be nine of us in all."

Quinn reached for one of the metal chairs and unfolded it, surprised to find it in nearly new condition. "How do you get things like this here?" But she knew, and answered her own question. "Traders."

"Yes."

Arturo helped her set up the chairs. They'd just finished when Mukdalla walked in through the front door, accompanied by her vampire husband, Rinaldo. Mukdalla smiled when she saw Quinn, and strode right over, giving her a big hug.

Quinn stiffened. She'd never been a hugger. Never been particularly comfortable with displays of affection.

Mukdalla released her quickly and stepped back, her smile less bright than before. "I'm glad you're okay, Quinn. Are you feeling better? Or at least in better control?"

"I'm getting there."

When she didn't expound on that, Mukdalla nodded. "All right. Well, I'm sure it will come." She turned to join her husband, who'd taken up watch at one of the windows.

Quinn felt Arturo's gaze and turned to find him watching her thoughtfully.

Soon, the others began to arrive. Amanda strode

in the door, accompanied by a Slava male and Neo.

"Micah took a different route," Neo told Arturo. "But he should be here in a few minutes."

Amanda led the Slava male to Quinn, a wide smile lighting her face. "Quinn, I'd like for you to meet my husband. This is Sam. Sam, Quinn Lennox, our sorceress."

Sam thrust out his hand, and Quinn shook it. "It's an honor to meet you, Quinn. We've been hoping and praying for your arrival for quite some time."

Quinn smiled uncomfortably. So many people's lives were dependent upon her, and not just in Vamp City. If she renewed the magic, how many innocent humans would be rounded up and killed for food and sport? But if she didn't renew it, people she'd met and come to like would lose their lives. Amanda and Sam, Neo and Rinaldo, Kassius and Bram.

"Thanks. I'll do my best." What else was there to say? She turned to Amanda. "Tell me about Zack. He's burning up, hotter than before."

The woman's mien turned professional. "His temperature is rising, I'm afraid. And shows no sign of stopping."

"Yet he still continues to feel fine. He's working out, for heaven's sake."

Sam gave his wife's shoulder a squeeze, nodded at Quinn, and went to join the men.

"That's typical with magic sickness," Amanda continued. "But that kind of body heat will still be a problem if it goes too high."

"His brain will fry."

Amanda's mouth compressed. "Yes. I'm afraid so."

"How quickly is that likely to happen?"

"I don't know, Quinn." She shrugged apologetically. "Nothing is ever certain when magic is concerned. But I'll be glad when you've renewed the magic. For a lot of reasons."

"Here comes Micah," Arturo said loud enough for all to hear.

Rinaldo started for the door. "Sam and I'll take watch." The two males headed out as Kassius and Micah walked in.

When they'd all taken their seats—some on the sofa and recliners, others, including Quinn and Arturo, on the metal chairs—Arturo began, glancing at Quinn. "Tomorrow is the equinox. Quinn's magic has been freed to some extent, hopefully enough to renew the magic of Vamp City."

"Thank you," Mukdalla whispered to the heavens, pressing her hands together.

"The problem we have now is twofold." Arturo leaned forward, his arms on his knees, his expression dead serious. "One, the magic must be renewed in the Focus. It might occur to Cristoff to keep watch there, so we'll have to scout the area fully before we take Quinn."

"Not *we*," Kassius said quietly. "Not you. You can't go near the Focus tomorrow, Ax. Cristoff cannot know you're involved."

"I shall remain out of sight."

"Far out of sight."

"Does the ritual have to take place at a certain time?" Neo asked. "Like midnight?"

Arturo shook his head. "Not that I'm aware. But there is a second problem. Quinn does not know the ritual that must be performed to renew the magic."

Sounds of frustration and disappointment peppered the small room, and it was clear that Neo, Amanda, and Mukdalla hadn't known.

"Sheridan Blackstone is the only one who knows the words," Arturo told them. "He was there, listening, when his father performed the first renewal after Phineas attempted to destroy his creation in 1878."

"Will Sheridan help her, then?" Neo asked.

Micah snorted. "That's the sixty-four-thousand-dollar question."

Kassius glanced at Quinn, his gaze sharp with knowledge. "I have something on Grant."

And she bet she knew what it was. When Arturo had delivered her to Cristoff after her first escape, Cristoff had demanded to know who set her free. He'd sent for Kassius since the werevamp could, through a bite, steal another's memories. After Kassius bit her, he'd told Cristoff the truth, to an extent, that two Slavas had set her free—Slavas she'd already sent home through a sunbeam. But Kassius had left out most of the details, like the existence of the tunnels beneath Gonzaga Castle known only to the Slavas. Tunnels created magically by Sheridan's brother, Grant. He'd also failed to mention to Cristoff that Grant had been the one who'd orchestrated her escape.

If Cristoff learned of Grant's involvement, there was no telling what he'd do to him.

Kassius smiled grimly. "When I get back, Grant and I will have a discussion about what I know and what he's going to do to secure my silence."

Arturo leaned back. "There's a good chance that Sheridan and Grant will be followed when they leave the castle for the Focus. We're going to need a diversion."

"I'll handle that." Micah smiled. "Cristoff will be certain the sorceress is right under his nose." He'd probably use glamour to make himself look like her. "We need to set a timetable. It's damned inconvenient that cell phones don't work in this place."

"What time shall I tell Grant to meet us at the Focus?" Kassius asked.

Arturo frowned. "Make it 5:00 P.M. That should give you plenty of time to get Grant and Sheridan in place."

"Cristoff will be frantic," Micah murmured. "The equinox dawns, and he has no sorceress."

"If word reaches Gonzaga Castle that the sorceress was spotted at Fabian's?" Kassius asked.

"Remind Cristoff that I will not stop hunting her until I've captured her. That will be enough."

"The moment this is over, any of us who've been spotted by Sheridan or Grant Blackstone had better disappear. Especially you, Kas." Micah's brows drew down. "Even if he doesn't have them followed, Cristoff will know the Blackstones were involved. The moment Cristoff threatens either of them, they'll give you up." He glanced at Arturo. "Even if Cristoff regains his soul through this, he'll never forgive a traitor. Ever."

Silence sat thick in the room for several moments before Arturo spoke.

"Quinn and I will remain here and work on her magic until time to go to the Focus. The better control she has, the better for all involved."

The discussion turned to logistics and diversions, and while Quinn listened, many of the names and places went right past her. Finally, the meeting was over.

Neo rose. "Rinaldo will stay and keep watch for you. Mukdalla's promised to send food back for Quinn."

As the others exited through the front door, Micah turned to Quinn, his eyes warm with concern. "Have you recovered?"

"For the most part. I think I'm just tired, now."

"Good." He flashed her a friendly grin and followed the others out the door.

When they were alone, Arturo turned to her, his eyes dark and fathomless. "Time for bed, *cara mia*. You are asleep on your feet."

But Quinn shook her head. "Not yet. I want to try to practice first." The sooner she learned how to control her gift, the safer they'd all be.

"If you're sure."

She smiled at him. "This moment, I'm sure. Five seconds from now, I might decide I'm too tired and go to bed." She looked around the ancient house warily. "We'd better go outside. If I try throwing power in here, I could bring this whole place down on top of us."

"If you bring the house down, so be it. It will have served its purpose. I'll make certain you get out safely."

She peered at him curiously, but then her tired brain caught up. "You're afraid my eyes will glow."

"Yes." He looked around the room, then pointed to one of the folding chairs. "Try to push that."

Quinn eyed it, clenching and unclenching her fists. The power still flowed beneath her skin, as it had ever since Vintry released it, but calmly now. Just a gentle current of energy. Narrowing her eyes, she wondered if she'd need an adrenaline spike to get it going. There was only one way to find out.

Lifting a single hand, palm out, she focused on the chair and willed it to move if only a couple of feet.

Nothing happened. *Dammit.* She'd thought she was past this phase.

With a twist of her lips, she tried again, imagining the chair slamming into the back of the hearth. Still nothing happened. When that first Ripper had attacked her, she'd had no trouble pushing him back. Then again, her life had been on the line.

"I have an idea," the vampire said behind her.

Quinn glanced at him over her shoulder. "Are you going to try to terrify me? My power seems to work best when I feel threatened."

He smiled as he joined her. "Would you believe me if I promised to tear out your throat?"

"Fortunately, no."

Coming up behind her, he slipped one well-muscled arm around her waist, and dipped his head to her neck.

"Are you going to bite me?" she asked, surprised. But she felt no prick of fangs, only the cool brush of his lips. And felt an answering shiver of pleasure.

"I am going to do what I've been wanting to do for hours," he said huskily. He turned her in his arms and kissed her thoroughly, his hand sliding into her hair, the other pulling her hips tight against his. When she slid her arms around his neck and opened her mouth to his, he slid his tongue inside with a groan, pulling her closer still. Passion erupted between them, a heady, wonderful pleasure that stole all thoughts, all worries, drenching her body in pleasure.

"This isn't helping me reach my magic," she said breathlessly, as his lips trailed kisses along her cheek and jaw.

"This *is* magic," he replied, his hands roaming restlessly across her back. "I need to be inside you, *bella*."

"There are vampires outside."

"They won't come in."

A burst of humor left her mouth on a sigh. "And you don't care if they do."

"I do not." His mouth nuzzled her neck. "I need to taste you, to feast on you, to worship your body in comfort and leisure without anyone's forcing our intimacy." As Fabian had last time.

And she needed that, too. Heaven help her, she needed him. That quickly, their kiss had stirred her into a frenzy of desire that sang in her blood, snapping and popping . . .

She stilled.

He lifted his head, peering at her with question.

"Hold on a second. Let me try something." When he slowly, reluctantly, released her, she turned once more to the chair, lifted her hand, and sent it flying into the wall.

"The passion?" he queried.

"I guess. It seems that my magic only works when *some*thing's stirring my blood."

He pulled her back against him, one hand sliding over her breast, the other between her jeans-clad legs. Quinn groaned, arching at the pleasure of his hands on her.

"All I need is you, Vampire," she gasped.

He growled low in her ear, his teeth nipping lightly at her earlobe, without fangs. His fingers slid against the crotch of her jeans, stroking, heating . . .

"You are my sun," he breathed, his breath warm against her cheek. His hand ducked under the hem of her shirt and burrowed up, his fingers sliding over her bra cup, tracing the edges, delving beneath to find the sensitive bud of her nipple.

She gasped at the sweet pleasure, arching against him as he pushed the cup aside, as he stroked her breast and plucked at the bud.

Suddenly, he was in front of her, on his knees, his clever fingers unfastening her bra clasp with one hand and her jeans button with the other. Her bra gave way. He brushed the cups aside, sliding his hands around to her back, pulling her close, then taking her breast into his mouth.

Quinn clung to him, sliding her fingers into his hair as she struggled for breath against the exquisite pleasure, his tongue stroking her nipple, his lips caressing the flesh of her breast, his warm hands sliding with tender care and increasing urgency over her back.

One of those clever hands returned to the front, unzipped her jeans, and slid down into her panties. A single finger dove deep into her body.

Her legs buckled, and he tightened the arm still around her waist, moving his mouth to claim her other breast. Hands in his hair, she held him tight against her as his finger slid in and out, in and out, his thumb circling and stroking her clitoris, driving her up and up and up.

She came with a cry, her legs buckling as the pleasure pulsed and throbbed inside her.

Finally, slowly, Arturo withdrew his finger from her body, his hand from her panties, his mouth from her breast, and stood. As she struggled to catch her breath, he straightened her clothing and stepped back, licking her essence off of his finger.

She watched him, bemused, and abuzz with the aftershocks of her orgasm. "I thought you wanted to be inside of me." He hadn't even slid his fangs into her.

The eyes that watched her were white-centered and white-hot. "You have no idea, *cara mia*." He turned away, arching his back, visibly struggling against his own needs.

"Then why . . . ?"

He turned back, his eyes slowly returning to normal. "In the Focus tomorrow, I will not be with you. Nor will your life be in danger. You must learn to call on the power without your emotions stirred."

"So you brought me to release so that I'd settle down."

"Yes."

"You could have joined me."

He smiled. "I could have. But then it would have been hours, not minutes, and you would have been asleep by the time we were through. I prefer to wait until I can take my time and make love to you properly. And I will take much time to do it." His eyes sparkled with heat, warming her body all over again.

"That kind of talk is not the way to cool me off, in case you're wondering."

His smile turned boyish and impossibly charming. "I am glad." He held out his hand to her. "Come. We shall attempt to push the chair together."

Bonelessly, she stepped forward and would have been perfectly happy to slide into his arms and stay there for a while. Maybe the rest of the night. Instead, she straightened her shoulders and corralled her thoughts, focusing on the task at hand. She didn't have much time to get this right. A single evening.

The realization hit her fully that she would get

one chance to renew the magic tomorrow. And if she failed, her beloved brother would almost certainly die.

The knowledge cleared her head as nothing else could have. "All right. Let's do it."

As she faced the chair, Arturo moved behind her and slid his arm around her waist again. Grasping the hand she'd been trying to push the chair with, he slid his palm across the back of her hand, his fingers slipping between hers.

"Concentrate, Quinn," he said softly. "Deep inside you is power, but it is not yet fully at your command." He squeezed her hand gently, brushing his cheek against her hair. "Close your eyes, *cara mia*. Now search inside yourself until you find the source of your power."

"It's a constant flow beneath my skin. If there's a source, I'm not aware of it."

"All right, then imagine that your arm is a laser gun."

Quinn laughed. "Seriously? Do you know how wrong that sounds coming from a man who was born in the fourteen hundreds?"

He nipped her ear lightly, but she could feel his smile. "We could call it a sword, but the effect would be much less satisfying."

"Laser gun it is."

"Now imagine the power you shoot from your laser gun is stored beneath the skin of your arms. They are one, and the loading is automatic. When you need the power, it flows directly from the gun barrels beneath your skin into your laser gun."

"I don't think laser guns have barrels."

"You are not concentrating, *cara mia*. Feel the

power. Feel it flowing into the gun, into your hands. Do you feel it?"

"Maybe?" It was so hard to know.

"Now try to shoot your gun." His fingers curled between hers, holding her hand, palm out, as the arm around her waist pulled her even tighter against his hard, lean body.

"On the count of three, no? One, two . . ."

Forcing her mind on the task, and off of that hard, lean body, Quinn visualized a laser gun, just as he said, imagined aiming it.

"Three!"

She imagined shooting it, saw in her mind's eye the power flying through her arm and out through her hand. And watched as the metal chair tipped over and clattered to the floor.

"I did it," she breathed, feeling Arturo's lips brush her hair. "Sort of."

"You did it, *cara*." His voice was rich with warmth and satisfaction. "Now shoot another."

This time, she aimed herself, Arturo's hand still laced with hers, and imagined the gun and the power firing without his verbal help.

The chair scooted back about two feet.

"Now send it into the wall, Quinn. Send it flying."

She glanced at him, twisting her lips, then imagined ramping up the energy in her laser, pumping it up like she might a water gun. Taking aim, she counted to three silently and *commanded* the chair away from her.

It slammed so hard into the hearth that a brick fell to the floor.

"*Bella*. Again."

She started to aim at a third chair, but at this angle

she'd send it straight through the window. "I need to move."

Arturo released her slowly, his arm sliding reluctantly away, and she moved to where she could aim the third one at the hearth. Concentrating as she had before, she succeeded easily, then sent another flying, and another.

Satisfaction overflowing, she turned to Arturo and blew the tips of her fingers as if she carried a smoking gun.

His smile dawned slow and brilliant, setting butterflies to flight in her chest. Oh, he was a gorgeous male, as dangerous as he was beautiful, in so many ways. But beautiful all the same.

"What now?" she asked.

The look in his eyes as his gaze traveled slowly down her body told her he was considering options he'd said would wait for later. But then he began setting up the chairs, apparently holding firm to his resolve.

A couple of the chairs, the last two she'd shot, wouldn't open fully anymore. Her blasts had gotten stronger as she'd gone down the line.

"Try your other hand, this time," he told her. "A good sorceress should be ambidextrous."

"You're sure about that?"

His eyes crinkled at the corners. "I am. Quite."

"Okay, then." When he'd stepped back out of the way, she lifted her left hand and willed the first chair to fly.

It tipped over with a soft clatter.

"Concentrate, *cara mia*."

"I know, I know." With a huff, Quinn started at the beginning, imagining the gun and the power, visualizing the energy flowing from her skin into the barrel, and . . .

The chair hit the hearth with such force that four bricks came crashing down. With a smug smile, she aimed again and sent a second chair flying, then lifted her right hand, too, and tried two at once. The right flew, the left only scooted a few inches.

"This is going to take practice," she muttered.

"Indeed." Out of the corner of her eye, she saw Arturo stroll over to a chest in the corner . . . a bar . . . and pour himself a drink.

When she'd knocked down two more chairs, she glanced behind her to find Arturo seated comfortably on the sofa, drink in hand, watching her.

"Enjoying the show?"

"Immensely." He lifted his glass in salute, then lowered it to take a sip.

Quinn snorted, then resumed practice until the mantel and all the bricks lay in a heap on the floor, the chairs little more than twisted metal.

Dropping her hands, she stared at the mess she'd made. *My God, I did this without touching anything. All power, all magic. My magic.*

Unease quivered in her stomach, the old loathing raising its head. She'd always hated being different. But she couldn't deny having the ability to make things move was incredibly satisfying. Still, she'd trade it all for Zack's life and health.

CHAPTER TWENTY-ONE

Arturo sipped his whiskey and watched Quinn as she set up the mangled chairs and flung them against the crumbling hearth, over and over, until there was little left of either hearth or chairs. He thrilled to the sight of her, to the power flowing from her fingertips, but more, far more, to the woman herself. She stood, shoulders straight, chin lifted, determination evident in every line of her long, sleek body. Her hair glowed like an angel's in the candlelight as her graceful hands lifted, pulverizing another pair of crumpled chairs.

Her beauty had moved him from the moment he first saw her, and that feeling, that odd pressure in his chest had grown steadily since. As had the aching need to touch her, to kiss her, to feel her sunshine and taste her sweetness. And there was sweetness there, though she held it close, sharing it only sparingly. With her brother, always. Perhaps with her brother's girl, though he'd yet to see her with Lily.

She was, he thought, an island, passing others by, rarely letting any of them get too close. In some ways, in the ways that counted most, he sensed that she was painfully alone. And he ached for her.

Micah had spoken to him in depth of the conversations they'd shared in the evenings when she'd thought him human, a writer. He'd made his friend repeat every word she'd spoken. And in almost two weeks, she'd told Micah little. She'd shared almost nothing of herself. Of course, she wasn't likely to confide that she'd recently escaped a vampire otherworld. But she'd been unwilling to share all but the most superficial information about her life and work. Micah had been forced to do most of the talking, creating an elaborate fiction about his own life.

More than once, Micah had returned to his apartment, shaking his head over something he'd slipped up over, yet she hadn't noticed the contradiction. She never did. She'd never seemed to be paying that much attention, as if she'd been present in body but not in thought. Holding herself apart.

Every now and then, when Arturo had her alone, she lowered her shields with him, just a little. She'd done so more freely before he set her and Zack free. She'd trusted him more then, before she realized her freedom was all a lie. He wanted . . . *needed* . . . her to trust him now.

So many things could go wrong tomorrow, but somehow he would find a way to keep her safe. And once the magic was renewed, he would set her free, in truth this time. Part of him wanted to go with her, to turn his back on his friends and his kovena, on his world, and spend the rest of Quinn's life with her.

But he'd do her no service that way. Outside of Vamp City, he was trapped in darkness and the shadows, unable to move freely until night blanketed the land. Still, he'd find a way to watch over her. Perhaps to visit her from time to time. She'd be safer far from his world. And he had too many ties here to leave it.

But as he watched Quinn arch her back, her hands on her hips, an ache moved through his chest, and he wondered if, when the time came, he'd actually be able to let her go.

Taking a sip of his whiskey, he rubbed his chest with his free hand. She'd awakened more than his conscience. She'd awakened within him feelings that had long lain dormant, feelings that were unlikely ever to sleep again. Because she'd stolen a part of him. And, in return, she'd given him a piece of the sun and lit a small, warm fire in his heart. There she would live for the rest of his long—and he feared, lonely—life.

Quinn was setting up the mangled remains of the chairs one more time when a rap sounded at the door. She threw a questioning look at Arturo, but he rose without concern, whiskey glass still in hand, and strode to open it.

Mukdalla handed Arturo a good-sized picnic basket. "Quinn needs to eat." She glanced Quinn's way, gave a small wave, then turned and left.

"I smell roast chicken and fresh rolls," Arturo murmured, just as the scents wafted her way.

"I smell Heaven. And I'm famished."

Arturo led her into the dining room, where a card table had been set up, flanked by two more metal chairs. Whole ones. He set the basket on the table, then pulled out a tablecloth, several covered dishes, two plates, napkins, utensils, and a couple of cans of cold Coke.

But when Quinn sat down and began serving up the food—two chicken thighs, potato salad, coleslaw—Arturo merely watched her, still sipping his whiskey.

"You're not going to join me?"

"Eat your fill, *piccola*. I have no need for the food, and you do."

"Trust me, Vampire, there's far more here than I could eat in three days. And we won't be here three days."

"No, we won't."

But still he made no move to serve himself, so she dug in. The chicken was delicious.

"Where will you go, once this is over?" he asked, taking the seat across from her.

She scooped up a forkful of potato salad and just stared at it. "I don't know," she replied honestly. And she didn't. For so long, she'd thought of nothing but getting Zack out of here and fleeing. But there were so many things wrong with this world, things that might or might not change when she renewed the magic. Whether or not she could make a difference, she didn't know. But part of her didn't like the idea of leaving, of running, when she might have the power to save the lives of innocent people.

And then there was Arturo. She met his gaze, her chest tight with unhappiness at the thought of never seeing him again. Their relationship—if she could call it that—was nothing if not complicated. He was a vampire, for heaven's sake. And she was an honest-to-goodness sorceress. What kind of future could they possibly have?

But there was no denying she would miss him.

He reached across the table to clasp her forearm lightly. "I want you to take my cell number. Or perhaps Micah's since I don't spend a lot of time in the real world. If you ever need anything, all you need do is call. I will help. Even if it's only to send money."

"Thanks, Vampire. We'll be fine."

"You and Zack."

She swallowed. No, not her and Zack. Zack would have Lily. Assuming . . . She looked up. "I can't leave without Lily."

"You must. Kassius will free the girl. And when she is free, she will know how to find you, yes?"

"Yes." Lily knew Zack's phone number. And if worse came to worst, she could always find him through the gaming sites they frequented.

She took the bite of potato salad and tried to swallow it past the fist in her throat. Because it wouldn't be her and Zack. Not once Lily was free. The two of them might go anywhere, probably to California as they'd planned.

And what would she do?

"Quinn." Arturo watched her with a softness that bordered on sadness. "Is there anyone else? Anyone other than Zack?"

She didn't need pity, dammit. "I'll be fine."

He just watched her, those dark eyes probing, assessing. Slowly, he lifted his glass. "To tomorrow's success, then. And to new beginnings."

He was in a strange mood.

She ate until she was full, devouring twice what she normally would have. Surprisingly, there was still food left over. "Your turn."

But he shook his head. "You'll need the rest later. The magic must be fueled."

Apparently, he was right.

As he sipped his drink, he studied her. "What other abilities do you suppose you might have?"

Quinn thought about it. She knew of one—the dark bubble she'd accidentally trapped the werewolf alpha in. As a kid, all she'd ever really done was push her stepmother a couple of times.

A sick knot formed in her stomach as she thought of the kid she'd almost killed in high school. A shiver went through her at the memory of that horrible day. It shouldn't have happened. It shouldn't have been able to happen. Except she knew better, now, didn't she? She'd been a sorceress, even then, if a barely functioning and wholly clueless one. That was the day she'd lost all her friends.

"What are you thinking, *cara*? They are not happy thoughts."

She shook her head, not wanting to discuss it. She'd never discussed it. And yet, maybe it was time. If there was anyone who would understand, it was Arturo.

She took a deep breath, feeling the anguish of that day, the horror of it, all over again. "It happened when I was in high school." She leaned back in her chair.

"You did not know what you were."

"I didn't, no." It was strange to think back, to try to see her entire life through a different lens. She'd never been who or what she'd thought she was. She'd never, in fact, been weird, not for a sorceress. But knowing that didn't ease the misery of that day.

"I was a good athlete," she began, wanting him to understand who she was back then. "I played on the girls' basketball team and ran on the track team. I had a lot of friends. Casual friends, probably, but I was well liked. I belonged. My best friend, perhaps my only true friend, was Owen. We'd known one another from the time we were in first grade. We'd climbed trees, made forts beneath his parents' picnic table with old blankets, and swum on the neighborhood swim team together. Even in high school, we were best friends, hanging out whenever we could."

Quinn crossed her arms, pulling them tight against her body as the hurt of the memory spread through her. "Four of us were hanging around in the locker area after school one day, waiting for track practice, when we heard a fight around the corner and went to investigate. The two boys . . ." Her breath caught, remembered anger and fear pressing against the walls of her ribcage. "One was a punk rumored to be a gang member. The other was Owen."

Arturo said nothing, but he watched her intently, hanging on her every word, and she continued.

"We all ran over, ready to defend our friend, but Owen didn't need help. He was a big kid and was winning. Until the asshole pulled a knife." She dug at her lip with her teeth, looking away, feeling the burn of tears. "I was so angry and so scared. I acted without thinking, Turo." She glanced at the vampire through the moisture in her eyes, then away again. "I grabbed the punk's arm, wanting to stop him, wanting to *kill* him. Five seconds later, the knife fell from his hand. Two seconds after that, he collapsed."

She was shaking, now. Why was she shaking after all these years?

"I think my eyes were glowing. Someone said something about that as they all backed away from me like I'd turned into a three-headed monster. Someone called 911, and the punk survived. The adults chalked it up to an undiagnosed heart condition, but the other kids wouldn't come near me again. Even Owen. I felt so guilty, so . . . *evil*. I knew I could have killed him. I knew it."

"But you didn't."

"No, but I could have. I almost did." She looked at him through a blur of tears. "How? How did I do it?"

For a moment, he said nothing. "You possess a very powerful gift."

Quinn snorted. "A dangerous one."

"Yes, though likely far less dangerous against immortal beings."

She thought about that. Vampires weren't likely to succumb to her touch, whatever it was. Was it wrong she felt relieved about that? She didn't want that *gift*.

"Have you tried to do it again?"

"Of course not."

"You should. The next time your life is threatened, try, *bella*. What have you to lose?" He watched her, understanding in his eyes. "It scares you."

"What if I can't stop it? For years, I had nightmares that everyone I touched fell down dead. Sometimes, I still do."

"That will not happen. You must want someone dead very badly to call the life from him like that. And I suspect, if you could remember what happened that day, you felt his life force coming to your call."

"I don't remember."

"It is never an easy thing when you first learn how to kill. Harder still, I imagine, when you are a child."

He rose and came around the table, holding his hand out to her. When she placed her hand in his, he helped her to her feet and pulled her into his arms, pressing her cheek to his shoulder, offering acceptance and understanding. He stroked her head, and she let him, needing this. Needing him.

"You are powerful, *carissima*, and that is a wonderful thing. You must not be ashamed or sorry for the gifts you've been given. Instead, you must learn to control them so that you use them only when you intend, and so that you never again inadvertently hurt someone."

"I can't exactly go around practicing *that*." Pulling back, she looked at him. "Unless you're volunteering?"

She said it with a smile, and humor lit his eyes. "No. That I will not volunteer for. But if ever again you are caught by someone who means you harm, do not hesitate to use everything you have against him, Quinn. Even that."

"I know. You're right."

He smiled and kissed her temple. "I usually am."

She lifted a brow.

He shrugged in a charming, self-deprecating fashion. "When you are six hundred years old, *usually* leaves a lot of room for error."

Quinn snorted and pulled away. "Shall I throw around some more chairs?"

"I would rather you try to make a bubble."

"I'm not sure that's a good idea."

"Why is that?"

"Because I don't want to catch you in it. And I don't want to get trapped in it myself." She cocked her head, considering. "Vampires can come and go from the Vamp City bubble at will. But not werewolves or humans. Why is that?"

He shrugged. "Perhaps because Phineas Blackstone wove that into the magic. Or possibly because that is the way bubbles . . . and vampires . . . are made. I would experience this bubble with you, *cara*.

We shall see, together, whether or not a vampire can leave it easily."

"What if I use up all of my power, then can't access it when I need it tomorrow?"

"A legitimate concern, certainly. But I suspect that the more you practice, the more you'll be able to do. Try it?"

She released a hard sigh and rose. "Okay."

Arturo came to stand behind her, sliding his arms around her waist. "Create your bubble, *tesoro*."

"Right." Taking a deep breath, trying to ignore the hard male pressed against her back, she lifted her hands . . . and dropped them again. How had she done this last time? Lifting her hands again, she closed her eyes, found again that river of power running beneath her skin and imagined it flowing into her hands as she created a bubble around them. On the count of three. One, two, *three*.

Power blasted from her hands, obliterating the card table, picnic basket, and half the wall behind it.

"Shit," she cried, pulling away from him, raking her hands through her hair. "I don't know what I'm doing!"

She heard his low chuckle. "Apparently not."

Whirling on him, she pointed a finger at his chest. "You laugh. You could have been sitting in that chair."

"I've come to realize that behind you is the safest place to be."

She huffed, then shook her head in a quick, clarifying burst. "All right, let me try it again." But after three more tries the sofa was lodged in the wall, one of the recliners upside down on top of it. And still no bubble. Thank God the ceiling hadn't fallen.

"I was tied to a stake when I called it the first time. And angry." Terrified. "The ability probably springs from my emotions, as everything else seems to do."

"It was not that way for Phineas Blackstone."

"Maybe not, but he was a powerful sorcerer with many years of experience."

"And you shall be powerful, too."

From all indications, he was right. And as mixed as her emotions were about being a sorceress at all, with power came strength—the strength to protect herself and others. And she absolutely wanted as much of that as she could get.

Arturo lifted a hand, his thumb stroking her cheekbone, the bridge of her nose, her eyebrow, his gaze growing more intense, as if he were studying her in minute detail.

"What are you doing?" she asked quietly.

"Memorizing your face. I shall miss you, *amore mio.*"

"Will you really let me go when this is over? Without a fight?"

A smile lit his eyes. "A fight I'm no longer likely to win." His expression sobered. "Yes, I will let you go. I will insist upon it." His hand cupped her cheek. "But I will not want to."

The breath caught in her throat, her chest hurting. "I'm going to miss you, Vampire."

His thumb traced her bottom lip. "And I you. Perhaps you will allow me to visit from time to time. If there is no other male in your life, or in your bed?"

"I think I'd like that." She pressed her cheek into his hand. His skin was cool again, but his eyes so warm. The thought of leaving him saddened her in a way she couldn't comprehend.

He leaned forward slowly, drawing out the anticipation as his lips brushed hers in a whisper-light touch, then moved against them more firmly, more insistently.

Need stirred inside her, and she began to tremble from the knowledge that this might be the last time they were alone like this. As if he heard her thoughts, or shared them, both of his hands slid into her hair, and the kiss turned harder, hotter, until her arms were around his neck, her mouth devouring his as his devoured hers.

The next thing she knew, she was in his arms, cradled against his chest as he rose and started up the stairs.

Her arms still around his neck, she kissed the corner of his eye, and his cheek, pressing her forehead against his temple. He smelled so good. Being in his arms felt so . . . right. For this moment, for this night, he was hers. Tomorrow could wait.

He carried her into a bedroom that had been furnished with two sets of bunk beds. Beds that, amazingly, appeared to have been recently made. But she remembered who this house belonged to. Neo. And she knew this must be temporary housing for escapees. A house now devoid of furniture on the main level, thanks to her.

Arturo set her on her feet in the middle of the room and took her into his arms, claiming her mouth as she claimed his. Heat rushed through her veins, weakening her even as it strengthened. Emotion pulsed inside her chest, a need, a desperation, to memorize every touch—the warmth of his lips on hers, the rough scrape of his tongue, the swelling of his fangs as they crowded his mouth, crowding their kiss, the firm brush of his fingers as they tangled possessively, tenderly in her hair. She vowed to remember every moment of this and everything about him—his warm, almond scent, his cool, crisp taste, the gleam of passion in his eyes as he gripped her head and rained kisses over every inch of her face.

He pulled back, still holding her in that gentle vise, his gaze traveling the path his lips had just taken. His eyes pulsed with longing, and the same sadness that throbbed inside her, the knowledge that this might well be their last night together, whether all went well tomorrow, or terribly, terribly wrong.

Quinn lifted her hands, cupping his jaw, running her thumbs over his cheeks as she memorized his face in return—the strong bones, the lovely gold of his Mediterranean skin, his dark hair, his straight nose, his full, beautiful mouth. And his dark eyes, golden brown in the firelight, centered white with hunger yet alive with tenderness and yearning.

His eyes beckoned her into their warm depths, promising the things that had so long been missing from her life—tenderness, closeness, affection. Acceptance. She'd known more of those with him than with anyone, including the parents who'd raised her. The thought of losing that again, of losing him, ripped something loose inside of her.

She didn't want to feel this way. She refused to need anyone. And she didn't. But Heaven help her, she would miss him.

"Vampire," she breathed.

He kissed her forehead, then pulled back, a softness in his eyes that melted her from the inside out.

"Turo," he said, whisper-soft. "You called me Turo, before and I would hear it on your lips again."

"Turo . . ." She smiled slowly, the pressure building against her ribs. "Make love to me, Turo. I don't ever want to forget."

His own smile bloomed, mirroring hers, his eyes deep wells she could drown in. "You will not forget." Slowly, he pulled off her shirt but left her bra, trailing his mouth over her shoulder, across her chest, into the hollow at the base of her throat, as if he would taste every inch of her.

She gripped his waist, tugging at his shirt, needing to feel his flesh against her palms. Pulling back, he released her to remove his shirt, meeting her gaze with that slow, seductive smile. Reaching for him, she pressed her hands against his kiss-warmed flesh, reveling in the hard play of muscles beneath her palms.

Leaning forward, she kissed his chest, tasting him, exploring, memorizing, adoring him as he had her, her lips on his chest, his shoulders, his biceps.

With a groan, part pleasure, part frustration, he unfastened her bra, then, to her consternation, turned her away from him.

"What are you doing?" she breathed, then understood when he brushed her long hair over one shoulder and pressed his mouth against her back shoulder blade. As his lips moved down her spine, his hands found her breasts, kneading them, playing with them as he held her close.

She slid her fingers over the backs of his caressing hands, running her palms up his forearms, touching him even as he touched, kissed, and fondled her. As his kisses reached the back waistband of her jeans, his fingers found her button and zipper.

"Step forward, *tesoro mio*," he said softly, his voice husky and sexy as hell. "Grasp the post of the bed."

Heat rushed deep into her body and, intrigued despite herself, she stepped forward. She glanced back at him. "What are you going to do?"

The small, devilish smile combined with the heat in his eyes had her pulse soaring, her body dampening, and her legs turning to jelly. Whatever he had in mind, she wanted.

Long fingers slid her jeans down to her thighs, then returned for her panties. "Step back, *cara*. Lean over."

Oh my. She did as he directed, feeling oddly more exposed with her shoes on and her pants around her knees than she probably would have if he'd first removed all her clothes.

His hands gripped her hips, his mouth continuing its tender mapping of her anatomy, covering first one nether cheek with his kisses, then the other, then spreading her wide and running his rough tongue in between, his fangs scraping lightly over her flesh.

Finally, *finally,* his tongue found the part of her body that awaited his attention the most impatiently. He stroked between her legs, delving his tongue inside of her until she was panting with need for more.

"*Turo.*"

He pulled back, and, a moment later, she felt his finger stroking her wetness. When it slid inside, she groaned with hot satisfaction.

"I need more," she gasped. "I need all of you."

His hands slid down the backs of her thighs, his touch less of tenderness, more of need, a hot, desperate need that matched her own.

She felt him rise, heard the zip of his pants. And then he was sliding inside of her—thick, and long, and gloriously hard.

"*Turo.*"

He swept her hair off of her neck and bit her suddenly, a piercingly sweet pleasure, and she cried out as he pulled, and she came, contracting hard and fast around him.

A moment later, he was gone, pulled out of her, and she was holding on to the bedpost for dear life, gasping for breath.

"What are you doing?"

"Lift your foot."

She did and he removed her boots and socks, one after the other, then pulled off her remaining clothes. He undressed himself and a moment later, he was sweeping her into his arms, laying her down on the narrow bottom bunk, bumping his head against the top as he followed her onto the small, cramped space.

He let out some kind of Italian swearword, then rolled his eyes at himself, making her giggle.

Laughter lit his eyes. "How I love that sound, *tesoro mio.*"

Grinning at him, watching him with incredible tenderness, Quinn parted her knees, and he settled himself between them, finding her, entering her again, with one smooth, perfect stroke.

Quinn cried out, arching into him, holding him close as he nuzzled her neck, then sunk his fangs, drawing her blood on a thrill of ecstasy. That quickly, her body began a second spiral up. But he pulled his fangs from her neck, instead brushing his warm nose against her cheek and laying more kisses on her cheek and jaw as he drove into her.

"Harder, Turo, harder."

He complied, his harsh breath in her ear as he drove her up, seeking his own release.

"*Bella,*" he groaned, his body tightening in that way she was coming to recognize, that way that meant he was close.

He pressed his cheek to hers, and she held him tight as they climbed higher than she'd ever gone, up to the sun, bathing in the warmth, the heat. A heat that flowed through her, filling her with light, with life.

She came in an explosion of color, her world fracturing and knitting back together different than it had been before. *She* felt different. Reborn.

Arturo collapsed, his face against her neck, his lips pressed to her shoulder. For a long time, they stayed like that. She didn't want to let him go, and he showed no sign of wanting to leave.

Eventually, he moved, though only to nuzzle her neck. "If you could live without food," he said quietly, "I would beg you to create a bubble for us alone. All I would ever need is you."

She kissed his temple. "I will miss you." And she'd never meant anything more in her life.

Slowly, reluctantly, he pulled out of her, then rolled to his side and took her with him. "Sleep, Quinn. I would hold you one last night."

Nestling against his warmth, Quinn's eyes grew heavy, and she gave in to the sweet exhaustion that tried to pull her under.

Her last thought as she fell asleep: When she left Vamp City, she would be leaving a piece of her heart behind.

Quinn woke to the feel of cool lips brushing against hers. Opening her eyes, she found Arturo bending over her, fully dressed.

"Awaken, Sleeping Beauty," he said with a small smile, warmth and something deeper in his eyes. Affection.

"Is it morning?" she asked groggily. How was she supposed to tell in this place?

"It is. And I must go."

She struggled to clear her mind, struggled to sit up. "It's the equinox."

"Yes. And Cristoff has gone off the rails and is demanding my appearance. Plus Grant and Sheridan Blackstone refuse to accompany you to the Focus."

"*What?*"

"They sent you a book." He lifted an eyebrow. "One they claim will tell you all you need to know, but it looks identical to the one Grant gave me for you before."

She smiled ruefully, understanding. "*A History of Witchcraft in America.*"

"Yes." He looked at her curiously.

"I can use it to communicate with them. It actually might work." By writing across the pages with the tip of her finger, she would be able to communicate long-distance with a sorcerer on the other end. A writing that none but another sorcerer could see. Sorcerer's text, Grant had called it. Sheridan could feed her the ritual that way.

"Do you have to go to Cristoff?"

"I must. If I fail to show, he could send guards to find me, and that we cannot have. Plus, if I am with him, I will know exactly what he has planned and can potentially talk him out of sending anyone into the Focus."

"But will you be able to leave in time?"

He stroked her cheek with the back of his fingers.

"If I am not, Kassius and Micah will get you safely to the Focus and back."

The bed began to shake suddenly, violently. Arturo disappeared. And a moment later, sunshine poured in through the uncovered panes of glass. Even half-blinded, the sunlight delighted her, then terrified her as the full import hit her.

The vampires . . .

"Turo?"

"Here, *cara*. The hallway remains in shadow."

She rose, dressing quickly, enjoying the brief visit of the sun even as she prayed that none of his friends had been caught in it. As she joined Arturo in the hall, the sunlight went out as suddenly as it had appeared.

"Your friends?"

"Safe, I hope. Kassius has been keeping watch the past couple of hours, but he's in little danger. With his wolf blood, he's able to tolerate the sun for short periods of time."

"I'm glad."

He nodded, then pulled her against him. "I shall return as soon as I am able."

"Is there any chance that Cristoff has figured out that you're his traitor?"

"Kassius says no. He still believes I am his loyal one, and he must continue to do so." He kissed her, slowly, thoroughly, then pulled back. "Be careful."

"You, too." He let her go and disappeared down the stairs.

She'd been awake five minutes and already things were starting to go wrong. Not an auspicious beginning to what might well be the most critical day of her life.

CHAPTER TWENTY-TWO

A light rain fell as Arturo rode toward Gonzaga Castle, his horse's gait slowing as water puddled in the road, turning the dirt to mud. The air was cool, almost brisk, and lightly scented with the diesel of the real world. An unnatural hush blanketed the land as day dawned dark as night, a hush filled with anticipation. And dread.

The equinox.

If Quinn succeeded, by day's end, Vamp City's magic would be renewed, and all would go back to the way it was before. Hopefully, to the way it was long before, before Phineas Blackstone's toxic magic began slowly disintegrating the consciences and souls of the city's inhabitants. Quinn's magic would be different, he was certain of that. Her goodness would have a cleansing effect.

He had to believe that.

Vampires were out and about this morning, riding in their carriages or hurrying on foot for one destination or another. But their heads were down, the exuberance with which they generally enjoyed life missing. All waited with bated breath for word of the sorceress.

Being away from her now, as time drew short, had not been his plan. But plans had a bad habit of going awry, especially where Quinn was concerned.

When he reached Gonzaga Castle, Arturo dismounted, tied up his horse, and climbed the wide steps to the front doors. He'd once loved this place. For decades, the White House had been the seat of the Gonzaga kovena, until the building's structure began to fail, and they'd been forced to build the castle. Though he enjoyed a home of his own too much ever to live within the close confines of the kovena, this had been his second home, the place where he'd come for companionship and friendship.

Now it was a prison to those, like Bram, who were trapped within Vamp City. And in the past couple of weeks, it had been a place he avoided, a deadly obstacle course to be maneuvered with the greatest of care lest his lies be revealed.

Guards opened the doors to him, bowing with deference, their expressions tense and unhappy though respect filled their eyes.

"Arturo," each murmured warmly.

"Gil, Jorge." Arturo entered the mansion's ivory marble foyer, surprised at the lack of activity and stunned by the fear hanging heavy in the air. He'd expected anxiety, yes. It was the equinox. But this was different. This was dark and rancid, the fear of vampires, not humans. And never had he tasted its like within these walls.

He followed the sound of low voices coming from the billiards room, accompanied by the tap of cue to ball and found, in addition to the two playing pool, half a dozen vampires lazing atop the velvet benches like whores after a good night. But there was no sense of happy repletion in the air. Nothing but that thick taste of fear.

Cristoff's angry shout carried from above, followed quickly by a man's cry of agony, and Arturo understood. Cristoff was a pain-feeder and fed well on the Slavas he brought in several times a day for his pleasure. But this cry was no feeding. And he'd wager the victim was no Slava. No, Cristoff released his fury on the guards he blamed for losing the sorceress.

At the far end of the billiards room, staring out the window, he caught sight of Bram and went to talk to his friend.

Bram heard him approach, threw back the whiskey in his glass, and turned to him. His gray eyes had a bloodshot, slightly wild look that Arturo didn't like. Blood splattered his gunmetal gray T-shirt and his jeans. And while vampire beards grew slowly, Bram had a healthy stubble that spoke of weeks of ignoring a razor, which was so unlike this male.

"Did you find her?" Bram growled, his mouth compressed, his jaw tight as if it had become welded in that position over the past two years.

"Briefly." Even a few weeks ago, he'd never have lied to him, one of his most trusted friends, but Bram was too close to Cristoff these days, and he couldn't risk it. "She was hiding at Fabian's Palace, but she's acquired the ability to disappear, and I lost her again."

"Dammit." Bram lifted his empty glass to his mouth, then scowled, clearly forgetting he'd already tossed back its contents. Instead, he threw the glass at the pool table, shattering it into a hundred pieces.

"*Amico mio,*" Arturo said quietly.

"I'm losing it, Ax." Bram ran both hands through close-cropped dark hair. "We're all losing it, Cristoff most of all. Even when he's not punishing anyone, he's feeding almost constantly, now. Blood, pain. Mostly pain. It's an illness, Ax. He can't stop."

"And you?" Arturo asked carefully.

"I'm not as far gone, not nearly. But the hunger grows. The more I'm around him, the more I feed, and the hungrier I become."

"Leave here. At least for a while."

"I have. I do. I wander the streets, but the hunger no longer comes upon me as a slow thing but hits me like a hammer. I'm suddenly violently hungry, with little control. I need pain. And I won't cause it, Ax. *I can't.*"

Arturo squeezed his friend's shoulder. "I know. I'm glad. It tells me your soul has not been compromised."

"Not my soul perhaps, not yet. But I'm losing my fucking mind. If this doesn't stop soon, I'm going to turn into as much of a raving sadist as our master."

"I'll find the sorceress. I'll see the magic renewed. I promise."

"If you don't . . . if you can't . . . don't let me become like him." Bram's gaze caught Arturo's, hard as steel. "Promise me, Ax. If I start causing the pain, you will end this worthless excuse for a life of mine. And you can do it. We both know it. *Promise me.*"

Arturo nodded. "It won't come to that."

"I hope not."

As Bram turned away, Arturo retraced his steps through the billiards room. As he crossed the foyer to the stairs, a second male began to scream, his cries in stereo with the first. Two of them. Below the males' cries, he could hear the softer sounds of female agony. An agony that weighed on his soul. When had he begun to block out the sounds of others' suffering? How had he gone so long without feeling . . . *and not known it*?

In a way, he missed that numbness. Life was far easier for a man . . . a creature . . . who must feed from humans when he couldn't feel the suffering of others. But that wasn't the man he was. Nor was it the man he wished to be.

With heavy steps, he climbed the stairs and strode down the hall to the massive doors of Cristoff's throne room. Stepping inside, he took in the sight, blinking, careful not to reveal his shock. Four of Cristoff's vampire guards had been strung up by their wrists. Two of them had been assholes loyal to Ivan even before the failing of the magic. Two had once been honorable males. Blood ran from the ears of all four, dripping from their jawbones onto their shoulders.

Six more guards stood at attention around the throne room, their backs ramrod straight, fear sharp in their eyes. For once, no other vampire joined their master in this feeding. The room was empty but for Cristoff and his guards.

Cristoff stood with his back to the door, facing his captives. As Arturo watched, the vampire master lifted his hands.

"Where is the sorceress?" he shouted, his voice hot with fury.

The captives eyed him with varying degrees of terror and resignation. But all were clearly in agony.

"I don't know," one gasped. "I had nothing to do with her disappearance."

In response, Cristoff raised his hands and pressed his fingers against the male's forehead. Seconds later, the guard was screaming at the tops of his lungs, the blood gushing from his ears and nose.

No wonder fear hung thick on the air throughout the castle. Every member of the kovena worried that he or she could be the next to hang from those chains as Cristoff sought his traitor.

Guilt lashed Arturo that innocent men were suffering for his own actions. He couldn't confess, not with Quinn's life on the line. But perhaps he could distract.

"Master."

Cristoff whirled on him, a wild gleam in his eyes that punched Arturo in the gut. A gleam quickly masked.

"News," Cristoff snapped.

Arturo spun his lies as quickly and cleanly as always. "I found the sorceress in Fabian Neptune's palace."

Cristoff's eyes lit with excitement. "You have her."

"No. She's acquired power, a gift of invisibility, or perhaps phasing. But she escaped, disappearing into thin air."

Cristoff's jaw turned to granite, his eyes narrowing, his face growing red with fury, and Arturo began to wonder if he, too, might soon be joining the guards hanging from the rafters.

Instead, the vampire master whirled back and palmed the heads of the two whom Arturo knew to have been decent males at one time. The pair screamed with an agony Arturo had rarely heard. The agony of having one's brain fried by a mind blast.

But Cristoff wasn't simply making them suffer this time. He held on to them as their screams intensified, as first one, then the other, fell unconscious.

No, not unconscious. Cristoff stepped back and Arturo watched, stunned, as the limp forms of the guards disintegrated, one after the other. Dead. He'd killed them, two of his own.

The fear of those watching surged a hundredfold.

Cristoff strode to the other two. "Tell me where she is!" But though they professed not to know, Cristoff palmed their heads as he had the first pair, and moments later, they, too, were gone.

The room turned silent as a tomb, terror pulsing beneath the hush. Slowly, Cristoff turned back to Arturo. "Where is she?"

Arturo met his master's gaze with a façade of calm certainty. "She's gone back to the real world. I nearly caught her this morning, then lost her when the sunbeams broke through, and she escaped through one of them."

"You saw it with your own eyes. Her escape from thin air." As Cristoff stared at him, the hot fury slowly left his eyes to be replaced with something far more disturbing. The gleam of fanaticism. *Madness.*

"I did."

"And did you see her disappear?"

"No. She was in the room, a small windowless bedchamber. There was no escape. And yet when I turned around, she was gone."

Inexplicably, Cristoff grinned, then motioned Arturo to follow as he strode toward the back hallway.

His pulse pounding unsteadily, Arturo complied. With his mind blast, Cristoff had always been one of the most deadly vampires alive. But he'd been calm, fair, and intensely loyal to his own. Today, he'd proved himself none of those things. Deadly, unpredictable, dangerous, now, in the extreme. And Arturo knew he'd been sliding toward this for a long time. Arturo had simply been unable to see it.

Cristoff led him to his own private bathing room, a room Arturo had once enjoyed the comforts of on a regular basis. The room was furnished in bright blue tile with fixtures of gold, the bath more pool than tub, a good ten foot by ten foot square. Steam rose from the citrus-scented water, and around the tub stood four scantily clad female Slavas, their jeweled nipples peeking out from beneath sheer sleeveless gowns.

Cristoff stripped off his robe and sank into the water. As he leaned back against the side with a sigh, he motioned to Arturo.

"Join me, *mio figlio leale*." My loyal son.

His heart heavy from what he'd just witnessed, Arturo sat on a nearby stool to pull off his boots.

"Tell me about the sorceress," Cristoff said, resting his arms along the sides of the tub, his tone warm. "Tell me everything."

Arturo undressed slowly as he took a moment to collect his thoughts, to decide what Cristoff really wanted to know, and to plan his lies. Then he slid into the heated pool across from his master until their legs were parallel, though not touching. One of the Slavas knelt at Arturo's side and began soaping his chest with soft, slender hands. Slender hands through which he felt no sunshine; hands that left him cold.

Slowly, he spun a tale, part truth, part fantasy. He told Cristoff about how he'd followed Quinn's trail to Fabian's, how Fabian had seemed genuinely surprised at her appearance, how he'd captured her and been shocked when she'd disappeared. He'd hunted her, of course, cleverly and untiringly. And again he'd found her, only to be forced back as the sunbeams broke through, sunbeams she'd taken quick advantage of to escape back into her world. No creature, not even a vampire, could leave Vamp City on a sunbeam. None but the sorceress.

Excitement and speculation lit Cristoff's eyes. "If she escaped Ivan, why would she return to Vamp City?" He answered his own question. "She was searching for her brother."

"Undoubtedly."

"Find him."

Arturo nodded. "Kassius is already hunting him. We'll find him."

Cristoff began to grin. "She's powerful."

"So it would seem. Where she came into that power, I do not know."

"It doesn't matter. Only that she has it. With that kind of power, she'll renew the magic on a null day. It matters not that we catch her today. Only that we catch her soon."

Arturo hoped she was half as strong as he'd portrayed in his fiction. She had power, yes. Power enough to throw furniture, but enough to save a magical world? That was yet to be seen.

Leaning back against the side of the tub, Cristoff closed his eyes. "You're the only one of all my vampires whose loyalty I have never questioned, my snake."

The words no longer warmed Arturo as they used to.

The vampire master waved his hand lazily. "Whiskey for me and my loyal son."

One of the Slavas immediately poured two tumblers, settling one in each vampire's hand.

Cristoff took a sip of his and opened his eyes, spearing Arturo. "You and Micah will find the sorceress in the real world, and you'll bring her to me. Quickly, Arturo, for we've not much time before this world crumbles around us. She will renew the magic. And then . . ." A satisfied smile bloomed slowly across his face. "And then she is mine."

Arturo swallowed. "What have you planned for her?" He tensed for the litany of tortures Cristoff had in mind.

But all his master said was, "You'll see, my loyal one. You'll see. And you shall rejoice."

Finally, Cristoff rose, taking the towel offered him. Arturo did the same, drying off and quickly dressing as one of the Slavas helped Cristoff back into his robe.

Cristoff picked up his whiskey glass and motioned for Arturo to follow him into the hallway, where two guards stood at attention. Arturo had never seen the kovena guards quite so rigid. Nor had he ever tasted such fear. One in particular, one of the newer guards, was shaking with it. Never a wise thing to do in front of Cristoff.

Cristoff slowed, noticing the visibly trembling countenance of the younger guard and the way he tried without success to meet Cristoff's gaze.

Eye narrowing, Cristoff peered at him. "What have you to hide?"

"N-nothing. I just . . . nothing!"

Cristoff turned to Arturo. "Do you think he tells the truth?"

Arturo considered, feeling the path beneath his

feet narrowing with every passing hour until he stood on little more than a tightrope. "Yes," he said blandly. "He was in the throne room earlier. I suspect he was affected by the executions."

With a considering look at the guard, Cristoff crooked a finger. "Come."

The young guard turned sheet white, but followed them down the hall to Cristoff's study. The vampire master placed his palm against the top right panel of the door. Soon the door rattled slightly, then sighed, opening. Only Cristoff had access to this room.

Arturo followed Cristoff into the room, the young guard trailing uneasily, his heart rate jackhammering, his fear flowing into Arturo's system like an infusion of sour wine.

Arturo had always loved Cristoff's study, with its walls lined with bookshelves, overflowing with tomes collected throughout Vamp City soon after it was created—duplicates of the real versions that would fetch a handsome price if money ever became an issue for the kovena. A brightly colored Persian rug covered the cold tile topped by a well-used brown leather recliner that sat before the hearth. Against one wall stood the chess table where he'd once spent untold pleasant hours.

In addition to the bookshelves, glass cases filled with relics collected throughout Cristoff's considerable lifetime dotted the room. The most prized, by far, was the jewel-hilted sword at the back of the room.

Escalla.

Cristoff motioned to the glass case in which Escalla appeared to float without tethering. "Retrieve the sword for me," Cristoff commanded the now-quaking guard.

Arturo's eyes narrowed, his own pulse quickening. For as long as Cristoff had owned the sword, he'd warned his vampires that Escalla had been charmed to respond only to his calling. Any attempt by another to touch it would mean death. Had that all been a ruse to keep them away from it? Or was Cristoff up to more of his sadistic play?

The young guard started forward uncertainly but conquered his fear and strode forward until he stood in front of the magical case.

"I . . . I'm not sure . . ."

"Reach in and take it out," Cristoff snapped.

The male did just that, his hand moving effortlessly, startlingly, through what appeared to be glass and apparently wasn't. But when he would have closed his fingers around the hilt, he froze. And suddenly he was encased in a mystical green fire that slowly melted the flesh off his bones. He screamed. A moment later, he turned to ash.

"I never could abide cowards." Cristoff strode forward, reached into the case, and pulled out the sword. He glanced at Arturo. "This is the most powerful weapon in the world, in the right hands." He chuckled. "In the right heart."

Arturo's own heart began to race as he stared at the sword whose destruction was presumably the only means of destroying the Levenach curse. Fortunately, there was no need for such a measure since destroying the weapon would be nigh-on impossible when he couldn't even touch it. Quinn's magic was almost certainly strong enough now to renew Vamp City, he was sure of it. And once she did, she would be safe. That was all that mattered.

"Go, my snake. Find the sorceress. Quickly!"

Arturo bowed before his master, aching at the loss of the Cristoff he'd once known and at the lives wasted this day. How many more would die before the magic was renewed? How long before Cristoff began to regain his soul?

If he ever did.

Lily drank her fill from the cool stream, then wiped her ice-cold hands on the skirt of the slave's dress she'd been given when she first arrived at Castle Smithson. The gown was long-sleeved and wool, and she thanked the heavens for it. The temperature had turned downright cold, and she'd have frozen to death if all she had were the T-shirt, shorts, and flip-flops she'd been wearing the morning she wandered out of the real world as she'd waited for Zack.

A dozen times a day, she wished she'd pulled on running shoes and socks that morning as she'd dressed for class. She'd lost her flip-flops early on and been without shoes ever since. Inside, being barefoot didn't bother her much, but out here, her feet were tender and sore. And ice-cold.

Still, cold, sore feet were a small price to pay for freedom. And, for the moment, she was free. She'd slipped out of the Trader's cart as it bounced through a shallow stream, soaking her bare feet and legs though sparing her dress, which she'd hiked up high. Stealing into the woods, she'd run for more than a mile, ignoring the pain in her feet, unsure which direction to go. Eventually, she'd come upon a small shack that looked as if it hadn't been lived in since 1870, and there she'd taken shelter for the night.

This morning, the realities of being on her own had begun to set in. Almost from the moment she'd arrived in Vamp City, the vampires had provided for her—food when she was hungry and a somewhat warm, somewhat safe place to live. With her freedom, she'd lost those. And, a born-and-bred city girl, she had no idea how to fend for herself.

Then again, even the most ardent survivalist likely had little knowledge of how to live in a land without animals except for the vampires' horses. A land where the only things that grew were dead trees.

She'd known, on an intellectual level, that food would be a problem, and had shoved a couple of slices of stolen bread into her dress pocket before she left. But she'd eaten one last night and the other this morning and was already hungry. And she was completely and totally out of food.

If she didn't find a way to escape Vamp City soon, she was going to starve.

The earth rumbled a split second before the shaking began. The water in the creek began to roll and splash, and she backed up, not wanting to get wet. The crash of a nearby tree had her hunching protectively as her heart began to hammer with excitement and hope.

Suddenly, the heavens opened. Sun poured down in a beam of light not twenty feet away. Her heart leaped and she ran for it without hesitation, praying she'd run right through into the real world. And, hopefully, not into the path of an oncoming car.

But when she reached the light and dove into the blessed warmth of the sunshine, nothing happened. In the shadows all around her, the dead trees stood sentinel, as if blocking her escape.

Her heart plummeted, and she fought back tears of disappointment. Trying one more time, she stepped out of the sunbeam on the other side, and back into the light.

"Please, let me through. Please!"

But while the sunshine warmed her chilled body, drenching her sun-starved skin and blinding eyes too long accustomed to the dark, no door opened. And minutes later, when the light went out and she was once more standing in the dark, hope shattered around her cold, bare feet.

There was no escape. Not this way.

And if not through a sunbeam, then how? She was so hungry.

The crushing disappointment weighed on her until it was all she could do not to sink to the ground and give in to the tears. But tears wouldn't get her out of Vamp City. And there had to be a way out.

How many times had she come to a point in a computer game where there appeared to be no way to win? She'd never given up because she'd known, if she searched long enough, she'd find it. There was always a way to win. She'd find it this time, too.

The snap of a twig had her heart rate skyrocketing. Her eyes had yet to adjust to the dark again, and the thought of something out there that she couldn't see had her blood running cold.

Slowly, her vision began to return, and when it did, she knew she was no longer alone. Dark forms dotted the hillside, standing between the trees.

Wolves. At least seven giant gray wolves.

The blood drained from her face.

"Werewolves," a female voice said a short distance behind her, making her jump. Too late, she realized that by standing in the sunlight, she'd undoubtedly made herself visible to anyone within a mile radius.

Lily glanced over her shoulder, not wanting to take her eyes off the wolves for too long, and caught a glimpse of a woman who looked to be close to middle-aged, at least midthirties. She wore a gown similar to Lily's, colorless in the twilight, and nondescript. Her hair, twisted into a knot at the nape of her neck, lacked a Slava's glow, but the belt around her waist, laden with a sword, hunting knife, and what appeared to be an old-fashioned waterskin, gave her the appearance of someone who'd been here a long, long time. As did the bow she held to her face, an arrow cocked and aimed at the nearest wolf.

Unless the Traders had snatched a survivalist off the streets of D.C., this woman was no freshie. Instinct told Lily she'd been here a while. Long enough to turn Slava, if she was human.

So if she wasn't human, what was she?

Vampire.

Lily watched the wolves, the saliva dripping from mouths lined with sharp, deadly teeth, and wondered if they, or the woman at her back, posed the greatest threat.

"They're starving," the woman added quietly, as if hearing her thoughts. "And you're fresh, tender meat. It's your choice—stay here and become dinner, or come with me."

Lily's body rocked from the force of her heart's thundering beats. It seemed she was about to become *someone's* dinner. But the vampire didn't have to kill her to feed from her. The wolves did.

Without a word, she turned and hurried toward the woman.

"She is mine," the woman called to the wolves. Several snarled. One howled. But to Lily's surprise, they made no move to attack. Was it possible that seven werewolves were really afraid of one vampire? And what did that say about Lily's own chances of survival?

She supposed she was about to find out.

CHAPTER TWENTY-THREE

Quinn paced the demolished living room of the safe house, clean now, after she'd picked up the mess she'd made while practicing her magic again this morning. Using the focusing technique Arturo had shown her last night, she was able to pull the power with more and more predictability. But whether the ability to throw chairs equated to the power to renew Vamp City's magic, she didn't know.

She glanced at her watch as she paced. It was after one o'clock. A short while ago, Mukdalla had brought her lunch and assured her that Zack was fine, that he and Jason had been in the gym almost nonstop since dawn. Quinn supposed it was as good a way for him to spend the time as any.

The low rumble vibrating in the floorboards made her freeze. Hoofbeats.

Her gaze flew to Kassius, who stood by the window.

"Arturo, returns," he told her. But as she started toward the door, he held up a warning hand. "Wait, Quinn. It's possible he's not alone. I can't tell."

But moments later, Arturo strode into the house. He acknowledged his friend with a nod even as he strode directly to her, swept her into his arms, and kissed her hard.

She kissed him back, feeling the tension in his hard body slowly ease. Finally, he pulled back, and she watched him with concern.

"What was that for?"

"I was in need of your sunshine, *cara*." He curved his arm around her waist and pulled her hard against his side as he turned to Kassius. "You understated it, Kas. 'Off the rails' does not begin to describe what I saw this morning. He is completely losing it."

Kassius's eyes were grave. "He gets worse by the day. What's his plan?"

"He is not concerned with Quinn's renewing the magic today. After the tale I spun, he's convinced she can renew it at any time."

Quinn watched him, curious. "What did you tell him?"

"That I watched you escape back into the real world through a sunbeam. He's ordered Zack found as a lure. I told him you were looking for him, Kas." Arturo searched her face. "Any more uncontrolled blasts?"

"No. I've been practicing, and I'm getting better."

"Good." He placed a soft, lingering kiss on her temple, then pulled away. "It is time to join the others."

The ride to Neo's was quick and uneventful. Quinn found Zack at the dining table sitting across from Jason, a massive half-eaten ham and turkey sandwich in his hands. His face was flushed, almost beet red, his hair damp with perspiration. His eyes, when he looked up at her, were sharp and bright, if disturbingly silver.

"Hi, sis. How's the training going?"

"Surprisingly well."

"Want to give me a demonstration?"

She gave him a wry smile. "Since my forte seems to be throwing and destroying things, I don't think Neo would appreciate it. At least not in the house." She sat beside him, resisting the urge to feel his forehead again. She could tell just by looking that his skin was burning. "How's *your* training going?" she asked, keeping her voice even with effort.

"Good," he mumbled around a bite of sandwich, then swallowed. He grinned as if he felt perfectly fine. Clearly, he did. "I'm getting stronger. Faster than I should."

"I've never seen anything like it," Jason said. "Maybe it's the magic fever, I don't know, but he's doubling his reps every time he lifts the weights."

Zack released his hold on one end of his sandwich to lift his fist and make a muscle. And, for the first time in his life, he had one. More than one. He wasn't bulked out by any means, but her brother's scrawny arms were no longer scrawny, after only two days of weight training.

"That's amazing." But she couldn't quite mask the worry in her tone. Building muscle that quickly wasn't natural. Neither was burning up with a fever that should have already killed him.

"Can I get you something, Quinn?"

Quinn shook her head at the sound of Mukdalla's voice. "No thank you, I'll get it myself." She found the sideboard set out with deli meats and cheeses, and made herself a quick and simple ham sandwich on white bread with a light smear of mustard.

She joined her brother but had taken only a couple of bites when Zack jumped up from the table. He gripped her shoulder. "Tell me before you leave for

the Focus, Quinn. I'll be in the gym, Jason, whenever you're ready. I want to try some more fighting
moves." He strode out of the room, a confidence in
his step that Quinn had never seen.

The ex-Marine met Quinn's gaze. "He's going to
wear me out."

Amanda, coffee mug in her hand, joined them, and
Quinn turned to her. "What's going on with Zack?"

She frowned. "Honestly, I'm not sure. His body is
changing much faster than should be possible. And
his temperature continues to rise."

"What's it, now?"

Amanda hesitated. "High."

"How high?"

"Almost 112."

Quinn gaped at her. "He should be dead."

"Yes." Amanda covered Quinn's hand with hers.
"You need to be prepared."

A searing pain spread through Quinn's chest at the
certain knowledge that at any moment, Zack's body
could fail beneath the unnatural heat. Any moment,
he could die.

"He'll be okay," she said, as much for her own
benefit as the doctor's. "Once I renew Vamp City,
he'll be fine." She had to believe that because the alternative was unthinkable.

Amanda nodded.

"Jason!" Zack called. "You coming?"

"I'm coming!" Jason smiled ruefully though his
eyes remained heavy with concern. "I don't think I've
ever had quite such an enthusiastic recruit. He's a fine
young man, Quinn."

As Jason went to join Zack, Amanda cradled her
coffee mug and peered at Quinn. "Are you okay?"

Quinn nodded though the real answer was no, and they both knew it. She wouldn't be okay until Zack was healthy again.

Quinn finished her sandwich in silence as Amanda wandered away. She was just rising when Arturo and Micah strode into the room.

"Join us, *cara*." Arturo held out his hand to her.

Quinn grabbed her plate, intending to run it back to the kitchen. But Mukdalla was walking through the room and intercepted her.

"I'll take it for you, Quinn. Go."

With a nod of thanks, Quinn joined the two vampires. "What's up?" They stood in a small circle to one side of the room.

"We're moving up the timetable," Arturo told her.

"Good. When are we going?"

"Now."

Her eyes widened. "Let me get the book. I have to give Grant a little time to get online with Sheridan." She hurried back to her bedroom and retrieved the worn hardback from beneath the mattress. Closing her door, she sat on the edge of the bed and stared at the plain and ancient cover. *A History of Witchcraft in America*.

Opening to the page where she'd first discovered Grant's mystical handwriting, she pressed her fingertip to the paper and wrote, "*Grant?*"

A soft rap on her door had her rising. She opened it to find Arturo, and let him in. He joined her, sinking onto the mattress beside her.

"Sorcerer's text, hmm?" He watched her curiously. "Is this how you and Grant planned your first escape?"

"Not exactly. But he did communicate with me

this way." She watched the page impatiently. "Grant has more power than he likes to let on, I think."

"Perhaps. But not enough to renew the magic of Vamp City. There is no doubt of that."

"And you think I do."

"I pray you do, *cara*. For if you do not, I will lose many friends."

Writing appeared suddenly on the page, a tight, handwritten scrawl overwriting the actual print of the book.

I am with Sheridan, now. How soon will you be in the Focus?

Quinn looked to Arturo in surprise.

He cocked his head. "What?"

She stared at him, then smiled with understanding. "You can't see it."

"See what?"

"The writing."

His brows drew down, and he looked at the page, studying it hard. "I see only a page in a book."

Grant had told her only a sorcerer could read the magical writing. "How soon will we be in the Focus?"

"He's ready?"

"Yes."

He rose. "We'll leave at once. A half an hour. Less, if all goes well."

She wrote the reply, then closed the book and joined him at the door. "I need to say good-bye to Zack."

He followed her to the gym, where Jason was showing her brother how to block an attack and . . . holy cow . . . Zack was doing it, and doing it well. He was changing before her eyes, just as Jason said. He was still skinny, but with his shirt off, she could see the slight play of muscles on a chest that had, just days ago, been devoid of any but the most basic.

"Zack?"

"Yeah?" He didn't even turn around. When she didn't immediately answer, he turned to look at her, then strode to her, his expression sobering. "Are you leaving?"

"Yes. It's time."

To her surprise, Zack grasped her shoulders. "What about Cristoff?"

"He doesn't know. We're doing this under the radar."

His hands tightened. "Are you sure?"

No, of course not. Anything could go wrong in this place. But she nodded. "We've got it under control."

Zack frowned, frustration tightening his features, and she wondered, once more, where her easygoing brother had gone. "One day soon, I'm going to be the one protecting you. Not them."

She slipped her arms around his waist and hugged him tight, feeling his surprisingly strong arms go around her in return. "Deal." Pulling away, she kissed his cheek. "Love you."

He kissed her cheek in return. "Love you, too, sis. Be careful."

She turned and found Arturo watching them.

"Ready?" the vampire asked.

"Ready." Taking a deep breath, she strode down the hall ahead of Arturo, prepared to meet her destiny.

Quinn accompanied Arturo and Micah outside, where Kassius and Neo waited, along with five saddled horses. "What's the plan?"

Arturo explained. "Kassius will escort you to the Focus and wait until you are finished. Neo, Micah, and I will circle the area, keeping watch and staying close enough to rush in if you need us but not close enough to be spotted with you."

Neo grabbed the reins of one of the horses and mounted. "I've scouted as far as the Crux. The coast is clear except for a pair of wolves on the hillside just inside. Friends of yours, I hope, Quinn."

Arturo pulled her against him. "Neo, Micah, and I will leave first. I want Savin's wolves to know what we're doing and, hopefully, to help us stand watch." He took her face in his cool hands. Even in the twilight darkness, he was a beautiful male, his eyes haunting in their intensity. "Be careful, *tesoro mio.*"

"You, too."

He kissed her thoroughly, if quickly, then turned to Kassius. "Protect her well."

"You know I will."

Arturo swung onto his horse as Micah mounted beside him, and the three started off as Quinn and Kassius waited, giving the others a head start. Kassius would take the fall as Cristoff's betrayer if they were caught.

Quinn glanced at the tall vampire. "You're a good friend, Kassius."

He was quiet for a moment before meeting her gaze, his eyes calm and sure. "I do this out of friendship, yes. But it's far more than that, Quinn. Someday, Arturo will lead our kovena."

She looked at him in surprise. "I didn't know that was part of the plan."

"Ax doesn't know it. He doesn't see himself as a leader, but the finest leaders rarely do."

"Do you have the gift of foresight? Have you seen the future, then?"

He shook his head. "It's not the future I see, but my wish that I express. The kovena needs Arturo. More than just the kovena. The true Arturo Mazza, whom you are only beginning to know, has the heart of a lion and the soul of a warrior for good. But, no, he'll not challenge Cristoff, not until he's convinced the master we once knew is not coming back. Not until he's willing to kill him."

"And that's not going to happen easily."

"No."

"Do you think someone as evil as Cristoff can really change back?"

Kassius said nothing for a moment. "I don't know, Quinn. I have known instances where a male has lost his soul and regained it again. But Cristoff has fallen so far that I'm not sure there's any coming back. I just don't know."

"If Arturo challenged Cristoff, would the kovena support him?"

"A challenge is a fight to the death. If Ax goes against Cristoff, one of them will die. The winner is the vampire master. Period. The kovena would bow to his power. Some will rejoice. Others will not because Ax won't allow the cruelty toward humans that they've become used to."

Kassius motioned with his head to the pair of mounts that remained. "It's time to go."

They mounted and rode in silence. As they entered the Crux sometime later, Quinn caught sight of several wolves on the hilltops and in the trees. Keeping watch? She lifted a hand in greeting, and one of them gave a shallow bob of his head.

They kept their mounts to a walk until they were well within the Crux, then Kassius stepped up the pace, urging his horse to a canter. Quinn followed. The sooner they completed their task and got away from here, the better. She saw no sign of Arturo or the others, but she knew they were close enough to help if the situation truly went to hell.

Cresting a small hill with dead trees on either side, she glimpsed a familiar flash of colored light that reminded her, as it had every time she saw it, of a small, grounded, aurora borealis. The Focus was a dome of writhing, brilliant color—fuchsia, orange, and blue.

A thrill of anticipation chased the chill of dread down her spine. The last time she'd attempted to renew the magic, she'd been with Grant and Sheridan Blackstone. The three had entered that dome together, but the magic had attacked her, and they'd failed.

If she failed again, today, one of the most potent of the power days, Zack might well be doomed. And Vamp City along with him. None of the vampires believed V.C. would survive the three months until the next of the power days, the winter solstice.

Kassius pulled up about a dozen yards from the Focus, and Quinn did the same. She dismounted, then pulled the book from the saddlebag where she'd tucked it earlier.

"Wish me luck," she said, eyeing that swirling mass of color with no small amount of trepidation.

"Good luck, sorceress," Kassius said quietly.

Quinn took a deep breath and stepped forward. The magic wasn't going to renew itself. As she approached the swirling color, she felt the same tingling on her arms that she always felt near the places where the two worlds bled through. But the magic here was far stronger. And as she stepped within that mass of color, she felt it, thick and heavy, coating her skin, stinging her flesh, as it had the last time.

"Let's get this over with," she muttered, and opened the book to the necessary page.

But when she touched the page, the book stung her and she jerked back. *What the heck?* She tried again, felt the same sting, but forced herself to continue, writing, *I'm ready.* The moment she finished, she rubbed her fingertip against her jeans, easing the sting. She was beginning to think magic was a bitch. Especially in this place.

She watched the book, glad that the swirling colors of the Focus provided adequate light for her to see. And a moment later, writing appeared in place of her own. *Say these words as best you can.* What followed was an almost indecipherable string of syllables that barely resembled words at all. *Awwer lkjo weeje loiwer orqim coijwe olk aers owera pwid.* Quinn stared at them with disbelief and a sinking feeling in the center of her chest as she remembered how quickly and effortlessly Sheridan had whispered the words last time.

As new words continued to scroll across the page, the first of them began to disappear.

"Shit." She began to sound them out, speaking them as quickly as she could. And as she spoke, the magic continued to dig at her, raking into her skin, burning, stealing her breath. And suddenly that cutting heat broke the surface of her flesh, pouring inside like a boiling syrup, *igniting.* The book fell from her hands, and she crashed to her knees.

Cara! Arturo's voice rang in her head.

Closer by, Kassius called to her. "Quinn?"

Her back arched with pain even as she felt the magic inside of her, even as she heard in her mind the words she must speak. Words nothing like the ones she'd been trying to sound out.

Forcing open her jaw, she repeated what she heard, a string of strange syllables that flew from her mouth as if she'd been born to them. The ground beneath her knees began to tremble, and she feared the sunbeams would break through again with Arturo, Micah, and Neo in the open.

Light flared up around her, light that appeared to be trapped within the Focus, blinding her. Thunder rumbled across the skies.

She could feel the power she sought there in the ground beneath her, but she couldn't . . . quite . . . claim it. And without that power, she could not renew the magic of this world.

"Come to me!" she cried, then returned to the words that flew from her tongue in a torrent of unknowable sounds. It was a language she didn't recognize. A language of magic calling to the forces of the earth.

The more she spoke, the harder she pulled at the magic, the more the pain burned and sliced at her until she was gasping for air between words, until sweat soaked her shirt and dampened her hair, until her eyes filled with dark tears and ran down her cheeks. She swiped at the tears, and her hand came away streaked with blood.

Quinn, you must stop. It is hurting you, cara. *Come out of there!*

"Sorceress, something's wrong. Get out of there."

But she ignored them both. She was here to renew

the magic, and she *would not fail*. Zack's life depended on it.

The storm rose up all around her, whipping her hair into her face, howling into her ears until she could barely hear her own screams.

So close. The magic was there, rising from the earth, inch by slow, painful inch. It was coming. She would succeed if she didn't stop, if she didn't quit. Sooner or later, *she would succeed*.

The sweat rolled down her temples. Her head spun. Magic pressed against her chest until she could hardly breathe.

Quinn! Arturo's voice cut through the violence of the storm. *You will kill yourself*, cara. *Come out. Please.*

"Can't," she gasped. "I'm so close."

Failure wasn't an option. Not when Zack's life hung in the balance.

Arturo flew off his horse and ran for the Focus, his vampire's speed far faster than any beast's. Unfortunately, his speed was of little use when he couldn't breach the Focus walls.

Through the swirling colored lights, he saw Quinn on her knees, arched in agony, the blood running down her cheeks. He felt her pain, almost more than he could bear, because it was hers.

"Quinn!" His hands fisted, raised as if to beat on the pulsing energy, stopped only by the certain knowledge that touching that energy would send him, and any but a true sorcerer, flying backward. "It will kill you, Quinn! Come out!"

But she no longer even seemed to hear him. Her

pain flayed him, her agony burned him alive. Her desperation clawed at him, her need to win this battle.

But at what cost?

"It is the curse that keeps you from succeeding," he called. It had to be. It was the curse that attacked her, that had attacked her the first time she attempted to renew the magic. Neither of the Blackstone brothers had been bothered by it. They weren't affected because they had no Levenach blood. Quinn alone possessed both Blackstone and Levenach blood.

That was the truth he'd finally figured out. Quinn alone.

"*Cara,* you must listen to me. The curse attacks you. The pull of the two magics will kill you. For nothing, *tesoro.*"

"It's coming. I can feel it coming."

Never had he met a more determined . . . *stubborn* . . . female. "You will die for nothing, Quinn. There is another way."

A way that he would avoid at all costs. Except this, except her life.

He glanced over his shoulder to where Kassius sat, still mounted, watching him with fathomless eyes. Shoving his fists against his forehead, he turned back, struggling to find a way to reach her.

He could not let her die like this. He could not let her die.

The agony was beyond bearing, Quinn's senses destroyed, her thoughts blown. *Save Zack* pounded through her head like a mantra. *Save Zack save Zack save Zack.*

Cara. Arturo's voice sounded in her head. She'd

thought she'd heard his voice in her ears, but couldn't be certain. *I no longer believe Zack's magic sickness is being caused by Vamp City's crumbling magic. It is the Levenach Curse that is harming Zack.*

She frowned. "How is the curse hurting Zack?" She barely whispered the words, but he seemed to hear. "He's not a sorcerer."

What if you are wrong, bella? We know that you possess both Blackstone and Levenach blood. What if your mother was the Blackstone, but it was your Lennox father from whom you inherited the curse? As did your brother. Then it is the curse that is killing him.

"You don't know that," she cried. "You can't know!"

This time his voice came clearly to her ears, every damning word. "I believe it to be true. I have suspected as much since we met with Tarellia. Kassius saw the struggling power within you, one strand of which Zack shared. We believed the one strand to be the crumbling magic. But her revelation that one was the curse made it all too clear. You are the only one in whom the two magics have blended."

The words pelted her like sleet, freezing her to the marrow of her bones. He'd known Zack was a Levenach since they met with Tarellia. He'd lied to her about the one thing that meant the most to her in the world.

The power she'd struggled so hard to hold on to slipped between her fingers as shock radiated across her mind. He'd told her over and over again that only by renewing the magic would she save Zack.

Though she'd lost her grip on the power, the pain still burned, still tore through her, ripping and cutting. But around her, the storm slowly died, the howl of the wind turned to an agonizing moan.

"Kassius." The name left her lips on a gasp.

"I am here, sorceress."

"The truth. For once, I need the damned truth."

There was a moment's silence, and she turned, blinking the blood from her eyes as she found him standing beside Arturo just outside the Focus, their faces garish masks of swirling colors reflecting the Focus's glow. Arturo's hands were fisted at his sides, frustration in every line of his face, his eyes ablaze in pain.

Kassius watched her with compassion. "Ax speaks the truth as far as we know it. When I bit you in Cristoff's castle, I sensed a connection between you and your brother and two powers struggling within you, one of which also attacked your brother. Tarellia's revelation that you possessed both Blackstone and Levenach magic explained much. As did a bit of research that revealed the historical basis of the name Lennox to be, in fact, Levenach. Your father is almost certainly a Levenach descendant. Renewing the magic of Vamp City should cure Zack's magic sickness, Quinn, but doing so is not the only way to save him. And it's not the way at all if it's going to kill you."

"We have to break the curse," she gasped, understanding. "Destroy Escalla." Her pained, furious gaze swung to Arturo. "You promised me you were through lying."

In the distance, a wolf howled. Closer by, a man shouted. "Gonzaga vamps have been spotted."

"*Cara*. Hate me, if you must, but come, now. When you are safe, and well again, I will happily allow you to slam me against every tree and brick wall in Vamp City. But come. Please!"

She was in too much pain to move, but this battle was lost. And she would *not* go back to Cristoff.

She struggled toward the Focus's wall. And then Arturo was sweeping her up, the wind flying through her hair as he ran. Darkness descended over her beaten, furious mind at last.

CHAPTER TWENTY-FOUR

Quinn woke feeling as if she'd gone five rounds with a Mack truck. Her head hurt, her body ached, her soul cried out with frustration. For a moment, she couldn't remember why.

And suddenly it all came rushing back. Standing in the swirling lights of the Focus, being flayed alive by the attacking magic. *The pain*. And for nothing. For nothing.

She'd failed. The power she'd needed to renew Vamp City's magic had remained just out of reach, refusing to come to her call. The equinox was all but over.

Zack . . .

He was still suffering the magic illness, still in terrible danger.

He was a Levenach sorcerer.

If Arturo could be believed.

Her chest ached, her teeth clenched at the fury curling in her stomach. After all the times he'd promised never to betray her again, he'd lied to her, *used* her to save his world, making her believe that renewing the magic was the only way to save Zack.

She caught a whiff of almonds. Her eyes snapped open, and she found him sitting on the end of her bed, watching her with enigmatic eyes.

"Get out."

He didn't move. "I did not lie to you, *tesoro*. I did not tell you everything because I could not."

She opened her mouth, then snapped it closed again. "I said, *get out*."

"Renewing the magic of Vamp City should have been enough to save Zack."

Dammit, she didn't have to lie here and listen to this. Pushing herself to her feet, she winced at the pain, echoes of what she'd felt in the Focus, as if the magic still hadn't let go of her.

Arturo thrust a coffee mug toward her. "Amanda sent this. It should rid your body of the effects of the magic. It will take the pain."

She stared at him. As much as she'd like to refuse his offering, she could barely stand up straight from the sharp blades ripping at her insides. Taking the mug, she downed its contents in one long series of gulps, then threw it at his head.

He caught it, of course, his vampire reflexes a dozen times faster than any human's. She briefly considered throwing *him* against the wall, but he wasn't worth the effort it would cost her.

She started for the door of the tiny bedchamber, but Arturo rose, easily blocking her way. When she glared at him, he lifted his hand, his expression begging her to hear him out.

"None of us anticipated that the curse would cause the magic to attack you like it did, *cara*. It should have worked. Zack should have been healed. I would have let you both go."

"You lied to me."

"I withheld my suspicions, that is all."

"Is it? Because you wanted to ensure I saved your precious hellhole of a world."

"Because I wanted to ensure you saved my friends!"

She just glared at him. "You could have told me the truth."

"Could I have? You told me yourself you did not know if Vamp City should be saved. If you'd known about Zack's curse, can you honestly tell me you wouldn't have considered going after Escalla instead of saving Vamp City?"

She opened her mouth to answer, then closed it again. Because she didn't know what she would have done. If Zack hadn't needed Vamp City saved, would she have tried to save it?

She just didn't know.

Arturo crossed his arms over his chest. "This is why I did not tell you everything. I could not trust *you*."

She looked at him in surprise, then scowled. "Get out of my way."

He didn't budge. "You are blind, Quinn. Blind to everything and everyone."

"I am not. Now, move, or I'm going to move you myself."

"You would have died in the Focus today if I hadn't fought to make you come out."

"That's not true."

"No? Look me in the eye and tell me you would have stopped trying to renew the magic when the pain became too much. That you would have given up at some point even if I hadn't been there."

She wouldn't have. Of course not.

"You'd have committed suicide before you quit."

"He's my brother!"

"He is more than that, *tesoro*," he said quietly. "He is your only reason for living."

The words were a slap. The pain fueled her anger. "I don't have to listen to this." Lifting her hand, she pushed him away from the door to crash against the side wall.

But when she reached for the doorknob, he flew back and spun her around, gripping her shoulders hard, his nose inches from her own, furious eyes staring into her own.

"Zack is all you care about. Your world is so damn narrow, Quinn, that if it does not involve Zack, it does not matter. Kassius risked his life to rescue you from Cristoff's prison. Amanda Morris and Neo have helped both you and Zack, plus they devote their lives to saving the captured humans. When the magic fails, they will die, Quinn. As will Sam and Rinaldo and Bram and dozens of others who *do not deserve to die*. But you give them no thought. They do not matter to you. None of them matters to you."

"What about the humans who will be saved if Vamp City dies? Humans who haven't been caught yet but will be in the coming days and weeks and months, not to mention the ones who are already here. *You* give *them* no thought!"

"There you are wrong, *cara mia*. I do give them thought. When you renew the magic, most of the vampires will reclaim their consciences and their souls. The barbarity will end. Some vampires will continue to feed and abuse humans—it has been so since the dawn of time. But the majority of Emoras will not."

He gripped her chin, and she tried to jerk away, but he held her fast, forcing her to meet his gaze. "You rail at me for lying to you, yet you lie to yourself. Your concern is not for the captives, Quinn. To some extent, yes. You are not without heart. But your primary concern is and has always been Zack, even at the cost of your own life. Have you ever stopped to ask yourself why?"

"He's my brother." She glared at him, the ache in her chest spreading.

"Have you considered what it would do to him if you died trying to save him? Have you ever considered *his* pain? You may think of yourself as devoted and courageous, but you protect yourself, Quinn, above all others, above anything and everything else. And everyone else be damned. Even Zack."

"Go to Hell." She jerked free of his hold, refusing to listen to this anymore. But when she would have focused the energy to once more push him away from the door, she couldn't. She couldn't even see clearly through the sheen of tears now blurring her eyesight.

He was full of bullshit. Nothing he said even made sense! But that spreading ache in her chest intensified.

She turned her back on him, needing to get away, but there was nowhere to go.

"*Cara.*"

"Go away." She swiped at the tears that were starting to leak out of the corners of her eyes. "You're wrong. I'm not protecting myself. I'm protecting *him*. It's the one thing I can do, the one thing I can give him."

"Can you not simply love him?" he asked softly. "Is that not enough?"

The pain in her chest intensified, the tears falling freely now. "He has so many people who love him. So many that he loves back."

"And you have no one else."

His words sliced her to the bone with their truth. She reached out a hand for the wall, curling her other arm across her stomach as the pain spread, as the terrible, aching loneliness she'd lived with a lifetime ripped through her, clawing at her heart. Zack loved her, she knew that. But she'd never been his whole world. And he was, and had always been, hers.

A gentle hand caressed her hair. A soft voice murmured in her ear. "You are not alone anymore, *carissima*."

He was wrong. She'd never felt more alone in her life. She didn't push him away, but neither did she turn and slide into his arms as the softest core of her longed to do. That way would only lead to more pain.

His finger twisted around a lock of her hair. "You push others away, do you know this?" he asked quietly. "Both Mukdalla and Amanda have attempted to befriend you, but you've rebuffed their efforts."

Quinn brushed at the tears that refused to cease. "I have not."

"You protect yourself, Quinn." He stroked her hair. "Understandably so. You have known too much betrayal in your young life. The mother who abandoned you by dying, the father who brought a woman into your life who could not love you, then sided with that shrew against you. The friends, the *best* friend, who abandoned you at the first sign of your differentness. It is surprising, *tesoro*, that you are as capable of love as you are, as starved as you were of your parents' affection. And you are capable of great love. It shines within you every time you look at your brother."

Quinn squeezed her eyes closed, trying to deny his words and failing. From the day Owen shunned her, after being best friends for most of their lives, she'd ceased to allow anyone to get close. Her subsequent friendships, even her relationships, had remained casual and superficial. The only one who'd truly gotten past her shields was the vampire at her back right now. A mistake.

"You are not alone anymore, Quinn. Within this safe house are many who have not shunned you despite your power. Who, in fact, care about you very much. Micah, Kassius, and Neo are all taken with you, much to my frustration. Mukdalla and Amanda both like you. They offer friendship, but you must open yourself to accept it."

"You make it sound so easy."

He stroked her hair. "It is. Wish for them to be your friends, and let them see the wish, and it will be so."

She pushed away from the wall and dried her cheeks, then forced herself to turn around and face him. He watched her with eyes soft as mink.

"You should have told me everything, Vampire. How can you ever expect me to trust you?"

"I am sorry, *bella*, but I had no choice. If you had been able to renew the magic, Zack would have lived. My friends would have lived. You would remain safe." His mouth tightened. "If you had chosen to hie off to steal Escalla instead . . ."

"You really think I'd have done that?"

"If you had decided it was the better course—that Zack's chance of survival was better that way, or that letting Vamp City die was the right thing to do—yes. I think you'd have done it. You proved that you have the heart and the stubbornness to do whatever you think must be done, no matter the risk to yourself, when you returned to Vamp City for your brother after making a clean escape."

With his thumb, he wiped a tear that still clung to her bottom lashes, his eyes sad, and soft as a summer breeze. "You are my weakness, *amore mio*. You may not put your own safety first, but I must. I cannot help my need to protect you any more than you can help your own to protect your brother."

Quinn met his eyes, the ache in her chest easing beneath his tender gaze. As angry as he made her sometimes, he'd shown her more affection than anyone in her life except, perhaps, the mother who'd given birth to her—a woman she had no memories of.

"Do you think Cristoff might destroy Escalla voluntarily if it's the only way to save Vamp City?"

"Possibly, though that sword is his prized possession." He played with another lock of her hair. "The only way he will ever destroy it is if he is utterly convinced doing so is the only way."

"Which means he'd first have to have possession of me." He'd force her to succeed in every way he could think of, and she had no doubt that sadistic monster would use pain, torture, and God only knew what else. Only once he was utterly unable to compel her might he consider destroying his precious sword.

Arturo's eyes darkened, his mouth hardening, his grip gentle yet firm when he grasped her jaw. "Promise me you will not even think about giving yourself up to him like that, Quinn. It would kill your brother to know what you suffered to save him. It would kill me."

"We'll find another way."

"Yes." The tension appeared to flow out of him,

and he tipped his forehead to hers. "Yes, we will find another way."

His hand slid to the back of her neck, and he exerted just enough pressure to have her closing those last few inches between them, bringing their mouths together in a sweet, drugging kiss. The future loomed, dark and ominous, and time was undoubtedly short. But she needed his touch, she needed the soul-deep intimacy she'd only ever found in his arms.

Her fingers went to the buttons of his shirt, and he made a sound in his throat of agreement, of need. They undressed one another with unhurried movements, the passion that was always present between them simmering at a low burn as he laid her down, half-beneath him, and caressed her body with long, tender strokes.

She slid her hands over his strong shoulders, kissing his jaw, his chin, pressing her lips against the strong cords of his neck. For long, long minutes, they touched one another, kissed one another, reveling in the feel of flesh on flesh. His hand slid between her legs, making her gasp with pleasure and open to him. As she spread her thighs, welcoming him, he rolled onto her fully. Catching her gaze, he entered her slowly, lovingly, completely.

Being with him was *right* as being with a man had never been right before. Yet there was still so much between them.

When their passion was spent, Arturo rolled to his side and tucked her against him, holding her close. Exhaustion pulled at her. She'd slept so little since returning to Vamp City. That and the Focus had worn her out.

Arturo's hand, warm as the summer sun, stroked

her arm, her hip, as gentle as a whisper. His lips pressed against her hair.

"Sleep, *cara*."

"We have to find Escalla."

"First you must sleep."

And held in the gentle warmth of his arms, she did.

Quinn awakened in the bed alone, feeling almost rested as she rubbed the sleep from her eyes and sat up. The room was dark but for the dim light from the oil lamps that lined the hallway and filtered beneath her door.

Rolling her shoulders, she glanced at the place where the lamp sat on the bedside table, imagined it igniting, and whispered, "Light." Nothing happened. Maybe calling fire would never be her thing, or maybe fire was just one of the many aspects of her gift she needed to learn how to control. The thought of the possibilities sent excitement winging through her blood.

Reaching for the Bic, she lit the lamp, then dressed quickly, needing to see Zack. Arturo's accusation that she thought of no one but Zack had cut too close to the bone. In some ways, he was probably right. Maybe in all ways. She'd never let anyone get close enough to see what she was, knowing they'd run.

But everyone here knew exactly what she was. And none of them had fled. Arturo, in fact, just kept coming back for more. He'd held her close most of the time she'd slept. Every time she'd awakened, he'd kissed her temple and told her to go back to sleep. Vampires needed no sleep. Yet he'd stayed with her, cradling her close, making her feel . . . cared for. It was a feeling, a softness, she couldn't afford. Certainly not from a vampire.

As she stepped toward the lamp, to douse it, she spied a wooden stake on the floor, which must have fallen out of her jacket. With a small smile, she lifted her hand and called it to her. It rose suddenly, wavered a moment in the air, then zinged straight to her hand. The practicing she'd done while Arturo visited Cristoff had paid off.

Slipping the stake into the breast pocket of her jacket, she went to search for Zack. She found him doing pull-ups on a bar hanging from the ceiling of the gym, his shirt off, the muscles of his chest gleaming with a fine sheen of perspiration. Muscles. Real, honest-to-goodness muscles. If it hadn't been for the bright red appearance of his usually pale skin, she'd have thought he looked wonderful.

He grinned when he saw her. "Hey, Quinn," he gasped between reps.

"That's twenty-five," Jason said, amazement in his tone. "Twenty-six," he added as Zack kept going. "Twenty-seven. Twenty-eight." At thirty-four, Zack finally dropped to the floor, barely winded.

Quinn stared at him. A Levenach sorcerer. Her little brother.

Jason tossed him a towel.

Zack took it, wiping the sweat from his face. "I heard the ritual was a bust."

"The curse is still holding back my magic. But I guess you heard that, too."

"Arturo told me."

"Is that all he said?"

The joy she'd seen in his eyes as he'd discovered

what his body could do died a swift death. "He said they haven't found Lily." His mouth turned harder than she'd ever seen it. "I'm going to find her."

All he could think about was saving Lily, just as all she could think about was saving him. Stubborn, one-track minds apparently ran in the Lennox family.

"When you're ready," Jason said evenly, "we'll go out together and hunt for them both—my wife and your Lily."

Zack met the Marine's gaze with a certainty she could hardly credit, and nodded. He was changing before her eyes. In more ways than one.

She thought about telling him about the Levenach-Lennox tie, knowing how much that would probably delight him. But other than bulking up at a surprising rate, he'd never shown any sign of magic or power. And it worried her that knowing he had sorcerer's blood might send his confidence even higher. Maybe too high, making him reckless. The fewer people who knew Zack was a sorcerer, himself included, the safer he'd be.

She headed back into the main room to find Arturo and found the doctor instead. Arturo's words came back to her, that she could make friends if she wanted to.

"Amanda."

The woman turned, a professional smile on her face that turned serious an instant later. "Zack's holding his own, Quinn. That's all I can tell you."

Quinn hesitated. She briefly considered confiding in her about the Levenach blood, then pulled the secret close again. "I guess the magic sickness works differently in everyone."

Amanda nodded thoughtfully. "I suppose it does."

Quinn opened her mouth, looking for something friendly to say. When nothing came out, she shut it again. Now probably wasn't the time anyway. "Have you seen Arturo?"

"He's upstairs."

"Thanks."

She took the stairs two at a time and found the door partly open, the sign that it was safe to be on the main level. Slipping through, she followed the sound of raised male voices. Kassius's, if she wasn't mistaken. And Arturo's.

"You must," Kassius said.

"Never."

As she stepped into the kitchen, Arturo looked up. Kassius turned away, his mouth hard with frustration.

"Want to fill me in?" she said, her tone letting them know they weren't being given an option.

Suddenly, the house began to shake. A shout went up outside. Micah darted in through the back, slamming the door shut. Silence settled like a musty blanket as the world stood still. But Quinn saw no light filtering from beneath the edges of the room-darkening curtains that covered every window.

"Take a look, *cara*," Arturo requested. "Carefully, please."

Quinn crossed to the window and pulled back the drape only an inch. The sunbeams visible were faint and distant. "Nothing close."

Arturo joined her, pulling the thick drape aside, and together they looked out.

Neo's house sat in the middle of thick dead woods, but the sunbeams were easy to spy through them, and she counted no fewer than eleven in the distance.

"It's getting worse," Arturo murmured. If a sun-beam broke through in Neo's yard, the vampires would be taking their lives in their hands every time they walked outside.

"What's the plan, Ax?" Micah asked.

Quinn turned away from the window.

Arturo moved to the counter to pour himself a splash of whiskey. "I shall destroy the sword."

"How are you going to get it out of the case, let alone out of Gonzaga Castle?"

Arturo took a sip. "I'll think of something."

"You're not going alone," Micah said, at the exact moment Kassius said, "I'm going with you."

"You will both stay out of it. Cristoff has killed four of his own, and those are the ones I know of. Stay here. Protect Quinn."

His friends' expressions turned incredulous.

"Absolutely not."

"What if you need glamour?"

Quinn watched the way Arturo fought to protect his friends and how they refused to send him into the lion's den alone. She envied him that kind of friend-ship. But she understood all too well the willingness to sacrifice for those one cared about. And she under-stood, too, Micah's and Kassius's unwillingness to remain behind.

It wasn't in her nature to hide any more than it was in theirs. Nor was it in any of their best interests to leave her behind. Because there was no denying that Cristoff was powerful, and it might well take their combined skills to pull this off. Going in one at a time, and *dying* one at a time, would help no one. They might be vampires, but these three males, these men, were her friends. An extraordinary thought.

And she didn't want any of them dying.

"We're all going," she announced, watching three faces swivel toward her with varying levels of scowls.

"No, Quinn."

"Absolutely not, *cara*."

"It's not safe, Quinn."

She met Arturo's unyielding gaze. "You said I needed to start working with others."

"Not *this* way."

"And that I need to open up to friendships. I've decided you're my friends, and I'm not letting you go in alone."

"*Cara* . . ."

"You need me."

"We need you to remain safe."

But she wasn't giving an inch on this. Taking a deep breath, she looked around, spying the fat, flickering candle that sat in the middle of the kitchen table. Concentrating, she called it to her. With a wicked sense of enjoyment, she watched the vampires' eyes widen with surprise.

Micah whistled. "Nice job."

"Perhaps you'll need a way to remove the sword from its case without actually touching the case."

Arturo glared. "You are not coming with us, Quinn. I forbid it."

"Do you?" she asked quietly. Did he still not realize they'd moved past the point where he could easily control her actions? Besides, she had other abilities that might be of use, others she'd practiced extensively while she'd waited alone for him at the safe house. Closing her eyes, she willed a bubble to form around the three vampires and herself.

At the exclamations of surprise, she opened her

eyes and smiled at the black void that now enclosed them, a darkness lit only by the fat candle still cradled in her hands.

"*Quinn* . . ." Micah exclaimed, knocking into one of the bubble's walls, which sent him careening into Kassius.

"What is this?" Kassius asked, clearly surprised.

"She can create worlds, as Phineas Blackstone could," Arturo muttered. "One that vampires apparently cannot leave at will."

Kassius pressed against one of the walls, but though his hand sank into its dark surface, he couldn't move through it. To her surprise, he began to chuckle. "Well done, sorceress." His expression sobered as he turned to Arturo. "I understand your reluctance to involve her, but she's right, Ax. She has power. And we'd be fools not to use every advantage we have."

Arturo threw his hands in the air. "I do not want *any* of you going with me."

"Looks like you got outvoted, Ax." Micah grinned. "All for one and one for all?"

"No!" Arturo's gaze swung to her, his eyes throbbing with an emotion she couldn't name. "You know what will happen if Cristoff gets his hands on you, again, Quinn. Must you always sacrifice yourself?" he asked quietly.

For moments, she stared at him, the air thick and pulsing in the void. "What happens if you fail? If Cristoff catches you, or if you accidentally spring one of his booby traps, you'll die. And your friends will almost certainly be implicated even if they're not with you. They'll die. And then it's up to me alone. Isn't it better to combine our strengths right from the beginning and maximize our chance of success than to risk dying one by one?"

Arturo shook his head, his stance mulish. "I will not fail."

"Ax . . ." Kassius eyed his friend calmly. "I think she's right."

"I have to agree, Ax." Micah glanced at the bubble above his head. "She's strong and getting stronger. But I'd suggest we take the time to develop a plan. One that uses Quinn's strengths. One that she can practice ahead of time."

Arturo glared at his friends, his frustration palpable. But he was beginning to waver, she could feel it. Finally, he turned to her. "Free them. I wish to speak to you alone."

This was coming down to a battle of wills, she could see that. And she was ready for it. Shifting the candle to one hand, she held out her other to Micah. When he took it, she nodded toward the wall. "Go."

Giving her a wary look, he reached out his hand and watched it disappear. Stepping forward, he left the bubble, releasing her hand at the last minute. She held out her hand to Kassius and he did the same.

When they were alone, she turned to Arturo. He stared at her for a long moment, his hard expression slowly melting to one of resignation and misery. He held out his hand to her. "Come here."

She gave in, placing her free hand in his, and he pulled her close, careful to avoid the candle as he buried his face in her hair. "I do not want to agree to this."

"I know." She stroked his back as he held her tight.

"You are coming to mean too much to me." His

words, and the depth of emotion behind them, burrowed into her heart, warming it, filling it.

"I need to do this, Turo. Not only do I owe that son of a bitch . . ." She pulled back, forcing him to look at her, to meet her gaze. "But this is what I was born to do. You know that as well as I."

He tipped his forehead to hers. "You are too strong for your own good, *tesoro mio*. And a thousand times too stubborn."

She smiled. "Better to work with me than to wonder what I'm doing behind your back, right?"

"Too strong." He cupped her jaw.

She stroked his cheek. "You've attempted to be my master."

"A spectacular failure."

She smiled. "You've been my protector and my teacher. But the student has learned much and is becoming strong. And while I still have a lot to learn, it's time we worked together, Vampire. It's time we became a team. Partners."

He sighed. She'd won, and they both knew it.

"You will be the death of me."

"I'm counting on being your ace in the hole."

He stroked her cheek, then gripped her jaw, his eyes as soft as they were intense. "Not partners. Teammates. And I am the leader of the team. I call the shots. You do not know that castle or its dangers. And I do."

"I can live with that as long as you don't try to protect me."

His jaw tightened. "No heroics, Quinn. I mean it."

She tugged on his hand, not quite ready to promise him anything more. "Come on, Vampire. Let's go. We've got work to do."

He followed her out of the bubble and back into the kitchen, where she placed the candle back on the table as Kassius and Micah watched, and waited.

Arturo started issuing orders. "Feed if you need to, then get ready to ride in an hour. We'll be returning to the safe house to hammer out a primary plan and at least two backups. Quinn will need adequate food to take with us. She'll be expending energy and power and will become quickly depleted. Micah is right, we must be fully prepared this time."

"All four of us?" Kassius asked.

Arturo nodded, his mouth twisting ruefully. "All four of us."

Kassius nodded. Micah gave her a small smile.

An answering smile lifted Quinn's mouth, then quickly fell away. Yes, she'd succeeded in getting herself included in this critical mission. A mission that required her to return to Gonzaga Castle and put herself once more within reach of a vampire who, if he caught her, would hurt her beyond imagining. A monster even the vampires feared.

She had power, now, at least. Abilities that she lacked before.

But whether or not they'd prove adequate against such evil was anyone's guess.

Want to know how it all began?
*A world of perpetual twilight,
a vampire utopia threatened with devastation . . .*
Keep reading for a peek into Pamela Palmer's
first Vamp City novel

A BLOOD SEDUCTION

Available now!

CHAPTER ONE

Perched on her stool in the chilly lab of the Clinical Center of the National Institutes of Health in Bethesda, Maryland, Quinn Lennox studied the lab results on the desk in front of her. Dammit. Just like all the others, this one revealed nothing out of the ordinary. Nothing. She'd run every blood test known to science, and they all claimed that the patient was disgustingly healthy. Utterly normal.

They lied.

The patient wasn't normal and never had been, and she wanted to know why. She wanted to be able to point to some crazy number on one of the myriad blood tests, and say, "There. That's it. That's the reason my life is so screwed up."

Because those lab tests were hers.

"Quinn."

At the sound of her boss's voice in the lab doorway, Quinn jumped guiltily. If anyone found out that she'd been using the lab's equipment to run blood tests on herself, she'd be fired on the spot. She set the lab report on her desk, resisting the urge to turn the paper over or slip it in her desk, and forced herself to meet Jennifer's gaze with a questioning one of her own.

"Did you have time to run the McCluny tests?"

Jennifer was a round woman, over forty, with a big heart and a driving need to save the world.

"Of course," Quinn replied with a smile. "They're on your desk." She might be running tests she shouldn't be, but never, ever at the expense of someone else's.

"Excellent." Jennifer grinned. "I wish I could clone you, Quinn."

Quinn stifled a groan at the thought. "One of me is more than enough." Certainly more than *she* could handle.

"Hey, you two." Clarice, in a T-shirt and shorts, a fleece hoodie tied around her waist, stopped in the doorway beside Jennifer. It was after 6:00 P.M., and most of the techs had already left for the day. Clarice was clearly on her way out since she'd taken off her white lab coat. But she should be, considering she was getting married in two days. A curvy redhead, Clarice had been one of Quinn's best friends in her first couple of years at the NIH. Before everything had started to go wonky, and Quinn had been forced to retreat from virtually all social events.

Clarice clapped her hands together, the excitement radiating from her so palpable that Quinn could feel it halfway across the lab. The woman practically had the words *bride-to-be* dancing in fizzy champagne bubbles over her head. "Are you two going to meet us at my apartment tomorrow night or down in Georgetown? Larry and two of his groomsmen are available to drive anyone who needs a ride home afterward."

The bachelorette party. Bar-hopping in Georgetown. Quinn nearly swallowed her tongue, forcing down the quick denial. No, she would not be going. Absolutely not. "It's easier for me to meet you there,"

Quinn replied. No excuse was good enough short of sudden illness. And it was too soon for that.

"I'll meet you at your apartment." Jennifer patted the younger woman on the shoulder. "You look radiant and happy, Clarice. Exactly how a bride-to-be should look. Not a bit the stressed-out crazy person so many brides turn into these days."

"Oh, I'm a crazy person, don't worry. I'm just happy-crazy."

"Stay that way. See you ladies tomorrow," Jennifer said with a wave, and disappeared down the hall.

Clarice came into the lab, now empty but for Quinn, and perched on the lab stool beside Quinn's. "I have a *million* things to do. Two million."

Quinn gave her a half-sympathetic, half-disbelieving look. "Then what are you doing here?"

"Procrastinating. The moment I walk out the door, I'll be moving a hundred miles an hour until I go to bed. If I ever get there tonight."

Quinn grabbed Clarice's hand. "I'm happy for you."

"Thanks." Clarice squeezed hers back. "I'm so glad you're going out with us tomorrow night, Quinn."

"Me, too," Quinn replied weakly, hating that she wouldn't be going. It had been so long since she'd enjoyed a night out, and this one promised to be a lot of fun. And she hated to disappoint Clarice. But she didn't dare go. Not to Georgetown. "I wouldn't miss it."

Clarice slipped her hand from Quinn's and hopped off the lab stool. "Enough procrastinating. I've got to get going."

"Get some sleep tonight."

Clarice rolled her eyes. "I'll sleep on the honeymoon."

"Larry might have other ideas."

With a laugh, Clarice disappeared around the corner.

Quinn turned back to her desk, folded the lab report, and stuck it in her purse, then pulled off her lab coat and glanced down at her clothes, her stomach knotting with tension. On the surface, she was dressed normally for the lab—jeans (purple), T-shirt (red), and tennis shoes (bright blue). The problem was, when she'd dressed this morning, the jeans had been blue, the tee yellow, the shoes white. The Shimmer had struck on her way to work this morning, as it did almost every day now. Why? Why did these things keep happening to her and no one else?

Heading out of the building, she began the long trek across the NIH campus to her car, not looking forward to the long slog through D.C. traffic to get home. Traveling to and from work on the Metro had been so much easier. But public transportation of any kind was out of the question now. What if they passed through a Shimmer? How in the hell would she explain such a color transformation to her fellow passengers?

By the time she reached her car, a ten-year-old Ford Taurus, she was sweating in the late August heat. Opening the car door, she stared at the pink interior, which was supposed to be slate gray, the knot in her stomach growing. With a resigned huff, she slid into the hot car and headed back into Washington, D.C., and home.

Her life had always been a little odd. Now it was starting to come unhinged.

Strange things had happened as far back as she could remember, though rarely. Only twice had they been scary-strange rather than silly-strange, like the color changes. And nothing had happened at all after that second bad incident, in high school. Not until a couple of years ago, when the Shimmers had begun playing with her.

A couple of weeks ago, the visions started.

Yes, her life was becoming seriously unhinged.

As she neared the Naval Observatory on Massachusetts Ave., she saw one of the Shimmers up ahead, like a faint sheen in the sunlight, almost like the rainbow that sometimes appeared in water mist. They were always in the same spots, never moving, never wavering—nearly invisible walls in various parts of D.C. that she'd always been able to see, always been able to drive or walk through without incident. Until recently. Now she avoided them like the plague, when she could. But there wasn't a single route to work that didn't pass through one.

Unfortunately, one cut right through the heart of Georgetown, which was why she couldn't possibly meet Clarice, Jennifer, and the others tomorrow. How drunk would they have to be to not notice her clothes changing color right before their eyes? Too drunk. It was far too great a risk.

As she drove through the Shimmer, the hair rose on her arms, as it always did, her car interior returning to gray, and her clothes and shoes returning to normal.

In some ways, she'd gotten used to the strangeness, but in a bigger way, she was scared. Because the changes were escalating in frequency, and she had a bad feeling that it was just the beginning.

She couldn't help but wonder . . .

What comes next?

Quinn unlocked the door of her apartment on the edge of the George Washington University campus and pushed it open. The warm smell of pepperoni pizza and the comforting sound of a computer gun battle greeted her.

"Oh, nice kill." Zack's voice carried from the living room, low and even. When had his voice gotten so deep? He was only twenty-two, for heaven's sake. A man, now. A computer geek who'd long ago found his passion in game design and, more than likely, the love of his life in his best friend, if he ever woke up to the fact that he and Lily were meant to be more than programmer buddies.

Quinn locked the front door behind her, set her purse and keys on the hall table, then strode into the living room, a room she'd furnished slowly and carefully, choosing just the right shades of tans and moss greens and splashes of eggplant to please her senses. But it was the room's occupants who pleased her far more. Zack and Lily sat side by side at the long table against the far wall, each in front of a computer. Behind them, the television news flashed on the flatscreen, the volume a low hum in the room. But neither of the kids paid the television any attention. Each fiendishly tapped away at a computer mouse, staring fixedly at his monitor. Beside Lily sat a plate with a single thick slice of greasy pizza. Beside Zack, two large pizza boxes. The kid never quit eating.

Lily glanced over her shoulder. "Hi, Quinn." A sweet smile lit pretty features framed by long, sleek, black hair.

"Hi, Lily."

Without glancing away from the computer screen, Zack grabbed a slice of pizza out of the top box. Overlong curly red hair framed an engaging face as he wolfed down half of it in one bite and appeared to swallow it just as quickly.

"Hey, sis," he greeted absently. Though only half siblings, they resembled one another rather markedly, except for the hair. They'd both inherited their dad's lanky height, green eyes, wide mouth, and straight nose. But while Zack had that mass of curly red hair, her own was as blond and straight as her late mother's. Their personalities, too, were nothing alike, which was probably why they got along so well. Zack personified laid-back serenity, while Quinn couldn't stay still to save her life. Something had to be in motion—her mind, her body—preferably, both.

Only two things truly mattered to her. Zack and her work. In that order. She liked her job, and she was damned good at it. But if Zack gave her the slightest hint that he'd like her to follow him to California after he graduated, she'd move. Just like that.

But he wouldn't. Zack had Lily, now, if he didn't blow it with her. He didn't need his sister. He'd never really needed her. Not the way she needed him.

"Whoa!" he exclaimed around a bite of pizza as some kind of bomb went off in the middle of the game. "Did you see that, Lily? Awesome."

Quinn grabbed a slice of pizza, then turned up the volume on the television and switched the channel to the local news.

"Another person has been reported missing in downtown D.C. in a string of disappearances that has police baffled. This brings the total number reported missing in the past six weeks to twelve. This

last incident is believed to have occurred near George Washington University."

"G.W.?" Lily asked.

But when Quinn glanced at her, the girl had already returned to her game, her lack of concern mired in the youthful belief that bad things only ever happen to other people. A view Quinn had never shared. Unlike most young adults, she'd never believed her world to be a safe, secure place. Never.

Quinn finished her pizza, then carried her laptop back to her bedroom and got online. Sometime later, she heard the front door close and glanced at the time. She'd been on the computer nearly two hours. Was Zack going out or coming back? Closing her laptop, she went to find out.

She found her brother in the kitchen, his head in the fridge.

"Did you walk Lily home, Zack?"

"Uhm-hm."

She grabbed a glass and filled it with water from the sink. "Want me to fix you something?"

"No, thanks."

Zack and Lily, both computer science majors at George Washington, had met their freshman year and become instant friends. They'd interned together this summer at a small Silicon Valley gaming company—a company who'd offered them both jobs upon graduation. Zack had mentioned that they might be doing some testing for the company over the school year.

"Were you guys playing or testing tonight?"

"Both."

Zack wasn't the world's greatest conversationalist. Nine times out of ten, she had trouble getting more than one or two words out of him, though every now and then she asked the right question, usually about gaming, and he talked her ear off.

He straightened, holding a small bottle of Gatorade. "Want one?" Her brother's eyes crinkled at the corners, the unspoken love they felt for one another sparkling in his eyes.

She smiled. "No thanks."

With that, he left the kitchen, his mind wholly engaged by whatever thoughts forever zinged around his head. He'd always been that way, seemingly unaware of anything around him. And yet he'd always been there for her. Always. Zack's love was the one constant, the one absolute, in her life. And always had been.

Quinn downed her water, then poured herself a glass of wine and followed him into the living room, curling up on the sofa, utterly content to listen to Zack's tapping at the computer keyboard as she read. She tried to give Zack some privacy when Lily was here, though she was pretty sure he'd never taken advantage of it in any way. As far as she could tell, Zack considered Lily a friend and nothing more. One of these days, he was going to wake up to the fact that his best friend was a beautiful young woman who happened to be in love with him. And when that day . . .

Quinn froze as a familiar chill skated over her skin. Her breath caught, the hair lifting on her arms. Oh, hell. She'd felt this same chill more than half a dozen times over the past few weeks. Only recently had she connected it to the visions.

She set her wineglass down so fast, it splashed onto the lamp table, then she lunged off the chair and crossed to the window with long, quick strides. But as she approached, she slowed, hesitating, her pulse kicking hard and fast. She knew what she *should* see, looking out the window—the dorms across the street, two dozen windows glowing with light and life, cars lining the street below. Her heart thrummed with anticipation and dread at what she *would* see instead.

Dammit, why does this stuff always have to happen to me?

With a quick breath, she stepped forward and lifted shaking hands to the windowpane, curving her hands around her eyes to close out the light from the room. And, just as she'd feared, she stared at an impossible sight. A line of two-story row houses, decrepit and crumbling, lit only by the moonlight falling from above, stood where the dorms should be. This street, unlike the real one, was unlit, unpaved. Uninhabited?

Three other times over the past weeks, after she'd felt that odd chill, she'd looked out the window to find this exact same scene. *Why?* If it weren't for all the other strangeness in her life, she might think she was hallucinating. Or going insane.

Maybe I am.

The sound of a horse's whinny carried over the sound of the real traffic, for the normal sounds had never died away despite the change in scenery. Her eyes widened. Maybe her imaginary street wasn't quite so uninhabited after all. She pushed up the window and leaned forward, as close to the screen as she could get without actually pressing her nose against it.

"Zack, turn off the light and come here." As soon

as the words were out of her mouth, she wanted to pull them back. She'd spoken without thinking. Then again, if he saw it, too . . .

Zack never did anything quickly, but the tone of her voice must have gotten through to him because he doused the light, except for one computer monitor, and joined her a handful of seconds later.

"What?" He folded his long length and peered through the screen beside her.

Quinn swallowed. "I thought I heard a horse. Do you see one?"

His shoulder brushed hers as he turned and looked in one direction, then the other. "Nope. Probably just one of the mounted cops." He straightened and returned to his computer.

Quinn pressed a fist against her chest and her racing heart. Just once, she'd like not to be the only freak on the planet.

The distinctive sound of a horse's clip-clop grew louder, overlaying the true traffic sounds. And then she saw it, pulling a buggy down that empty dirt street, a dark-cloaked figure holding the reins. A moment later, incongruously, a yellow Jeep Wrangler burst onto the scene, swerving around the carriage, causing the horse to sidestep with agitation. The buggy driver shouted with anger. And then the strange sounds and sights were gone, and Quinn once more stared at the dorms and cars that were really there.

"*Lily's missing.*"

At the sound of Zack's frantic voice through the cell phone the next morning, Quinn leaped from her lab bench, her free hand pressing against her head. "Are you sure?" *God.* The disappearances!

"We were going to meet out front and walk to class together like we always do. But she never showed up. And I can't find her."

"She's not picking up her phone?"

"No. She texted me to say she'd be here in five minutes, but that was fifteen minutes ago, and she's not here. She's not anywhere, Quinn. I've been walking around looking for her."

"Zack." She'd never heard him sound so frantic—she'd never heard him sound frantic at all. She scrambled to think of a logical, safe explanation for Lily's disappearance and couldn't come up with a single one that fit Lily's serious, responsible nature. "Have you called her mom?" Lily lived with her parents about six blocks away.

"I don't know her mom's number."

Crap. "Do you know either of her parents' names?"

"Mr. and Mrs. Wang."

"Zack. There have to be hundreds of Wangs in D.C."

"I know."

"Where are you?"

"Starbucks on Penn."

A couple of blocks from their apartment. "Stay there. Inside. I'm on my way."

Thirty minutes later, after handing off her work to a fellow technician, racing to her car, and flying through more nearly red lights than she cared to admit, she found Zack right where he'd said he'd be, his body rigid with tension as he paced. He looked up and saw her, the devastation in his expression lifting with relief. As if she could fix it. *Oh, Zack.* His

T-shirt was plastered to his body, his face flushed and soaked with sweat. He loved that girl, she could see it in his eyes, even if he didn't know it, yet. If Lily was really gone, her loss was going to slay him.

And his grief was going to slay Quinn.

She took his hand, squeezing his damp fist. "Where have you looked?"

"Around." His eyes misted, his mouth tightening painfully. "She's not here, Quinn."

"We'll find her."

But he wasn't buying her optimism any more than she was. The cops hadn't found a single one of the missing people, yet. Not one.

"Do you know where she was when you last heard from her?"

"She was close. Within a block or two of our apartment."

Quinn cocked her head at him. "Doesn't she usually buy coffee on her way to class?"

"Yeah."

"Where?"

He blinked. "Here."

"Have you asked if they saw her?"

His face scrunched in embarrassment. "No." He pulled out his cell phone as he walked up to the counter, stepping in front of the line and holding out his phone and, she assumed, Lily's picture, to the barista. "I'm looking for my friend. Did she get coffee here a little while ago?"

The man peered at the picture. "Yeah. Lily, right? She ordered her usual mocha latte no-whip."

Zack turned away, and Quinn fell into step beside him as they pushed through the morning-coffee crowd and left the shop. She squinted against the glare of the summer sun. "She went missing between here and the street in front of our apartment. It's just two blocks, Zack." And the chances they'd find her, after Zack had already looked, were slim to none.

Together, they walked down the busy sidewalk, dodging college kids, locals, and tourists as they searched for any sign of Lily or what might have happened to her. Quinn's chest ached, as much for Lily as it did for Zack. His anguish, thick and palpable, hung in the steamy air.

When that familiar chill rippled over her skin, it startled her. *Oh, hell. Not here. Not now.*

They were nearly to the block their apartment sat on, the street where, just last night, she'd seen an old-fashioned horse and buggy. In the dark. Surely she wouldn't see it in bright daylight.

Her pulse began to race in both anticipation and dread. What if she saw that strange scene again? What if, as always happened when she peered out the window, she suddenly couldn't see the real world? Would she start running into people? Maybe walk in front of a car?

She grabbed Zack, curling her fingers around his upper arm.

His gaze swung to her, hope wreathing his face. "Do you see her?"

"No. I just . . . I don't feel well."

His brows drew down, and he pulled her hand off his arm and engulfed it in his larger one, closing his fingers tightly around hers.

Hand in hand, they crossed the street, pushing through a throng of backpacked college kids, and walked around the construction barricade that was blocking her view of her building. As they cleared the barricade, Quinn swallowed a gasp at the sight that met her gaze. Superimposed upon a small section of her apartment building, to the left of the entrance, was what appeared to be a house of some sort. Or row house. It was set back and partially illuminated as if by a spotlight, surrounded by shadows. A crumbling, haunted-looking house that wasn't really there.

Holy shit. She pulled up short.

"You see something."

Zack's words barely registered, and she answered without thinking. "Yes."

"What?"

His excitement penetrated her focus. "I'm not sure." But she started forward, her gaze remaining glued on that impossible sight. The shadows fully blocked the sidewalk, extending almost to the street, as if the vision were three-dimensional, as if a slice had been cut from another world, a square column, and dropped into the middle of hers. But the house didn't appear to actually stand within that column. In fact, the column didn't appear to quite reach the front of her apartment building at all. It was as if the shadows acted as a window into the world where the house sat, alone and abandoned.

She frowned, trying to make sense of it. Why, when the scene appeared at night, was she able to see what appeared to be the entire landscape of . . . what? Was it another world? Another time? No, it couldn't be another time. Not with a Jeep Wrangler racing across the landscape.

Why could she see it when no one else could? And, clearly, no one else could. People were walking right through those shadows as if they weren't there.

She had no intention of doing the same. With her luck, her face and hair would turn purple.

Zack squeezed her hand. "What do you see, Quinn? Something to do with Lily?"

"I'm not sure. Probably not," she replied out of habit, not about to admit to her weirdness. If Zack knew about it, he'd never said a word. And if he didn't, if he'd remained happily clueless all these years, well, there was no need for him to find out now. "Just give me a moment, Zack." She let go of his hand. "Wait here."

Quinn eased forward, dodging a couple of college kids as she neared that strange column of spotlight and shadows. It wasn't a spotlight, she realized, but sunlight illuminating the front stoop of a house that stood only about twelve feet away. Mold and mud splattered the ancient brick; glass, long since broken, left gaping holes for windows; and the front door hung askew, dangling on one hinge. On that door, a tarnished lion's-head doorknocker sat cockeyed and snarling at unwary visitors. Visitors long gone.

It looked so *real*.

The column itself was only about six feet wide, yet the house sat farther back than those six feet. To either side of the spotlighted front stoop, shadows and darkness lingered, like a nightscape cut by a beacon of sunlight. Yet people continued to flow through that shadowy column, oblivious. Unaffected.

"*Lily's pen.*"

Quinn hadn't even realized Zack had followed her until she saw him reach for the bright green ballpoint pen lying on the sidewalk just inside the shadows.

"Zack, no."

Instinctively, she grabbed his bare forearm just as

his arm . . . and her clutching hand . . . dipped into the shadows. Energy leaped at her through the hand that held him, attacking her with an electrical shock that raced over her body like crawling ants, shooting every hair on her arms and head straight up.

Her breath caught, her eyes widened. Her brain screamed, *Let go of him!* But her fingers couldn't react in time, and, suddenly, they were both flying forward.

Into nothingness.

At Avon Books, we know your passion for romance—once you finish one of our novels, you find yourself wanting more.

May we tempt you with . . .

- **Excerpts** from our upcoming releases.

- Entertaining **extras**, including authors' personal photo albums and book lists.

- Behind-the-scenes **scoop** on your favorite characters and series.

- **Sweepstakes** for the chance to win free books, romantic getaways, and other fun prizes.

- Writing **tips** from our authors and editors.

- **Blog** with our authors and find out why they love to write romance.

- **Exclusive content** that's not contained within the pages of our novels.

Join us at
www.avonbooks.com

AVON

An Imprint of HarperCollins*Publishers*
www.avonromance.com

Available wherever books are sold or please call 1-800-331-3761 to order.

FTH 1111

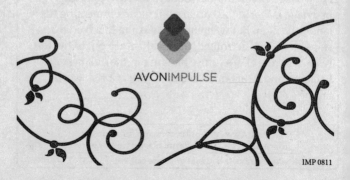